By Gaelen Foley
Published by Ivy Books

THE PIRATE PRINCE
PRINCESS
PRINCE CHARMING
THE DUKE
LORD OF FIRE
LORD OF ICE
LADY OF DESIRE
DEVIL TAKES A BRIDE
ONE NIGHT OF SIN

One Night of Sin

A Novel

Gaelen Foley

IVY BOOKS • NEW YORK

One Night of Sin is a work of fiction. Names, characters, places, and incidents are the products of the author's imagination or are used fictitiously. Any resemblance to actual events, locales, or persons, living or dead, is entirely coincidental.

An Ivy Books Mass Market Original

Published in the United States by Ivy Books, an imprint of The Random House Publishing Group, a division of Random House, Inc., New York.

Ivy Books and colophon are trademarks of Random House, Inc.

ISBN 0-345-48009-0

Printed in the United States of America

Ballantine Books website address: www.ballantinebooks.com

OPM 9 8 7 6 5 4 3 2 1

This book is dedicated with all my love
to the one person without whom
I'd never have become a writer. . . .
Thanks, Mom.

Georgiana's Brood: THE KNIGHT MIS

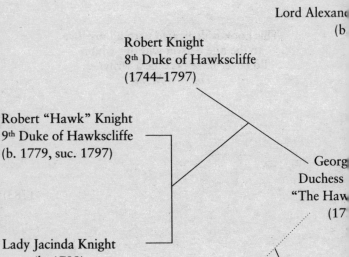

Lord Alexan
(b

Robert Knight
8th Duke of Hawkscliffe
(1744–1797)

Robert "Hawk" Knight
9th Duke of Hawkscliffe
(b. 1779, suc. 1797)

Georg
Duchess
"The Haw
(17

Lady Jacinda Knight
(b. 1798)

Samuel O'Shay, prizefighter
"The Killarney Crusher"

Lord Johr
(b

THE KNIGHT SERIES:
#1 *The Duke*
#2 *Lord of Fire*
#3 *Lord of Ice*
#4 *Lady of Desire*
#5 *Devil Takes a Bride*
#6 *One Night of Sin*

CELLANY

r "Alec" Knight
786)

Sir Phillip Preston Lawrence
Shakespearean actor

na Knight
Hawkscliffe
cliffe Harlot"
–1799)

Lord Damien Knight

(twins, b. 1783)

Lord Lucien Knight

Lord Edward Merion
Marquess of Carnarthen

ack" Knight
781)

Dotted lines denote Georgiana's lovers.

Pleasure's a sin, and sometimes sin's a pleasure.

—LORD BYRON
Don Juan, Canto I, stanza 133

CHAPTER
∞ ONE ∞

London, 1817

*F*iery swords of lightning clashed across the sable sky. Great rolling clouds flung down a warning spatter of rain. Thunder growled in the distance, but the only sound in the dark, empty street was the frantic percussion of the girl's running footfalls.

Every step jarred her in her thin kid half boots. Her dingy skirts swirled about her legs, threatening to trip her. Fleeing the glow of lanterns on the broad avenue, she raced up a murky side street, her long hair tangled and wild. Her pale young face was stark with terror as she glanced over her shoulder and pounded on, her fists clenched, her breath raking harshly through her gritted teeth.

With a small gasp, half a sob, she pitched around the corner ahead into a coal-black alley and immediately pressed backward out of sight into the shadowed alcove of a doorway. There, she held perfectly still, but for the panicked heaving of her chest. *Don't move. Don't even breathe.*

They were only seconds behind her.

The riders came with the storm at their heels—relentless, inescapable as the approaching tempest. Another throaty snarl of thunder vibrated the windowpanes of the darkened building where she hid. She huddled down against the bricks, trying to make herself smaller, for when the low rumble faded, another sound still remained—softer, but more terrible by far.

Clip-clop, clip-clop, clip-clop.

The relentless cadence of hoofbeats grew louder. Becky Ward shut her eyes with a grimace of fear, a bead of sweat rolling down her cheek. The narrow alley funneled the sound of their approach: the squeak of well-oiled leather, the jangle and hiss of deadly blades, guns, pikes, and pistols—weapons that did not even have a name in English.

Not that the riders had been sent to kill her. *Oh, no,* she thought bitterly. The prince wanted her brought back to him alive. If she had one advantage, that was it.

She yanked in the muddied hem of her skirt a split second before they came trolling past the mouth of the narrow alley. She stood trembling in the muggy heat of the summer night, holding her breath, agonized with waiting as they stopped mere yards from her hiding place.

They nearly had her, and, expert trackers, the Cossacks knew it. Prince Mikhail Kurkov had sent four of his best warriors after her, though many more were at his beck if these should fail. From where she stood, she could see the looming silhouettes of the second pair.

Huge, menacing men with thick beards and elaborate moustaches, the battle-hardened Cossack soldiers wore dark gray coats over baggy trousers, which they tucked into their black riding boots. Beneath the brims of their foreign-shaped helmets, their inscrutable faces were browned and leathery from life in the saddle, their slightly slanted eyes cool and efficient. It was said they were descended from the Huns.

One sniffed the air, trying to scent her out, while the others glanced around, murmuring questions and replies to each other in a low, rapid tongue that she could not decipher. She swallowed hard as they split up to continue searching for her in pairs. The first two continued onward while the second turned their swift, rugged horses around and headed back toward the wide, lamp-lit thoroughfare, whatever it was called. Oxford Street . . . Piccadilly? Becky wasn't sure. When they had gone, she nigh collapsed with exhausted relief, leaning all her weight against the locked door behind her.

For a fleeting moment she allowed herself to shut her eyes.

Another hairbreadth escape.

After four days of this, on the run, hunted from town to town as she had made her way southward to London, she did not know how much longer she could last. She had not eaten all day and had reached a foggy-headed state of fatigue. Fear seemed to be the only thing keeping her awake; but closing her eyes brought no respite, for it immediately called back the crisp, awful image stamped on her mind of her mighty cousin's crime. How could Mikhail have done it, killed that man in cold blood?

Worst of all, she felt in part responsible. *If only I had not tried to interfere. . . .*

She flicked her eyes open again with a shudder, and her hand crept instinctively to the tiny seashell she wore on a ribbon around her neck. Somehow she drew another small dram of courage from her final token from her father. *Must press on.*

She had to reach the Duke of Westland before the Cossacks found her.

As lord lieutenant of Yorkshire's West Riding, it was His Grace's duty to handle Mikhail, since the murder had taken place in his jurisdiction. Becky had not bothered with any of the lower-ranking justice officials because of her cousin's high rank; none but a very powerful man would dare to stand against the half-Russian prince, who had also recently inherited her grandfather's British earldom. Old Westland was known for his courage and integrity; she clung to her faith that he would bring Mikhail to justice—provided she could gain an audience with him in order to report the crime.

She knew how shallow aristocrats could be. After four days on the run, looking more beggar than lady of the manor, she was having doubts about whether she would even be received. The thought of being turned away at the door was too awful to contemplate. Westland had known Grandfather, she reminded herself. They had been political rivals rather than allies, but surely her grandsire's name would be enough to make the great Whig duke listen.

Unfortunately, she had never been to London before in her life and had no idea where to find this place called St. James's Square, where she had heard the duke kept his Town residence. The squad of Cossacks dogging her every step were not helping matters, for Mikhail did not intend to let Becky expose his brutal crime. No, he had other plans for her entirely.

Accustomed to submissive serf girls, the prince had become obsessed with trying to control her. With his hand around her throat and his cruel, hot whisper by her ear, he had made it clear how he would punish her defiance. *I will teach you to obey, loobeemaya.* Grandfather's death had made him her legal guardian, but Mikhail was dead wrong if he thought he owned her like some sort of chattel. She'd rather die than be subjected to the brutal ravishment he had promised. The thought drove her on with grim resolve.

Gliding out of the alcove, she went cautiously to the edge of the alley and peered out. The Cossacks were gone. Glancing left and right, she slipped around the corner and continued on her way.

She hoped it wasn't much farther, for her feet ached and she was starving. How many fancy garden squares could one city have? she wondered, but at least the elegant environs of the West End seemed much safer than the seedy tenement areas she had traversed at dusk. Now, however, past midnight, it was too dark to make out the street signs posted high on the sides of buildings. She stared and squinted at them as best she could, knowing that hunger and exhaustion would make it much too easy to become disoriented in the maze of this vast, dirty, bewildering city.

Oh, she missed her wide Yorkshire skies and silent, windy moors, and most of all, she missed her bed.

A sudden stab of lightning split the sky. Becky flinched, shrinking into her olive-colored pelisse. The churning clouds overhead were poised to launch their assault. She knew that she had to take shelter. It was futile to continue now. The intelligent thing to do was to find some unobtrusive place to hide from the Cossacks for the rest of the night and to escape the approaching storm's fury.

In the morning when the light returned, she would be able to read the street signs again. She could even ask for directions when people appeared—not that she had had much luck in that vein. She glanced down at her rumpled, muddy clothes with a great sigh.

Thanks to her current state of dishevelment, every respectable-looking person she had approached for directions had brushed her off and quickly walked away, taking her for a beggar—or worse. Appearances, it seemed, mattered a great deal more in Town than they did in her rustic village of Buckley-on-the-Heath. She had even been proffered a most disgusting proposition from a well-dressed man old enough to be her father when she had walked by.

Startled by the lewd offer, she had fled, only realizing afterward that while she might have considerable freedom in the country, in Town, a girl walking alone—especially after dark—was universally mistaken for a harlot. That was why no one would help her.

Even the heartless jeweler whose shop she had ventured into upon first arriving in London had obviously reached the same conclusion. When she had nervously presented the great ruby secreted away beneath her clothing and asked how much it was worth, the jeweler had looked her over in her bedraggled state as though he suspected her of stealing it. He asked to see the authentication papers; Becky had never heard of such a thing, and in any case, had been compelled to flee her home without any forewarning. There had been no time even to gather some money or food or an extra set of clothes, let alone the proper documentation. Then she realized what the blackguard had been about—trying to swindle her.

With barely a glance at the enormous ruby, the jeweler had haughtily informed her it was a fake. Becky had been infuriated. He might think her a country bumpkin, but her mother had not raised a fool.

The Rose of Indra had been in her family for two hundred years. It was all the inheritance she could claim from her coldhearted noble relatives, and her only hope of saving her home and village from Mikhail. A fake, indeed! She had stormed out, disgusted, then decided to go straight to the Duke of Westland's instead. The great Whig lord would just have to help her get a fair price for her precious jewel, in addition to helping her prosecute Mikhail for his crime. She only hoped that Westland would not take one disparaging look at her like everyone else had in this pompous city and turn her away, because if that happened, she had nowhere else to go.

She refused to give in to despair. Somehow she would survive. Why, Yorkshire folk were as ruggedly self-sufficient as they were mistrustful of outsiders, she told herself. She would jolly well survive on her own, just like Mama had taught her.

Yet, deep down, if truth were told, she was beginning to have a terrible feeling that her cause was hopeless. Mikhail was too powerful, too well-connected, too rich. There had been too many near misses so far over the past few days when his personal army of battle-hardened warriors had nearly caught her. As her fatigue deepened, she knew she was bound to make a mistake—one that could cost her, her freedom, her home—not to mention her virtue. *I hate this city. I'm going to die here.*

Reining in a fresh surge of desperation, she dragged her hand through her tangled hair and forced her thoughts back to the problem of finding shelter for the night before the storm hit. She knew she had to hurry. The treetops behind the high, spiked walls of the rich Londoners' private gardens swayed and rustled. The air felt heavy with the weight of pent-up rain.

Folding her arms across her middle, she kept forcing one foot ahead of the other, her bleary stare traveling over the neat cobblestone streets of the slumbering neighborhood, with its tree-lined lanes and occasional lampposts giving off hazy orange globes of light. There was nowhere, nowhere, to go.

Flat-fronted town houses offered no shelter behind their bristling wrought-iron fences. She wouldn't even have minded sleeping in a hayloft, but the alley passageways leading back to the stables were locked up tight. This was no way for the granddaughter of an earl to go about, surely, she thought in rueful exhaustion.

Down one street, up another. She made a halfhearted effort to scale a garden fence behind a stately darkened town house. She could see a dainty little gazebo in the garden that would have served her well, but she couldn't fit between the tall wrought-iron bars, let alone make her way over their sharpened tips. Moving on, she turned a corner and, much to her surprise, arrived in yet another garden square. Hope rose.

She walked over to the fenced-in center park, read the engraved copper plaque, and scowled. *Damn.* Not St. James's. The sign said Hanover Square. She looked around in misery, not sure where to go from here.

A volley of thunder in the distance stirred ancient memories of her earliest childhood at sea on Papa's ship. She glanced at the lowering sky. Under normal circumstances, she wasn't scared of much in life, but the shattering boom of cannon fire and the bloody, screaming, splintering destruction that she had seen those broadsides bring during the tenderest years of her childhood had left her permanently scarred with a fear of loud noises. Turning her face in to the wind, she brushed her blowing tresses out of her eyes and bleakly surmised it was going to be a bad night.

At that moment the storm broke in earnest, unleashing thunder crashes, lightning, and a torrent of rain. She let out a startled cry, the cold, sudden downpour jolting her into motion.

Dashing across the street, Becky took shelter in the first spot she found, trespassing or no. On the corner, a grand town house on the scale of a mansion offered a stately portico framed by fat white pillars. All of the windows of the house were dark at this late hour, and even if the owners were sleeping, she reasoned, they could not be so heartless as to mind her ducking under their portico to weather out the worst of the storm.

A moment later she was wiping the rain off her face and looking out at the elegant square from the mansion's front porch. *It should suit well enough for the night,* she thought. The porch had low walls on the sides to help hide her if the Cossacks came past. A pair of spiral-shaped bushes in large urns flanked the front door.

Breathing a sigh of relief, she leaned against the house, then slid her back slowly down the wall in sheer exhaustion and sat on the flagstone floor. Shrugging deeper into her pelisse, she drew her knees up to her chest and wrapped her arms around them, watching and listening to the rain.

How alone she felt. *Nothing new in that.* Scowling to ward off self-pity, she reached into her pocket and reluctantly took out her last morsel of food: a lone peppermint candy that she happened to have on the night she'd had to flee. Picking a piece of lint off it, she put the round hard candy into her mouth and sucked on it slowly, trying to make it last as long as possible. Her stomach protested at the meager offering.

She glanced at the locked, bolted door of the mansion-house with its fine, brass, lion-mask knocker and wondered about all the food they must have inside, the big, fluffy beds. . . . The thought made her even more miserable. Leaning her head back against the brick wall, she only meant to close her eyes for a moment or two.

She never intended to fall sound asleep.

The worst of the storm had passed an hour ago, subsiding into a vigorous, soaking pour. Watery spheres of gaslight from the wrought-iron lampposts along Oxford Street illumined blowing sheets of rain. The streets of the West End appeared deserted—but for one elegant black town-coach that came rolling through the bluster and blow, drawn by a blindered team of midnight-colored horses.

The mood inside the coach was one of wicked merriment, its passengers four of the undisputed rulers of Society, bon vivants of the first order: tall, athletic, good-looking men in their prime with a reputation for thrill-seeking and hedonism. Impeccably dressed, they sprawled on the silk-upholstered seats while the snug space of the carriage brimmed with their lively repartee.

"Will you stop rattling that damned dice box?"

"No! I've got to warm it up so I can win back what I lost on the Molineux match. I'm going to take your money tonight, my friend. And yours."

"You're not content with having stolen my mistress? How is she, by the way?"

"Fine, except you spoiled her utterly. Damned expensive wench. Do let me know if you want her back."

"No thanks."

Sardonic laughter abounded; the four archrogues were heedless of the weather.

Highborn libertines connected to the best families of England, they took their pleasures where they willed and were each entirely accustomed to the pampered life of the aristocracy, every whim catered to by armies of servants from the day they were born. They had met at Eton as lads and had been fast friends ever since. Despite the edge of danger they presented, having fought a total of some fifty duels among them—the collective number of females they had seduced ranged into the thousands— the high world courted them.

Their presence at a party made it fashionable; their snub spelled doom.

Tonight they had favored the hostess Lady Everley with their late arrival at her ballroom. The Everley ball was one of the last of the Season before the high world removed to Brighton for the rest of the summer in its restless search for pleasure.

Having graced the ball just long enough to set tongues wagging and to half scare, half titillate a few doe-eyed debutantes into nearly swooning with their subtly inso- lent attentions, they had finished their drinks and made their bows with their practiced air of bored superiority, which was, of course, largely for show.

In roguish manly company again, haughty pretensions cast aside, they were bound for Lord Draxinger's town mansion in Hanover Square for a late night of cards and gambling.

Another carriage-load of their acquaintances would be coming along behind them, but the earl wanted to get home first to make sure his staff was up and awake, and prepared to entertain his friends with his usual lavish hospitality.

Later in the night, no doubt, they would send for the harlots.

Lord Alec Knight knew the routine because it was always the same.

Staring out the carriage window at the rainwashed streets, all dark and empty, the golden-haired leader of their set barely listened to his friends' rowdy exchange.

Alec did not know what was wrong with him tonight.

He would have gone home if he thought he would have felt any better there, but he knew the malaise would only follow him.

"Are you dicing tonight with us or are you still sworn off hazard?" A pause. "Hullo? Knight?" An elbow nudged him in the ribs. It jarred him from his brooding.

Alec turned to Fort with an air of distraction. "Hm?"

"What is the matter with you tonight?" Drax exclaimed at his absent manner. "I say, you've been acting strange for days!"

"Aye," Rush agreed, the raven-haired heir to a marquisate. "I thought you were going to skewer Blakewell, training with the épée at Angelo's today."

"If he doesn't work on his parries, next time I will," Alec said coolly.

"What about Harrington? You nearly killed him, too."

Alec scoffed. "His footwork's atrocious."

"You must give him credit for trying. You're too fast for him."

"Then he's got no business stepping into the piste with me." Alec shrugged and looked away.

"Jesus!" Rush laughed. "It's only practice, Knight."

"Leave him alone, Rush. He's in a mood again," Fort said.

"No, I'm not."

"He's always in a mood these days."

"I'm not in any damned mood!"

"What is it, then? A toothache?"

"How the hell should I know?" he muttered. *A rut,* he thought.

"If you ask me," Fort told the others, clapping Alec on the back, "all the dear lad needs is a willing lady— no, pardon—a lascivious, rampant wench to dance the goat's jig on his lap for an hour or two. Help him to forget a certain Miss Carlisle. I'm in earnest!" he protested as the others laughed and heartily assented.

"Good advice! Get wapt, my boy. You'll be right as rain in no time."

"Cheers, to a vigorous humping," Drax declared. " 'Tis the only cure for whatever ails a man."

"You think I haven't tried that?" Alec answered.

"When?" Rush demanded.

Alec heaved a sigh and looked away.

"Admit it, man! You've been a monk ever since her wedding, and that, to put it mildly, is unlike you."

Drax leaned forward. "Tell us what's the matter, old chap. We are your friends. Heartbroken?"

"Hardly. She is happy: I am happy for her. End of tale."

"Problem with the tackle, then? Bit of the clap?"

"God, no! Jesus, Draxinger! Nothing like that." Alec scowled and shifted in his seat.

"He's not eighteen anymore," the ever-loyal Fort said

in his defense, his hazel eyes twinkling. "I'm sure we all know better than to go into battle without armor."

"I daresay," Alec muttered.

"Well, then?" Drax's ice-blue eyes searched his face in concern.

Alec stared at him, and then merely shook his head. He had always been their leader in mischief, so how could he tell them that, these days, their constant pursuit of pleasure had begun to seem intolerably, well . . . pointless to him?

They all kept going through the motions, he knew not why. And unlike his mates, he had made mistakes—serious mistakes—spurred on by the nameless hunger that would not be satisfied, try as he may to chase down any reckless impulse of excitement.

But as lost as he might be, complaining seemed beneath contempt. All the world envied him and his friends their glamorous existence at the pinnacle of Society. Women wanted them, and men wanted to be like them. Surely this aching hunger for more was wrong. Even after his losing streak at the tables, Alec knew he still possessed more than a human being could reasonably ask of life.

Then again, when had he ever been a reasonable man?

His comrades awaited his explanation, but he shrugged it off, loath to discuss his disenchantment. If he did not speak of it aloud, perhaps it would go away. "No doubt you're right," he said after a long moment, a jaded half smile curving his lips. "I probably just need to dock a bit of prime tail."

"Good lad! That's the spirit."

"Pemberton's wife was throwing herself at you all night—"

"No, no, this calls for a professional." Rush reached into his pocket with a grin and tossed over the latest edition of an infamous little volume called *The Whore-*

monger's Guide to London. "The evening's bill of fare, my lord?"

"Here, have a drink." Drax, owner of the equipage, opened the satinwood liquor compartment beside him, selected a bottle by the light of the tiny interior carriage lamps, and then passed Alec a crystal decanter of fine French brandy.

Alec accepted it with a nod and downed a determined swig, then passed the bottle on to Rush.

Meanwhile, Fort picked up the *Whoremonger's Guide* and held it up to the little flickering lamp, squinting at the pages upon pages of names and addresses. "Ah, yes, now, let us plan the night's menu," he said cheerfully. "For the hors d'oeuvre, I believe I shall start with the Summerson twins—"

"Excellent choice," Drax chimed in.

"And for the first course, hmm, this Spanish señorita called Bianca sounds intriguing—she's new, but I've heard good things. As for the remove, Kate Gossett is always very tasty—"

"God, I love her," Rush vowed. "What a dairy she's got in her bodice."

"Magnificent bosoms, yes. Second course, all four of the Wilson sisters, I should think—"

"No, no, I'm tired of them," Rush protested. "Something different, something new."

"Yes," Alec echoed softly. *Something new.*

As his friends' jaunty arguing about nothing in particular resumed, he considered their advice. Perhaps they were right. Perhaps a night of lust was all that he required, for even more than gambling, Alec loved sex, relished sex, lived for sex. It was love that he avoided like the plague.

Drumming his lips thoughtfully with his fingertips, he mentally riffled through his long list of sophisticated ladies and love-starved Society wives who regarded a wild, sweaty night with him as the high point of their year.

Perhaps.

But he was even bored of the pleasant sport of cuckolding his betters, and that was a very bad state of affairs. The thought of another meaningless rutting with some hard-eyed harlot threatened to bring back his "mood."

He would have never admitted it aloud, but whores as a breed made him uncomfortable ever since his own lucrative arrangement with Lady Campion some months ago; fallen women pricked, he supposed, what little conscience he still possessed.

He had laughed about his services to the wealthy baroness at the time, even bragged about it to his mates—she was delightfully insatiable and, better still, made his gambling debts go away. Their scandalous arrangement had raised eyebrows, but he had gotten away with it, of course. He was Alec Knight. He always got away with everything.

Unlike his recently exiled friends, Lord Byron and Beau Brummell, one felled by scandal, the other by debt, Alec had fought for and kept his golden throne as a ruling prince of Society in spite of everything. It was style and money and class that made the man, after all, hardly virtue.

His family also had been scandalized at his brazen affair with the infamous baroness, but they should've expected something like this when the clan's patriarch, Robert, the Duke of Hawkscliffe, had cut off his funds in a final attempt to bring their wild baby brother to heel. Well, Robert giveth and Robert taketh away, Alec thought, but he refused to be controlled by his family's wealth. No, with his expert bravado, he would never admit to a whit of repentance for having played the stallion for Her Ladyship.

And yet, somehow, these days, it wasn't so easy to look in the mirror. Not when he knew damned well that his wickedness had cost him a fair slice of his self-opinion and the esteem of the only girl who had ever meant a thing to him.

After twenty years of unswerving devotion, dear, steady Lizzie, his younger sister's best friend, had forsaken him for his old schoolmate Devlin Strathmore, with a final warning to Alec, her former idol, that he had better change his ways before he ran his whole life aground in pure self-destruction.

Well, there was nothing to be done for it now. Lizzie was a good girl, better off with Dev, and that was that.

Besides, as Alec cared for her like a sister, their flirtation had always felt slightly incestuous to him: Even a sinner like him had to draw the line somewhere.

Propping his elbow on the ledge of the carriage window, he lifted his hand with a heavy motion and wiped away some of the wet fog on the glass with the heel of his fist.

Strathmore was best for Lizzie. Alec had accepted that. The pair were perfectly suited and very much in love; the viscount was prepared to love her in a way that Alec had barely dared contemplate. He had not liked losing to his rival, but he had, of course, behaved like a gentleman in the end. How could he do otherwise? Deep down, he knew he was not good for Lizzie. He suspected he was not good for any woman, since he seemed much too capable of driving them insane.

He preferred not to think about it. He only knew that, ever since their wedding, the newlyweds' bliss only seemed to underscore his deep-seated ennui; their irritating joy somehow made the hard glitter of his high life look like fool's gold.

Resting his cheek on his hand, he stared out into the jet-black night when he suddenly spotted two figures on horseback in the rain. He perked up slightly with his usual dangerous curiosity.

The riders were coming up Oxford Street from the opposite direction, and he took note of them because they were the only other people he had seen about in this foul weather and at this late hour.

As the carriage approached, passing the riders near one of the brilliant gas streetlamps, Alec got a fair glimpse of the two uniformed men. Fierce-looking fellows, heavily armed. *Probably looking for whores, as well,* he thought cynically. Indeed, they appeared to be looking for someone, peering down every alley and byway as they rode slowly down the street, scanning the shadows.

Odd, he mused, but marking the odd shape of their tall, brimmed helmets, he understood. *Foreigners,* he realized belatedly as the carriage passed them by. *Probably lost.* The metropolis had been crawling with foreign princes, generals, and dignitaries and their entourages ever since the close of the war. All of Britain's former allies against Napoleon were wildly popular in London society these days.

He considered halting the carriage to offer directions, but the foreign soldiers had vanished into the rainy darkness again before Alec could even determine if they were Germans, Russians, or Austrians.

"Something wrong?" Drax inquired.

"Oh—no." Alec shook his head and put the trifling mystery out of his mind, determined to renew his interest in the night's revelries. "Pass me the brandy."

Before long the coach rolled into Hanover Square and halted before the large, darkened town house on the corner. Drax's town mansion was a stately redbrick affair of four stories and three window bays, distinguished from all the other houses on the square by its covered portico over the entrance.

As soon as the carriage stopped, the gentlemen jumped out without waiting for the groom to get the door.

Indeed, while the coachman up on the box set the brake, rain coursing off the brim of his top hat, the liveried groom posted in the rear barely had time to take the hanging lantern off its hook before jumping down off the gleaming wet coach and hurrying to light the walkway for the young earl and his stylish guests.

Drax brushed the servant off, taking the lantern from him. "Never mind us, see to my horses," he ordered as he reached into his waistcoat for his house key.

"Aye, milord."

Drax held up the light, ushering his guests ahead of him.

The rain-slicked pavement diffused the lantern's glow like polished ebony as they hurried up to the covered porch. With the lamp's flickering glow behind him, the shadows were deep; Alec strode in the lead, as usual, and so it was he who nearly tripped over the prostrate form of a sleeping female on the ground.

"Good God!" He put his hands out quickly at his sides, preventing his friends from doing the same as they ducked out of the rain and crowded under the portico's shelter.

"I say!" Rush exclaimed, before quickly recovering from his surprise. "Well, there you are, old boy. A gift from the gods. Go to it."

"Shh!" Fort whispered with a wicked glimmer in his eye. "She's sleeping!"

Alec turned to Drax with a frown. "Do you know her?"

"Never seen her before in my life." Pushing the others aside, the earl lowered himself gracefully to one knee beside her and held the lantern nearer so they could better see their delicate-featured foundling. "What a beauty," he murmured.

Alec relinquished his place at the front without comment as the other two bent down on either side of Drax, Rush sweeping his ebony cloak back over one shoulder and crouching down beside the girl, Fort leaning down slowly to brace his hands on his thighs. He tilted his head a bit, studying her.

"Nice-looking girl," Fort remarked with his usual gift for understatement.

Alec hung back, on his guard. *Perfect. Another whore.*

She was sound asleep, breathing sweetly, like some enchanted fairy-tale princess awaiting her true love's kiss—except for the smudge of dirt on her cheek.

Instead of a glass coffin for a bed, she had naught but the cold, hard ground. The sight of such a fair young creature reduced to such conditions caused a strange, tender pain in his heart. The thought of his nights with Lady Campion brought a twinge of guilt, like a clothing thread catching on the scab of a barely healed wound.

No, they were not so different, he and the sleeping girl on the ground. Perhaps it was that realization that made him keep his distance, a reluctant and unwanted sense of kinship. While his friends crowded around her, Alec leaned back against the opposite pillar, folding his arms across his chest. "She's a little young, don't you think?"

They ignored him, warming to their sport.

"The abbess must have sent her over for the party," Drax whispered.

"She's early."

Rush flashed a satyric grin. "Maybe she was eager to get started."

"So, Alec, old boy." Fort looked askance at him over his shoulder. "How do you feel about brunettes?"

He snorted, eyeing her uncertainly. The wench was

lovely, no point denying that. Her skin was like cream, her lashes black velvet. Her slim figure was wrapped in a knee-length olive-drab pelisse as she lay on her side on the damp flagstones, her head resting on her arm, her dark chocolate hair pooled around her.

"Slumber of the innocents," Rush purred.

"Right," Alec drawled.

Fort frowned at the angle of her neck. "That can't be comfortable."

Alec supposed not. He surveyed her slowly, from her tangled tresses to the couple of inches of black-stockinged calf visible between the top of her battered half-boots and the mud-spattered skirts of her plain, light blue walking dress. Cynicism flickered in his eyes at the deceptive air of innocence wafting around her like the scent of roses.

Nobody was truly innocent in this world, so why should he give a damn if his friends ogled her as though she were an object, a thing?

He rolled his eyes, losing patience with them—and himself. "Are one of you going to wake the chit or are we going to stand here gawking at her all night?"

"He's right. We must get her inside. I shall thrash my butler for making this sweet creature wait out here," Drax clipped out. "Let's pray she hasn't caught her death."

"That would be a waste," Rush agreed. "Luscious little thing, ain't she?"

"Hard to tell beneath the grime," Alec muttered.

Rush sent him a wily grin. "Perhaps we should give her a bath."

"Burn her clothes while you're at it. Quite disgraceful," Drax said, wrinkling his long straight nose.

"Yes. We'll wrap her up in satin sheets." Rush reached down to touch her hair, and something in Alec stirred violently.

He scowled. "Why don't you give her some room?"

They all turned, looking startled at his sharp tone.

"You're going to scare her if she wakes up and finds you breathing all over her like that," he said matter-of-factly.

"We're not going to scare the chit," Rush scoffed.

"Alec's always right about women," Fort reminded them in a murmur.

"Yes, best leave this to me, Rushie, old boy. Bloody damned bull in a china shop, you are." Gingerly, Drax touched her fragile shoulder. "Miss? I say, miss?" He shook her gently. "Wake up, my dear. Hullo?"

Alec watched her awakening in spite of himself. *Entrancing creature.* Yes, he'd give her that.

There was something so vulnerable in the way her sooty lashes fluttered drowsily. Her head lolled a bit, her lips parted slightly; then her eyes flicked open—luminous violet, jewellike in the lamp's glow.

"Good morning, sleepyhead," Rush greeted her softly.

Her beautiful eyes widened.

Finding his friends crowded around her, the girl sat up abruptly with a frightened gasp, visibly dazed and disoriented with slumber. At once, she scrambled back against the wall, panic flashing across her lovely face.

The three of them laughed, but Alec could tell that she was frightened, still half asleep and not sure what was going on. He knew he should speak out, but he didn't want to get involved. Not when the pitiful sight of her caused a pained, muddled tenderness to stir and churn in the region of his solar plexus. He wanted to look away in boredom—but he found he couldn't do that, either. Instead, he watched her in brooding hunger and mentally counted the days since he'd last had a woman. He let out a low exhalation of starved need.

So much for his recent efforts to be good.

* * *

As her sleep-blurred vision cleared, Becky found herself surrounded by three large, strange men looming over her in the darkness, their handsome faces distorted into lecherous, leering gargoyle masks by the twisting shadows from the lantern's flame.

They smelled of liquor, and though their voices were cultured, she was frightened by their hard, aggressive stares and speculative smiles. She knew in an instant what they wanted. She had seen that look before—in Mikhail's cold, gray eyes.

With her cousin's threat of force still ringing in her ears, and fragments of dark, violent dreams still lingering in her head, she pressed her back to the wall, her heart pounding. "L-Leave me alone. I haven't done anything wrong."

"Of course you haven't, my dear," purred the cool, lean gentleman in front of her. He had ice-blue eyes and a thatch of short, flaxen hair with a tinge of red in it. "Don't be alarmed. I am Lord Draxinger and these are my friends." He offered her an elegant, pale hand. "I believe you wish to come inside?"

She eyed him warily, not trusting his show of gentlemanly polish nor his offer of hospitality. Not by a mile.

"Don't be shy, love." The big, raven-haired fellow to his right moved forward, reaching for her as though he meant to scoop her up in his arms. "Let me help you."

"Stay back!" she cried, warding him off.

He knitted his thick, black eyebrows in surprise, taking pause at her warning. "My dear girl, I am Lord Rushford—you've probably heard of me. Now, come inside," he commanded with a managing smile. "We're going to get you nice and warm—"

"Don't—touch me," she ordered him through gritted teeth.

The two lords exchanged a startled look, and then laughed.

"There, there, my dear. Don't be afraid," the third fellow interjected soothingly. He had leonine features and thick, wavy hair the color of mahogany. "They're just trying to be friendly."

"Can't you blackguards see you're scaring her? Give the girl some room."

Only now, when he spoke, did Becky realize there was a fourth man with them.

Surrounded by lusty-eyed devils, she lifted her gaze and spied the golden-haired angel lurking in the background, outlined by silvery rain.

Fallen angel.

She drew in her breath, caught off guard by the vision of unearthly male beauty. Good God, in all her days, she had never beheld his equal.

An elegant creature of dark radiance, formally dressed, he was leaning with one shoulder against the other pillar several feet away, his arms folded across his chest. He kept his distance, as though wary of her, or aloof, or as if he merely found her beneath his concern.

Yet pinned in his celestial-blue gaze, she felt a strange tingle run through her body.

Tall and muscular, he had the lean, sculpted build of an athlete: an air of quick, restless energy behind his outward languor. His finely chiseled face was square-jawed, high-cheekboned, intense—a flawless composition of severe male perfection.

Perhaps she was still dreaming, but with the glow of heaven still upon him, she half expected to see mighty wings sprouting from his broad shoulders. But, no, she realized, her pulse quickening with unsettled awe as she looked into his otherworldly eyes and read the taut need in his stare; the devil himself had begun as the first among angels. Blissful sin personified.

Temptation in the flesh.

"Come inside with us, my dear," Lord Draxinger spoke up, startling her out of her trance.

"Yes, have a drink," Lord Rushford murmured, reaching out again to cup her cheek.

She knocked his hand away with a savage motion and shot to her feet. "Don't touch me!"

The third man laughed at her fierce show of spirit. Becky glared at him.

"You know, I think she fancies me," Lord Rushford rumbled, staring at her.

When he stood up slowly from his crouched position, rising to his full height, Becky had to tilt her head back to meet his fiery gaze. She felt the blood drain from her face.

Lord Rushford pressed closer; she shrank back against the wall. He planted his hands aggressively on the bricks and lowered his head. "Tell me your name, you impertinent vixen."

"Easy, Rush. You've had a bit too much to drink," said the cool-eyed angel in the corner, but the black-haired man was fixed on her.

"Get the door," Rushford ordered the other one as he took her arm.

She felt cornered. Her heart thumped like that of a trapped rabbit. "Please." She swallowed hard. "Let me go."

"No, no, my dear. You must come inside and have a drink with us," Lord Rushford said in a tone that brooked no argument. "I insist." His grip was not rough, but it was unyielding.

Country girl or not, common sense told her she was doomed if she let these men take her inside. Staring at her towering captor, all of the strain and terror of the past week swirled in her mind, pounded in her blood, funneled down into a fierce point of rage.

No, she thought as her fury surged. She would not tolerate this. They were *not* going to do this to her. With senses blurred by fear, instinct pounded in her veins—fight or flee. As Lord Rushford leaned nearer with a vain grin, boldly bent on kissing her, Becky attacked without warning.

She stepped forward suddenly and kneed him hard in the groin. He yelped in startled pain and let her go as he lurched to the side. In the blink of an eye she shoved the brown-haired man violently out of her way, and when Lord Draxinger reached for her elbow with a condescending, "Now, now, my dear," she hauled back her fist and punched him in the jaw as hard as she could.

She dashed out of the portico and ran at top speed into the night, instantly drenched in the pouring rain.

For a full second Alec could not even react for sheer astonishment. He was rarely surprised anymore in life, especially by females, but the girl's attack left him flabbergasted. Fort was laughing his head off, applauding her attack and yelling, "Bravo, my girl!" but Alec could only stare in shocked amazement at the sight of the other two members of his exalted set laid low. Rushford bent, wheezing, over his offending organ, while Drax rubbed his jaw with a groan and spit out a bit of blood.

"Chit knocked my damned tooth loose!"

All of a sudden, Alec laughed aloud. Good Lord, the chit had thrashed them, neat as a ninepence! How many women of England, their past conquests, would have paid in gold to see the great seducers thus unmanned? Alec was not among the casualties of the little hellion's rampage, so he could appreciate the humor in it; but although she hadn't touched him, she had certainly jolted him out of his "mood." He was already in motion, dashing out of the portico's shelter with a hell-raising grin.

"Where are you going?" Fort called as he ran out into the rain.

"To make sure she's all right!"

"Her?" Rush croaked. "What about us?"

"You deserved it." Squinting against the rain, Alec spotted the mysterious waif sprinting away down the street. "Miss!" he yelled, starting in her direction. "Come back!"

She cast a frightened glance over her shoulder, but just kept running. Plainly, she had no intention of trusting them now. Alec sent his friends a scowl. "I told you not to scare her."

Then he set out after her at an easy jog, his longer paces allowing him to gain on her at once.

"Careful, old boy!" Fort yelled after him merrily. "Girl's dangerous."

"I like dangerous," he replied under his breath. Indeed, he was eager to see what she might try to do to him.

He cast aside his initial prejudice about her kind. The lass had spirit, aye, pluck to the backbone. He had to know her name. She was a challenge, and challenges, like surprises, were so very rare in his life. More than being merely intrigued, though, he was concerned about her, too—perhaps, in spite of himself.

He was not entirely sure now that their first assumption had been correct, that she had arrived in advance of their usual summons for the *filles des joies*. She hadn't been dressed like one, hadn't smelled like one, doused in cheap perfume. She'd worn no rouge, no tawdry fake jewels. And she was sober.

Either she had just woken up and hadn't yet known what was going on when his friends had besieged her with their excessive attentions, or there was another explanation for her naive alarm.

Alec intended to get to the bottom of it, solve her little mystery. It was not as though he had anything better to do.

Ahead, the girl paused on the corner, beginning to tire. Looking one way and the other, as though she wasn't sure which way to go, she glanced behind her and now saw him chasing her. She jumped back, recoiling.

"Leave me alone!" she cried shrilly, though he was still half a block away.

"Wait! I just want to talk to you!"

She let out a furious sound and fled again, darting to the left.

With a glint in his eyes, Alec poured on the speed, drawing easily on his large, unused reserves of physical strength honed over many years of near daily training at the best fencing and boxing clubs in London. The puddles were deep as he splashed through them in his flat black shoes. He was still dressed for the ballroom in black trousers and tails, but the driving rain quickly soaked his shoulders and chest, sousing his favorite white silk waistcoat and plastering his hair to his head. Breathing harder with his sprint, he tugged off his cravat and threw it aside.

As he turned the corner onto Bond Street, a carriage-load of Drax's expected guests passed him, hailing him in surprise, but he ignored them, absorbed in the chase.

He had a feeling he would not be going back to Draxinger's for any cardplay tonight. No, he was already contemplating another kind of play altogether, the wondrous game of skin to skin. God, he needed it.

He had gone too long without. He had not had a woman since well before Lizzie's wedding to Strathmore on Midsummer's Eve. Rejected by the one girl he always thought he'd marry—if and when he was ever ready to settle down—Alec had not had the heart to resume his Don Juan ways.

Until tonight.

What the hell was he waiting for? His body ached for a woman's touch. He made up his mind as he pounded on through the rain that this mystery girl would do as well as any. Besides, it would indulge his vanity to succeed where his friends had failed.

Passing a row of quaint shops with darkened bow windows, their shutters and doors locked up tightly for the night, the girl's pace began to flag, as though she could not keep going much longer. She cast another anxious glance over her shoulder and saw him catching up.

Alec was almost upon her now, only a few yards behind, close enough to see the fury that flicked over her dainty features at his determined pursuit.

"Go away, you fiend!"

"No," he panted cheerfully. She had yet to learn of his famed stubbornness—and he had yet to learn her name.

With a small yowl of pure feminine frustration, she rushed over to the nearest storefront, a haberdasher's, and seized the only weapon she could find.

Snatching the long-handled candlesnuffer off its metal holder on the wall, she whipped around and swung it at him. "Stay back!"

"Oh-ho!" he laughed as he approached slowly. *I like this girl.* "What are you going to do with that thing? Put my lights out?"

"Keep your distance or I'll brain you! I'll do it, I will!"

He disobeyed, of course, stalking toward her another step or two as he caught his breath. "Easy, kitten—"

"Don't you 'kitten' me!" *Whoosh!*—the metal bar sang through the air in her grasp. Her dark tresses flew; the dirt-streaked skirts swirled around her trim figure as she swung her weapon with admirable ferocity straight at Alec's head.

He ducked, his fencer's reflexes yanking him under the arc, but the nearness of the miss left him astonished all over again. Women had been threatening to kill him for years, but none had actually tried it before.

"Jesus!" he exclaimed, and then started laughing again. He couldn't help it.

Her face flushed. "Don't you dare laugh at me, you coxcomb! I'm not afraid of you! A hero's blood flows in these veins, I'll have you know!" she cried wrathfully, trying—rather adorably, Alec thought—to scare him away. "My father fought beside Nelson at Trafalgar!"

He held up his hands. "I surrender! Don't hurt me!"

"Ugh, you—" Another massive crash of lightning overhead cut off her words and sent her darting under a nearby awning of one of the shops that lined the street.

Alec followed eagerly, but when he joined her, she was already in position to defend the small rectangle of dry territory she had claimed.

With her weapon at the ready, she begrudgingly allowed him to step under the cover of the striped tin awning.

The shadows were deeper in their shelter. He smiled wickedly at her as he approached. "Well, isn't this cozy?"

The warm rain drummed upon the awning's painted tin, dampening the sound and casting an air of intimacy over their taut standoff.

The girl backed up a step uneasily, adjusting her grip, more than willing, it seemed, to try again to break his head if he made one false move.

Alec was on his guard and half smitten—though that meant nothing. He was known to fall in love six or seven times a day. *Beautiful eyes,* he thought. He studied her by the distant streetlamp's glow through a haze of rain. Big, stormy eyes full of fight and spirit, their violet hue a rare and fascinating color. Her thick dark hair was slicked back with the rain, accenting the delicate sculpture of her face. Raindrops starred her lashes and turned her plump lips to dewy roses. Dirty little stray. Ravishing.

And he wanted her.

He dared not tell her so, however, for fear of the risk to his health. Indeed, his amusement at her ire was bound to get him clobbered, but he could not wipe the roguish grin off his face. Finally, a distraction worthy of him. "You're rather handy with that thing. Have you ever thought of playing cricket? Our team could use you at the Lords."

She let out a dainty growl of exasperation. *Whoosh!*—again. He leaned back from the waist as the candle-snuffer sailed past his chest. He could have grabbed it, but then she would have run and his fun would end.

"What's wrong with you?" she cried, obviously vexed by her miss. "Why won't you leave me alone?"

"But mademoiselle, I only came to make sure you're all right—and, of course, to apologize for my friends' rude behavior," he added with his purest choirboy stare. He offered a charming smile of humble male contrition along with it, but she eyed him warily, as though she wasn't buying it. Well, she soon would. They always did. "They didn't mean to frighten you—"

"I wasn't scared!"

"Of course not." Alec's lips twitched with the effort not to smile at her bravado. "Still, it wasn't very nice of them to disturb your slumber."

She raised her weapon in menace. "Are you making fun of me again?"

"Why, no," he answered softly. "I'm flirting with you, my dear."

CHAPTER
❧ TWO ❧

"*O*h," Becky said slowly, not quite sure what to do with this information. She flicked her fingers more firmly around the metal rod of the candlesnuffer, though, securing her grip—just in case he tried anything.

The man's smile was knowing, irresistible. "There's really no need for further violence, is there? Haven't you left enough wounded men in your wake?"

"They deserved it," she bit back hotly.

"Yes, they did," he agreed, advancing another step, his hands held out in a soothing, conciliatory gesture. "But I didn't treat you that way."

She remained on her guard, but conceded that at least that much was true.

"What's your name?"

"You first."

He seemed startled by the command, then shrugged. "Alec." He lowered his hands to his sides, making no move to come closer. "Lord Alec Knight, at your service." He sketched a courtly bow, his hand on his middle. She wasn't sure if he was still mocking her: His heaven-blue eyes danced. "You needn't be afraid," he added softly. "I mean you no harm. I know my friends gave you a bit of a start, but on my honor, you are quite safe with me."

Becky eyed him warily. Safe, she thought, was a relative term. One thing was certain, though. There was nobody like him in Buckley-on-the-Heath. She had never met a man before who called her *mademoiselle*. Indeed, it seemed that in Lord Alec Knight and his companions, she had gotten her first glimpse of that fabled, nocturnal race, the London rakehells.

All the more reason to keep him at bay. His kind made a sport of ruining females. At least that's what she had heard. And yet . . .

Blame her adventuring soul for it, she was a little intrigued.

Scrutinizing him cautiously, she decided that she did not sense any actual menace coming from Lord Alec Knight. Tall and strapping as he was, he could have ripped away her weapon if he'd had a mind to. No, by the look of him, any woman in this man's radius was in a different sort of danger altogether.

Everything about him spelled heartbreaker. He had the face of an angel, a sinner's smile, and the cool, hard stare of a jaded pleasure-seeker who didn't give a damn about much of anything.

His weapons of seduction were formidable . . . that caressing gaze . . . that low, beguiling, slightly scratchy voice . . . that roguish playfulness—and, oh, that gorgeous face.

He had cast off his cravat, exposing the manly architecture of his throat. Without his neckcloth to hold his loose white shirt closed, the frilled V of his collar had parted down to the first button of his waistcoat, revealing the beguiling little notch between his collarbones and a tempting expanse of damp, gleaming skin.

Becky tried not to look.

Oh, yes, he probably had no trouble at all leading unwise women astray like the very Pied Piper. But although she averted her gaze, she could still smell the enticing cologne that clung to him; the rain and his exertions had heightened his scent. She could feel the heat of his muscled body from where she stood.

"What's your name, sweetheart?" he murmured, a practiced line delivered with smooth persistence, as silvery miniature waterfalls cascaded off the awning's edge behind him. A boyish pout skimmed his full, kissable lips. "You promised to tell me yours if I told you mine."

"I didn't promise you anything," she informed him.

The flicker of mischief in his laughing blue eyes admitted to his attempt at trickery. He flashed a smile. "I must know, all the same." He edged closer, the irresistible softness of his deep voice coaxing her trust; she resisted for all she was worth. "Tell me. I shan't go away until you do."

"In that case, it's Becky," she muttered, but did not offer her last name. The less he knew about her, the better.

Fortunately, her first name alone seemed to satisfy him just fine. "And why, Becky dear, were you sleeping in Draxinger's doorway?"

Her pride bristled. "Maybe I was tired." *Maybe I had nowhere else to go.*

"The butler wouldn't let you inside?"

What was he getting at?

"Why should I bother the butler?" she countered in a prickly tone, her pride smarting at the condition in which those rich, haughty fellows had seen her. They must think her low, indeed.

"You could have knocked on the door," he chided with a smile. "The servants would have let you in if you had simply said the abbess sent you over for the party."

Abbess? Becky furrowed her brow and stared at him, and then her eyes widened as understanding dawned. *Oh, Lord . . . !* So, that's why his friends had been so outrageously forward! It made sense now. Becky was appalled to realize that, along with his cronies and everyone else in this horrible town, Lord Alec Knight believed she was a whore.

And that, she thought angrily, was the only reason he was still standing here.

He didn't care about her in the slightest. He was only after a bit of fun. "Come back to the house," he coaxed her in a silky tone. "You just stay close to me. I won't let the lads bother you."

Torn between outrage and disbelieving humor at what a very bad day she was having, Becky shook her head slowly, stubbornly, emphatically. But her heart pounded.

Oh, this was rich. Finally, someone showed her a glimmer of concern in this hateful city, and now she understood why.

She was about to correct his error when she suddenly stopped herself, recalling how everyone she had asked for help today had simply brushed her off. Surely, if she told this bona fide London rakehell that she was an honest girl—if he surmised he was not going to get what he wanted—then he, too, would leave her standing here alone again, starving, hunted, lost. The thought of being left out here in the streets again, by herself, in the middle of the night, was somehow worse than Lord Alec's shocking assumptions.

Worse by far.

So, at that moment, instead of speaking up, she did what any canny country Yorkshireman would do and kept her mouth shut.

No, let him believe of her what he willed. It didn't really matter in the grand scheme of things. With her survival at stake, she was well past caring about her reputation. Somehow his golden presence made the night seem a little less black.

"Come, Becky," he coaxed her gently. "You'll catch your death out here in the wet. I can see you shivering."

He glanced at her weapon. "Why don't you put that thing down?"

"Keep your distance!" she warned, but she could feel her defenses growing thin.

He smiled almost tenderly, studying her in the darkness. "Why do I get the feeling you haven't been doing this for very long?"

"I—I—" She had no idea what to say. Did he mean *whoring*?

"It's all right," he murmured indulgently, his glance flicking over her body. "You needn't be embarrassed of your inexperience. In fact, I'm glad to hear it. You're much too pretty to be out on the streets, my dear."

The compliment flustered her. Well, it must have been dark indeed if he thought that in her abysmal condition.

He put his hands in his pockets, regarding her with a thoughtful gaze. "How long have you been in Town?"

She swallowed hard. This much she could answer truthfully. "Oh, about . . . eight hours."

He raised his eyebrows in amusement. "So long?"

She nodded. "I just arrived this afternoon."

"From?"

"Yorkshire." Her candlesnuffer dipped in her grasp as a lump of homesickness rose in her throat. Her chin trembled as she thought of her village and her beloved home, the ancient rambling Tudor hall at the edge of the heath. How she missed Talbot Old Hall, with its countless gables, climbing ivy, and four oak-carved angels standing guard atop the dramatic hammer-beam roof with swords and shields.

His eyes glowed. "A Yorkshire lass. How delightful. I'm from the north, myself. Born and bred in the Cumberland hills. Country lad," he teased.

She could not help smiling ruefully at his claim and the unlikely image of this glossy London sophisticate scything hay or shearing sheep.

"Well, that's a first," he remarked in a low tone, studying her. "You have a beautiful smile, Becky." His leisurely stare moved over her. "My my, dimples and all."

She blushed, but then he shook his head and sternly took her to task. "This isn't Yorkshire, *ma cherie*. You cannot proceed this way in Town. You could get hurt. Badly."

He did not know the half of it.

"I'm not afraid," she vaunted; a knee-jerk reaction, in truth, for of course it was a lie. She supposed such bravado was deeply ingrained in her from a lifetime of having to prove herself.

He smiled knowingly. Drifting closer, he casually placed one well-groomed hand on the side of her candle-snuffer. She failed to protest, mesmerized momentarily by his elegant fingers' deft caress along the smooth wood.

He probably had an expert valet who buffed his nails for him in a monthly gentleman's manicure, she thought. Hypnotic hands.

His nearness made her strangely weak. She could do nothing, enthralled by his glittering gaze and strong, sensitive hands; he took her weapon gently out of her grasp and set it back in its holder, easily disarming her—in more ways than one.

"That's better," he whispered. "Now we can be friends."

When he turned to her again, she stared at him uncertainly, filled with an odd longing to put herself in his beautiful hands. *Help*, she thought. *Please help me.*

He reached out and with a bold, slow, seductive caress, traced the line of her jaw with his fingertip. She quivered; the response surely amused him.

"So what do you think of our fair metropolis, after a full eight hours on London soil?" he inquired casually.

"Honestly?" At his encouraging nod, her confession tumbled from her lips. "It's horrid," she wrenched out, her voice breaking to a wretched whisper, her chin starting to tremble. "I hate it with all my heart."

Her vehemence clearly startled him, but then he furrowed his brow and drew her closer. "Oh, darling, no. Shh, there. Don't cry." He put his arms around her, soothing her with his whispers; she stood there numbly for a moment, neither moving closer nor pulling away.

The contact routed her defenses, taking her greatly off guard. It had been so long since anyone had held her. Years. That thought alone made her want to cry. She closed her eyes.

"Shh," he whispered.

She did not know him, but she was so weary, and the delicious strength that she felt in his arms and muscled body as he embraced her, invited her to rest against him. *Safety.* When he bent and kissed her brow, she simply melted, leaning her forehead against his lips, half asleep on her feet.

"Becky, my sweet." His mouth skimmed her hairline and then he whispered, "Shall I take you home?"

"I can't go home," she said miserably, exhaustion and his kindness making her eyes well up with tears. She shut her eyes more tightly, not wanting him to see.

"So, it's like that," he answered thoughtfully, drawing what conclusions, heaven only knew. When he spoke again, his tone was mild, his breath warm against her brow, a sophisticated murmur. "Actually, you see, I meant . . . to my place."

Oh, God. He thought she was a harlot and was now genuinely propositioning her for the night. "Sir, I really don't think—"

"Look at me." He tipped her chin up with his fingertips, and when he stared evenly into her eyes, the world disappeared. "I'm not going to hurt you. You know that, don't you?"

She nodded slowly.

He wiped the single tear off her cheek, which had escaped her willful effort not to cry. "I understand better than you know, believe me. I can guess how it all played out. Some heartless cad back in Yorkshire had his way with you." As he spoke, he slowly rubbed away the smudge of dirt on her cheek with the pad of his thumb. "Your parents threw you out. It probably wasn't even your fault. Now you're alone. You've got nothing, no one."

Tears threatened afresh at his last words, because those, at least, were true. Unbearably so.

He shook his head with gallant tenderness. "We've all been down on our luck, my love. This isn't the end. Don't lose heart." He kissed her head again. "Come home with me tonight. As a gentleman, I cannot leave you out here alone to fend for yourself. I'm sure there must be some way I can help. You're very beautiful, you know. You'll find no shortage of protectors. Yes, you'll make your fortune, my girl, and when you do—" He pulled back, gave her a roguish smile, and chucked her gently under the chin. "I hope you shove it down your parents' throats."

Becky stared at him with fresh tears in her eyes. Tears of gratitude. He had it all wrong, of course, but she smiled tremulously at his defiant encouragement, one rebel to another. No meek sufferer, it was very much in the spirit of the way she looked at life.

Maybe he was not entirely uncaring.

She managed a taut nod and took a deep breath. "Thank you," she whispered as she blinked her tears away.

His smile turned wily. "As for the fool who caused your ruin, I can guarantee you one thing: He never pleasured you as I can." He moved closer, and then he touched her mouth, running the pad of his thumb slowly across her lower lip. "You look hungry," he whispered. "I could feed you." He lowered his head as though to kiss her, but Becky found the breathless strength to turn away, her heart pounding at his velvet beguilement.

"Why do you resist?" he asked, his murmur rich with decadent sensuality. He stroked her cheek. "Come home with me. We'll take it nice and slow. I'd never rush you, sweet babe. I won't do anything you don't want. I'm going to make you feel so good, Becky. Let me take care of you tonight." He tucked her hair gently behind her ear. "You won't regret it." Her heart raced; his silken touch was maddening as he caressed her cheek and the curve of her neck. "What is it you desire?" he breathed. "Just tell me. Anything you want."

She swallowed hard, trying to hold on to her defenses as he made her body tremble. Well, that sounded terribly sincere, she thought. Yet his practiced seduction proved powerfully intoxicating.

Intoxication often brought with it a fool's courage, and Becky, in a surge of daring, decided to play along for a moment, perhaps out of simple fascination to find out how all this business worked. Or perhaps because he had already succeeded in arousing her. "Anything?" she countered skeptically.

"Well," he amended with a languid half smile. "Within reason."

His hand wandered lower, trailing slowly down the center of her chest.

She glanced down at it. His gold and onyx pinky ring glinted in the distant lamplight. Such deft, expert hands. No man had ever touched her there before. A few had tried. She had slapped them.

She did not slap Lord Alec.

She didn't even want to. He was too fascinating, too

gorgeous, too charming, too smooth. Her mind felt drugged with his coaxing; she had a feeling she was in deep over her head with this man, but at the moment she didn't even care.

"You see, if it's plain riches you want, you're better off with Draxinger," he purred, drawing little shapes on her breastbone with his middle fingertip. "I daresay you've won his heart already, aside from the small matter of knocking his tooth loose."

"You're not rich?" she ventured boldly, lifting her chin.

"Sorry, no," he answered in amusement.

"You seem rich."

"I try." His eyes danced as he shook his head sadly. "I made a fortune gaming and I lost it."

"Ah, that's a pity." Her voice sounded a trifle breathless despite her playful bravado.

"I know."

"So, make another."

"Good idea," he said dryly. "I hadn't thought of that."

"Why not? If you can do it once, you can do it twice, can't you?"

"When one falls down a deep, dark hole, *cherie*, one must crawl out of it as best one can. After that, one isn't so inclined to throw caution to the wind. Besides, there's such a thing as luck, and lately mine's all bad."

"You met me," she pointed out, mustering up a saucy smile. "Perhaps your luck has changed."

He laughed aloud at her assertion. "I like your style, my girl."

"I am in earnest. I was born lucky. It's true."

"If you'll forgive my saying so, you don't look all that lucky to me." He pinched her cheek playfully, and then lowered his hand to his side.

His frank words startled her, then she broke into rueful laughter, in which Lord Alec joined her. It felt so good to laugh and smile after the past few days' ordeal. She shook her head, lowering her gaze. *What am I doing, flirting with him?* She couldn't seem to help herself. Her blush deepened as she realized she was behaving like a romping country hoyden, exchanging banter with the fine lord, just asking to be ravished.

Very forward, indeed. Dangerous, too. But it didn't scare her. Not compared to the Cossacks. It only made her blush, and she was glad it was dark so he could not see the way his sensual stare turned her face pink.

You'd better tell him it's not going to happen, her better sense warned. But then he'd leave, and now she found herself wondering what it would be like to kiss him.

"What's going on in that pretty head of yours?"

She lowered her gaze, fighting a smile. "I have no interest in Lord Draxinger," she murmured, peeking at him from beneath her lashes. "For whatever it might be worth."

"Ah. Well. There's always my other friend, Rushford. The one you kicked."

"No!"

"He'll be a marquess one day."

"I don't care. He's a pagan and a brute!"

"Yes, well—no. Not really. Very well. Sometimes." He chuckled, attempting to defend his friend. "He's just not used to girls who don't swoon at his glance."

"Neither, I wager, are you," she shot back, then bit her lip after the pert remark. *Oh, dear.* She cleared her throat. "My point being that, er, *you* didn't act like a brute."

Lord Alec raised his eyebrows mildly. "No. Well. It does not matter, anyway, I'm afraid. I am sorry to say Lord Rushford is a . . . trifle cross at you at the moment. I fear the family line may be in peril after you nearly gelded him. Besides, he's already got a mistress. On the other hand, of course, he will be bored of her by week's end, so perhaps if you bide your time—"

"No thanks." Becky gave him an arch look and folded her arms across her chest. "What about that third fellow? Who was he?"

"Fort? Yes, Lord Daniel Fortescue. Capital chap, but you don't want him. He's a mere younger son, like me."

"Younger son?"

He nodded. "In my case, the youngest of five."

"Good heavens, you've neither fortune nor title?" she taunted with a smile.

He shook his head sardonically. "No, but I do have a number of talents that I think would astonish you."

Something in his stare made her believe it. "Really?" she forced out weakly.

"Mm." He nodded.

"Like what?"

He flashed a reckless smile. "Come home with me and you'll find out."

Lord, he was too much. She bit her lower lip, captured by his cobalt eyes. Truly, he was the most beautiful man she had ever seen in her life, an Adonis, nay, Apollo. A sun god with hair of tarnished gold and eyes as blue as the deepest ocean.

She forced herself to look away, feeling breathless and slightly overheated.

"Well?" he whispered. "What's it going to be, girl?"

"You're very bad, aren't you?" she murmured, stalling for time as she struggled to relocate her wits.

"On the contrary, my love, I am extremely good," he whispered. "Why do you fight this? Don't you like me?"

"I like you."

"I'm not going to beg."

"Lord Alec—"

"I want you. Stop playing games."

She turned as red as the cross on the Union Jack. What in blazes had she gotten herself into? What was she to say? Then a distant sound snagged at her attention.

Clip-clop, clip-clop, clip-clop.

Her eyes widened; she felt her blood run cold. *Oh, no.* Ignoring Lord Alec entirely for the moment, she mustered her courage and forced herself to look, peering into the darkness in the direction of the sound.

By the dim illumination of the wrought-iron lampposts, she spotted two of the riders about a block away, but coming closer steadily, as undeterred by the blowing rain as mechanical automata. Even from a distance, she recognized the distinctive shape of their brimmed helmets and the familiar motion of their heads turning as they glanced from side to side, scanning each intersection they passed.

A wave of dread washed over her. *Too late.* Running now would only draw their attention.

"Becky? God's teeth, I've never had this much trouble persuading a lass in my life—"

"I'm persuaded!" As she jerked her frightened gaze back to his chiseled face, it occurred to her all of a sudden that he might be her only hope of evading capture.

Magnificent specimen that he was, Lord Alec had lots of lovely muscles, to be sure; he was tall and walked with a strut, she had noticed. But she did not want him to try to fight the Cossacks—God, no. She already felt responsible for one man's death back in Yorkshire.

Now, as she looked up at him, the cocksure glint in his dark blue eyes made her worry he might think that he could take the Cossacks on. But Mikhail had told her how his soldiers were plucked from their mothers' bosoms as children to be molded into warriors, trained to mete out death. If, when they came to seize her, her lusty Knight tried to interfere or challenged them out of some misguided sense of aristocratic chivalry, Becky had no doubt he would be promptly slaughtered.

She could not bear it. He was the only person who had been nice to her—in a fashion—since her arrival in London. No, she would not get this man killed, too. She did not want him involved at all. But as the Cossacks passed the third lamppost, her doom was in sight. She turned back warily to her companion. She did not want Lord Alec challenging those brutes, but perhaps there was a way that he could hide her.

After all, the Cossacks were looking for a girl alone. Everyone in this town seemed to think she was a hussy, anyway. . . .

"You've persuaded me," she whispered again.

"Thank God," he muttered. "For a minute, I thought I was losing my touch."

What a time for all his jesting! As he reached to caress her face, Becky cautiously captured his hand. A smoldering glow leapt to life at once in his cobalt eyes. She managed to smile at him, though uncertainly, and linked her fingers through his, drawing him with her into the shadows. She held his gaze with a virginal, come-hither stare.

Surprise flickered in the depths of his eyes at her initiating this move, but he came willingly enough. He looked intrigued. "You're full of surprises, do you know that?"

You have no idea. "Am I?"

"Mm." With long, strolling paces, he allowed her to lead him back into the darkest region beneath the awning, into the recessed doorway of the shop, tucked between a pair of bow windows.

Her heart thudding, she backed against the locked, green-painted shop door, and then boldly reached out and stroked him, her fingertips carefully exploring his chest. "It's kind of you to worry for my safety."

"Well, Becky dear, I must confess, my motives are not entirely pure." He pressed closer in a way that would have upset her ten minutes ago, but now she welcomed the nearness of his big strong body, shielding her from view of the street.

She lifted her chin, meeting his hungry stare. Nervously, she wetted her lips with the tip of her tongue. He watched with a look of absorption.

"Would you like to kiss me, Lord Alec?" she asked in a breathy voice.

"Very much," he answered huskily. "Plain old 'Alec' will do, love. Told you, remember? Mere younger son."

"I daresay there is nothing 'mere' about you, Lord— I mean—Alec." Sliding her hands up his chest, she wrapped her arms around his neck, praying that even if the Cossacks noticed two people kissing in the shadows, they would never guess that one of them was their quarry.

He slipped his arm around her waist. Becky's heart skipped a beat and then pounded against him. With his other hand, he tipped her head back. But then, instead of claiming her lips, he paused, gazing thoughtfully into her eyes.

"What is it?" she whispered. Would the blasted man please hurry before she was spotted?

"I can't tell if you really want this," he said. "You quite confuse me, little girl."

She gazed at his sensitive mouth, made for deep, wanton kisses. "I do." Heaven help her, it was true. "More than you know." She met his searching gaze in stark vulnerability. She had never been this close to a man before; his body against hers was almost enough to make her forget all about the Cossacks.

"You're shaking," he said.

"I'm just—a little cold." In truth, it was part terror,

part desire, that swirled through her veins, a dizzying concoction.

"Then I must endeavor to warm you." He tightened his embrace with a sportive growl and rubbed her arms briskly. Then his hands grew still, gently cupping her shoulders. He opened his coat and gathered her inside of it, physically taking her under his wing. The clean, manly scent of him permeated her senses. "Better?"

With her arms around his lean waist, she nodded, smiling shyly at him.

Alec stared into her eyes. "Try to trust me, *ma petite*."

"Very well," she whispered slowly.

He gripped her hips in a sensual hold and drew her closer against his hard body—his chest, his belly, his thighs against hers. The excitement of his possessive clutch made her catch her breath. Then he lowered his head in silken menace, still watching her in the darkness at close range. Her heart fluttered wildly, but if she had expected a rough semi-ravishment, he devastated her with his gentleness. She closed her eyes, shivering with exhilaration as his lips brushed over her mouth in a light, exploratory caress. Leashed passion thrummed between them.

"Mm," he breathed, a throaty sound of pleasure that roused a burst of eager sensations within her. She had never experienced anything like it. "Very nice."

She felt a bit like a delicate marzipan on the dessert plate of a connoisseur, and could hardly wait to be devoured. It was agonizing, blissful.

The world, the Cossacks, all but disappeared; there was only this magnificent stranger and the wonderful sense of safety in his arms. He made her think how nice it would be to forget all about her quest and simply slip into the role he had assigned her.

Wicked.

She held her breath in sheer anticipation to see what

he might do next. The tip of his lordly nose skimmed her cheek as he inhaled the scent of her skin, taking his time with her, his warm breath tickling the corner of her mouth as he played. Her pulse raced. His hand was hot as he cupped the side of her neck, flirting with her earlobe. Then he kissed her bottom lip, nibbling ever so gently.

She moaned. *"Alec."* Remembering abruptly to breathe, she gasped in delight, and when her lips parted, he stole his chance with smooth expertise, moving more intently into her mouth, and as before, when he had kissed her brow, she melted.

As the hungry moments passed, his skilled hands roamed up and down her sides in searing caresses. She groaned, giving way in her amazement and yielding as he kissed her more deeply. The slow, luscious licks as his tongue stroked hers sent joy arrowing down her spine until her very toes curled. God, who was this man? she wondered as her world spun. *Delectable creature.*

He had the body of a god, the soul of a satyr, but the kiss he gave her was the work of a virtuoso. Clearly, he had done this before. Many, many times.

She, however, had not.

She clung to him, not a very convincing tart, she feared, for she was weak-limbed and trembling, her heart slamming. Fear infused her passion, lending it a reckless edge as the towering Cossacks rode past slowly on their warhorses.

Their fierce eyes scanned the doorways and dark alleys for a frightened, solitary girl; with barely a glance, she imagined they dismissed the young "unfortunate" plying her trade in the shadows with a dissipated blond nobleman.

Becky doubted she was even recognizable, inflamed with wanton desire for her heavenly fallen angel. Even the pleasant scratchiness of his blond day-beard chafing against her chin filled her with pleasure. All of her discoveries this night had thrown her into a state of astonishment. From the moment she had opened her eyes to find herself surrounded by his smartly dressed friends, it was as if she had awoken in a world about which she had heard rumors, but had never given much thought. A most enticing world of privilege and pleasure, luxury and lust.

Mrs. Whithorn, her housekeeper back home, had been telling her for years that she was a wicked girl, going to hell, just like her mother. Perhaps there was some truth to it, after all. It was all that could explain her ripeness for his temptation.

When Alec put her hands on him, as though he needed her touch just as badly as she had needed his kiss, she obliged with burning eagerness, fondling his sculpted abdomen and stroking his bare neck. She ran her fingers through his rain-dampened hair.

He, too, had abandoned himself to passion's spell; she could feel it in him, hear it in his needy moan, soft and low. He groaned her name and tilted his head the other way, kissing her again with sweet, drowning depth. He wrapped his arms around her, gathering her closer still.

Long after the Cossacks had ridden past, they remained where they were, their lips joined, their hands all over each other, until Alec suddenly stopped himself, panting roughly. "Ah, God, I'll die if you don't let me make love to you."

She couldn't answer. She could barely catch her breath.

"Please, Becky, say yes." He kissed her neck, lighting fires of temptation in the core of her body. "I need you."

His insistent male whispers roused a soft moan from her lips. Exhaustion had taken its toll, as well, so she knew that perhaps her judgment was a bit skewed, but after yet another close call, her confidence flagged. She knew it was time to be grimly honest with herself. How much longer could she realistically outrun them? It was a miracle she had made it this far, in truth, outnumbered as she was. If, or perhaps more accurately, *when* the Cossacks captured her and dragged her back to Mikhail, she already knew the punishment that awaited her. He had promised her a vicious rape. The great Prince Kurkov had not helped to drive Napoleon from Europe by making idle threats. But, oh, she knew a way now that she could trump him, if disaster struck.

If she failed in her quest and his Cossacks seized her, then let the brute do his worst; if she had the nerve tonight, she could have already robbed him of his prize by giving her innocence away freely to a man of her own choosing.

To Lord Alec.

She barely knew him, but one kiss had shown her he was skillful and gentle, and anything was better than having her body torn asunder by her own cousin's brute force. Oh, Mikhail would be so furious, she mused in defiant pleasure while Alec kissed her neck and blurred her starved senses with his powerfully potent attentions. It was madness to antagonize Mikhail. He'd probably kill her for it, but better to be dead than to find herself the captured plaything of a murderer.

By God, it would be worth it just to see the look on his face.

Just then, Alec pulled back a small space, flushed and tousled, his cobalt eyes smoldering with passion. "Let's go," he whispered urgently.

With a tremor of yearning in the pit of her belly, she closed her eyes.

"Don't deny me. Come on, Becky. Say yes. You and I have got to finish what we've started—"

"Yes."

He paused, then let out a shaky exhalation like a small laugh. "Praise God."

She dragged her eyes open and warily beheld his smoldering seductive smile, but she glanced away self-consciously, blushing after what she had just agreed to.

Alec planted a boyish kiss on her flaming cheek. "Such blushes," he murmured fondly. "You are so adorable."

She scoffed a little at his sweet words, unused to such flattery. He straightened up again and left her to collect herself for a moment while he did the same, sauntering to the edge of the awning. He rested his hands on his lean waist and looked out at the rain. "Lord, what a mess."

Becky leaned her head against the locked door behind her, still rather dazed. She glanced down the street again and noted in relief that the Cossacks were nowhere in sight. The weather was still temperamental, however; the wind blew swiftly, and torrents of rain drummed the pavement.

Alec turned to her, his tall, strong silhouette outlined against the downpour. He held out his hand and waited for her to take it.

For a moment she just stared at him in musing fascination, this man she intended to take for her first lover. Surely Mrs. Whithorn was right: She was every bit as impetuous as Mama. This was without a doubt the most reckless thing she had ever done in her life, but events had driven her to it.

Heaving herself upright, she shyly left the safety of the doorway and ventured over to Alec's side. He gathered her near. Her body still pulsated with mysterious longing for this beautiful stranger, her senses wildly attuned to him. She supposed there were brides who knew their new husbands no better than she knew Alec Knight.

Arranged marriages were common—and, apparently, for him, so were reckless trysts with ladies of the night.

Well, she was not her brother's keeper. In London, she had heard, they liked gossip, but folk from Buckley-on-the-Heath minded their own affairs and thanked others to do the same.

If Lord Alec was a loose-living, pleasure-seeking rogue, that was his business—and quite to her advantage, under the circumstances. Indeed, she very much intended to enjoy herself and to keep her secrets; for as charming as he was, he was obviously a libertine, hardly the sort of man she could confide in. He did not want to know her problems, and that suited her well enough. She much preferred to keep her troubles to herself rather than to learn point-blank that although he would join his body with hers, he didn't care about her any more than her relatives did.

No matter. She was used to relying on herself alone. This night would be a splendid experience as long as she remembered to guard her heart. He was only in it for himself. And so was she. Well, that was fair, was it not? she thought uneasily.

Alec took off his formal black tailcoat and put it around her shoulders. "Come." He looked soberly into her eyes. "Ready?"

She nodded bravely.

Trusting herself to fate and Alec Knight, she put her hand in his.

They ran.

Alec was thankful for the downpour, cooling the hot, keen edge of his ardor. He could not wait to bed her. Rarely had any girl so captivated him. He had wanted novelty, and God knew he had found it. There was no telling what the chit might do or say next. She was an entrancing blend of courage and vulnerability, and so damned beautiful. He knew it was highly decadent of him, but he adored her inexperience, savoring it as a rare delicacy. He had loved turning her reticence to fire.

It was just like wooing a virgin—with none of the guilt.

But one thing was certain. The chap who had ruined Becky had better pray he never crossed his path, because Alec knew he would not hesitate to thrash him soundly for it. On second thought, perhaps that was a tad hypocritical, since he fully intended to enjoy her himself. Very well, he conceded. *I'll thank the chap first, and then beat him senseless.*

They hurried on, hand in hand.

There was enchantment in the night, in the thunder that rang with their laughter as they dashed through the rain, in the silvery miniature cascades that rolled down their bodies and slicked their skin, in the diamond droplets that adorned their hair and eyelashes and made their lips and faces gleam. They splashed their way through deep puddles, leaving bubbles in their wake.

"Are you holding up all right?" he asked her over the loud ceaseless hiss of the rain slapping the pavement.

She nodded.

Alec frowned, concerned about the effects of the inclement weather on the girl's health, but it would have taken longer to reach the hackney stand, so they went on foot; it was only a few blocks down Piccadilly to his bachelor rooms at the exclusive Althorpe.

The original Baroque mansion, Althorpe House, had long since been divided into a few bachelor apartments. Behind it, situated around the green pleasant space of the lamplit courtyard, were several long, neat row houses built as luxurious private apartments with all the modern conveniences, eight to a building, four on each floor. Alec, naturally, owned one of the most desirable apartments with the best view.

When Becky and he arrived, the liveried porter at the property gates trudged out of his booth and went to unlock the way for them.

Waiting for him to do so, Alec glanced at Becky in persistent solicitude. She stood shivering beside him, wrapped in his oversize tailcoat like a good little soldier. Not a word of complaint. This girl was tough, he thought admiringly, but he could not stop worrying about her like a blasted mother hen. She was so pale in the darkness.

With that night-dark hair and eyes like amethysts, she possessed a haunting beauty, but her pallor troubled him. He noted the shadows under her eyes, the hollows beneath her elegant cheekbones. She looked very tired, and young, and fragile; and Alec found himself besieged by the most baffling need to take care of her. No, he would not lay a finger on her until he was sure she was all right.

When the porter hauled the creaking gates open to admit them, he gathered her closer with a protective arm around her shoulders. "This way, sweet," he murmured, escorting her into the courtyard. "We're almost home."

Home.

The word pained her, but she hurried to keep up with Alec's long, brisk strides as he led her to a handsome brick building marked *F.*

"My rooms are back this way."

They tracked wet footprints through the marble-tiled foyer as he led her through it and up the five stairs to a gracious mezzanine level. Here they left the staircase, going down a corridor that led toward the back of the building.

Becky followed with a sense of wonder and taboo, taking in all the strange sounds of rowdy male life going on behind the closed, numbered doors. Bass and tenor voices argued about racehorses and prizefights. Baritone laughter. She smelled smoke from pipes and cheroots.

"I hear music," she murmured.

"That is the Honorable Roger Manners," Alec explained in a confidential but humorous tone, glancing at the ceiling. "Practices the pianoforte for two hours every night. Annoys the blazes out of the other chaps, but I am a great lover of music."

"That is fortunate."

"Fortunate, indeed, since his chambers are right above mine. If he had taken up the trumpet, I fear I should not be half so accommodating." He reached into his waistcoat and fished out the key to his rooms. Becky held her breath, her heart pounding as he turned the lock. It clicked back with a low *snick*.

Alec glanced at her in question, reading her eyes, as though trying to assess if she was quite sure about this, but in the moment's somber silence, a sudden, hungry growl from her belly startled them both. Becky clapped her hands to her middle, her eyes widening.

"God's teeth, was that your stomach?" he exclaimed.

She turned red, mortified. "I—I think it was the thunder."

"Becky, sweet," he chided with a pained wince. "You're starving, aren't you?"

She bit her lip for a second, then nodded ashamedly. "I haven't had anything to eat since last night."

"You should have said something!"

"I don't wish to be any trouble."

"Nonsense, you couldn't be any trouble if you tried." He shook his head at her, then opened the door to his chambers. "Now, then, what am I going to feed you?" he mused aloud as he led her inside unceremoniously, tossing the key and the other contents of his waistcoat onto a thin-legged Sheraton table by the wall. "I shall send out to Watier's. We'll order a feast."

"Honestly, I'm not that picky." She walked in cautiously behind him.

"Well, I am. Welcome."

Their echoing footsteps suggested the spacious dimensions of the hall even before he lit a fine beeswax candle. The flames rose one by one atop the silver candelabra on the table, rolling back the darkness to show her the elegant space he called home.

Goodness, she thought. He claimed he wasn't rich?

There were gleaming white plaster cornices, a fireplace with a veined marble chimneypiece, and a huge bay window. The crimson walls contained exquisite paintings that hung on little chains from the brass picture rail beneath the gilded frieze. The man had very fine taste, she thought, rather awed. The sophistication of his home made her feel like an utter hayseed.

Small jeweled objets d'art adorned the mantelpiece, but she gasped at the sight of two painted Grecian urns on display inside a pair of recessed statuary alcoves.

"Are those real?" she blurted out in amazement, the rude question popping out before she could stop it. "Sorry." She covered her lips belatedly with her fingertips.

He smiled blandly. "Athens, fifth century B.C."

"Good heavens," she breathed. *Don't touch anything.* She tucked her hands into the pockets of her damp pelisse and stared all around her. The chaise in striped satin looked wonderfully inviting, but she dared not sit down on the furniture in her wet, dirty clothes.

"Make yourself at home, my dear." He went striding across the glossy parquet floor. "Sitting room through the French doors there." He pointed to a pair of closed double doors on the other side of the room, then opened a door on the left. "Bedroom's here. Follow me."

Her eyes widened as he disappeared inside. Lord, he

wasn't wasting any time! He had promised not to rush her—

"Becky, come here, pet."

She sidled over to the threshold of his bedchamber and peeked inside, a dozen nervous excuses on the tip of her tongue, but he quickly beckoned to her from a smaller room attached to the far wall of his sprawling bedchamber.

"Come into the dressing room. I think you will appreciate this."

"But—"

"Hurry. I have a little treat for you."

"What kind of treat?" Her heart pounded, but she was too intrigued to refuse. She tiptoed through his bedchamber, then stopped and stared in amazement at his towering domed bed. It nearly filled its arched, curtained alcove, only leaving enough room for several candle stands.

Elevated on a carpeted plinth, its plumed crown ringed with roses and winged cherubs nearly touched the ceiling; a profusion of sumptuous draperies flowed down from the dome to swathe the headboard in velvet opulence. The foot of the bed was curved inward like a rounded couch, with wooden bed-steps at the center of the sinuous contour. Large, gilded mirrors on both walls of the alcove reflected the gold and scarlet expanse of the kingly mattress.

No, one could not call that thing a bed, she thought with a gulp. It was an altar, a shrine to the mysteries of Eros. *Oh, Lord, what in heaven am I doing?*

Suddenly, from the dressing room, she heard a creaking noise followed by the steady splashing sound of pouring water.

"Becky, in here!" Alec called.

What in blazes? Hurrying past the hungry maw of

that wide bed, she joined him shyly in the dressing room, peeking in with caution.

"Voilà," he said with a smile, then she gasped as he gestured to an extravagance the likes of which, she was quite sure, had not been seen since Nero's day.

She stared in openmouthed wonder at the built-in bathing tub of dark green marble ensconced in an arched, curtained alcove like the one that housed the bed. It had, to her disbelief, two taps jutting out of the wall with engraved tiles that labeled one, CHAUD, the other FROID. Water was pouring out of both spigots amid a cloud of steam.

"Warm bath, my dear?"

"But—what—how?" She looked at him in question.

He smiled at her bewilderment. "We have piped water from a cistern for the cold tap. For the hot, the kitchen boiler lies on the other side of this wall. A pipe concealed inside the wall carries the heated water right through from the boiler to the bath, you see?" He reached across the tub and casually knocked on the tiled wall.

"Ohhh."

"It's new. Very rare. Actually, this is why I moved here. Only a few of the ground-floor apartments have them."

"Positively decadent."

"I know," he purred with a leonine smile. "I'm a sensualist, what can I say?"

"You're spoiled," she murmured in wonder.

He slanted her a sudden frown. "I'm sure I am not spoiled," he riposted in a somewhat prickly tone.

Had she struck a nerve? Becky tore her gaze from the steaming bath and looked at him in surprise. "I was only jesting."

"Humph." He rose languidly from the edge of the tub, showing her a glimmer of his high-society hauteur.

"If there is one thing in this world that I treat with dead seriousness, *cherie*, it is pleasure." He gestured toward the bath with a courtly flourish. "Enjoy."

"Pardon?"

"Soap. Towels." He pointed to these items on the shelf nearby while the water continued splashing merrily into the tub. "Just turn the handles on the taps when it's filled. You're welcome to use my dressing gown when you're through." He nodded to a long robe of paper-thin, royal blue silk hanging on a peg.

"But Alec—"

"But nothing, *ma petite*. I will not permit you to expire of a fever from the storm like some tragic heroine in a pantomime. I want you out of those wet clothes, posthaste—perhaps you shall require some assistance in disrobing?" he offered, turning back to her, one eyebrow raised suggestively as his glance skipped down over her body.

She looked down at herself abruptly and realized her wet clothes were clinging to her in a most indecent fashion. "I—I can manage, thanks."

"I don't mind," he added with lavish generosity. "I'm fairly handy at undoing a lady's stays—"

"I'm sure."

"I set a record for speed once in that very art."

"Did you?"

"Yes, it was a wager. I had to do it blindfolded, both hands tied behind my back. Forty-five seconds."

Her eyebrows lifted high. "How?" she asked faintly.

"Using my teeth." His smile was tranquil, slightly treacherous. "I like winning wagers."

She gulped.

"Now, if you want someone to scrub for you, I am happy to volunteer—"

He took a step forward; she jumped back.

"Alec!"

Alec stopped himself with that choirboy smile. "Right. I'll just be going, then."

Becky shook her head at the scoundrel, but could not help smiling warily as he retreated. His blue eyes danced with mischief as he strolled to the door, sketched a bow, and withdrew. For a long moment she stood there uncertainly, then dragged her hand through her hair. It took her a moment to recover from his whirlwind presence, but then he popped his head back in the door.

"Yell if you need anything. Don't hesitate."

"Go away!" she scolded, laughing.

"Right. Sorry. Leaving." With a sparkling look full of pretended repentance, he withdrew again and closed the door.

Still chuckling, Becky glanced around at his tidy dressing room: the mirrored vanity with its array of shaving accoutrements, small cologne bottles, pewter-handled hairbrush, toothbrush, comb. She eyed the soap and thick, puffy towels longingly, then stepped closer to the tub and peered in to see how full it was.

Feeling the delicious steam rising to her face, she chewed her lip indecisively, and glanced at the dressing room door behind her. "Are you still gone?"

"Yes!" he called from some distance through the apartment, then asked hopefully, "Do you need me?"

"No."

"Hurry! I'm bored."

"Yes, sir," she muttered, though it was impossible to mind the order, given his lavish hospitality. She let out a weary sigh, beginning to relax already. After several days on the run, huddling down in barns at night to snatch a few hours of sleep and coming out smelling of animals and hay, not to mention getting spattered with mud from passing carriages on the road, a bath would work wonders to restore her sense of normalcy.

Going over to the dressing room door that Alec had

left open a crack, she tried to close it, but to her dismay, it would not shut properly.

"Sorry, the latch is broken," he called from an outer room, apparently hearing her efforts to make it stay closed. "Don't worry, Becky, I won't spy on you. Tempting as it may be."

She snorted in answer to his droll remark. "Very well, I'm trusting you!"

But only up to a point.

Pressing the door closed as best she could, she went over to the bathing tub, rested her foot on the edge of it and drew her skirts up over her thigh with a wary glance over her shoulder.

The tiny suede pouch that held the Rose of Indra was firmly tied to the garter around her thigh. Quickly, she untied the leather strings that had secured the acorn-sized ruby and glanced around for a place where she could hide the jewel for the night. Lowering her foot and brushing her skirts back down again, she tiptoed over to the mahogany dresser, bent down, and silently opened the bottom drawer.

Tucking away the great ruby behind neat stacks of her host's muslin cravats and white lawn and cambric shirts, she closed the drawer again, satisfied that her inheritance, the hope of her village, was securely squirreled away till morning.

This done, she turned to the magnificent bath with a sparkle of anticipation in her eyes. Why, she could wash up and look a good deal more respectable when she left tomorrow morning to call on the Duke of Westland.

There would be time enough tomorrow to shoulder her worries again. For tonight, she would cast her cares aside, needing time to recover. Catching a glimpse of her pauperlike reflection in the mirror, she let out a wry snort and continued undressing.

* * *

Meanwhile, Alec waited in wet clothes for the victuals to arrive; waited, indeed, for three quarters of an hour. Waiting was not generally his forte, but he could be a patient man when he knew the reward would be worth it.

After his lengthy hiatus from the world of amour, he intended for both of them to take their time tonight. Savor it.

He was eager to get out of his wet clothes, but for that, he needed the dressing room. He was restless and dashed uncomfortable, but had no intention of barging in on his fair guest's privacy, all the same. That would have been exceedingly bad form, and invasive. It was important that Becky feel safe in his keeping. Women gave themselves so much more passionately when they were given enough reassurance.

Inexperienced as she was, he was prepared to go to great lengths to put her at ease. Curiously, he found he didn't mind.

At last the errand boy returned with a large basket of food elegantly draped with a checked napkin from the club, a small bottle of champagne, and a baguette peeking over the side. Alec handed the windblown lad an extra two shillings for his pains, took back his dripping umbrella, and closed the door. At once the room filled with the delicious, savory scents of Watier's best fare.

He set the basket on a pedestal table in the center of the room, poured two glasses of Beaujolais, and went to inform his pretty foundling that her gourmet feast had arrived. With the wineglasses dangling from one hand, he mused upon the pleasant task of looking after someone else for a change, instead of circling endlessly against the devils in his head.

Sauntering into his darkened bedchamber, he had only gone three paces into the room when the candlelit vision ahead stopped him in his tracks. The dressing room door had swung open a few inches, thanks to its broken latch, so it was purely by innocent accident that he caught a fleeting glimpse of Becky's naked loveliness.

She had gotten out of the bathing tub and was languidly drying off, running that thick white towel all over her body.

The chivalrous part of his brain gave the order to turn away—but somehow his limbs refused to obey, the command overridden by his awestruck male senses.

Good heavenly Lord.

Transfixed, his dazed stare trailed over her white hourglass figure. Her wavy sable mane hung heavily past her alabaster shoulders to kiss the sweeping line of her back. His gaze sank lower helplessly. Sweet hips, a derriere just plump enough to make his mouth water. Long, elegant legs that he needed wrapped around him, now. With a smooth motion, she slipped on his blue dressing gown and glided out of his line of vision.

A jolt of lust throbbed through him belatedly. He suddenly remembered to breathe. Abruptly, he loosened his hold on the wineglasses before he snapped the stems.

He fairly held his breath, listening: He could hear her moving about in his dressing room, humming softly to herself. The tender sound made him quiver like the tickle of light fingers running down his back. He forced his glazed stare away from the crack in the door, his pulse galloping.

After a moment, he managed to fight the lion of carnality back into its cage for the time being, then struggled to recall his purpose in coming here in the first place. The vision of her silken body had chased every thought from his head.

Ah, yes. The food.

"Becky?"

"Hullo." She appeared in the doorway with a relaxed

and sensual air, combing out the tangles in her long wet hair. Her cheeks glowed from the warm bath and there was a golden-violet luster in her eyes.

Alec swallowed hard.

The cloth belt of his dressing gown cinched her narrow waist, and with an inward moan, he recalled all too vividly that there was nothing beneath that fine blue silk but warm, white skin and heavenly curves. He could almost taste them.

"Your, uh, dinner's here."

"Bless you," she purred. "I feel so much better already." She accepted a wineglass and took a sip. "Mm. You were right. The bath worked wonders."

"Good." Slipping his arm around her slim waist, he leaned down, captured her lips, and gave her a soft, slow kiss. He could not resist. She tensed at first, but he felt her yield after a moment, resting her hand on his chest. "Go and eat," he murmured, releasing her with some reluctance. "Food's on the table in the other room."

"I can wait for you."

"Go on, you're hungry. It's all right." Brushing past her, he set his wineglass on the dressing table and then began unbuttoning his waistcoat. "I've got to get out of these wet clothes. Of course," he added slowly, "you may stay and watch if it pleases you."

Shrugging off his waistcoat, he tossed it carelessly over the wooden towel stand nearby and offered her a smile.

Becky's heart was racing, her lips still tingling from his unexpected kiss. His silk dressing gown caressed her skin; already she felt wrapped in his pleasing male scent, entangled in his web of desire.

She wasn't really going to do this, was she?

The thing of it was, there was hardly any graceful way

out of it now. And as he continued undressing for her, she was not sure she wanted to.

She stared at him for a long moment, trying not to look shocked and virginal.

"You love to tease me, don't you?" she asked after a moment.

"Who, me?" he whispered coyly.

Mrs. Whithorn's voice in her head promised fire and brimstone, but Becky did not budge. She held her ground, trying to prove, perhaps, that she could be sophisticated and worldly, too.

Alec watched her watching him, and then her gaze traveled down his body. She could not help staring at the way his thin white shirt clung to his skin, wet linen hugging every muscled line of his broad shoulders and lean waist. He was even lovelier than she had thought. When she looked into his eyes again, she read an invitation there that took her breath away.

No, she was not ready to touch him yet.

With the leisurely air of a man biding his time, he sat down on the vanity stool and pulled off his shoes, chucking them aside. He stood up again, his bare feet long and princely, cushioned by the thick Persian carpet.

He reached for his wine, took a sip, and then shrugged his black suspenders off his shoulders. He started to take off his shirt, but paused. "Do you want to help?"

"No."

His eyes danced. "Suit yourself." Then he peeled his shirt off over his head, and Becky stifled a gasp at the glorious flex and play of sculpted muscle. He sent her a speculative glance, the promise of undreamed pleasure smoldering in his eyes.

So, he wasn't an angel, after all. No, she concluded, her heart beating faster as he helped himself to a towel. He was a veritable Greek god—all smooth and strong and perfect. No angel could inspire such wicked thoughts. Her hand trembled as she lifted her goblet to her lips and took a steadying sip of wine, but she could not help staring as he patted the towel over the flowing lines and broad dimensions of his damp chest, then ran it lower, caressing oh-so-invitingly the intricate rippling fretwork of his taut belly, lapped by unsteady candlelight.

Who could have guessed that the male physique was endowed with such beauty under all those starchy cravats and layers of tailored clothing—shirt, waistcoat, jacket? She was entranced and wondering if he'd mind if she kissed every hard plane and curve. She'd make a ring of kisses around his adorable belly button. . . .

She took another feverish gulp of wine, thinking that she really ought to leave now. His black pantaloons were still damp from the rain and bordered on indecency—skintight, vaguely see-through, outlining every delicious inch of him—including regions that no young lady had any business staring at. Good Lord, were all men that big down there?

He turned away, finally finding a remnant of modesty, but when he peeled his trousers off, Becky choked on her wine at the sight of his sleek hindquarters, bare as the day he was born.

Far more beautiful than any statue, he straightened up, kicking off his trousers. "Are you all right?" he asked as she kept coughing. When he turned to her, buck naked and completely at ease, Becky inhaled a couple of droplets of wine and shook her head violently. He started toward her. "Do you want a clap on the back?"

Retreating, she flung up her hand to ward him off. "I'm fine," she croaked. "Just fine—thanks."

"You're sure?"

"Positive," she wheezed, then whirled around and fled the room with the golden vision of him emblazoned on her mind in all his primal glory.

Her hasty exit must have puzzled him, but a second later his jolly laughter followed her, resonating from the dressing room.

"Shy, Becky-love?"

"Oh, do stop!"

"Teasing you? Never!" he called back amiably. "I think I've found a new hobby."

She tried to scowl in his general direction, but somehow she couldn't stop smiling.

CHAPTER
❦ THREE ❧

Reaching the salon, Becky immediately spotted the source of the mouth-watering food smells wafting on the air—the dinner basket waiting for her on the round pedestal table. Her eyes lit up and she strode over to it without hesitation, tearing away the checked cloth covering the basket.

She oohed and aahed over each wonderful delicacy that she removed from it—bread and a hunk of good Cheddar, a jar of pureed soup, cold sliced meats neatly wrapped in cheesecloth, a bevy of slightly warm dry puddings, two peach tarts, strawberries, even a bottle of champagne. She found the silverware, napkins, and fancy china bowls and small dishes that Alec had left on the table, and quickly began fixing a plate for each of them, ravenously sampling everything.

With their feast laid out before her, she was tempted to devour it single-handedly, but she supposed that would have been inexcusably ill-mannered. Pained with waiting, she glanced toward the bedroom, but Alec was still in the dressing room changing into dry clothes.

Curbing her hunger, she decided to take a discreet peek around. Lifting the candelabra off the table, she wandered across the large main room, admiring his Old Masters and his Grecian urns with their beguiling, elongated figures so intricately worked. Trailing her hand along the scrolled arm of the luxurious Roman couch upholstered in striped satin, she approached the French doors to the sitting room and nudged one open, but when she lifted the candelabra and peered inside, she was taken aback to find the parlor bare.

No furniture. No rug. Just a lonely expanse of parquet floor and an empty picture rail that ran the circumference of the room beneath the ornamental frieze. She frowned and closed the door again. As she turned around slowly, perusing the main room again, she began to see the empty spaces where she realized more pieces of his spare, leggy, claw-foot furniture had once stood, though they had been well-camouflaged by a white statue here, a deftly placed potted fig tree over there. On the walls, she now detected slightly darker rectangles where the silk wall-hangings had not faded from the sunlight because they had previously been covered up by now vanished pieces of art.

Well, perhaps those things had been sold off to help him climb out of that sinister-sounding "deep dark hole" that he had mentioned. Recalling what he had said about making and then losing a fortune at the gaming tables, her first thought was one of sympathy at the realization that the proud aristocrat was doing his best to keep up appearances—obviously of penultimate importance here in Town, as she had learned today when everyone had shunned her.

But then alarm suddenly flashed through her. If he was having financial difficulty . . . *Oh, no.* Her glance flicked toward the dressing room. What if he found the Rose of Indra hidden in his dresser drawer? If he chose to take it from her, she doubted she could stop him. He was bigger than she, and stronger.

She was already marching toward the dressing room, determined to get him out of there, or at least to distract him if he was still lingering over his toilette.

You could choose to trust him, instead, a small voice in her head offered. Perhaps it was conscience.

Indeed, if she took that route, Alec, judging by his cultured furnishings, might even be able to determine how much the jewel was worth, whether its value was sufficient to buy back her home from Mikhail. But Becky couldn't do it.

Trusting people was usually a losing bet, she had learned in life. Better to rely on oneself alone. Then no one could let you down.

She hurried on, determined to keep a good man honest, but just as she stepped into the bedroom, her suave host emerged.

"I thought you'd be eating by now." Ambling toward her, Alec was bare-chested, a towel draped carelessly across his shoulders. He had donned loose baggy trousers of natural linen—in the style called Cossack trousers, ironically enough. He was still tying the drawstring as he sauntered toward her, his bare feet silent over the parquet floor.

"I . . . I waited for you." She scanned his face in guarded suspicion, but quickly concluded by his guileless look that he had not found the ruby.

Thank God.

"I see," he said amiably. "So, you were coming to tell me to hurry up."

She smiled, the tension slowly easing from her. "Those weren't to be my exact words, but the sentiment's the same."

"Here I am."

"Come, your soup is getting cold." She captured his hand and tugged him over to their feast.

"You don't have to share with me, Becky. It's for you."

"You're much too generous. I could never eat all this by myself."

"Ma'am," he murmured, politely pulling out a chair for her at the table.

She gave him a gracious nod and took her seat. With a warm smile, he sat in the chair next to her, his thighs sprawled loosely.

"I hope everything is to your liking. Watier's is famous for their dinners here in horrible, hateful London Town."

She sent him an arch smile. "It's all very good," she replied as she lifted her spoon to her lips. "Almost as good as my own country cooking."

"You can cook—food?" he exclaimed.

Nodding, she pointed with her spoon to the place she had set for him. "Eat."

He did not obey; she had a feeling he rarely did. Instead, he propped his elbow on the table and just watched her with an odd little smile on his face.

"What is it?" she asked with a spoonful of soup halfway to her lips.

"Hm?" he murmured.

"You're staring."

"You're the only woman I know who can cook food," he said matter-of-factly, then took the towel off his shoulders and used it vigorously on his still damp hair.

Becky couldn't help smiling when he was through. He looked so adorably tousled and boyish.

"Shall I open the champagne?"

"Oh, would you?" she asked eagerly, then confessed, "I have never tasted any before."

"Well, then, you must do so without delay." He rose and undertook the task. "If you intend to make your fortune as a fine London courtesan, my girl, you're going to have to get used to the stuff."

She offered no reply, guiltily letting him maintain his wrong assumptions.

She was trying not to think yet about what lay ahead

tonight, and she had the distinct impression that Alec knew she was nervous and was determined to soothe her with his teasing and his easygoing charm.

She supposed it was going to hurt, despite his skill as a lover.

Her mother had died when Becky was fourteen, still too young to have certain matters explained to her; and the ultra-pious Mrs. Whithorn probably didn't know the facts of birds and bees, herself; but whatever instruction the female adults in Becky's life had left neglected, the brazen country girls in her village had explained in wicked, astonishing detail.

Sally, the red-haired tavern wench, and Daisy the milkmaid, both fetching, knowing, brazen girls, were local experts on the subject of the "amorous congress." Any male with whom one of them dallied had to be sampled by the other, as well. The two girls were both rivals and friends, and thoroughly relished sitting around and debating their comparisons afterward, much to the scandalized delight of the other young people in Buckley-on-the-Heath. The older folk pretended to be oblivious to the younger set's explorations, for, after all, mating was a key part of country life, from the butterflies courting amongst the meadow flowers, to the kestrels coupling violently in midair, to the orderly annual breeding of Farmer Jones's prize sheep. Sex was everywhere. God knew there was little else to do in rural England, except work.

Though Sally and Daisy had both gone up to the hayloft with nearly all the local farm boys and, of course, their favorite, the local squire's insufferable eldest son, Becky had never even felt tempted. The extent of her experience was through hearing her lowborn friends' accounts, and truthfully, she did not believe everything they said. She just liked being included in the conversations.

Well, she concluded, if Sally and Daisy had lied just for fun—and she wouldn't put it past them—no doubt Alec would show her what she was supposed to do.

She did trust him that much.

He was very easy to be with, she thought, watching his every move with deepening feminine interest. Aye, if the lads back in Yorkshire were scruffy ponies, he was a haughty, temperamental, blooded stallion—very fast, very beautiful, and highly dangerous.

He read the champagne label with an approving nod. Untwisting the wire and coaxing the cork partway out with his thumb, he sent her a devilish half smile. "Center of the ceiling medallion."

"What?" She followed his upward glance, then realized what he was about—making a game of shooting the cork out of the bottle. Her laughter relieved some of her tension. Lord, the man could make a party out of a twig and a ball of twine.

She shook her head and boldly challenged him: "Never."

He lifted his eyebrows. "I see. The lady doubts my aim. Do you want to bet?"

"Dashed right I will." She looked around for something to wager with. "I'll bet you . . . one strawberry that you cannot hit the center of the ceiling medallion with that cork," she declared, holding one up between her fingers with a flourish.

"I'd rather win a kiss instead."

She shook her head firmly. "Strawberry or nothing."

"You drive a hard bargain," he said, taking aim. "Tallyho."

Pop!

The champagne cork sailed through the air like a Congreve rocket and collided with the ceiling medallion, then bounced violently to earth.

"Oh, blast," she muttered, losing the bet.

"I thought you said you were born lucky." He strolled back to the table with the frothing bottle in his hand.

"Well, I'm lucky when it matters."

"Tilt your head back and open your mouth," he murmured, strolling back to the table with the frothing bottle in his hand.

The order startled and intrigued her. She ignored the frisson of arousal that his wicked tone sent through her veins and, daringly, did as he told her. Alec poured a small draft of the foaming liquid into her mouth and watched hungrily as she swallowed it.

"What do you think?"

She tasted it carefully, wrinkling her nose. "I like the bubbles, but 'tis a bit sour, isn't it?"

" 'Dry' is the term, *cherie*. Have some more." He poured out two narrow champagne flutes. "You'll find you may quickly acquire a taste for it."

"Are you trying to get me tipsy?"

"It never crossed my mind." He slipped her a sly half smile, then held up his glass. "A toast."

She followed suit and looked at him in question.

"To the bold and beautiful Becky—you do have a last name?"

"Ward," she blurted before considering the matter more thoroughly. *Blast.* She hadn't really wanted to tell him that. The less he knew about her, the better.

"To you, Miss Ward. I predict that you shall take the Town by storm. In fact, I will make sure of it— personally," he added with a wink.

She gazed at him wistfully for a second. "Thank you for your kindness to me, Alec. I don't know what I would have done tonight without you."

He looked away with a careless laugh and a hint of color rising in his manly cheeks. "Oh, it's nothing, I'm sure. It's easy to be kind to a beautiful girl."

Good Lord, had she just made the libertine blush? He

avoided her gaze and busied himself making sure they both had plenty of champagne, but the brief tint beneath his angular cheekbones spoke volumes of the real man behind the jaded facade.

He has a good heart, whatever his faults. All the more reason not to confide in him, she thought gravely, gazing at him. All the more reason not to risk getting him killed. She had already seen Mikhail slaughter one man.

"You're supposed to drink now," Alec instructed with a determined return to his rakish indifference. "I toast, you drink, you see. A simple ritual."

"Right." She slipped him a knowing smile and sipped her champagne. "Ah, I must pay off my wager! Hold out your hand, good Sir Knight," she commanded in a playful tone worthy of his own roguery.

He obeyed, for once.

"Now, claim your reward." Ceremoniously, she placed a strawberry on his waiting palm. It sat there, plump and scarlet, like a priceless ruby.

Or a tiny delicate heart.

His long, sandy lashes veiled his blue eyes as he stared down at it for a second, his expression so guarded it was impossible to know what he was thinking. Then he recovered with a devilish grin, tossed the strawberry up into the air and caught it in his mouth.

Becky gazed at him warily as he ate his prize in one bite. He washed it down with a swig of champagne from the bottle, and she was struck with the thought that a girl would have to be foolhardy to give her heart to a man like him.

When he flirted, he was furthest away.

"Something wrong?" he asked, lifting his eyebrows in his urbane way. *You can't reach me,* his firm defenses seemed to taunt her from the depths of his blue eyes, like great shining silver walls of steel within him.

She shook her head, mystified. "Just a little tired. And still hungry," she added.

"Well, eat, girl. Enough of your missish manners. I know you're starving." He took her fork, stabbed some meat and cheese with it, and then offered it to her.

Becky smiled at him and accepted the bite.

Do hurry, he thought, enjoying feeding her but growing a trifle impatient. The sooner she was done eating, the sooner he could take her to his bed.

The little hellion fascinated him. After all his Society ladies with their fancy airs and haughty affectations, her naturalness enthralled him. He watched her devour pudding and meat, bread and cheese, gulping down champagne like it was water, and found himself growing decidedly aroused. He hoped her other appetites were equally lusty.

Finishing her meal at last, his fair young guest slumped back in her chair and rested both hands on her stomach with a contented sigh.

He regarded her in amusement. "Feeling better?"

"Worlds. Thank you so much." She leaned at once across the table, draped her arm around his neck and kissed his cheek. "You will be my hero forever."

"Have another drink, Becky-love," he purred.

"You think I'm only saying this because of the champagne?" she retorted, lounging back in her chair again.

He did not answer. A tipsy, half-naked girl in his rooms suited Alec just fine.

Instead, he reached over and stroked the curve of her face with one knuckle. "It's good to finally see some color in your cheeks."

"Thanks to you," she murmured. She did not protest his light, exploratory caress; indeed, his touch visibly relaxed her.

Alec savored the rose-petal softness of her cheek and

fought the urge to tell her she was too damned beautiful for any man's sanity. He liked the way the curling tendrils of her midnight mane framed her face and tumbled down her dainty shoulders.

With a heave of will, he sat back in his chair, waiting for her to come to him. He would not rush her. He would not. He stroked his lips in thought as he stared at her.

"So, why do you insist on claiming that you're lucky?" he inquired, at which she laughed a little, skimming her lips back and forth along the rim of her wineglass with a musing motion that quickened his blood. Did she even know how badly she tempted him?

"Now, there is a tale to impress even you, Lord Alec." She slanted him a mysterious smile. "It has to do with my middle name."

"Which is?"

"Guess," she ordered.

"No."

"I'll give you a hint: It starts with an *A.*"

Alec smiled with a speculative gleam in his eyes. "Alexandra—similar to mine."

"No."

He raised his eyebrow. "Anne?"

She shook her head.

"Alice. Arabella. Agnes. Agatha?"

"No, it's not an actual *name.*"

"Ah . . . Anise? Alphabet? Azalea?"

"No, no, think more . . . geographical."

"America? Atlas?" He stole a naughty glance at her breasts. "Alps?"

She laughed. "You beast! I think you need another hint—"

"No, don't tell me. Now I am determined to guess it. It's Arundel. Ascot?"

"No."

"Blast. I was going to bet a shilling on you in the Derby."

"Ha."

"I've got it!" he said suddenly. "Africa!"

"Finally, you're on the right continent, at least."

He narrowed his eyes in thought. "I see. Someplace hot. Exotic."

"Mm-hmm."

"Fits you," he murmured, raising his glass to her again in practiced gallantry.

She stretched her legs out under the table, her calf briefly caressing his shin. "We'll be at this all night if I don't give you another clue," she said.

"Well, we can't have that. All right."

"My father," she said meaningfully, "was in the navy."

"Oh, yes. I recall you mentioning something about that while you were threatening to brain me with the candlesnuffer."

"It made a tolerable weapon, I thought."

"God knows you used it well. Father in the navy . . . hot place. Of course! It's Aboukir! Aboukir Bay, at the head of the Nile. You must have been born in the year of the battle."

"Actually, sir," she informed him with a rather tipsy lift of her chin, "I was born *in* that battle. God save the Queen," she added.

He watched her in amusement, which she apparently mistook for disbelief.

"It's true! While my father was on the upper gun-deck of the HMS *Goliath* helping to blow up Boney's fleet, Mama was in the sick bay giving birth to me."

"Really?"

"Yes!"

"I see. So, you're lucky to be alive, is that it?"

"No, no, it's a much more cheerful reason than that," she scoffed.

"Born in a battle?" he murmured admiringly. "That explains a lot about you. Do tell."

"For weeks our ships had been scouring the Mediterranean in search of Napoleon's fleet, for the French just kept running and hiding, whisking away just ahead of us at every turn. But then, in the same hour that my mother went into labor with me, the French fleet was sighted in the Bay of Aboukir. They were riding at anchor, their sterns to our guns, defenseless—with no escape route. After weeks of searching, we had stumbled across the enemy purely by chance, like finding a needle in a haystack.

"Papa declared to Admiral Lord Nelson that it *must* have been the fortunate star of my birth that had brought them that stroke of good luck, for my arrival in the world was the only thing that was different from every day that they had been on the hunt. And it's true," she added proudly, "because the Battle of the Nile was, aside from Trafalgar, our most glorious victory. It ruined French sea power and changed the course of the war."

This girl astonished him.

"Thank God you had the foresight to be born then," he said abruptly.

"Yes, I know. Otherwise, we'd all be speaking French." She grinned and took a swig of champagne.

Charmed to the point of distraction, wanting nothing so much as to scoop her up in his arms and kiss her senseless, it took Alec a moment to recover his wits.

"What the devil was your mother doing on board a warship?" he asked. "Surely the navy has rules against that sort of thing."

"Well, my dear Lord Alec," she said confidentially. "I'm sure you're very innocent about such things, but there are rules and then there are *rules*. Officially speaking, we were never there. Nor were the several dozen other women who lived on board the ship with their husbands. That was the problem, you see. Mama was very beautiful, and Papa's commanding officer took a fancy to her. She would not tell my father of his superior's advances," she added wistfully. "She did not want him to do something rash and jeopardize our livelihood by harming his career—let alone call the man out to duel, which he surely would have done. Papa was very dashing," she informed him. "Instead, Mama gave him the excuse that my education was being neglected with such an unconventional upbringing. After that, she and I took rooms in Portsmouth and became landlubbers."

"Landlubbers," he echoed in quizzical amusement.

"Yes. I haven't seen the sea in years," she added pensively, staring at nothing. "Sometimes at night I dream about it, miles and miles and miles of waves." She paused. "Mama died the summer I was fourteen. She fell ill caring for a poor family of the parish."

Alec laid his hand over hers in a silent offering of comfort. "I'm very sorry."

"It's all right. She was wonderful to me while I had her. They both were."

"What's this?" he murmured, leaning closer to capture the tiny pink seashell that hung from a ribbon around her neck.

Her sudden, lovely smile dazzled him. "Do you like my little shell?" One would have thought it was a flawless diamond, for all her pride in it.

"Very pretty. Did you steal it from a mermaid?"

"Papa gave it to me the last time I saw him." Sadness crept into her voice as she spoke. "Mama and I bade good-bye to him at Portsmouth, the last time he went away. He said that I could hold this seashell up to my ear and, anytime I wanted, I could hear him whisper inside it, 'I love you.' "

Alec looked into her eyes.

With the seashell still resting on his fingertips, he was flooded with such a wave of protective male instinct that he barely knew what to do with himself.

Parents dead. No wonder she had ended up on the streets. "Come here, baby," he whispered, releasing her trinket and sitting back slowly in his chair, offering her his lap. "Come on," he ordered softly, taking her hand and drawing her to him.

She came to him with uncertainty in her wide violet eyes. He wrapped his arms around her, gathering her onto his lap. "It's going to be all right." He pressed her head down onto his shoulder and stroked her hair. "Why don't you stay with me for a while?" he murmured. "I won't let anything bad happen to you."

"Alec." She trembled a little as she breathed his name. Raising her head from his shoulder, she pulled back a small space and stared into his eyes; her own, liquid pools of emotion, their glowing violet hue like sun-kissed clouds at dawn.

Her beauty, he knew, would long haunt him.

"You are the sweetest man," she breathed. Cupping his cheek in her hand, she closed her eyes and gently kissed him.

Alec quivered, breathless with the butterfly caress of her silken lips against his, healing him, enticing him, redeeming him. The ends of her sable hair tickled his skin; he pulled her closer, winding his arm around her, splaying his hand across her hip, kneading her. The feel of her firm young flesh was luscious to the touch, sheathed in his silk dressing gown.

Capturing his face between her soft hands, Becky tasted him more deeply. Alec opened his mouth, welcoming her tongue's delicate explorations; and with that, the two of them simply picked up right where they had left off beneath that awning.

Alec couldn't get enough of her. After a few moments she let him turn her on his lap so she was facing forward, straddling him, both of them engrossed in kissing and caressing. Her bare feet curled around his calves. His hands roamed hungrily up and down her back.

The candles flickered, creamy drops of melted wax rolling down their shafts; the music from his neighbor's pianoforte floated through the ceiling, while the rain drummed the windowpanes. Alec's heart slammed in his chest as he focused all his attention instead on the tender neophyte in his arms and his own strange longing to protect her.

His fascination with her took him by surprise, God's truth; he had not expected to find this sense of connection. Maybe he could keep her, just for a while, he thought as his right hand ventured under blue silk, exploring the juicy thigh that hugged his hip.

He had never taken a mistress of his own before. Surrounded all his life by more women than he knew what to do with, there had never been any need. But she was different, he mused, shuddering at the unbearable softness of her skin. So eager, so sweet. The gentle way she stroked his belly was driving him insane. The delicious heat of her body called to his blood like a siren's song.

Half maddened by her position astride him, her legs spread, the humid warmth of her core permeating his groin and teasing his ferocious erection, he could think of nothing else but parting that dressing gown and taking her right there on the dining table.

"Darling?" he panted, finally finding the strength to break their kiss.

"Alec," she answered breathlessly.

The way she moaned his name made him smile. He hadn't even really started pleasuring her yet. He cupped her lovely face between his hands, relishing the sight of her like this, utterly aroused for him, her violet eyes smoldering, heavy-lidded with desire, her cheeks aglow with passion's flush. It seemed he had finally succeeded in warming her up. The girl was on fire. His pride swelled, along with other regions of his anatomy.

The dressing gown he'd lent her had come loose in a deep V that ended at her navel. He trailed his fingertip down the center. She flinched with want, her chest heaving under his light caress. "Becky," he whispered slowly.

"Yes?"

"Shall we go to bed?" When he reached her navel, his touch traveled back up her bare flat midriff again, but he veered off to the right at her chest and ran his fingertip up along the lower curve of her breast, moving with exquisite slowness over the pebble-firm point of her erect nipple.

She gasped and closed her eyes, enjoying the sensation, her inhibitions lowered by champagne. Encouraged, he squeezed her nipple gently between forefinger and thumb, and licked his lips at her sigh of delight, half ready to explode before he even got inside her.

"Becky?"

"What?" she murmured dreamily.

"I need you, kitten. Come to bed and love me."

"Alec," she groaned again.

"Please."

He was the living, breathing definition of irresistible.

His kisses had made her more drunk than the fancy French champagne, she thought, insofar as she could string a thought together. She felt the massive readiness of his body throbbing with insistent demand against her pelvis, and did not suppose a refusal at this late juncture would have been very well received. She was not sure that she was capable of uttering one, anyway.

She was lost and drowning in the deep blue ocean of his eyes, and it was wonderful. Any threat from Mikhail seemed naught but a bad dream. She had gone to the Blessed Isles with Alec.

She may have begun this night with calculation, but now there was only the honeyed sweetness of his gaze and the fierce primal need he had awakened in her.

This moment might be her last chance to change her mind, but his powers of persuasion were too great for her to withstand.

It was all over when he started kissing her earlobe, whispering to her. "You're so different, Becky. So beautiful. So soft." His fingers still flirted with her nipple while his other hand cupped her head, his thumb caressing her jugular.

With his mouth's warm caress at her ear, she closed her eyes and bent her head, kissing his broad shoulder. His skin was bronzed velveteen beneath her lips. When she tasted him with the tip of her tongue, he quivered. She grew intoxicated by her power to make him respond to her touch in the same way that she responded to his. Aye, whatever mysteries lay in store for her in that other room, she wanted her initiation to be with him.

And she wanted it now.

She slid her palms slowly up his muscled biceps to his shoulders, then wrapped her arms around his neck and held him close. "Make love to me, Alec," she breathed.

He stood up, lifting her with him. She clung to him, her hands locked behind his neck. He made her feel so feminine, carrying her into his bedchamber as if she weighed no more than a feather. She just stared at him, half besotted; she left her last maidenly doubts by the door. He walked across his chamber toward the magnificent alcove. Becky could feel the invisible draw of the ornate towering bed behind her, like another presence in the room, as if the carved cupids round the gilded dome were watching. The mirrors reflected the three candles that burned there, bathing the velvet-draped alcove in a wash of flickering light.

"Nervous?" he asked softly, nuzzling her nose with his own.

"N-No."

"Liar," he whispered. "It's all right. You won't regret it."

"I know."

He set her down on her feet at the bottom of the mahogany bed-steps. Her heart pounding, Becky turned slowly to study their opulent playground for the night.

Alec touched her chest, slipping the silk dressing gown off her left shoulder. She blushed in lingering modesty, not wanting to part from it quite yet, not that it hid much now, with the cloth belt undone. The robe hung open, but her arms were still threaded through the capacious sleeves; the garment half flowed off her, loosely garlanded through the crooks of her elbows to drape behind her like an elegant India shawl.

This pleased Alec, judging by the lustrous glow in his eyes.

"You are an exquisite woman," he whispered hoarsely. He lifted her hand from her side and kissed her knuckles, then escorted her slowly up the bed-steps.

Becky hesitated at the top step and turned to gaze at him uncertainly.

His stare was gravely worshipful. No man had ever looked at her that way. She bit her lip and put her resistance aside for once and for all. There would never be another night like this, she knew. The future was dark, but come what may, this honeyed memory would be her secret, her own delicious indiscretion.

Her heart beat faster as she crawled toward the headboard and then sat in the middle of the vast mattress, bracing her hands behind her. It was very cozy under the bed's sweeping draperies. She glanced up at the underside of the dome and found it whimsically painted with blue sky and puffy white clouds. How very *Alec*, she thought, looking at him again with a lazy smile.

Her position afforded her a breathtaking view as her sun god came walking up the bed-steps with an air of predatory languor. He went down on his knees at the foot of the mattress and stared at her as he approached on all fours.

Anticipation gave her such a tremor that she suddenly was glad he wore those loose linen trousers. She was still quite intimidated by that part of him that she had first encountered full-on in his dressing room.

His knowing half smile soothed her fears.

"Trust me," he whispered as he moved atop her, his advance coaxing her onto her back. Her heart pounding, she lay back slowly under him, resting against the satin bolsters of the headboard.

Alec reclined on his side, partly atop her. Below the waist, all of him was pressed firmly against her body. Distant piano music and the light beating drum of rain on the window glass infused the charged silence in the alcove. Propping his elbow on the bolster by her head, Alec rested his cheek in his left hand; his right went exploring.

When he touched her, an indecent wave of relief rushed through her. She luxuriated in his caresses. Closing her eyes, she drew in her breath and dropped her head back, reveling in the gentle warmth of his hands and the coolness of the rain-scented air against her bare skin. She could not bear for him to stop.

His hand glided over her body until she was quivering. His mouth followed, first at her throat, her pulse hammering in the artery beneath his lips. He became more aggressive, claiming her neck in a deep, openmouthed kiss, all but biting her. She surrendered completely to him in climbing ecstasy.

"Take this off." His order was taut, rugged. He pulled at one sleeve of the dressing gown. She was quick to obey, sliding her arm out of it and letting the luxurious garment whisper down onto the mattress behind her in a pool of blue silk.

Alec's fiery stare devoured her nakedness. "God, Becky," he ground out. "You are . . . just what I've needed so badly, so long."

"Am I?" she breathed.

He nodded with a wicked glance, and moved atop her. Becky abandoned herself to kissing him, savoring that gorgeous mouth, but he left her lips after a moment, moving lower. Much lower.

Not an inch of her body did he leave unexplored—the delicate skin in the fold of her elbow, the little notch at the base of her throat, the bend of her knee, the gentle slope of her foot, the soft curves of her inner thighs, and her breasts, which seemed designed for his cupped palm. He studied and learned every curve with an intimate mastery.

Her pulse was pounding, her back arching under his touch; she drew in her breath in delight when he laid his middle fingertip on the hardened jewel of her womanly center. She had not known that this was what she needed until he stroked her.

"So wet for me," he whispered, sliding his fingers inside her. She moaned in sweet anguish, bringing her hands up to her breasts as he pleasured her. "May I?" he asked huskily. She gasped his name in helpless hunger. Her chest heaved as he lowered his head, her nipples swelling eagerly as his lips approached, but rogue that he was, he played with her a bit, driving her mad. He blew gently on each turgid crest before he gave her the relief of his warm, hungry mouth.

She ran her fingers through his golden hair while he suckled hard, his hand stroking deeply between her thighs. "*Oh, Alec, Alec.*" She gripped his broad shoulders and tipped her head back in delight as he flicked little rings around her nipple with the tip of his tongue.

"You had better not come yet," he warned in a velvet murmur, denying her his hand as he moved up to kiss her neck.

She wasn't sure what that signified, but she was happy to let the man do to her whatever he fancied. If this was ruin, she had no use for respectability.

Alec eased down onto her, settling heavily between her thighs. She trembled with yearning as she clung to him, moaning a little at the depth and urgency of his kiss. Her hips rose with a shocking will of their own, caressing his giant hardness through the single layer of his clothing. He groaned with pleasure at that, and so she did it again, and he responded with a wild kiss, gently grasping her nape beneath the soft mass of her hair.

He drove his pelvis hungrily against hers as their tongues mated, their kiss ever deepening. She smoothed his silky forelock, which fell forward in his eyes, all the while intoxicated by the kid-leather softness of his supple, muscular chest against her. The hands with which she touched him, the body she pressed against him, every inch of her exalted with heightened sensitivity.

"Lie back for me, Becky." Quivering like a lusty stallion, he nuzzled her fevered brow. "I want you now. I need to be inside you."

She pulled back a small space and looked into his eyes. In the candlelight, they had darkened to the brooding blue of sapphire seas. She knew the time had come.

"You will be gentle with me, Alec?" she whispered, petting his hair.

"Of course I will, sweeting. Of course I will." He cupped her face in his hand, the pad of his thumb caressing the corner of her mouth, as he offered another kiss of drugging depth and patient solicitude.

As his kiss eased her worries, he laid her back slowly on the bed, staring into her eyes. The blue robe was still unfurled beneath her.

She had one final chance to change her mind when he reached over to fetch something from a trifle-box on the candle stand, but perhaps, at heart, she was as much a gambler as he, for she let the moment come and go without regret.

"What are you doing with that?" she whispered as he fitted a thin, filmy sheath of some sort over his towering erection.

"Making sure we're both protected, my love," he said softly, and tied the ribbon at its base with shaking hands.

"Oh," she murmured, though she did not understand. The man obviously knew what he was doing. In any case, the question fled her mind when he lay slowly between her legs.

She had never been so acutely aware of every inch of her own skin, and certainly was wildly aware of every inch of him. There was only sensation and sweetness and his mesmerizing blue eyes, his gaze that reached deep into her soul. His lashes swept downward; he lowered his head, his soft lips nuzzling her shoulder. She slid her arms around him with a small, impatient sigh.

He took her face between his hands and gave her slow intoxicating kisses. These deepened, his tongue delving into her mouth until she was in rapture, her whole body filled with an eager uncontrollable trembling to have him inside her.

He reached down, his searching fingers assuring her body's readiness. Becky held her breath, her heart slamming in her chest. He rested his fingertip lightly on her pleasure center as he pressed into her, claiming her, inch by throbbing inch. "Oh, sweeting," he moaned, though he barely had half of it in yet. "Is that gentle enough?"

Her only answer was a soft, amazed groan. She ran her hands down his velvety sides, enthralled by each flowing ridge of powerful male muscle.

"Are you ready for more?"

"Yes," she panted.

"Do you want all of me now?"

"Alec," she wrenched out. His hand glided all the way up her body, up her belly, chest, and throat, until he captured her chin very gently.

"Open deeper for me, sweeting. Relax. I'm not going to hurt you. I need you to take it all. Oh, Becky, I'm dying for you." She obeyed, relaxing inwardly as best she could, accepting his fevered kisses while he slid closer, penetrating her with a ragged groan. "Becky." She gasped at a small burst of pain within as they were irrevocably joined. He remained still, buried to the hilt within her.

His fiery lips lingered at her brow. "Take your time, sweet," he soothed in a hoarse whisper. "We've got all night if you want it." He glanced down at her, propping his elbows on either side of her head. He caressed her cheek with the backs of his fingers. "Are you all right?"

She nodded with a hard swallow, her world spinning, her pain dissolving fast. Her reeling senses made the cupids seem to swirl around the dome above his bed; from the corner of her eye, she glimpsed Alec's reflection in the mirrors by the bed, the full length of him atop her, the beautiful sweeping line of his bare back. She closed her eyes while he nuzzled her cheek and stroked her breasts, rousing her anew.

When she sought his lips again, he understood she wanted more. He obliged her smoothly and at once, rising up on muscled arms above her to give himself with slow, deep strokes full of leashed male power and tenderness.

His hips rode urgently between her thighs, every inch of contact blissful as their bodies moved in a full-length caress from the soles of her feet on his muscled calves, to her hands gliding up and down his rib cage, to the heated rhythm of his chest and belly rocking against hers, and the deep, hot moistness of his tongue in her mouth. He possessed her completely in that moment, claimed her.

He groaned against her lips as she raked her nails slowly down his back and grasped his lean buttocks.

"Becky, you're driving me wild." He cupped the back of her thigh and raised her body slightly, sighing with pleasure as this brought him deeper into her body.

"Alec, slower," she begged him, exploring this whole new sensation of deep delight.

"Better?"

"Yes, oh . . ."

"And this?" Several minutes later he arched back, leaving just enough space between their bodies to slip his hand down between them. He touched her center with a feather-light contact, using the pad of his thumb.

If he would have moved, she'd have screamed, on the precipice between mindless pleasure and pain, but Alec was much too splendid a lover for that. His patient stillness allowed her to set her own pace, rising against his delicate touch and sinking again on his big wonderful cock.

"Good?"

"*Yes.*" She slid her arms around his neck, pulling him closer.

"I meant it when I said that you could stay with me," he whispered, lipping her nose and then the curve of her brow. "Come into my keeping."

Becky went still; he remained inside her.

"I mean it. I'm not as rich as Draxinger, but at least I'm not as rude as Rush."

She laughed breathlessly at his murmured jest, which in turn roused a sharp gasp of pleasure from him, as laughter made her body clench him more tightly within her.

"Oh, God, Becky," he said dizzily. "You—do things to me. I can't explain it."

"Good things?"

"Very good. Wonderful things," he answered barely audibly as he lowered his head and kissed her with renewed intent.

"I can't stay, Alec."

"Of course you can. You must," he purred. "Think about it."

When she realized that after this night she could never see him again, she suddenly wanted to cry. She could never let Mikhail find out that Alec Knight had been the one. She held him harder, clutching him with a new and private desperation.

"Oh, God, you're delectable, Becky," he breathed a few minutes later, his muscled chest damp and heated against hers. "It's heaven inside you." She sensed his taut control beginning to fray, but he fought to hold back, letting her take her pleasure of him. "Look into my eyes when you let go. I want to feel it with you. I want to watch you come. That's right, Becky. Just let it happen."

All of this was miraculously unexpected, but she only then began to realize that the best part lay ahead as pleasure turned to bliss, and bliss to ecstasy.

Her cries climbed in volume and in pitch. Their pace slowed; his strokes deepened. Her body felt made of pure light, pure love, as she held Alec's sweetly tortured stare.

"Oh, Becky. I need you."

"Alec."

"Yes," he panted, half a growl. He swooped down fiercely and claimed her mouth in a wild and fevered kiss, his arms locked tight around her body. He thrust into her like the end of the world was upon them, again and again, his own violent climax prolonging the exquisite shudders that racked her body. His gasps raged, hot and jagged by her ear, until he collapsed atop her, breathing hard.

Becky was out somewhere in the universe. A million tiny stars twinkled in her blood; in the silken darkness, she floated on the night's tranquil hush.

Alec turned his head on their shared pillow and gave her a tousled, heartbreaking smile, one she knew she'd remember for the rest of her life. He just shook his head and pulled her closer.

Spent and still breathing heavily herself, Becky's arm felt like lead as she lifted her fingers and dragged a weary caress down the side of his sweat-dampened face. Alec captured her hand and pressed an ardent kiss into her palm. Then he took a deep, cozy breath and hugged her with a lazy trace of a smile, pressing her head against his chest.

Becky accepted his possessive embrace with quiet joy, and soon drifted off to sleep, listening to the slow, strong beat of his knightly heart.

She did not know how she would leave on the morrow. She only knew she would not risk this man.

Not for all the world.

CHAPTER
∽ FOUR ∽

*F*iltered sunlight and summer breezes wafted into the peaceful bedchamber the next morning. As Becky drifted back to awareness from a deep and restful slumber blissfully devoid of frightening dreams, the first thing she noticed was that the rain had stopped.

Then she listened to the lulling rhythm of soft, deep breathing nearby and turned her head on the pillow, gazing for a long moment at the beautiful man sleeping beside her.

Alec.

His name alone, two soft sensuous syllables, flooded her body with remembered pleasure. She lay quite still, simply enjoying the contentment that filled her, and the rich newfound sense of connection to him, and indeed, to herself.

Now, why did it not surprise her that the scoundrel hogged the bed? A fond, private, highly satisfied smile played at her lips as she studied him, curbing the urge to caress him. *So sweet.*

Alec slept on his stomach hugging a luxurious swansdown pillow, the sheets tangled loosely around his long, muscular legs, his blond hair fanned across his angular cheekbone. The flowing, fluid lines of his bare back and big, loose shoulders made a wistful sigh escape her.

It was hard not to touch him when she knew the velvet warmth of his skin and the safety of his embrace—

and harder still to know she must leave him. It would be so easy to snuggle into his arms and laze the day away, but she knew she mustn't wake him.

He would ask too many questions. He might even try to stop her. There was no point in making this any harder than it already was. Her village was still under Mikhail's iron fist, and she did not want Alec Knight involved.

No sense dawdling, she thought, staring sorrowfully at her sleeping prince. The longer she lingered, the better the chances he would wake. Pressing up gingerly from the mattress to avoid disturbing him, she only moved about four inches before her hair snagged on something, stopping her. She winced and looked over to find that his fingers were wrapped in her long hair.

The tug on her scalp pained her but she found a certain humor in her predicament as she carefully disentangled her tresses from around his strong, lax hand. She had to free a few strands from the signet ring that he wore on his left pinky, but soon managed to untie herself from his unconsciously possessive hold.

Brushing the gold sheets off of her hips and legs, she silently slipped out of his bed and crossed, nude, to the dressing room, the blue dressing gown abandoned, still entwined amid the sheets. Walking caused her a bit of soreness south of her navel, but overall, she felt wonderful, strong. Renewed, refreshed, ready to fight another day.

The water now lay cold and sluggish in the marble bathing tub. She cleaned away the small streaks of dried blood that remained from her initiation and then got dressed. She was a little surprised that she felt no regret whatsoever for her exploration into passion the previous night. It was not as though a child might result—she had finally divined the purpose of Alec's condom.

Her clothes were still a bit damp after their soaking in

last night's storm, but at least the good rinsing had left them cleaner. In between putting on articles of clothing, she helped herself to half of the remaining peach tart, eating with her fingers, and devised her plan of attack. Today, come what may, she would find her way to St. James's Square and tell the mighty Duke of Westland all that she had witnessed on that horrible night when she had been forced to flee.

Becky had met the stately and quite handsome middle-aged duke on two occasions in the past, for he owned a palatial hunting lodge several miles away from Talbot Old Hall. All the same, she doubted he'd remember her. Westland and his entourage only visited during grouse-shooting season, but when he came, he sometimes hosted musical evenings or afternoon teas, where he and his terrifyingly elegant daughter, Lady Parthenia Westland, received the local gentry like proper aristocrats.

As token lady of the slightly ramshackle manor nearby, Becky had been invited, too. When in Yorkshire, the Westlands sometimes condescended to attend the occasional country assembly ball, as well, though Becky had thought the glamorous Londoners seemed to be holding back yawns, despite their efforts to be gracious. Thanks to the local gossip at those balls, she had learned about His Grace's town house in St. James's Square. Today all she had to do was find the place, then muster the nerve to go knocking on the Westlands' door.

Dressed at last, her hair combed and pinned up as neatly as possible given her haste, she glanced cautiously into the bedroom and made sure Alec was still sleeping soundly. Then she tiptoed over to the mahogany chest of drawers and opened the bottom one without a sound.

Reaching in past his neatly folded stack of snowy white cravats, she felt around until her fingers closed around the Rose of Indra in its little leather pouch. She withdrew the ruby from its hiding place and then tied it securely around her garter once more.

When her sole inheritance had been retrieved, she stood up, smoothed her skirts, and pulled on her knee-length pelisse. Glancing at herself in the mirror, she shook her head. She couldn't believe she had to face Parthenia Westland looking like this. She had done her best, but still looked like some sort of wayward servant girl.

The duke's daughter, white-blond, sharp-featured, and entirely blue-blooded, was everything Becky was not—everything Grandfather had wanted her to be, but impetuous Mama had run away with her sailor man, and Becky had been the result.

Ah, well. At least her hair was clean. Even Mrs. Whithorn grudgingly acknowledged that it was her best feature. Giving her reflection a resolute nod, Becky pivoted and marched herself out of the dressing room, knowing she must be on her way.

Passing through the bedroom, Becky knew it was risky, but she could not help returning to Alec's side. She went silently into the alcove, squeezing herself up the narrow space between his giant bed and the wall. She just wanted to take one last tender look at him.

She stood over him, staring at him in lonely sorrow. *I don't suppose I'll ever see you again.* She ached as she gazed at him. Perhaps there was some way she could contact him once Mikhail had been brought to justice. On the other hand, she was not sure if Alec would want that. He was, after all, a bona fide London rakehell.

With a pensive half smile, she recalled his roguish taunting last night under that awning when she had threatened him with the candlesnuffer. *What are you going to do with that thing, put my lights out?* It was terrible to leave him without saying good-bye, but she dared not linger. She was not sure she could withstand the temptation of those deep blue eyes. Her hand moved forward to caress his golden hair, but she stopped herself, her eyes misting. *Good-bye, angel man,* her heart whispered.

Then she slipped out quietly.

Alec awoke at the sound of the closing door. He lifted his head from the pillow and squinted against the light in the direction of the entrance hall.

"Beck?" he called in a scratchy voice, but there was no answer.

For a few seconds it didn't quite sink in—then he saw her place beside him empty and let out a shocked expletive. He jumped out of bed, hastily yanking the sheet around his waist. Racing into the entrance hall, he threw the front door open.

"Becky!"

She was on the stairs, having just reached the landing down the hallway. She glanced back in guilty shock, then ran, disappearing from his view.

"Becky—come back!" He rushed out of his apartment into the carpeted mezzanine hallway. "Where are you going?"

She ran, not looking back.

Standing there, staring after her, Alec was so stunned by her desertion that it took his breath away.

And then he was furious.

He would not stand for it—being left behind like he mattered not a whit. By God, nobody made love to him like that and then went sneaking off without so much as a by-your-leave! It was one thing for him to do it—how many mornings, after all, had he tiptoed out of London's various luxuriant boudoirs, slipping out on his drowsing ladies to avoid any weepy good-byes? He would not tolerate it being done to him!

He was utterly confused, only half awake, and left to

wonder what he had done wrong to make her go. He had treated her like a princess last night! For God's sake, he, Alec Knight, had actually offered to make her his mistress. How could she just leave him without a word?

Was the beautiful but tenuous bond he had felt between them nothing but a figment of his imagination?

Well, she was not getting rid of him so easily. He thrust out his jaw in angry determination. *I'm going after her.*

Since he could hardly rush out into the courtyard of the Althorpe wearing nothing but a bedsheet and a scowl, he stomped back into his apartment, when a thought struck him. *Blazes, I hope she didn't rob me.* The Disciples of Venus had a certain reputation for thieving, and he had not yet paid her. He yanked open the drawer of the console table where he usually kept small sums of money for convenience's sake. Maybe she had finally started acting like a proper whore—

The money was still there.

The sight of it jarred Alec and completed his confoundment. What kind of harlot ran off without collecting her pay? Something strange was going on here. Was it her pride that had made her go? Her way of acknowledging that what they had shared last night was more than commerce? But if she felt it, too, then why wouldn't she stay? And more important, where was she off to?

A fresh wave of that same baffling protectiveness he had felt toward her last night rushed through him when he thought of her venturing into any of the Town's various brothels for work.

"Damn it," he whispered, unable to stomach the thought. There were decent establishments that treated their girls fairly, but there were horrible places, as well, where the girls were drugged, beaten, and barely fed. Becky was too new to London to know the difference.

If she didn't want him as her protector, fine, he

thought, bristling, but he had to make sure she arrived in safe conditions. She was getting his help whether she liked it or not.

He slammed the front door, rushed into his dressing room, and began hastily throwing on his clothes. *Perdition!* he thought as he pulled on his boots. *Reckless chit!* Perhaps she thought her winsome smile and those magical eyes were enough to snare her a high-ranking peer with deep pockets, like his brother. Why should a girl like Becky make do with a mere younger son?

He marched out of the dressing room, but knowing the cutthroat regions of London where some of those seedy brothels lurked, he grabbed his sword and pistols from the fanciful half-moon commode in his bedchamber. Pausing to buckle the holster on around his waist, he paused, gazing at the bed as he adjusted his weapons at his hip.

Becky.

The very thought of her made him ache and throb and yearn for he knew not what. Scanning the bed where she had surrendered so sweetly, his gaze landed on the blue dressing gown, unfurled in the place where she had slept. He recalled it staying beneath her there when he had taken her on the bed, and now a dark blotch in the middle of the blue silk captured his full attention.

What the devil?

He went closer, reached down warily and grasped the robe. Holding it up, he stared at it for a long moment without comprehension, thunderstruck.

In the middle of the field of royal blue silk there was an unmistakable crimson stain. The sight of it nearly knocked the wind out of him. His jaw hung slack. Blood.

No.

His first thought was that he'd hurt her. She had asked him to be gentle but he'd been too rough. But that was impossible. He had taken pains—

No, no, no, no, no.

Not a—

The pieces slammed together in his mind.

Her trusting gaze. Her innocent laughter. Her shy kisses.

No. I didn't. I wouldn't!

Be gentle with me, Alec. His own instinctive tenderness with her, as if his body sensed a truth hidden to his jaded mind's assumptions.

Virgin.

"Christ!" Alec dropped the thing with a wild gasp as though it had burned him. His heart lurched, then began pounding madly. How could he not have felt her barrier? But—*the condom.* A string of expletives exploded from his lips and ended with a self-directed "Fool!"

The reputed greatest lover in all England had not even realized last night that he had despoiled a virgin. He never tangled with virgins. Never!

But if she wasn't a whore, then who the hell was she and where was she off to?

He wasn't even sure now if Becky Ward was her real name. All he knew was that he had blundered and that he was bound by honor to make it right. *Good God, I might actually have to marry her.*

He could not even think about that yet or he might drop dead of an apoplectic fit.

He swallowed hard, his heart racing. One thing at a time. First he had to find her. Already in motion, he threw the bloodstained robe back onto the bed and raced out. Yet again, the mysterious waif had him chasing her—and that was new, indeed. Usually it was the other way around. Not this one. How much of what she had said last night had been a lie? *The jig is up, my girl, and when I catch you I'm going to wring your deceitful little neck.*

Dashing down the stairs, taking several steps at a

time, he ran out into the courtyard, glanced to the right and left, but did not see her.

"Becky!"

"Ah, so she's your little morsel, is she? Figures."

Alec whirled to find his piano-playing neighbor ambling across the courtyard, idly swinging his walking stick and smoking a cheroot.

"Did you see which way she went?"

"Why, yes. She asked me the way to St. James's Square." Roger Manners pointed his walking stick at the Piccadilly gate.

"Thanks." Alec nodded and raced after her, his heart pounding, but he was more puzzled than ever as he left the quiet, cultivated grounds of the Althorpe and rushed out onto the busy thoroughfare. *St. James's Square?* What could she want there?

He suddenly caught sight of her ahead and hastened to follow, but on second thought decided to hang back and watch her so he might find out what the little minx was up to before he confronted her. One way or another, he would get to the bottom of this. Now he really wanted to know why she had been sleeping on Draxinger's doorway.

If she had stuck around this morning scheming for marriage, that he could have understood, because despite his own racy reputation, he was still a family member of the mighty Duke of Hawkscliffe. It didn't get much more blue-blooded than that, and Alec knew that if he ever did decide to marry, his eldest brother, Robert, would certainly restore his income from the family fortunes.

But obviously that had not been Becky's scheme, so why on earth would any chit in her right mind throw her virtue away on a total stranger and then sneak away in the morning? It made no blasted sense.

From time to time he saw her stop to ask directions

from various people on the streets. Now that he knew the truth, Alec tensed with an almost obsessive protectiveness each time she did, but she was sensible about whom she approached.

It was not long before he trailed her into the stately garden square. He eased around the corner, watching from a wary distance as she searched out the house numbers, then stopped when she faced the enormous town house of the Duke of Westland.

Alec knew the residence because he had attended several social events there in the past, including the fair Lady Parthenia's debutante ball, where he and Fort and Rush had tried to trick Draxinger into wooing Westland's daughter by making a rakish wager about which of them could thaw the ice-princess.

Everybody knew that Draxinger and Parthenia belonged together. Drax had been a goner from the first time he laid eyes on the elegant frost-maiden, but neither of the two equally haughty creatures would make the first move. The lads' attempt to push Drax and Parthenia together had not worked, though, and when her father found out about their bet, he had taken a severe dislike to Alec and his friends.

Across the square, Becky advanced bravely to the Westlands' front door.

What on earth is she doing? What business could a Yorkshire hoyden have with a leading Whig lord? He knew by her slight, charming Yorkshire burr that at least that much of her tale was true.

Leaning on the corner, Alec had to maneuver a little to be able to see her through the green leafy boughs of the plane trees planted in the square's central garden. As she came into view, he saw her pause on the doorstep, square her shoulders, and take a deep breath, steeling herself with a valiant air.

She knocked soundly on the door.

* * *

The Duke of Westland's drawing room overlooking Berkeley Square made General Prince Mikhail Kurkov a trifle homesick for his beautiful palace on the Moika River in St. Petersburg, for despite rumors to the contrary, he was, on occasion, a civilized man.

He faced the ugliness of war without flinching when he had to, but between battles he appreciated the finer things in life as much as any educated nobleman.

The airy, spacious room was beautifully appointed. Bright morning sunlight streamed in through large arched windows and danced on the silver tea service laid out on the round mahogany table buffed to a high sheen. Light yellow walls complemented couches and armchairs upholstered in a lavender striped silk.

Any minute now he expected his feckless young cousin's arrival. He was already in position, prepared with a reasonable explanation to shoot down her predictable accusations. Did she take him for a fool?

It had been but a trice to learn where she would go, to whom she would turn. Mikhail had big plans, and he did not intend to have them undone by a mere slip of a girl. Upon arriving at Westland's house, the first thing he had done was to put a word discreetly in the butler's ear.

"My good fellow," he had murmured, "if a young lady with dark hair should come to the door while I am visiting with His Grace, would you please detain her as quietly as possible? Her name is Miss Rebecca Ward, a kinswoman of mine. I am her guardian, you see. My grandfather's recent death entrusted her . . . but, ah, how shall I say?—fair Rebecca suffers from an unfortunate malady of the mind."

"Oh, dear. I am very sorry, Your Highness," the butler had said with a sympathetic nod.

"She may try to follow me here. In recent days, she has shown a tendency to break away from her caretakers, trying to follow me wherever I go. This is, of course, very dangerous for her. She is unable to care for herself. If she were to wander off in the city, we might never find her again." Mikhail had shaken his head regretfully. "Perhaps I am too tenderhearted, but I cannot bear for her doctors to restrain her. She cries so piteously. It is enough to break a man's heart."

"I'm sure it must be a terrible burden, Your Highness."

Mikhail had sighed and nodded like a saint. "I do not *expect* that Rebecca will follow me today, but this morning she did seem particularly agitated. Telling her nurse I am the devil. Very sad."

The butler winced and shook his head sympathetically.

"It is not her fault, of course, but I should not wish to bring any embarrassment to your master's doorstep. Her fits tend to cause a scene. If Rebecca does appear, I would ask that you have your footmen lay hold of her and send for me at once, so that I can take her home. You need not worry—I would not say she is dangerous— she is only a young girl. But she can be a bit violent. Her doctors say she suffers from hysteria."

"We will see to her with compassion, if the young lady should arrive," the butler had assured him with a bow.

"Thank you," he had answered, slipping a fiver into the servant's pocket with a quick smile. "Your staff will not discuss her condition, I trust."

"Never, Your Highness. I will make sure personally that they do not."

"Good man."

The obliging fellow had then escorted Mikhail to the breakfast room, where the Duke of Westland had agreed to receive him.

And so, staked out here and lying in wait for her,

Mikhail was irked, but not unduly alarmed, by his little cousin's success thus far. True, Rebecca had eluded his men for nearly a week and had made her way to London in good time, but he had frankly expected as much, for they shared the same superior Talbot blood. The chit had merely exhibited—in miniature—his own fundamental competence in achieving his chosen aims.

All the same, she was only twenty years old and a female, a basically insignificant being. It was inconceivable that a rosy-cheeked country lass could be of any real threat to him.

No, he would soon have the temperamental young beauty in hand, and when he did, they were going to have a *discussion* about her snooping, her meddling, and her insubordination.

Then he would teach her a lesson she would not soon forget.

As with drilling soldiers or breaking horses, he merely had to show her who was in control. Westland, for his part, suspected nothing. The duke innocently believed that he had only come to discuss politics.

If Westland had been startled when Mikhail arrived so early without an appointment, the duke was too impeccably well-mannered to let his astonishment show. After all, they had been introduced just a week ago through Countess Lieven, and Westland had extended to Mikhail an open invitation to drop by anytime if he wished to discuss the latest bills in Parliament.

Mikhail knew full well it was too early to come calling, but he could not risk Rebecca getting here before him; besides, as a foreigner, he could plead ignorance of London ways. That, along with his high rank and the fact that the Whigs frankly needed him, had silenced any curious comment on Westland's part regarding his unexpected visit.

Mikhail had soon discovered upon arriving that the

duke was a man who appreciated the work ethic of any aristocrat who did not loll abed till noon but got down to business straightaway. When the butler had shown him into the breakfast room, Mikhail found Westland sitting alone at the table, back from his morning gallop and dressed with smart reserve; eating his breakfast, sipping coffee, reviewing two newspapers, and preparing for the day's meetings all at the same time—and making it all look quite easy.

Now they had repaired to the drawing room, where Westland was amiably determined to persuade him to join the Whigs instead of the Tories.

Ever since Mikhail had inherited his British grandfather's earldom, the Whigs and Tories had been fighting over him. It was quite amusing. As an outsider to English politics, they knew he could go either way.

His grandsire had been a staunch Tory, like all the past Talbot earls, but as far as the world could guess, his first loyalties might lay with his boyhood friend, Czar Alexander of Russia, and the Czar could not have made his preference for the Whigs any plainer on his last state visit to this quaint little island.

The Tories were now in control, but the Czar firmly believed their days in power were numbered and that the future of England lay with the Whigs. •

Mikhail agreed. Not that he really gave a damn for either side. It was only a question of which could be more useful to him. The obvious answer was the Whigs, but he intended to make them work for it. If their party would indeed control England's future, then it was imperative that in time he get control of them.

"We envision great changes in the future," Westland continued with admirable conviction. He proceeded to explain.

Mikhail barely listened, keeping one ear on the front door, a bit on edge with this whole situation. He nodded his head and seemed to deliberate, but he had hammered out his plan long ago.

He would gain a foothold among the Whig elites and use it as insurance on his life if anything went awry when the plot was carried out back in Russia. Such enterprises were delicate.

Czar Alexander suffered from enough paranoia to keep scores of spies on the lookout to sniff out rebellions before they occurred—as well he should be, after what had happened to his father. Mikhail's own uncles had helped to overthrow the brutal, bloodthirsty Czar Paul.

If the present coup succeeded, Mikhail knew that he would soon be called back to Russia to help restore order. They would need him to help run things with the iron fist that he was famous for. The army loved him, and at their head, he would consolidate his power.

If the plot failed, however, and he were implicated, he would simply deny everything—he was too smart not to cover his tracks. How could they blame him, after all, when he was a thousand miles away here in England? Yes, if things went wrong, he would have already ensured his own survival by embedding himself inside the Whig party as an advocate for Russian interests. Mikhail knew that the Czar would be a fool to prosecute him when he alone would be in a position to influence English politics in ways that benefited Mother Russia and harmed her enemies. From trade agreements to military alliances, the Czar would have to see that if he left Mikhail untouched, Russia could reap considerable rewards from British industry and sea power. It was a foolproof plan, with only one little fly in the ointment.

At that moment, the little fly came knocking on the Duke of Westland's door. Mikhail turned his head toward the sound and narrowed his eyes.

* * *

Waiting for the door to be answered, Becky had never been so nervous in her life. She was mentally rehearsing her words to the august lord lieutenant when the great white door before her creaked open. At once, the imperious-looking butler raised his bushy white eyebrows.

"Good morning, young lady." He opened the door wider and nodded at someone behind him.

Becky gave him a slight curtsy, her heart hammering. "G-Good morning, sir. I . . . have come to see the Duke of Westland."

"Very good, my dear. Everything will be well, I'm sure," he said gently. "Do come in. Step inside and take a seat. That's right."

Becky eyed him warily as she stepped inside. He was awfully obliging for the butler of a duke, she thought. She had been sure she would've had to argue at some length to be granted an audience with the great Westland.

"Thank you," she said cautiously, wondering if the old butler was a bit senile as he smiled and smiled.

"There you are," he said dotingly. "Right this way."

Her spine stiff with wariness, Becky followed him into the opulent entrance hall, wondering why he studied her in such a bizarre fashion, as though she were a wild animal in a menagerie.

Two beefy footmen in livery stood at attention nearby, while a wide-eyed maid in a cap and apron was posted at the foot of the staircase. The girl was staring at her, too, as though she were some species of exotic beast. The butler sent the maid a commanding nod, and she went scampering up the stairs.

Something very strange was going on.

Becky regarded the butler dubiously. "You will let me see the duke?"

"Of course, my dear. Whatever you wish." The old

butler offered her his arm and led her over gingerly to a cushioned bench by the wall. "You just sit right down here for a moment while we fetch His Highness."

She tensed instantly. "You mean His Grace?"

"Of course, Miss Ward, my mistake. Just so."

Becky stared at the butler, her face turning ashen. "I did not tell you my name yet."

The two footmen advanced like living pillars as she pressed up from the settee.

"Do sit down, miss."

"What is going on here?"

"There there, my dear. Soon you will be safely at home again."

"Home? I want to see the Duke of Westland!"

Before the butler could reply, she looked up, hearing someone rushing down the stairs. Her blood curdled in pure disbelief as she recognized those iron footfalls.

Mikhail.

She did not wait for visual confirmation. *I've got to get out of here.* With a mighty shove, she pushed the butler violently into one of the big footmen and ducked under the swiping arms of the other, who lunged forward and tried to grab her. The returning maid shrieked as Becky bolted for the door.

"Rebecca!" Mikhail bellowed, running down the stairs. "Get back here!"

She did not look back, banging the front door open on its hinges and leaping off the stoop.

Once more, she ran.

Alec pressed away from the corner of the building as Becky came racing back outside mere seconds after having gone into Westland's town house. To his astonishment, she took off at a full-out run, her long hair flying, her skirts hitched up to avoid tripping over them. He almost called out to her when a man rushed out of the house after her.

He was tall and lean, with dun-brown hair and a short, narrow beard that encircled his hard mouth. He looked familiar.

"Rebecca!" he clipped out in sharp, foreign tones.

Who is that? I know him. He looked about forty and was dressed in military uniform, with white breeches, high black boots, and a coat of midnight-blue with brass buttons and gold epaulets. He marched after Becky with a few long, aggressive paces.

"That is enough foolishness, Rebecca. Get back here—now! You're coming home with me!"

Alec bristled.

She ignored him, flying out of the square.

The uniformed man barked an order in some foreign tongue, and instantly, from around the side of the building, streamed four towering Cossacks.

Of course—Prince Kurkov.

Countess Lieven, the wife of the Russian ambassador and a leading hostess of London society, had been singing her countryman's praises all through the Season, and making sure the steely-eyed war hero was welcomed into the first circles of the ton.

Not a difficult task, for with the wild popularity of Czar Alexander, there was nothing more fashionable than a Russian nobleman these days. Indeed, the creatures were all the rage—except for the matter of their serfs, of course, which made them, for the broad-minded English, as problematical as the Americans with their slaves.

Personally, Alec had no opinion of the foreign prince except a faint, cynical amusement at the way he paraded around Town with his Cossack retinue as if he were the Czar himself. But what on earth did the fierce Prince Mikhail Kurkov have to do with Becky Ward?

Staring in confusion, Alec remembered the two soldiers he had passed in the carriage last night, the ones he thought were lost. Those hats, yes. He recognized them now. Cossacks.

And here they were again.

Kurkov clipped out an order and the Cossacks snapped into motion, four of them pursuing Becky at a rapid clip. He remembered her sleeping on Draxinger's doorstep—not far from where he had seen the soldiers. Had they been trolling the streets last night searching for her even then? But why?

Virgin.

"What the hell is going on?" he whispered under his breath. *Is that why she came home with me? Merely to escape them?* He feared he knew the answer, and his heart sank. *Oh, Becky, you didn't have to sleep with me to have my help. I'm not that bad.*

Just then the trim, patrician Duke of Westland himself appeared in the doorway. "Good heavens, Kurkov. What's all this about?"

Alec was already moving in the direction that Becky had fled as the prince left the chase to his men and returned to the front steps, but he overheard the prince. "I am very sorry for this disturbance, Your Grace. My young cousin is very ill. . . ."

Cousin?

"Her mother was unstable, you may recall. Rebecca has inherited an unfortunate distemper of the mind."

Alec did not hear the rest of Kurkov's dubious explanation. He might not have all the facts about her, but Becky Ward was one of the sanest people he had ever met. The girl wasn't mad and she certainly wasn't ill.

What she was, he thought grimly, was in trouble.

Trailing her pursuers, he moved through the park under the cover of the trees while the perplexed Westland invited Kurkov to wait inside until his men retrieved her.

Becky's hopes were crushed, panic and sheer despair threatening to overwhelm her as she pitched around another corner and sprinted through the quiet, pleasant neighborhood. What in God's name was she going to do now? How could the cursed brute have gotten to Westland's ahead of her? But she already knew the answer to that. Mikhail must have driven straight from Yorkshire while she had been forced to take a winding course in order to stay ahead of his men.

Determined to do just that again, she glanced back and saw the quartet of Cossacks separating into pairs behind her again. They split up to head her off, following their usual protocol.

She gulped for air and raced on. Pounding down the clean cobblestoned street, she scanned her surroundings frantically for a place to hide, but all she saw were rows of tall, tidy houses and a few spindly young trees here and there.

Nothing.

She fled on, ignoring her body's soreness from the momentous event of the night before. If Alec with all his gentleness had done this to her, then Mikhail meting it out as a punishment would have surely left her bruised and torn and curled up in a ball for a week. She shoved the horrible image out of her mind.

Her cousin could go to hell as far as she was concerned, the killer.

A shout from behind her alerted Becky that the Cossacks were closing in. By pure will, she surged ahead with a burst of speed. Perdition, these brutes were determined, she thought grimly, fighting back her terror. As the Cossacks gained on her, she darted into the mews behind the row of houses she had just passed.

The alley was narrow, but she discovered a warren of small stables and carriage houses that could provide any number of hiding places. She slipped into the first open stable door that she came to and crouched down in the shadows inside an empty stall.

She heard a stable-hand whistling to himself as he swept the aisle at the other end of the barn, then the ominous footsteps of the Cossacks approaching, their boot heels ringing harshly in the narrow space of the mews.

While she waited out of sight, holding her breath, she could hear them coming closer, hear their guttural exchange.

The sound of rustling straw from the next stall startled her; she turned her head sharply, but then a friendly equine snuffling revealed her only possible means of escape. Dare she . . . ?

Horse-stealing was a hanging crime.

Mikhail's men accosted the stable-hand down the way, doing their best to find the English words to ask if the man had seen a dark-haired girl run by. *I've got to get out of here. Now.*

"What's that you're saying? What, a girl? No, sir, ain't seen no girl," he answered jovially. "What are you fellows—Germans, then? Hail to old Blücher, what-hey?"

She crept out of the stall, emboldened to see that the horse had wandered outside into its own small corral. The tall bay was already wearing a leather halter. Becky commandeered the lead rope draped over one of the fence posts to use as reins. Nervously, she climbed over the fence and approached the animal.

Glancing to her left, she saw a pair of Cossacks continuing their search for her down the row of stables. They had gone past her hiding spot and now their backs were to her. All they had to do was turn around, however, and they might have seen her climbing up onto the post and rail fence, using it as a mounting block as she slid onto the horse's back.

The bay took exception, sidestepping and tossing its head. Becky clung on tenaciously, trying to bring the animal under control without letting the Cossacks hear her. Unfortunately, she had more pluck than experience. She had never ridden astride before, let alone bareback; she soon realized the bay would throw her before it allowed her to lean down and open the gate.

"Damn you," she whispered. "Whoa! Halt, boy. There's a good boy."

" 'Hoy!" the stable-hand suddenly yelled. "Get down from there! What do ye think you're doin' with that 'orse?"

She glanced over recklessly and saw the stable-hand in the doorway. He dropped his broom and ran toward her, his shout alerting the Cossacks.

"Jump, you worthless blackguard!" She squeezed the horse's sides with her knees and gripped its mane, holding on for dear life.

The bay reared. Becky felt herself sliding down toward its haunches, but hung on harder. *"Go!"* She gave it another angry kick the second its front legs slammed back down to earth. It didn't like that at all—and then they were off.

The horse took three fast, bouncy steps then went airborne, tucking its forelegs up high as it sailed over the fence. She gasped, her eyes widening as they soared; the earth fell away far below her.

The landing on cobblestone was so hard that it rattled her teeth.

Disaster struck. She dropped the lead line in her automatic lunge to hold on more tightly to the horse's mane. Now she had no means whatsoever of controlling the animal.

Worse, her mount's stubborn delay had given the Cossacks the moment they needed to rush ahead in time to block the only exit from the mews, the same way she had come in.

Waving their arms, they spooked the horse. Becky nearly fell as the animal careened to the side, but the stable-hand caught the lead-rope, and the next thing she knew, the Cossacks were pulling her down off the animal's back.

She fought the one who had her more securely, while the other silenced the stable-hand's protests with a threatening glower.

"I guess that's the chit you was lookin' for!" the groom muttered.

"Help me!" she cried, thrashing as one Cossack wrenched her arm behind her back. "They're trying to—"

"Help you?" the sturdy old stable-hand retorted. "You bloody little horse thief. Hangin's too good for the likes o' you! Whoa, boy!" he yelled as the angry bay tossed its head, jerking the lead-rope out of his hands.

The horse bolted, galloping out of the mews.

"Look what you done now!" the groom shouted at Becky, his face turning red. "You'll pay for this, my girl! You'll pay dear!" With that, he ran out of the mews after the animal, leaving Becky caught between the Cossacks, fighting to no avail.

"Let go of me!" she shouted.

Each of them took one of her arms, turning her around roughly to return her to Mikhail, but as all three turned to face the entrance of the mews, Becky's eyes widened.

The Cossacks paused, too, obviously taken aback to find a bristling, broad-shouldered archangel blocking the only exit with a sword in his hands, the morning sun shining on his golden hair, and blue eyes blazing like the wrath of heaven.

CHAPTER
∞ FIVE ∞

"*A*lec," Becky breathed, paling. "What are you doing here?"

"What does it look like, my dear?" he growled, his stare pinned on his captors. "Rescuing you, of course."

"No!" she wrenched out. "Stand aside. Leave, Alec! They'll kill you. I don't want you involved in this! You shouldn't have followed me."

His cool, hard gaze flicked to hers; Becky flinched, for he looked at her as though she had betrayed him. Those eloquent blue eyes needed no words to reproach her for keeping secrets and sneaking away without even saying good-bye.

And yet here he stood. Ready to fight for her.

Little did he know it would be suicide.

She struggled against her captors with renewed fury and rising hysteria at the thought of them leaving him dead in this alley the way they had killed that other man in Yorkshire—his beautiful body lifeless, his fiery spirit quenched—all because of her.

The soldier on her left wrenched her arm up hard behind her back. She grimaced and nearly spat on the man in her fury.

Alec swore when they hurt her, moving closer.

"What are you doing?" she cried.

"They shall not take you."

"It's too late. Just go! Please, Alec. These are Cossack

warriors." She swallowed hard. "They'll kill you, and if they don't, there are a dozen more at my kinsman's command who will track you down and finish the job. Just—walk away, I beg you."

His shrug was barely perceptible. "We Knight brothers don't abandon our friends," he said, his tone barbed with withering irony. "Your little secret's out, my love. We need to talk."

"Get out of here!" she fairly screamed at him, but he was unmoved.

"If you think I would leave you after what happened last night," he said to her with his stare pinned on the Cossacks, "then you have completely misjudged me."

She closed her eyes for a second in frustration and searing embarrassment now that her ruse had been found out. This was not supposed to be happening. She could not believe he had followed her! "Please, Alec. This is my fight."

"Well, it rather looks like you're losing, *cherie*. I'm here to even the odds."

"Oh, God." Blast his male pride! *He's going to die right in front of me.*

When she forced her eyes open again to face the nightmare, Alec had fixed his spear-tipped stare on the larger of the two Cossacks. "Let her go and I'll spare your life."

The two big warriors laughed at his warning snarl.

Alec's chiseled jaw tautened. The angle of his sword changed, its point homing in on the level of the larger Cossack's heart. "I said," he repeated, "let her go."

"Alec—"

"Do shut up, Becky. You and I will discuss this later. For now, I am mainly interested in them. What do you want with her?"

"They don't speak English."

"Oh, I think this ugly brute understands my meaning perfectly," he said, his eyes narrowing at the larger man.

He was right, she saw. The Cossack knew he had been challenged. Glancing darkly at his comrade, he shoved Becky into the other man's arms, then went toward Alec, drawing his sword.

So, his future bride not only thought him the lowest sort of cur, forsaken of all honor, but she also doubted his ability to take this ugly pair. Well, he'd show her. Damn right. It was time to prove to her, to himself, to his great brothers and all the world what rakehell Alec Knight was really made of.

"Come on, you damned Hun," he muttered, holding his ground as he watched the Cossack advance. In the warrior's heavy-lidded eyes he saw the fires of countless battles reflected back at him, centuries of rape and pillage dating all the way back to Attila.

His heart thundered, but he swore to himself he was ready for this. This was no practice, no orderly duel. He must fight now as he had never fought before.

For Becky's sake.

Whoever the devil she was.

He noted with a swift glance in her direction that she was giving her remaining captor a hell of a time. *Good girl.* She might be a damned lying vixen, but she did not lack for courage, that one.

The other Cossack struggled to drag her away, but Becky was doing all in her power to slow his progress, fighting him every step. The man's shins would be covered in bruises. He already had her claw marks on his leathery cheek, but he looked on the whole undeterred in his mission.

Alec knew he would have to make as short work of the first man as he could if he were still to rescue her, and by God, if he survived this, the chit had some explaining to do.

Then the first Cossack chopped at his head with a mighty arc of steel, which Alec parried. The earsplitting clang of blade on blade bounded off the high, narrow walls of the mews; Alec felt the impact of that first blow vibrating the very bones of his wrists, while his sword shuddered with tension.

The Cossack laughed at him, his words low and garbled as they struggled inches apart: "You'll die, English."

"Not alone," he replied.

They flung apart, then the battle started in earnest.

Never had Alec been put on the defensive so quickly. He swung and thrust again and again, but could not seem to make a decent hit on his opponent. He hung on with dogged determination, but grew angrier each time he had to duck one of the Cossack's thunderous blows. The fight whirled faster, their blades flying, a hail of blows striking louder, stronger; the whole of his mind was focused intensely on his foe.

They circled, parted, clashed again.

Alec had just begun to identify a few of his opponent's tendencies that he might exploit when his heel caught an uneven cobblestone behind him. He saw his life flash before his eyes as he fell, but his instincts must have already planned his recovery before he could give it any conscious thought, for the moment he hit the ground, he rolled and thrust in the blink of an eye, and snarled with satisfaction as his blade sank deep into the warrior's thigh.

The Cossack roared.

Becky gasped, staring.

Alec sprang to his feet and out of arm's reach as the Cossack clutched one hand to his injured leg. The warrior slowly lifted his gaze from his wound and gave Alec a look that promised Armageddon.

With a cocky little smile, Alec beckoned him on.

* * *

"Frankly, Your Grace, it has been the most distressing situation." Mikhail turned away from the window and shook his head, wearing a mask of brotherly concern for his errant young cousin. "I fear the child has inherited her mother's instability of temperament, only in the daughter, it's even worse."

"How so?"

Pulling himself restlessly away from the window, Mikhail went to the table and accepted a strong cup of tea with a nod of thanks. "I am sure you must have heard about the scandal that ensued years ago when Rebecca's mother, Lady Mariah Talbot, eloped with Captain Ward against her father's wishes."

"Yes," the duke conceded. "They say your grandfather never forgave her for it, even after Captain Ward had perished at sea."

"As my grandfather's solicitors have assured me, that rumor is indeed true. Which explains why I found my poor young cousin living like a peasant in Yorkshire. Shocking, really." With a bewildered shake of his head, Mikhail took a seat across from the duke on one of the striped armchairs. "Whatever affliction of female hysteria came to Rebecca by blood was no doubt worsened by the conditions in which she was raised. She is nearly one-and-twenty, but her prospects have been as neglected as her education."

"Really?"

"She has been allowed to run wild, literally. She spends most of her time walking out on the moors!" he exclaimed with an air of perplexity. "She has seen nothing of the world beyond her village, speaks no French, has none of the usual accomplishments of a young lady of her birth. She can barely make a curtsy. Not to speak ill of the dead, but I fear my grandfather was too hardhearted in his grudge. The girl's father was unsuitable, yes, but that is hardly the child's fault. It's not as though she were illegitimate. It was a legal marriage, by all accounts."

"Quite. Well, yes, alas, I cannot disagree with you on the point of Lord Talbot's hard-heartedness." Westland offered a wan smile. "Your grandfather was one of the old hard-line Tories who opposed tooth and claw every reform we Whigs brought before the Lords."

Mikhail nodded with a glum snort. "I believe it. When I learned that his will had named me as Rebecca's guardian, I went to fetch her, knowing it would be a challenge to oversee the process of marrying off an eligible young lady, but I never expected anything like this. All I sought was to bring her to my London house and introduce her quietly around Society until a suitable husband could be found for her, but Rebecca went absolutely mad over being forced to leave her precious Yorkshire. At first I thought it was merely feminine moods, but within a few days of our arrival in London, it became clear that there was something, well . . . wrong with her."

Westland shook his head sympathetically.

"I have made some inquiries," Mikhail confessed in a lower tone, lying deftly through his teeth. "One of the former mad-doctors to King George has agreed to examine her."

"Tragic."

Mikhail summoned up a rare smile. "Forgive me, Your Grace. I should not have burdened you with all of this, but I can only continue to apologize for the way she burst in on your home and abused your servants."

"Not at all, not at all, dear chap. I only pray the girl is not a danger to herself."

"If it is not too much trouble," he added hesitantly, "I would be most grateful if we could keep this matter quiet, to spare Rebecca's dignity and my family's good name."

"Of course, Kurkov. Say no more. If the young lady is disordered in the mind, she needs help, not needless mockery. I do hope your men won't be too rough with her," he added, glancing toward the window with a frown. "She is so young."

Mikhail twitched, but suppressed his angry certainty that it was not his men Rebecca needed to worry about on that point. She would pay for embarrassing him like this. "I have given them strict orders to forbear her curses and to use minimal force."

Westland absorbed this with a satisfied nod and took a sip of his tea.

Pleased that he had sufficiently discredited his young cousin so that no one would believe her now even if she tried to report what she had seen, Mikhail followed suit, hiding a cold, narrow smile behind the rim of his cup.

Just then a crystalline voice sounded in the hallway. "Papa! Papa, I need your opinion on something!" Lady Parthenia Westland came striding into the drawing room at that moment in a rustle of white muslin. "Papa, I am meeting with the Charitable Ladies this afternoon to finalize arrangements for the Brighton whist drive and I can't decide if we should serve chicken or woodcocks at the Winner's Ball—Oh!"

The duke's daughter suddenly stopped at the sight of Mikhail. Her long-lashed eyes widened in surprise, while the sunlight gleamed on her white-gold hair. It was sleek, smooth, and shiny as platinum, fashioned into a sophisticated knot at her nape.

Mikhail rose abruptly to his feet, tongue-tied by the diamondlike elegance of her beauty.

"Oh, I'm so sorry!" she exclaimed, lowering the pad and pencil that she held in her hands. "Forgive my intrusion. Papa, I did not realize you had a visitor." She nodded to Mikhail. "Good morning."

He bowed.

"Do come in, darling," Westland said. "It's quite all right. Allow me to present Prince Mikhail Kurkov, the Czar's friend."

"Prince Kurkov? Oh, it is an honor, Your Highness," she said, gliding closer with an intrigued smile. "One cannot go about in Society without hearing reports of your valor in the war." She offered him her hand.

He bowed over it with precise formality, one hand resting on the hilt of his sword. "The honor is mine, Lady Parthenia."

She sketched an answering curtsy worthy of an artist's brush, then wafted over to her father's side. Mikhail watched her, decidedly impressed.

Westland gave her a fond squeeze around her shoulders. "Well, now, chicken or woodcocks, eh? These are weighty matters beyond my ken, daughter. Perhaps Prince Kurkov has an opinion."

"Do you, Your Highness?" Parthenia turned to him with a bright and friendly smile.

Mikhail stammered, thrown off balance. Menus for entertaining were hardly his forte, but more astonishing by far was his sudden realization that he was looking at his perfect bride.

Healthy, he could see in a glance. Good breeding stock, superior bloodlines. Impeccable manners, and beautiful enough to impress even the Czar.

Most important, marrying Parthenia Westland would cement his alliance with the elite Whigs.

Stunned by his good fortune, he could barely manage a shrug, slipping readily into the familiar role of a blunt, simple soldier. "Forgive me, Lady Parthenia. I know not."

"My thoughts exactly," Westland agreed.

"Oh, Father," she chided him fondly, and then turned to Mikhail with a speculative air, tapping the blunt edge of her pencil against her chin. "If you would not think me too forward, sir, might I ask if Your Highness enjoys a bit of cards now and then?"

The question startled him, coming from such a demure creature. "Why, yes, my lady. Not intemperately, of course, but there is much waiting during a war, and cards are a common pastime amongst soldiers in their tents and officers in the mess."

"Just what I had hoped to hear!" she replied, dazzling him with her smile. She turned to her father. "May I ask him about the whist drive, Papa?"

"Oh, go on," Westland muttered, obviously quite the doting papa. "If you must."

Parthenia turned to Mikhail again. "Each year, Your Highness, the Ladies' Charitable Society, of which I am a part, arranges a whist drive by the seaside town of Brighton to raise funds for our charitable foundation benefiting navy widows and their children."

"Admirable," he answered with a nod.

"Unfortunately, the difficult times our country has suffered of late have greatly increased the need for aid, and so, this year, we are determined to expand our charity to include widows and children of men from all branches of the military. To do so, we have doubled the entry fee from last year, but on the other hand, I can assure you the annual Brighton whist drive always guarantees great excitement and notoriety for those who make it into the final round."

"All that enjoyment for only ten thousand pounds," Westland said drily.

Mikhail nearly choked. "Ten thousand pounds?"

"Too steep for you, sir?" she teased with a jaunty grin.

Startled by her charm, Mikhail laughed and glanced

at her father. "I see why they put such a pretty lady in charge of signing up the players."

"An indecent sum of money, is it not?" Westland agreed. "Only such smiles could induce a man to go along with such folly." He pinched his daughter's cheek with sardonic affection. "I swear to you, I did not want my little girl involved in such wranglings, but she is difficult to say no to."

"So I see."

"Oh, hush, Papa. It's for a good cause, as you well know. Don't be fooled, Your Highness. My father is signed up for it, as well," she added matter-of-factly. "And that means it *must* be respectable."

"Wasted funds. I am hopeless at cards."

"Oh, Papa, winning is not the point. It is a *donation*."

"As long as they don't match me up with a damned Tory for a partner."

She laughed and turned prettily to Mikhail again. "I do hope Your Highness might consider it soon. There are only thirty-two seats in the game."

"For the thirty-two richest men in England," the duke remarked.

She gave her father a scolding tap on the arm. "The Regent's playing, too."

"Well, he'd hardly miss a chance to squander England's coffers," Westland muttered.

"If you can avoid being eliminated through all four rounds," she explained, "the winner and his partner get to split the prize of 320,000 pounds—minus ten percent for the poor, of course."

"A small price to pay for the chance to please Lady Parthenia." Mikhail offered up this flattery with a Continental bow. "I shall be honored to participate, my lady. Count me in."

Westland gave his daughter a doting pinch on her cheek. "Well, that was easy, wasn't it?"

*   *   *

As the battle in the mews raged on, Becky could not believe what a skilled fighter Alec was. He was magnificent. More than that—fearless. She was astonished at his skill, speed, and ferocity with a sword. He had been right. She had underestimated him, and she was sorry for it.

The second Cossack was still trying to drag her away, but she kept looking back in worried amazement as Alec held his own and then some against one of Mikhail's fiercest warriors. "Ow! Get your hands off me!" she muttered to no avail, tripping over an uneven cobble in her efforts to resist the Cossack's pull.

Suddenly, a bellow of pain rose from the embattled men behind them. Both she and her captor stopped struggling and turned to see which man had been hurt.

Her eyes widened, hearty pride rushing into them. Alec had stabbed the giant Cossack again, this time in his biceps.

The Cossack cursed him in his native tongue, but Alec merely watched him with glittering eyes. He was in full control of the fight now and appeared in some dark way to be enjoying it. Becky's captor, watched the fight for a few seconds in apparent confusion and rising anger.

His nostrils flared, as though he scented real danger to his comrade now. Perhaps loyalty to his fellow soldier weighed even more heavily on him than Mikhail's orders, for after a moment's hesitation, the second Cossack sent Becky a pitiless glance, and then he was in motion once more, dragging her toward the horse's now empty corral.

He reached for one of the lead-ropes draped over the post.

"Oh, no, no, you don't—stop it! Damn you!" In short

order she was tied to the fence post, her hands bound in a very Gordian knot at about shoulder height.

She fought her bindings. "Alec, look out!" she yelled as the second Cossack entered the fray, going to his wounded comrade's aid.

He arrived too late to save him, though, for at that moment Alec plunged his sword into his first opponent's belly with such exquisite form that it looked as if he had practiced it for a dozen years, like a deadly ballet.

Becky shuddered and looked away as the soldier bellowed and fell to his knees.

Alec withdrew the blade and spun gracefully to meet the next opponent as the first one toppled facedown, but the second Cossack did not intend to make the same mistake.

Instead, he reached for his pistol.

Alec dove as the Cossack fired, but Becky heard his curse of pain and knew that her hero was hit; taking cover by pure instinct, she flung herself behind the post that she was tied to. Landing on the ground, Alec brought up his pistol in answer and fired back at the Cossack.

Boom!

Becky was glad the Cossack was facing forward, because she did not want to see where exactly Alec's bullet had struck him. She only saw the man's big, uniformed body jerk, the sudden movement so violent that his odd-shaped helmet fell off.

The Cossack grabbed at his throat, his scream cut off before he could make one. Then he went crashing to the ground.

She closed her eyes tightly and leaned her forehead against the fence post, shaking the whole length of her body and unnerved by the deafening silence in the alley.

Her heartbeat was a crazed staccato; she suddenly felt rather dizzy, slightly nauseated. She knew the Cossack's bullet had hit Alec, but she did not know how badly he was hurt, and for a second could not bring herself to look. This was exactly what she had feared.

The worst part was her ridiculous, infuriating sense of helplessness: Trussed up like a Christmas goose, she was unable to free herself or use her hands. If Alec was down, there was nothing she could do to help him. It was unbearable. *God, let him be all right.*

Just as she gathered the courage to look, she felt a hand touch her arm and let out a shriek, nearly jumping out of her skin.

"Shh, it's only me," Alec panted.

"Are you hurt?" she asked frantically. "You were hit—"

"Just a scratch." He glanced down at his left arm. His coat sleeve was torn at the top, nearly at his shoulder, and she saw blood seeping through the dark blue broadcloth. "Damn," he said, "I liked this coat."

"Don't you dare make a joke at a time like this!" she wrenched out.

"Shh, calm down, it barely grazed me. Come, we've got to get out of here," he murmured, but his eyes were dark and troubled as he worked swiftly to untie her wrists.

His hands shaking slightly with the aftermath of the fight, he fumbled with the Cossack's puzzlelike knot only for a moment before losing patience and simply slicing the ropes in two with his blade.

The second she was free, Becky hugged him hard around his waist, pressing her cheek to his chest.

"Shh. It's all right. They can't hurt you now," he whispered, holding her just for a heartbeat. She nearly cried out at the denial when he pried her back a small space and tilted her face up to meet his gaze.

His chiseled face was taut, his mouth a hard, unsmiling line. "Hurry, we must go. There were two more sent after you. The sound of gunfire will draw them here any minute now. Can you run?"

"Yes, of course." She forced a nod, feeling braver now that she saw he was not too seriously injured.

"This way." Alec grasped her hand firmly and cast one last regretful look at the dead men in the mews. "For the record, Becky, I have no idea who you really are or what the hell is going on, but you're going to explain it to me, do you understand?" he ordered in a low tone. "You owe me that."

The cool, leashed anger in his glance cut her, but she really couldn't blame him.

"Come on," he murmured. "We'll cut through the stables." Scanning the area, he tugged her forward by her hand.

Behind them, they heard deep, foreign voices calling out from the direction of the street as the other pair of Cossacks approached, searching for both their quarry and their companions.

Alec and she exchanged a grim look, then stealthily slipped away.

Westland's butler marched into the drawing room with an anxious look. "Beg pardon, sirs, my lady. One of Prince Kurkov's officers below has asked to speak to His Highness."

A taut glance passed between Mikhail and Westland, but they did not speak of the unpleasant matter of Rebecca in front of Lady Parthenia.

The duke strode over to the window, glanced out, then shook his head at Mikhail, relating the negative answer in silence. Mikhail absorbed this, then sent the butler a grim nod.

"Tell him I'll be right there."

"Very good, Your Highness." With a short bow, the butler exited.

Mikhail glanced at his host apologetically. "I should be on my way, in any case. I have imposed for too long. Your Grace. Lady Parthenia." He stared for a moment longer at the duke's radiant daughter, and then bowed to her again.

"He is an odd man, isn't he?" Parthenia whispered to her father after the tall, imposing prince had marched out.

The duke shrugged and gave her a fond smile. "He is a soldier. And a Russian. Their ways are different than ours. In all, though, I think well of him. And I daresay His Highness thinks well of *you*," he teased, tugging a light spiral curl on her nape as he strode past.

"Oh, Father, you and your matchmaking," she scolded his retreating back.

"I would like to meet my grandchildren before I die, Parthenia," he said breezily as he went off to continue with his morning's correspondence. "The chap's a prince, after all. You could do worse."

Parthenia considered this, left standing alone in the drawing room. Then she drifted to the window and looked down cautiously at Prince Kurkov conferring with his exotic retinue of guards. How fierce they looked!

She could hear them talking but did not understand a word. He *was* rather handsome, she supposed. He was not an exciting, though irritating, challenge like Lord Draxinger, but at least Prince Kurkov behaved like a grown-up, which was more than she could say for the earl and his fast-living friends.

She snorted at the thought and then shrugged the matter off, leaving the window to figure out the rest of the meal for the grand Winner's Ball to be held at the conclusion of their whist drive fund-raiser.

Meanwhile, outside the Westlands' house, Mikhail

could not believe what he was hearing. "You're telling me she got away?"

"Your Highness, it's—worse than that," Boris said grimly.

"How—worse?" Mikhail growled.

The Cossack's gaze fell to the ground.

"Well?" Mikhail demanded.

Pytor answered for the sergeant: "Ivan and Vasily are dead."

"What?" Mikhail turned to him in furious incredulity.

In a low voice Pytor quickly explained how they had found the pair, one shot, one nigh disemboweled.

"Did anyone see anything?" Mikhail demanded.

"A groom saw the girl. He claims she tried to steal a horse, but Ivan and Vasily pulled her down off its back. The horse ran off and the groom had to chase it. He saw nothing further. When he came back, they were dead. We have not yet located anyone who might have seen what happened in the interim."

Mikhail shook his head, stunned. God's bones, two of his best warriors were dead! He took a deep breath, shaking off his astonishment. "It is impossible she could have done this on her own. Someone is obviously helping her. Whoever he is, find this man and kill him."

"Yes, sir. Gladly." Boris jerked his head up with vengeance burning in his dark eyes.

"As to your comrade's bodies, get rid of them at once," Mikhail added. "I do not want the English authorities asking questions. And whatever happens—*whatever* happens, do you understand me?—Rebecca must not be permitted to speak to Westland. I want this house kept under watch at all times; she will no doubt try to meet with the duke again, and when she does, you will intercept her. She may try to approach them elsewhere, so if Westland or his daughter leave the house, follow them—discreetly, please. Neither of the West-lands must ever perceive that they are under our surveil-lance."

His glance flicked over his men's traditional Cossack uniforms. "I want you all in English civilian garb from now on. Try to blend in, for God's sake, and keep your eyes out for the girl. When you have her, bring her to me."

His men bowed in obedience.

Mikhail started to walk back to his waiting state coach, then paused. "On second thought, kill her if you get a clean shot," he amended. "That little bitch just be-came more trouble than she's worth."

Kurkov and his men might have the advantage of numbers, Alec thought, but he knew the territory, every nook and cranny of the West End and surrounding dis-tricts, and he used this knowledge to spirit Becky away from danger.

All bravado aside, however, he knew he was in a state of delayed shock over what had just happened. His head was in a whirl, the aftermath of battle still coursing through his veins.

He could not believe he had just killed two men be-fore breakfast. What on earth had he rushed into this time? *Look before you bloody well leap.* Had past disas-ters at the tables taught him nothing? Having to marry this fair deceiver was a dubious enough obligation, whoever she was; he hoped he would not also go to jail on her account.

"We've lost them by now, surely." Becky stumbled after him as he strode on through the shadowy maze of old crooked alleys tucked behind the stately fronts of stuccoed houses. He was in no humor to slow his paces so she could keep up.

"Alec, you're hurt! We must see to your arm," she insisted over the chiming of nearby church bells tolling the hour of eleven. "We have to stop the bleeding."

"I'm fine," he growled, tugging her by her hand.

"No, you're not." Becky halted, planting her feet to counter his forward momentum. She matter-of-factly showed him her hand.

It was bloodied from holding his.

Reluctantly, Alec paused and glanced at his injury. The blood had run all the way down his arm.

With a worried, guilty wince, Becky examined his wound, but he roughly shrugged off her ginger touch.

"It doesn't matter," he grumbled. "After all," he added with a bite in his tone, "what's a little of my blood after you shed yours?" He walked ahead. "Come on, we have to keep moving."

Behind him, he heard her inhale slowly through her nostrils in a quiet struggle for patience, but it seemed she wasn't touching his remark with a ten-foot pole.

"Alec. Be reasonable. If you keep losing blood at this rate, you'll be too weak to fight *or* to run if they spot us again."

He stopped for a second, anger pulsing in his temples, then pivoted and looked coldly at her. "You lied to me."

She tensed, going visibly on her guard.

"I found the blood on my robe this morning, Becky. Your blood. Don't tell me you're on your cycle because I know that isn't true. You're a goddamned virgin. No, correction—you *were*. Until last night. Until me."

Instead of answering him, she looked away and clamped her mouth shut, perhaps mortified that her ruse had been discovered, then she folded one arm across her waist in a defensive posture. He could almost see her clam up, shut down, dig in her heels; and then she tried to brazen it out.

"So?" she muttered with an insolent, one-shouldered shrug.

For a second he couldn't speak at all. "So?" he echoed, thunderstruck.

"It's not as if you care," she said.

The piercing challenge in her glance left him tongue-tied. Her battened-down stare reflected all of his mistrust and anger right back at him, despite the scarlet blush that raged in her cheeks.

Alec reached out and gripped her shoulders. "Why, Becky? Why didn't you tell me you were a virgin?" he whispered harshly, resisting the urge to shake her. "I wouldn't have touched you if I had known. I didn't force you! You could have said no at anytime and I'd have stopped. I took you for a harlot—and you knew full well that's what I thought, but you didn't see fit to tell me otherwise! Instead, you made a fool out of me. Do you even realize the consequences of what you've done?"

"You're hurting me," she informed him, tight-lipped and mutinous.

He instantly released her from his grip, but stayed close, looming over her. "Tell me what the hell is going on. Enough of your stubbornness. Why are they after you? Is your name really Becky Ward?"

"Yes. That is my name. That much I can tell you. But no more. Come. I'll bind your wound for you, then I'll be on my way. There." Avoiding his gaze with a will, she nodded toward the unassuming little church on the corner. "We'll go sit down in there so I can tend you. It doesn't look as though there's anyone on hand to bother us. That cut needs attention, and soon."

"No." Alec shook his head slowly. He would show the little hellion what stubbornness was. He was famous for it himself. He folded his arms across his chest. "I'm not going anywhere until you tell me what is going on. I deserve to know why I just killed two men back there, and—God's bones!—I'm entitled to know why someone is trying to kidnap my future bride."

"Bride?" Her eyes shot open wide. She finally looked over and met his furious glower. "*What* are you talking about?"

"You know damned well, Becky-dear. That's right. You're my headache now, and God knows what we're going to live on! What were you thinking, girl? I'm in no position to take a wife! Now I find out that the woman I'm bound to marry has a foreign prince for a cousin and Cossacks out to kill her, so pardon me if I seem out of temper!"

Her jaw had dropped. She stared at him for an astonished heartbeat, then shook her head slowly. "I see you've lost your mind, my lord."

"Would it were so! What, did you think me so bereft of honor that I would debauch a virgin and then throw her to the wolves?"

"Don't be absurd. I'm not marrying you!"

"Yes, you *are*," he growled, fire and brimstone in his eyes. "My honor demands satisfaction. I may be many things, *cherie*, but I have never been a ruiner of virgins."

"Oh, God, you are completely overreacting!" she huffed, plainly flustered.

"I'm sorry if you don't like it, but if you had told me the truth last night, this might have been avoided."

"How could I?" she retorted frankly.

"What's that supposed to mean?"

"Please! I saw for myself how you and your friends treat women. I understood perfectly well that I was nothing to you but a fleeting entertainment—a whim. But for me, this whole thing happens to be a matter of life and death."

"You're not making sense."

"How could I have trusted you with something so serious when it was plain to see you were only having fun? You gave me no reason to believe you'd even care."

"Oh, be fair. I was good to you—"

"A gracious host, yes."

"And lover, I suppose? You did trust me enough to come willingly to my bed!" he nearly shouted, his face flushing with fury.

"That's different."

"How? Do you judge me so incapable of helping you? A stupid stallion only good for a roll in the sack? Is that it? Because if that's what you really think of me, then you give me the greatest possible insult—"

"I didn't say that, Alec. Don't put words in my mouth. Look, there is no need for all of this. Your bachelorhood is quite safe. It's obvious that marriage is not what you want, so rest assured, I have no intention of marrying you—nor can I, legally, without my guardian's consent. I don't turn twenty-one until the first of August, and believe me, he would never allow it."

Alec stared at her. "I take it you're referring to Kurkov."

Her eyes widened; she searched his face with renewed wariness. "You know Mikhail?"

"I'm Alec Knight, *cherie,* I know everyone. Everyone but you, it would seem."

She avoided his reproachful stare again with a quick, uneasy glance at the carriage that went clattering past them down the cobblestoned street.

"I saw where you were going, you know," Alec added in a lower tone once the noisy vehicle had passed. "You were trying to get in to see Westland, but you can't do that now, can you? Kurkov got there first. So, what are you going to do next?"

She shook her head wearily and dragged her hand through her thick dark curls. "I—I don't know. I'll think of something."

"Why Westland?"

No answer.

"So stubborn," he whispered. "We're going to have to

work on that. What did you want with old Westland, Becky? Shall I repeat the question a third time?"

"You can stop asking me questions altogether because I am not going to answer them."

"Why is Kurkov after you? We can do this all day if you want."

"It isn't any of your business!"

"The bloody hell it's not!" he thundered so loudly that it drew the attention of a pair of uniformed nursery maids pushing their prams on the opposite side of the street. The women looked at them in alarm, then quickly hurried by. "Didn't you notice I just saved your life back there? I think I'm entitled to know!"

"Yes, I did, and no, you're not! I'm trying to keep you alive, Alec! That bullet missed your heart by inches!" she cried, holding up her fingers a short span apart. "Next time you might not be so lucky."

"Lucky?" he cried, feeling insulted. "That was skill, I'll have you know."

"Oh, forget this! I'm leaving. Hang your grandiose honor, and your fatheaded male pride, too. I'm doing this for your own good. Bind your blasted wound yourself."

"Where do you think you're going?"

"Anywhere you're not! And don't follow me again!" With that, she turned on her heel and set off without him again.

Alec rolled his eyes heavenward and checked the urge to follow her and drag her back, knowing that physical coercion would only drive her further into her shell. "So, you're just going to walk away—ruined?"

She whirled around with sparks shooting from her eyes. "What do I care for ruin with a squad of Cossacks at my heels?" She turned her back on him again and trudged on, shaking her head, feminine fury bristling in every line of her posture.

"God, grant me patience," Alec said under his breath. Robert, Lucien, all of his brothers had promised that one day he'd meet a girl as intractable as he.

He hated it when they were right.

"Now who's being unreasonable?" he called after her in a tone full of male superiority. "You've got no money, Becky. No place to go. You don't even know your way around Town. What if those brutes come after you again?"

"If?" She slowed a step, let out a weary snort and shot him a wry look over her shoulder. "You mean *when*. I don't know, Alec. It's not your problem. I'll manage somehow. After all—" She took a deep breath, bolstering her courage with a lift of her chin. "Right is on my side."

"So am I," he said softly, staring at her retreating back.

Infuriating creature!

Alec clenched his jaw, baffled by such trenchant rejection from a female. More than frustration, insistent panic began to snake through the back of his mind as she sought once more to abandon him.

Something about this girl just touched a nerve in him.

"What about last night?" he blurted out in taut anger. "Was everything between us just a lie?"

She was not so far away that she didn't hear him, and his words stopped her in her tracks. He saw her spine stiffen, and then she put her head down.

Alec caught up to her, but she would not look at him. "Don't do this to me, Alec," she said. "Please just let me go."

"I can't do that, Becky. I won't. We are bound together now. By blood. Last night you gave me your virginity. Today I took two lives to save yours. These are monumental facts, not something you can simply walk away from and ignore." He laid his hand on her shoulder and turned her gently to face him. "How is it that after all of this you still cannot confide in me?" he asked in a softer tone. "I'm no saint, God knows, but am I so very bad?"

"It isn't that," she whispered in a fragile tone.

"What, then, sweet?" When he brushed her hair gently behind her ear, she quivered, the electrical attraction between them crackling just beneath the surface, so ready to be stirred to life. "Tell me. Don't shut me out. Let me fix whatever's hurting you."

She looked at him with a soulful stare, showing him her crimson-smeared palm. "Don't you see, Alec? I don't want any more of your blood on my hands. There's still a chance for you to escape, to avoid getting tangled up in all of this with me."

"No, my darling." He cupped her face between his hands. "That chance is past," he said with finality as he held her in an even gaze. "I *am* in it now, whether you like it or not. Don't protect me. Just tell me what we're dealing with."

Becky did not want to accept it, but finally had to admit that what he said was true. She had dragged him into it with her, and she hoped to God that both of them did not soon regret it.

I didn't mean to, she thought woefully. She had tried to keep him safe.

Alec, for his part, did not appear daunted by whatever they might face. It seemed that the warrior within the elegant hedonist had been aroused. Stationed immovably by her side, he towered over her, his feet planted wide in a fighter's stance, ready for action, his strong thighs and broad shoulders thrumming with bold vitality; the climbing sun burnished his golden hair, and his deep blue eyes held her in a calm gaze. Revolving darkly in their depths, she saw fierceness, intelligence, and a perfect willingness to serve out treachery, even death, to her enemies.

Even last night, he had not been so seductive as he was in this moment without even trying, she thought with a small shiver of awe. The pure valor with which he offered himself reached even deeper into her guarded heart.

No, she realized, looking at him with new respect, this was not a man who needed her protection.

He was right, she conceded grimly. She needed Alec's help whether she liked it or not—whether it was fair or not. Her village was counting on her. She could not just think of herself, her pride, or even his well-being. The problem was larger now that Mikhail had gotten to Westland ahead of her. God only knew what lies her cousin had told the duke and his staff about her, for the butler and footmen had certainly treated her like an escaped lunatic.

Maybe Alec, with all his worldly shrewdness, could help her make a new plan. In truth, the thought of an ally when all hope had fled was most welcome, especially one who did not seem to know the meaning of fear, and had proved himself astonishingly expert with a sword.

She let out a low exhalation, seeing that she had no choice now but to swallow her pride and do what was hardest for her: Ask for help.

Trust.

He reached out to embrace her. He gave her a tender, manly little smile and clasped his hands around her waist as though he'd hold onto her by whatever means necessary. It bothered her that she could no longer fight this battle on her own. But then he bent his head and pressed a kiss to her temple, surrounding her with his delicious strength, and his nearness filled her with an indescribable comfort.

"Listen to me, you stubborn little mule," he whispered, nuzzling her. "From now on, let us decide together what is best for both of us. Perhaps I spoke too rashly. Neither of us can lay down the law for the other—as much as we might like to," he added drily. "I'm afraid we're both too strong-willed to take no for an answer."

They exchanged faint, cautious smiles of a truce.

"I will not impose marriage on you if you'll jolly well quit trying to escape me."

"But Alec—"

"Hear me out. You do not lack for courage, God knows. You've got more heart than I have ever seen in a woman before, and I admire that. But do not seek to protect me, little one. I can take care of myself—and you." When he tipped her chin up with his fingertips, she looked guardedly into his eyes. "Still, don't forget we can marry legally in Scotland."

She blushed at his persistence with the notion. There was no way she'd believe it was what he really wanted. "No." She shook her head. "There is no time."

"Perhaps when this is over."

She looked away, but felt him studying her. "Perhaps."

"Refuse me if that is your will," he said after a moment, "but you must then allow me to satisfy honor by other means: Accept the protection of my sword." She looked up at him and trembled at the white-hot chivalry that glowed in his eyes. "I will do aught in my power to help you," he vowed. "My only condition is that you tell me the truth."

Absorbing this, she gave him a grave nod. "Very well," she forced out with a hard swallow. "I will tell you all."

"Good." He released her slowly from his possessive hold around her waist. "Perhaps you will start with what I am most interested in knowing."

"What's that?"

"Why you gave yourself to me last night." He rested his fingers lightly on her shoulder and prevented her from turning away. His touch felt a trifle domineering, but Becky yielded after a moment, eyeing him warily. He shook his head, his cobalt eyes searching her soul like a lantern's beam sweeping the night. "You paid too high a price for food and shelter. Did you really think it was the only way you'd get my help?"

She bit her lower lip and thought out her answer carefully before replying. There was such a thing as male pride, and if she was going to let herself rely upon his help, it was best not to anger him. "I . . . wanted you. You must be used to that."

"Not from untouched maidens. No, Becky. Don't spare my feelings. You have made your misgivings about me quite clear. Even I know I'm not *that* irresistible," he said with a faint trace of world-weary humor. "Go on. What else? There's more you are not telling me." His perceptiveness startled her. His mouth twisted cynically. "I'm a gambler, remember? Reading faces is what I do."

Becky struggled with her uncertainty, then closed her eyes. "I want to tell you, but you'll be so angry. I'm afraid you will do something rash."

"Like what?" he asked coolly.

"Challenge him," she whispered, slowly opening her eyes again.

"Kurkov?"

She nodded.

"I'm not afraid of him."

"Well, I am! I know what he's capable of, and you should be, too, if you're wise. Do you know how many battles he's fought in?"

Alec's touch was gentle, but his eyes were stormy as he took her face between his hands and held her stare. "What did he do to you?"

Tears rushed into her eyes at the terrifying memory, much to her surprise. But Alec's gentleness was implacable, his solicitude inescapable, and finally her resistance crumbled. "He—He threatened to force himself on me. He said he would teach me a lesson I wouldn't forget, and that when he was done with me, he'd marry me off to someone horrid. I didn't want it to be that way," she whispered, holding him in an imploring stare. "Not for my first time."

Alec's nostrils flared.

"So I chose you instead," she confessed. "Because you were kind to me and you tried so hard to put me at ease and . . . you made me laugh when I hadn't smiled in days." Her chin trembled a bit with her refusal to cry. "I'm sorry if that means I used you, but I couldn't let him have that victory over me. He's taken everything else, you see. I couldn't let him take my pride."

Alec's mouth was a grim pale line. She had seen him annoyed, seen him exasperated, and seen him murderously intent on battle against the Cossacks, but not until this moment had she seen him utterly enraged.

He did not say a word.

He turned away, closed his eyes briefly with a noisy inhalation and, for a swift, harsh moment's silence, struggled for calm. "I won't let him touch you, Becky." His sapphire eyes flicked open again, gleaming with steely resolve. "That son of a bitch will not lay a finger on you," he said through gritted teeth. "Not over my dead body."

"That's exactly what I'm trying to avoid!" she cried, pulling away in a fresh wave of anguish. He caught her by her elbow, hushing her, to no avail. "You don't know how treacherous he is—I do! I saw him kill a man in cold blood, Alec! That's why I went to Westland's house! The duke is the lord lieutenant for West Yorkshire. I want Mikhail arrested! I want to see him hanged."

"So, that's why he's chasing you. To silence you before you can expose him for this crime?"

She nodded emphatically. "Yes."

"Well, at least it is beginning to make sense now," he murmured. Squinting against the climbing sun, he looked away, gathering his thoughts.

After a moment, she noticed that he was bleeding again, and told him so.

He glanced down ruefully at his wound. "Actually, if your offer of help still stands, my arm hurts like hell. Have you got anything we could use to wrap it?" His frank admission seemed to Becky aimed at putting her at ease again, as much as anything else; perhaps he recognized how intimidated she was by his icy, silent fury at Mikhail.

"Petticoat," she said with a sniffle. "I could tear a few strips off."

"So, then . . ." He lifted an eyebrow ever so slightly, offering her a cautious half smile. "I might get to see your ankles?"

An answering smile spread slowly across her face as she held his gaze, shaking her head. "You really are too much."

"Pride m'self on it." He gave her a roguish wink and sauntered past her, leaving her to marvel at his talent for making her feel better with an irreverent jest, a smile, a droll remark—and his kindness for caring enough to try.

He could kill with zest and alacrity, but his heart was gold.

Knight, she thought, gazing at him.

"Come along, *petite*." He took her hand as gracefully as though he were leading her to the dance floor of a ballroom. "We can go and sit in the church like you said, and while you doctor me up, I want to hear exactly what you saw."

She nodded and went with him.

"And, Becky?" he added, pausing. He stared up at the sun-splashed steeple. "Try to have a little faith in me." He sent her a guarded look. "I might just surprise you."

She lowered her head, chastened.

With a touch that brooked no denial, Alec cupped her elbow with his other hand and shepherded her across the street to the little sanctuary, steering her to safety yet again.

CHAPTER
∽ SIX ∽

Alec had not been inside a church since Lizzie's wedding to Strathmore, but even a sinner like him, he thought now, had to take pause upon walking onto holy ground, having just despoiled a virgin and killed two men in violent combat. Hatred simmered in his heart for this man she called Mikhail. So, the great Prince Kurkov thought he'd force himself on Becky? He could hardly wait to shove a sword through the man's heart.

Following her through the giant oak doors and into the chapel's silence, Alec's mood was dark and brooding. They passed a stone baptismal font carved with scallop shells at the back of the sanctuary, then stepped into the silent nave.

It was peaceful and cool inside.

Filmy sunlight permeated the white vaulted space above them; closer to earth, a long gray aisle led up to the plain altar between rows of dark mahogany pews. He heard his fair companion let out a steadying exhalation, and sent her a sober glance.

"This way," Becky murmured, taking his hand.

They passed through dusty sunbeams and into soft shadows as she led him toward the dim recess of a tiny side chapel. Watching her walk ahead of him, her delicate frame, her tousled hair like ebony silk, Alec felt tenderness and fury battling for rule inside him. He was prepared to make a joke to soothe away the fear he had seen in her eyes, and equally ready to tear someone's heart out to protect her.

Well, he had wanted something different, he reflected. *Careful what you wish for.*

The girl had his heart and mind, his entire being, in an uproar. Some of the things she said outside had unnerved him with their perceptiveness. The "boys will be boys" defense that usually procured female forgiveness for Alec and his friends seemed to hold no more water with Becky Ward than it had for Drax with Parthenia Westland.

At least he understood now why Becky had refused his dutiful offer of marriage. She was a few months shy of being old enough to wed of her own volition. But Alec recognized that it was more than that.

The lady, it seemed, did not hold him in the highest opinion.

She liked him well enough, he supposed. The physical attraction was definitely mutual, but he was not sure he had her respect, and that made him feel as though she had thrown down the gauntlet to him, daring him to prove himself worthy of her. It was not the sort of challenge he could walk away from. And, his mind whispered, if he could earn her respect, perhaps he could win back his own. He didn't even want to think about what stalwart Becky would say if she knew about Lady Campion.

What a piece of work the little battle-maiden was, he thought with an amused glance at her face as he moved to where she bade him sit, in the first box-pew in the side chapel. The girl had knocked Drax's tooth loose and nigh gelded Rushford with her knee, yet he himself had been foolish enough to think he could get away from her unscathed.

The chit had a gift for taking a man's vanity and handing it back to him, sliced and diced. It stung to know that she had judged him an amoral scoundrel and had only slept with him because he was the lesser of two evils.

Any man but Kurkov would have served her purposes last night.

Fortunately, he did not make a habit of trusting women. This one had a devious streak that was bound to keep him on his toes. Yet he could not think ill of her.

Odd.

Her spontaneity disarmed him; her force of character was unequivocal. With a haughtier upbringing, she could have been *the* queen bee of the Season.

Becky closed the pew's little wooden door behind her and joined him. Before them, a chipped and glassy-eyed wooden Archangel Michael clad in Roman-style armor and golden wings was skewering the serpent, pennants flying from his lance.

Alec looked curiously at Becky as she propped her foot up on the kneeler, stole a furtive glance around to make sure there was nobody on hand to see, and lifted her skirt out of the way, revealing a bit of her white petticoat beneath and a lovely curve of leg.

He rested his arm along the back of the glossy wooden pew and savored the show with a wicked smile. "You really are an interesting young lady," he remarked as she struggled to rip a length of cotton from her petticoat to bind his wound, scowling when she couldn't break through the sewn hem. "So innocent and yet so . . . very naughty."

"Will you stop flirting and put those muscles to use?" she whispered.

"Your wish, demoiselle, is my command." He leaned closer and obliged. Grasping her hemline in both hands, he tore through it with a powerful yank; but perhaps he was still on edge after his battle against the Cossacks, for he unintentionally exerted more strength than the job required and, suddenly, the cotton tore in a high slit all the way up to her thigh.

His immediate rush of roguish pleasure at the sight of her creamy skin above her high white stockings was replaced by curiosity when he glimpsed an object secreted away there, a small suede pouch tied to her ribbon-garter.

She gave a small gasp and went very still as Alec clamped his left hand atop her bare thigh. His right closed around the leather pouch that held some hard object, about the size of an acorn. Lord, what was she hiding now?

"What's this?" He glanced up suspiciously and met her anxious gaze.

Her heart pounding, Becky looked into his blue eyes and thought about the gambling debts he'd mentioned, his missing furniture, his admitted lack of funds—but if the two of them intended to stay alive, she knew they had better start trusting each other.

The man had saved her life today. She owed it to him to make the first move.

"Open it," she murmured, placing her faith in him as he had asked, despite the fact that the ruby was all she had. Without it, her hopes were lost. "See for yourself." She nodded at him, folding her arms nervously across her chest.

She bit her lip in agitated silence as he spilled the Rose of Indra out of its suede pouch into his palm.

"Good God!" he whispered, staring at it. He looked up at her in alarm. "Where did you get this?"

"It's mine. It's my inheritance. May I have it back, please?"

His eyes darkened with new understanding at her question, and new indignance. "You think I would take it from you?"

"It's all I've got," she answered uneasily. "I need whatever sum it can bring to save my home and village from Mikhail."

Alec handed it back to her without further comment, but he needed no words to make his displeasure felt. Well, he was insulted again. What was she to do about it? She had tried to please him by letting him see it.

She felt better the instant the jewel was in her possession again. Better safe than sorry. She tucked it into her bodice. "It's called the Rose of Indra. It's been handed down to the women in my family for many ages. It came to me through my mother. You see, Mikhail does not know it exists. I shall sell it and use the money to try to purchase Talbot Old Hall anonymously."

He sat back slowly, his probing stare still skeptical. "Perhaps you'd best start at the beginning."

She nodded. "Five days ago—early Thursday morning— it started like any ordinary day," she began. Clutching her petticoat in both hands, she worked to tear a strip off, and set it aside to use as bandaging. "I was in the kitchen garden checking on my herbs and vegetable beds when a group of the local villagers showed up at Talbot Old Hall to bring me their complaint."

"Talbot Old Hall?"

"My home," she admitted with a homesick pang. "At least it used to be. Now I'm not so sure. When Grandfather died, Mikhail inherited it—and all the other estates, as well."

He tensed. "Your grandfather?"

"The Earl of Talbot," she said, bracing herself for his reaction.

Alec just looked at her. Then he leaned forward, slowly rested his elbow on his knee, and held his head in one hand. "You are of noble birth," he said in a constricted tone.

"Yes."

"And last night I debauched you after several bottles of wine."

"Er, yes. That rather sums it up nicely, I'm afraid. Well, you needn't look so glum," she attempted. "It's not as if I didn't want to be debauched."

He slanted her a warning look. "Continue."

"The Talbot clan has always had its fingers in international business and diplomacy," she said. "Shipping interests, ties to the East India Company. Mama used to say there were only three rules in her family. Though few in number, they are ironclad, each one assigning family members their proper roles: The eldest son is the dutiful earl and shall vote Tory in the House of Lords; all daughters marry into the peerage; and all younger sons are funneled into diplomatic service for the Crown. Talbot sons have pressed the family's glory to all the foreign courts of Europe and beyond," she said cynically. "Indeed, to the farthest reaches of the earth—from Canton and Calcutta to Constantinople. And Russia, too."

"Thus the foreign cousin who's a prince," Alec said as he sat up properly again and stretched out his long legs under the pew in front of him.

"Exactly." She nodded unhappily, only slightly mollified by the knowledge that the title of Prince was used differently on the Continent than it was in England. In Europe, princes ranked slightly higher than dukes, but were still lower than grand dukes and archdukes. In England, of course, *prince* was reserved strictly for royalty.

"My mother had two brothers," she explained. "Michael, the eldest—he was to be the earl. Mikhail is named after him. He died of a fever at the age of forty, never having succeeded to the title, for Grandfather was still alive. My mother, Mariah Talbot, was the middle child, and Jonathon was the younger son. Many years ago, Jonathon joined the Foreign Office, per family tradition, and as a dashing young man, was made an attaché to the British ambassador to the court of Catherine the Great. In Petersburg he met a beautiful Russian noblewoman, Princess Sophia Kurkov, distant kin to the Czar. Her brothers, it was said, participated in the coup that overthrew Czar Paul—the father of Czar Alexander. Czar Paul was said to be utterly mad."

"I know who Czar Paul was," he retorted. "It so happens I do follow more than Society gossip."

Becky looked away. *I am not going to bicker with him inside a church.* "At any rate," she said, with, in her opinion, admirable patience, "having that shrewd Talbot eye for gain, Uncle Jonathon wooed and married Princess Sophia; Mikhail was the result. Through one of his Russian uncles, he gained the title of Prince. Through his father, he has now gained the Talbot earldom, as well. It's a pity Uncle Michael had no sons, but he died before he even managed to procure a wife."

"My condolences."

She snorted. "I wouldn't have known him from Adam. If I even have other kin, I do not know them. The whole family pretends I don't exist. We have no connections beyond the blood in our veins. I only found out about Grandfather's death because they remembered to invite Mrs. Whithorn, our old housekeeper, to the funeral." She lowered her head. "They have obviously forgotten I exist."

Alec frowned, studying her. "Well, that is very unkind. Why should they ignore you that way?"

"Because Mama broke the family rules," she answered ruefully, lifting her head to meet his protective gaze once more. "Instead of fulfilling her duty and marrying a lord, she eloped with my father, a mere navy officer."

"And thank heavens she did, or we'd all be speaking

French," Alec teased softly, echoing her tipsy words of the night before, and clearly signaling that he was on her side, even if her kin were not.

She sent him a grateful smile. "Which I cannot do, by the way."

"What, speak French?"

"Yes. My lack of accomplishments was one of the things Mikhail upbraided me for. Apparently all the Russian nobles at the Czar's court speak in French instead of Russian—is that not strange? I might have learned it, I suppose, if I had applied myself, but why should I study their tongue when they killed my father? Papa would have turned over in his grave. 'Bloody frogs,' he'd say. 'Hang 'em all.' "

"I have a brother or two who'd agree." Alec smiled wryly as she tore another strip off her petticoat and set it aside to use for cleaning and bandaging his wound.

"Grandfather never forgave Mama for eloping. Papa's valor at sea didn't matter. Even his commendation from Admiral Lord Nelson was not enough to break that proud old curmudgeon's grudge against the pair. After Papa died, we did our best to survive, but unfortunately, the navy was in such dire financial straits, holding wages in arrears, that it was impossible to collect my father's pension or any of the money owed us. We had no other means of feeding ourselves. Mama hated it, but she had no choice other than to go crawling back to her family for help."

"That must have been hard."

"We were lucky that Lord and Lady Talbot agreed to receive us at all. Grandfather wanted to throw Mama out on her ear upon sight, but Grandmother appealed to him on grounds of the family's reputation. How would it look if they were to let one of their own starve in the streets? So, it was decided that we would receive aid, but, of course, we were not welcome at His Lordship's

Berkshire palace, the seat of the Talbot earls. Instead, to minimize the family's embarrassment, we were bundled off out of sight to the remotest of the earl's secondary estates—Talbot Old Hall, in the West Riding. It's quite in the middle of nowhere," she said fondly. "An ancient hunting lodge on the edge of the moors."

"Sounds bleak."

"No, it's wonderful," she averred. "It's peaceful and quiet, and the landscape is magnificent. I wish you could see it, Alec. Buckley-on-the-Heath is not smart and fashionable like Town, but to me . . ." Her gaze wandered wistfully across the ceiling as she imagined the tiny village square, as familiar as her own reflection. "To me, it's home. The first real home I ever had. And now Mikhail is going to destroy it. I daresay destroying is all that he knows how to do."

Her thoughts drifted back to her first glimpse of her cousin, storming past the ivy-clad gatehouse and thundering up the drive with his Cossack retinue, his baggage wagon piled high, as though he intended a long stay. A sense of doom had come over her on sight of her formidable new guardian, but she had never anticipated the threat to her village, her home, or herself.

"I had expected him to leave quickly. After all, the old Hall is not exactly the finest of the Talbot estates. Before Mama and I moved in, Grandfather used it merely as a hunting box. And yet, Mikhail seemed to settle in. It didn't make any sense. Each day that passed, I grew more suspicious that something strange was going on. I didn't understand it at the time, but now I realize it was the very remoteness of the Hall's location that suited him—a perfect, secluded setting far from the prying eyes of the world where he could plot and scheme in secret."

While Alec mulled it over, Becky got up and went over to the small stone basin of holy water by the entrance of the chapel. "I hope this isn't sacrilegious," she whispered as she cautiously wet some of the cotton strips from her petticoat.

Alec pulled his shirt down off his wounded shoulder so she could attend to the nasty cut on his arm. "I've never had a wound cleansed with holy water before," he remarked, giving her a teasing glance. "Perhaps it will make me invincible."

She sent him a dark look. *I hope so.* Dabbing tenderly at his injury with the wet cloths, she set about explaining exactly what had happened the previous Thursday, when everything had begun to go so wrong. . . .

Thursday morning, Yorkshire

Becky stood in the shadow of Talbot Old Hall, her lashes bristling, her jaw clenched as she watched the frightened villagers go shuffling back down the sunny drive. She had done her best to soothe them; it all rested on her now. She pivoted and strode back briskly toward the house, tucking a long, waving tendril of her hair behind her ear.

The breeze and her determined walk sent her light calico skirts swirling around her legs. Above her, stark against the cloudless blue sky, the rooftop angels carved in oak stood guard with swords and shields, one at every corner of the ancient, fantastical house. The Hall had countless gables jutting this way and that, their upper stories jettied out in late medieval fashion. Ivy climbed thickly up the walls, encircling the diamond-paned windows.

Gusting inside, she marched through the dark, oak-paneled entrance hall, past Mrs. Whithorn, who seemed tempted to protest but held her tongue when she saw the fierce look on Becky's face.

Striding down the shadowy main corridor toward the

great hall, she passed the gun-room and the massive Elizabethan staircase with its intricately carved pine-apple newel-post and the familiar sixteenth-century portrait of an ancestor called Lady Agnes, who wore a sly, knowing smirk and a magnificent ruby as big as a walnut.

The ghost of Lady Agnes was said to haunt the Hall, and as a child, Becky thought she had seen the gray lady once floating across the minstrels' gallery, but now that she was grown, she had decided that the elegant specter had been naught but a figment of her imagination.

With the villagers' protests still ringing in her ears, Becky continued to the end of the corridor until she arrived at the threshold of the great hall, mentally girded for battle; when she saw her royal cousin puffing idly on a long-handled pipe, however, she stopped in her tracks, taken aback by this latest incivility.

So. Now he was smoking in the house.

As if his groping her on the staircase last night after dinner had not been bad enough! She gritted her teeth.

The man had no respect for anyone. No, all the world were serfs to His Highness. Back in Russia, he owned some twenty thousand human beings. Free-spirited as she was, she could barely wrap her mind around it.

Clenching and unclenching her fists for a second, she wiped her sweating palms discreetly on her skirts, ignored her pounding heart, and with a lift of her chin, resumed her businesslike march into the vast, drafty room before he noticed her standing there fumbling for courage.

Her slippered footfalls patted firmly across the cool gray flagstones, echoing beneath the soaring vaulted ceiling with its ancient chestnut beams against ivory plaster.

The sound drew Mikhail's attention.

If he knew he was an unwelcome guest, he showed no

sign of it, looking perfectly at ease now that he had been fed his breakfast, quite the king of all he surveyed.

Seated on a cushioned bench at the dark, heavy oak table where he had just finished his late breakfast, and wearing nothing but loose trousers and a luxurious dressing gown, the prince looked over the edge of his newspaper at her, then slowly lowered it, watching with predatory interest as she passed.

His cool perusal made her uneasy as she crossed to the bay of mullioned windows at the other end of the room and opened them to rid the air of his pungent pipe-smoke. The summer breeze blew in, carrying with it the heathery freshness of the open moors. How she longed to be out walking on the heath today, untroubled by all of this!

But through the window she could see the source of her ire—the small, foreign army bivouacked in the meadow behind her house. The Cossacks were only just beginning to stir from their drunken bout of marauding in the village last night, though it was half past ten. They made an exotic sight there in the English meadow, sleeping off their vodka amid the butterflies and daisies.

Ever since her cousin had arrived with his private Cossack army, it was as if her tiny village had been under enemy occupation, and there was no one who could rescue them.

Some of his soldiers had slept on the ground around their campfire, others with their heads resting on their rugged ponies' backs. They had formed a sort of teepee out of the deadly, sixteen-foot lances that Mikhail had told her they trained with from childhood until they became experts in the art of skewering infantry—to say nothing of their skill with every other weapon known to man.

"Cousin." Mikhail's deep, accented voice broke into

her thoughts. He sounded amused. "You seem agitated."

Becky turned around slowly, unsure how to begin without exploding, only hoping she did not look as tense and startled as the stags' heads and other hunting trophies mounted on the walls.

Mikhail cast his newspaper aside with a patronizing chuckle. "So serious. What ails you so on this fine summer morning, my little English rose?"

She refrained from rolling her eyes at his attempted charm and stared evenly at him, advancing slowly as she spoke. "Your men spent last night terrorizing the village. Again."

"Is that right?" He looked at his newspaper.

"Yes." Becky stalked toward him as she rattled off the list of their latest offenses. "They drank to excess, ransacked the tavern, attacked the serving wenches, terrified the people in the square, and beat up the poor village half-wit because they thought he was making fun of them."

"And?" Mikhail asked boredly.

"Something must be done!" she exclaimed. "Will you not speak to them? Their behavior was outrageous! Cousin, your men are a danger—"

"Of course they are a danger!" he said lightly. "That is the reason they exist." He tapped the ashes casually from his pipe. "Do not fret, Rebecca. It was a misunderstanding, I am sure. They meant no harm. This is simply what they are bred for. They are Cossacks, used to warfare. They are merely bored—as am I." He rose from the bench with an easy motion and strolled toward her.

"You refuse to curb them?" she murmured, staring at him in amazement.

"I will do so, *if* and *when* the situation warrants. No sooner, and certainly not on your orders."

She stood there, stunned by his indifference. Exhaling

smoke in her direction, Mikhail smiled when she gave a small cough.

Waving the smoke away, Becky felt her resentment bubbling over. "I do not know the custom in your home-land, cousin, but in England it is considered rude to smoke inside the house."

"It is my house," Mikhail said mildly.

This frank reminder of her new reality took her off guard. "Right," she forced out, lowering her head. What he said was quite true, though for some reason she kept forgetting that fact. It counted for nothing that she had lived here for over a decade while Mikhail had ar-rived but a fortnight ago.

He was Grandfather's rightful heir and that was that. The Old Hall belonged to him now. And, her mind whispered in warning, so did she. *Careful,* she cautioned herself and took another delicate step back as his sly smile widened.

"Leave my men to me, *loobeemaya,*" he murmured, and she nearly jumped out of her skin when he lifted his hand to her cheek without warning. "The more interest-ing question by far is, what am I going to do with you?"

"I don't know what you mean." She held very still, fighting the urge to pull away, instinctively fearing to make any sudden moves around him.

Her fear seemed to please him. His thumb stroked her cheekbone, sending unpleasant chills down her spine. "Shall I take you to London, I wonder? Bring you out in Society? Find a suitable husband for you, perhaps? Countess Lieven is a great friend of mine. Perhaps she'd be your sponsor."

She pulled away nervously as lust stirred anew in his eyes. "I do not wish to go to London. Mrs. Whithorn says it is as bad as Sodom and Gomorrah."

He tilted his head back and laughed. "Charming. Mrs. Whithorn is quite right, fair creature. Yes, I think you will be much happier right here . . . with me. I would much rather keep you all to myself." His gaze traveled over her body, then he glanced discontentedly around the great hall. "The only problem is this house."

"What do you mean? What's wrong with it?" she asked, thrown off guard.

"I do not care for it. Dark, dank, drafty. Bloody medieval. I am thinking of tearing it down, building anew. Something grander, more modern." He looked at her again. "What do you say to that?"

"Tear down Talbot Old Hall?" she breathed, the color draining from her face.

"You object?"

"Mikhail, this house has stood in this spot for centuries! It is . . . my home," she added softly.

"Well, if that's how you feel, then perhaps you should try and persuade me. Come, Rebecca." He stared at her. "Persuade me." When he started to pull her closer, she yanked out of his hold.

"You are indecent!" she hissed, then whirled to make a speedy exit, but her cousin grabbed her arm, dragging her back to him. "Let go of me!"

His smile was cool and taut. "Where is this famous English hospitality of which I have heard so much? You have done little to make me feel welcome, cousin. I am idle—and you are lovely."

"Take your hands off me!"

"Why won't you give me a kiss? We've got to start somewhere—"

"I said no!"

She slapped him hard across the face.

Mikhail stopped. His eyes flared with fury at her reckless blow, then, without hesitation, he hit her back, backhanding her across the face.

Becky flew, landing on the floor a few feet away and

only just managing to catch herself with hands planted wide.

"How dare you raise your hand to me?" he thundered. "Don't you know who I am?"

"Oh, yes." Though reeling from the blow, she lifted her gaze in enraged, full-out rebellion. "A brute."

His chest heaved where the V of his dressing gown lay open. "Do you have any idea what would happen to a Russian girl if she dared try that?"

Becky could not guess the answer and was not sure she wanted to know. She climbed to her feet unsteadily, still a bit stunned by the blow. She could not believe he had hit her.

"I would have her flogged until she begged for a night in my bed," he informed her in a snarl.

Just try it with me and see what you get. Though quaking, she held her ground. "I am not your serf."

"But you *are* my chattel." His arm shot out before she could escape. He gripped her hair and dragged her head back, forcing her to meet his blazing stare. His hot, stale breath filled her air. "Our grandsire's death made you my possession by law till you turn twenty-one, remember? One way or the other, girl, I will teach you to obey."

"Go to hell!"

"Ah, so it's to be defiance? Your choice. You can take the yoke easy, of your own free will, or fight me every step of the way—it matters not to me. Don't think our kinship entitles you to any special treatment," he panted in her ear. "I know all about how your mother disgraced herself with scandal; to me, you're little more than a whore."

"You bastard! Don't speak about my mother—" She shrieked when her renewed struggles only brought more pain.

He wrenched her scalp, pulling hard on her hair. "I'm

afraid I am not like your English gentlemen, Rebecca. I'm not afraid to play rough. Did you know I have a harem back in Russia?" he asked mildly. "It's very common among men of my class."

She grimaced in disgust; his pale eyes gleamed.

"Yes, fourteen beautiful young serf girls of every coloring and temperament, about your age. I do miss them," he added with a worldly sigh. "A man has needs. But of course, I could not bring them here. On English soil, the law would have them freed. Fortunately, I have you, thanks to Grandfather, and I shall train you by the same methods I used on them. It works, you know—my system—though it gets a little bloody now and then."

She sobbed and furiously blinked back tears, unwilling to give him that victory over her.

"I always win in the end, Rebecca, so heed me well. If you wish to save yourself a great deal of misery, I suggest you make it your purpose in life to do exactly as I say. It is mine alone to decide what you may do at any hour of the day, where you may go, whom you may see, what you may eat, what you shall wear, how many goddamned times a day you blink. Get used to it," he whispered in her ear, then roughly released his grip upon her hair and thrust her away from him.

She stumbled away in humiliated terror while Mikhail folded his massive arms serenely across his chest. "Go to your room for the rest of the day. I will send for you when I am ready to hear your apology. Right now, I am not in the mood."

"Apology?" she gasped, still reeling.

"You struck me and insulted my men. You will explain to me why this was wrong when I call for you this evening. Understood? Now, go." He turned away, dismissing her with an idle flick of his jeweled hand.

She was trembling all over, her mind a blank. Only

one thought crystallized clearly in her mind: "Leave this place," she uttered.

"You're still here?" he asked in an ominous tone, turning around slowly. "Very stupid. Yet I'm impressed."

Her temper snapped. "Leave my home!" she screamed, keeping the furniture between them. "And take your filthy barbarians with you!"

When he strode toward her, his robe flowing out behind him, she fled. She streaked past Lady Agnes's portrait and went pounding up the stairs, her heart hammering.

Mikhail stayed at the bottom of the staircase. "I am the master of this house now!" he roared after her. "Either learn to obey me or get the hell out!"

That's an easy choice. Gaining the safety of her bedchamber, Becky slammed the door. For a moment she stood there trembling, listening to make sure he was not still pursuing her. Hearing nothing, she slumped against the door in a dazed and trembling state of shock at what had just passed. Her mind could not absorb that her legal guardian had struck her.

He intended much worse still to come.

Her hands were cold, her stomach in knots as she realized she could not stay here. Her own home—and yet she had no choice but to leave it. He had made his revolting desire plain enough. It was his house now. She would rather be evicted than humiliated, terrified. Raped.

At that moment, a muffled click from the door behind her nearly made her jump out of her skin. It was followed by Mikhail's low sneering voice penetrating through the wooden seam between the lintel and the door: "I'll be back at midnight to hear your apology. Then your *training* will begin. You'd better hope you please me, *loobeemaya,* or I'll marry you off to the worst man I can find."

Laughter.

Her throat closed, the curse she wanted to scream at him muted. She stared at the door. As she listened with pounding heart, his heavy footfalls receded down the corridor. He was gone.

Cautiously testing the door, she discovered that he had locked her in. Now she was his prisoner in earnest. . . .

Alec hoped his rage did not show too plainly on his face as Becky paused broodingly and finished cleaning his cut. *Training?* he thought, his temples pounding with wrath. *Training?*

For his part, he could hardly wait to teach that blackguard a lesson the likes of which he would never forget.

She shrugged, veiling the cauldron of emotion in her eyes behind her lashes. "So I started packing."

No wonder it was hard for her to trust him, Alec thought. He wouldn't trust anybody, either, if he were in her place.

"How's that feel?" she murmured, staring at her work.

He made a vague mumble in answer, more concerned with her tale, but he was glad to see that the bleeding had stopped. "Continue, please."

She tore a fresh strip off her petticoat. "After Mikhail's threats, I knew that I had to get to safety quickly, but I feared my cousin might retaliate against any of my neighbors who agreed to give me aid. Also, it would have been very easy for his men to seize me if I stayed nearby. So I resolved to retreat to the next town where I could take a room in a lodging house and hide until I had worked up a plan to get that monster out of my home and his Cossack brutes away from the village."

"But you said he locked you in."

"Yes. So he thought." Carefully wrapping a strip of cotton around his biceps, she slipped him a wry smile.

"The house is riddled with secret passageways that have been there since the days of Queen Elizabeth and Bloody Mary—there's even a priest-hole behind the great hall's hearth. Mrs. Whithorn herself thinks the secret passages are just an ancient rumor, and Mikhail certainly doesn't know they exist, but I explored them often as a child."

"Aha. Good girl."

"In any case, since my cousin had threatened to tear the Hall down, I didn't dare leave my most valuable possessions behind."

"This ruby?"

"No, I had not yet learned of its existence. My father's navy medals and Mama's love-letters to him. They were stored in the attic. I knew I had to sneak up there and retrieve them before I could possibly leave. . . ."

It had been years since Becky had gone into the Hall's secret corridors, but fortunately, she still remembered the whole procedure. Moving with brisk efficiency, she lit a small lantern and marched past the windows into the narrow dressing room adjoining her bedchamber.

At once, she crossed to her large oak wardrobe—empty now, since all her clothes were packed—and opened the doors. Reaching inside, she ran her hand along the right inner corner until her fingertips found the little latch in the back panel seam. With a wary glance behind her, she turned the latch and then pushed the wardrobe's back panel forward. It creaked and opened into a yawning black hole in the wall, just large enough for an average-sized person to slip into.

Becky raised her lantern and did just that.

Thrusting her lamp and an exploratory foot through the dark hole first, she stepped down gingerly into the narrow space. Ducking her head as she entered, all was exactly as she remembered from childhood—the shivery darkness, the same clammy draft moving like a ghost down the pitch-black corridor. Before proceeding, she pulled the doors of the wardrobe shut behind her, then glanced left and right, got her bearings, and headed for the attic stairs.

Cobwebs tickled her face while many-legged crawling things fled before her lantern's beam. She followed the passageway with silent steps, took a right turn, and continued until she came to the ladder leading to the upper levels of the house. Grasping the dust-coated rungs, she began to climb. She passed the openings that gave access to the third and fourth floors, mounting upward until she reached the fifth and topmost level of the house. Just when the sense of claustrophobia was beginning to oppress her, she emerged from the secret passageway through another disguised door hidden behind an ancient flag hung on the wall.

She came out into the hallway near the short wide stairs that led to the attic. As soon as she pried the attic door open, a wave of stale, musty air rushed out. She turned away, wrinkling her nose at the smell and coughed. Then she stuck her head through the door and peered in, lifting her lamp. *Please, no bats.* Nervously, she glanced around. If the creatures were there, she did not see any, not by her lantern's glow nor by the wan daylight filtering in through the single dirt-clad window. Satisfied, she went in.

Up in the attic, time had stood still. Beneath its slanted ceilings and exposed beams stood towers of bins and trunks and boxes with a slim path cleared between them. Becky tiptoed down this path, her wonderstruck gaze traveling over the eccentric array of objects stowed here: a pair of old whicker panniers, abandoned toys, odd-shaped snowshoes.

Odd pieces of a rusty suit of armor were strewn across an old table, steely gauntlets and a fierce-looking helmet with a black horsehair tassel. There were moldy old court robes where a clan of mice proliferated, a broken chair, a rolled carpet leaning upright in the corner. Though anything of real value had been removed years ago for storage in her grandfather's Berkshire mansion, the attic still held remnants of a few hundred years' worth of world travels by various Talbot diplomats. Faded paintings. Exotic vases. A dusty model of the Coliseum.

Her roaming gaze stopped on the massive bombé dresser against the wall. *That's what I want.* The huge Baroque piece stood taller than she did; its bowed belly easily contained two hundred tiny drawers. The question was, in which drawer had she put Papa's medals? Mama's love-letters would be with them, tied with a faded ribbon.

Setting her lantern down, she began searching the miniature drawers for her prized possessions. Each one held some odd, whimsical treasure: weird looking keys, old invitations to a Hunt Breakfast, a tiny book of illustrated Bible stories for children, a small whistle whittled out of wood, a thin forget-me-not bracelet made from someone's braided lock of hair, a tiny silver bird figurine. One drawer she opened contained a thriving colony of strange insects. She shut it quickly, and soon thereafter found the items she had come for.

Simple curiosity made her open one last drawer that she had not explored, though her lantern oil was running low, which meant that she must hurry. Pulling it farther open, she peeked inside and found a very old-looking wooden box small enough to fit in the palm of her hand. She lifted it out of the drawer and, after blowing away a puff of dust, found a name carved in the fine wooden lid: *Agnes Mariah Talbot.*

Why, that was Lady Agnes in the portrait at the foot of the great stairs! The ghost she had seen as a child. With her heart beating faster and gooseflesh rising on her arms, Becky opened her Tudor ancestor's little trinket box.

Inside, it was lined with cream velvet. It had clearly been designed to hold something precious, but all it contained at present was an ancient-looking piece of paper folded in a square. Gingerly, she unfolded the two-hundred-year-old note.

A seal with faded colors at the top of the page marked it as some official sort of document. Dark, jagged handwriting flowed across the page, the language fraught with Shakespearean-style spellings that slowed down her efforts to decipher it; but she soon discovered that the paper explained the origins of the great ruby brooch that Lady Agnes wore in her portrait. Apparently, it had been a gift from a Ceylonese prince to one of the Talbot diplomats who had made a perilous journey to the East Indies some two hundred years ago in order to promote trading ties with the Spice Islands. Becky was startled to learn that the intrepid Lady Agnes herself had gone on this journey and had charmed the ruling despot from whose ruby mines the jewel had come; henceforth, the Rose of Indra was to be passed down through the female line of the Talbot family.

Which meant that it would now be hers.

For a moment she pondered this in awe, then could not help but feel a twinge of bitterness that such a treasure should have been lost. She had no other inheritance. Why, if she could get her hands on that ruby, it would surely be worth enough to buy Talbot Old Hall from Mikhail.

As she scanned the document, a postscript scrawled across the bottom of the page in a clearly different hand gave a tantalizing hint of what might have become of the Rose of Indra. The spellings were more modern and the words appeared to have been hastily penned: *The*

*Roundheads are coming and soon shall besiege us. The
Rose has been hid amongst the lilies.*

So, she mused, some quick-thinking ancestor had
managed to hide the jewel from Cromwell's forces during the Civil War. No doubt it would have been confiscated, along with any other valuables that were found.
In those days, the Talbots had sided with the Cavaliers.
The lilies? She turned the oblique message over in her
mind. If there had once been lilies planted at Talbot Old
Hall, they had long since withered, but then her eyes
widened. *No, no—of course!*

The old gatehouse.

Over the years, the approach to the Hall had been
changed; the gatehouse sat at the end of the overgrown
place where the old driveway had once joined the country road. It was a squat stone outbuilding covered in ivy
and crumbling with age, but atop its little mansard roof,
as a nod to the first Talbot lords' Norman origins, the
fortified gatehouse was topped with a copper finial in
the lily-shaped form of the fleur-de-lis.

Amongst the lilies . . .

Could the Rose of Indra still be hidden somewhere inside the gatehouse? How wonderful if it were true, she
thought, her pulse racing with excitement, her eyes
agleam at the intriguing possibility. If the jewel was still
hidden somewhere in the gatehouse, and if, with all her
good luck, she could find it, then maybe, just maybe, she
could work through a trustworthy bank to buy the Hall
and oust Mikhail from the premises forever.

It was a very long shot indeed, but right now it was
the only hope she had, and if it worked, she could make
everything better, not just for herself, but for all of
Buckley-on-the-Heath. She had to try.

Tonight.

* * *

"Well, you obviously managed to find it," Alec said after a long silence.

Tucking the end of his bandage in securely around his biceps, Becky nodded, avoiding eye contact. She detected his closer scrutiny; she could feel his shrewd gambler's gaze reading her face.

"You saw something in the gatehouse that you did not expect to find." His blue eyes flickered with intrigue. "Something you were not supposed to see?"

She swallowed hard and nodded. *Something terrible.* Turning away in hesitation, she gazed at the statue of the archangel battling the serpent.

"Becky?" he murmured, drawing back her attention with a gentle caress on her arm.

She turned with a tumultuous stare, her heart clenching as she gazed at him. "If I tell you the rest, you can't back out anymore."

"I don't want out, Becky." He took her hand. "I'm on your side," he said softly. "Everything you've told me makes me all the more committed to helping you."

She leaned closer and pressed a lingering kiss to his cheek. "Thank you."

He nodded, and then she related the conclusion of her dark tale. . . .

The night was eerily still as she slipped outside and hung back for a moment, clinging to the shadows as she scanned the area for Mikhail's guards. The Cossacks were nowhere in sight. Becky prayed they had not returned to the village to cause more trouble.

Satisfied that the coast was clear, she darted toward the thicket where the gatehouse was obscured, her small bag of supplies bumping against her side as she ran. It held little more than a candle and tinderbox for light and a small digging spade.

Sprinting through the kitchen garden and across the

carriage drive, her footfalls made quiet crunches on the gravel before she reached soft turf again and raced on.

Once more she had used the secret passageways to exit the house unseen, waiting until full darkness had fallen. Now all her thoughts were focused on finding the Rose of Indra. *Among the lilies . . .*

Ahead, the woods loomed, indigo-shadowed, mysterious; above, ragged clouds wound around the crescent moon.

She braced herself as she entered the woods, but had to slow her pace, fighting her way through vines and brambles. It was so very dark that she almost missed the humped roof of the gatehouse slumbering under its ivy blanket. Changing course, she picked her way toward it, climbing over a fallen log, then jumping when an owl hooted from somewhere nearby.

At last she crept up to the stone gatehouse, moving cautiously around the outbuilding until she found the side that had once faced the road. Her gaze pierced the night's gloom to home in on the door. She walked toward it, her heart beating faster.

Inside, it was pitch-black, probably untouched for a hundred years except for her childhood explorations over a decade ago. She lowered her bag to the floor and bent down to take out the tinderbox. Feeling for the flint in the darkness, she managed to strike a flame and quickly transferred it to the candle.

Cupping the teetering fire with her hand to protect it from the gentle draft she felt upon her face, she lifted the light and gazed at her surroundings. The front room was quite bare, with naught but a fireplace and a steep flight of rotting steps leading to the loft above. But as her gaze continued to travel around the room, her confidence grew as she scanned the frieze adorning the interior of the gatehouse: white plaster lilies on a purple ground. Surely the ruby was still hidden in here somewhere.

She followed the frieze around the room, searching for any more clues about where the jewel might be hidden. As her gaze traveled around the heights of the room and over the elaborate cornices, it came to rest on a modest roundel situated between two small high windows shaped like fleurs-de-lis. The barest silver glimmer of moonlight shone through them. Below the frieze, the roundel was only about as large as a dinner plate and bore the Talbot family crest. Something drew Becky to it.

She crossed to a large old storage trunk by the wall and climbed up onto it, setting her candle on it beside her. Then she stood on tiptoe and reached up with both hands to see if she could remove the roundel from the wall.

It was a struggle, and bits of plaster dust fell into her eyes, but she blinked them away and pulled hard. The roundel came off the wall. Steadying herself from the sudden jerking motion, she set it down, leaning it against the wall near her feet, then peered up at the circle of plaster she had exposed, hard and brittle and ivory with age.

Nothing.

She poked at it with her hand, but there was no secret hiding place, no tiny vault where a jewel could be stored. *Blast.* Determined to continue her search, she got down off the trunk, but her toe kicked the roundel and it rolled away like a discus. As she picked up her candle again, she glanced at the errant roundel and something caught her eye as it made several swirling passes a few feet away and landed on the floor, faceup.

Furrowing her brow, Becky picked it up and slowly turned it over. A hushed gasp escaped her lips. A small leather pouch was attached to the back of the roundel, fixed there by a little hook driven into the wood and tied in place by two suede strings.

Her heart began beating impossibly fast. With shaking fingers she untied the strings and opened the pouch, emptying its contents into her hand.

The fat, bloodred ruby slid out of the pouch and fell into her waiting palm.

She stood there, openmouthed, staring at it. It was real! The Rose of Indra! Somehow, finding it exceeded her wildest imaginings. She let out a tiny screech of glee and twirled once on her heel in sheer joy, but then heard a noise.

A low, animal sort of groan.

She froze and held her breath, listening. It came from the adjoining chamber. Gooseflesh crept down her arms as she realized that someone—or something—was in there. Perhaps a wounded animal, for she sensed a creature in pain. Perhaps one of the barn cats had been in a fight and fled there to lick its wounds.

But the scraping sound that followed could not have been made by a little cat. *Oh, Lord,* she thought, her heart pounding. Perhaps some aged vagrant had taken shelter in here to escape the workhouse, for hard times besieged England. If so, he had nothing to fear. She could offer him something to eat.

Steeling her courage, Becky approached the door that connected the two small chambers and lifted the light.

"Hullo?" she called softly, but immediately upon opening the door, she smelled stale urine and the faint tinge of blood. A stirring in the corner drew her frightened glance. "Wh-Who's there?"

"Aidez-moi," came a parched, raspy whisper.

"Show yourself!"

Her knees turned to jelly as a human silhouette unfolded itself in the shadowed corner and rose with a pitiful movement, stepping cautiously toward the light. Becky beheld a barefooted man in torn trousers and a loose white shirt hanging off him, much stained, with ruffled sleeves.

A gentleman's shirt.

"Dear God." She laid her hand across her mouth and stared, her eyes wide.

He had dark hair that had gone shaggy; he was tall and powerful of frame, but badly underfed. His face was gaunt, hollows under his high cheekbones, just above the edge of his rough beard.

His dark eyes filled with terror as he glanced toward the window, then again at her, imploringly. *"Aidez-moi, s'il vous plaît, mademoiselle."*

She recoiled against the door. "You're a Frenchman!"

"Non, non! Je suis Russe. Je suis Russe."

"What? Roose? Your name is Roose?" She heard the shrill note of alarm in her own voice, but she couldn't help it. Her heart was pounding wildly.

He struggled to make her understand. *"Non!* Rooseeah. *Je suis de* Rooseeah."

"Roose-ee-ah?" she echoed in bewilderment. "Russia? Oh! You're a Russian?"

"Oui! Je suis Russe!" More babble.

Becky shook her head frantically, understanding none of it. "What are you doing in my gatehouse?"

He rattled off two or three silky-smooth paragraphs in French, enough to convince her by his lordly bearing that he was no commoner, but she could not understand a word.

He fell silent at her blank expression, then dropped to his knees with an anguished stare and bowed his head, half weeping, needing no further language to make it plain that he was begging for her help. It was then that she realized the man's hands were chained behind him.

Appalled comprehension filled her mind. So, this was what Mikhail was hiding. This was why her cousin had lingered so long in Yorkshire. Why the prince was holding this man prisoner in the gatehouse, she could not fathom, nor did she care. The foreigner could be dangerous, but it was a chance that every instinct bade her take.

Moving with brisk efficiency, she made a swift search of the room and located the keys to his manacles hanging near the door in the outer room. Striding back into his cell, she approached cautiously.

Becky showed him the key with a warning look. He closed his eyes with an expression of complete obedient desperation, then turned, giving her his hands. He smelled awful, and the raw condition of his wrists was appalling.

Her hands shook as she fumbled to free him.

The second he was free, he took the candle and instantly blew out the flame. Becky backed away from him, mistrustful in the dark. He grabbed her elbow and turned her toward the door with an order that she couldn't understand.

"What are you doing?" she demanded, then obeyed his belated hush as she heard the distant sound of male voices. *Someone's coming!*

The Cossacks.

No doubt coming to check on their prisoner. Becky glanced toward the window as the color drained from her face; the Russian's angular countenance filled with murderous intent. She did not understand the words, but his questioning murmur was enough of a cue: *Where do we go?*

They had to get away.

She grabbed his sleeve and pulled him with her, leading the dazed man out of what had been his prison. Once more she stepped out into the blowing woods. The Cossacks' voices were growing louder. She glanced around with her pulse pounding. If she could get him to the house, she could hide him inside the secret passageways, but when she tried to urge him in that direction, he refused.

He pointed, indicating the approaching Cossacks, not yet visible. He shook his head and backed away from her.

"Fine," she muttered. They could make a run for it. One of her neighbors down in the village would have to help them. Big Samuel, the blacksmith, or Mr. Haskell, the apothecary. He used to be an army man, he would not be too frightened of Mikhail.

"Come on," she whispered, leading the pitiful creature deeper into the woods. Barefooted, he stumbled on the rough ground, thanks to his weakened condition. In his strength, he would have been a formidable man.

As they disappeared into the woods, behind them the Cossacks must have found the gatehouse empty, for they sent up the alarm, harsh male shouts ringing throughout the area they had just evacuated. She could imagine them running through the gatehouse, and knew that in another moment they would be on their trail.

Becky and the captive ran faster, thorns and branches tearing at them as they rushed by. They hit the open moors and ran full out, though the Russian's steps were already flagging.

"Come on, you can do it! I know these moors like the back of my hand!"

He seemed to grasp her meaning as she urged him on. Past the woods, the treeless heath with its low scrub and gently rolling ground provided their pursuers an easy mark when they finally spotted them. Becky screamed when the bullets started flying over their heads, but the Russian was cool, putting her ahead of him.

A lord, a gentleman, no doubt.

The Cossacks must have summoned Mikhail himself, for she now heard her cousin's voice far behind her barking orders at his men in Russian.

Then his voice carried to her on the night, a long, echoing howl.

"*Rebeccaaaaaa!* Rebecca! Get back here!" Mikhail bellowed after her.

Their captive let out a garbled cry as a massive report from a rifle ripped through the air, bounding off the moors' gentle rises. The man she had just freed went sailing facedown into the turf, shot in the back.

She let out a shriek and jolted down to her knees beside him. "Oh, my God! God!"

He could barely lift his head, and she knew he was dying as he pointed furiously to the horizon, needing no English to make his order clear: *Go!*

He tore off the small silver religious medal that hung around his neck and pressed it into her hand. Weeping, she closed his blankly staring eyes, then clenched her jaw and rose again, staring in tearful rage at the armed men by the treeline.

A glimmer of moonlight showed her Mikhail's outstretched arm, gesturing to the men to hold their fire. Some of the other Cossacks were just leading their horses onto the scene.

"It's too late, Rebecca!" he shouted over the moors. "Come back now of your own will and nothing will happen to you. Don't make me chase you!"

You monster, she thought, her eyes burning as she turned her back on him.

Two of the Cossacks mounted up but she was already in motion, running faster than she had ever moved in her life. She had a fair head start on them and knew this terrain much better than they did. The boggy ground and countless holes made by the various animals of the brush gave a person on foot the advantage over any rider who did not wish his horse a broken leg.

She leaped over a large stone and dashed down the familiar dip of a gully, following the fold of the landscape and using the cover of darkness to escape. Every pounding footstep reverberated from her ankles all the way up to her teeth, but she raced on, her legs pumping furiously beneath her.

"*Rebeccaaaa!*"

She ignored him, barreling on.

Her cousin's voice grew fainter, but his final threat chilled her to the bone: "You make one move against me and I will *burn your village to the ground!*"

As she came back to the present and the stillness of the little church, Becky felt the dark shadows of those memories still clinging to her.

Alec watched her with a brooding stare, mulling over her words. She glanced at him sorrowfully and searched his face, trying to gauge his reaction. If he didn't believe her, she did not think she could go on. She bit her tongue, however, and waited for him to break the silence. Rather than speaking, he slowly reached over and took her hand between both of his.

Tears rushed into her eyes.

She moved toward him, and he pulled her into his arms. Trembling with soul-deep gratitude, she closed her eyes and took strength from his embrace.

"Oh, Alec, I feel so awful. That's why I didn't want to bring you into this, you see? I'm already responsible for that man's death."

"No, sweeting, you tried to free him!" he exclaimed in a tender whisper. "You tried to help. They're the ones who took his life." His hold on her was firm yet gentle, and she could feel the fierce protectiveness in his touch as he stroked her hair. "You probably gave him the only chance he could have had to get away. You did the right thing."

"I tried, but it wasn't enough."

"Most people would have run. You stayed despite your fear and got him out of there."

She shook her head. "How could I have been so blind? I can't believe it was going on right under my nose. I still have no idea who he was or why they were holding him. Do you know what the worst part is? I dropped the medal he gave me somewhere out on the moors. Whoever he was, now his family will have nothing at all to remember him by. I tried to find it, but they were coming after me so fast . . . I had to run. It's probably still out there somewhere, rusting. I just feel so awful."

"You did all you could. You mustn't blame yourself, Becky." He kissed her head. "Everything's going to be all right. We'll get your home back for you, and then we'll get everyone in your village, if need be, to help scour the moors until we find it. Your cousin's not going to get away with this. I promise you that."

Struggling against tears, she hugged him tightly. "I'm scared, Alec." She buried her face against his neck.

"I know, sweetheart. But you're not alone in this anymore, do you understand? Whatever happens, we will face this together. And I'll tell you something else." Cupping her cheek, he leaned closer and kissed her forehead. "I'm not letting you out of my sight until this is resolved."

"You're not?"

"No." He shook his head slowly, trying to coax a smile from her. "I am appointing myself your royal bodyguard, my lady. I trust that you are pleased."

It worked. She succumbed to a hapless smile and blushed, dropping her gaze. "I am." Reliving the still vivid nightmare in the telling of her tale, she was all too happy now to accept his protection in lieu of his forced, dutiful offer of marriage.

"Good." Turning away with a resolute nod, Alec

stood and took charge, climbing out of the pew to prowl restlessly across the chapel. "Very well, then. We must determine the best way to proceed."

Watching him, Becky could not think of anyone she would have rather had as an ally. "Mikhail has come to London now, as you've seen, but I'm sure some of his Cossacks are still stationed in the village or even at the Hall in case I try to come back."

"Well, you're not going back until it's safe." Alec shrugged the tension out of his shoulders. "First off, you're sure the property is not entailed?"

"Certain of it," she answered, nodding as the creaking of the great church doors alerted them that the faithful had begun drifting in early for the noon service. "It can be purchased—if my cousin can be induced to sell it."

"Or tricked into losing it somehow, hm?" he murmured wickedly.

"What do you mean?"

Alec was already onto the next thought, still pacing. Arms folded across his chest, he tapped his lips with his finger in thought. "But . . . if we prosecute him first and succeed in getting him convicted of a felony, his property will be forfeited to the Crown, and then it will be even more difficult for you ever to get your home back. Either the royals will keep the Hall for their own private use or will put it up for auction, where you will surely be outbid and outspent. After all, an ancient manor near a grousing heath would no doubt prove quite appealing to the shooting set, also given its historical significance. Best not to call attention to the place, or that'll drive the price straight up."

"I hadn't thought of that." She frowned. "So, what should we do?"

"Seems to me we should work on getting your house back first and *then* bring your cousin to justice. The sooner we get the house away from him, the sooner his troops will clear out of your village. It shouldn't be too difficult, since it sounds like he's not that keen on the property, anyway. We just have to figure out where to hide you in the meantime and how to get the best price for that jewel. May I see it?" he asked respectfully.

She nodded and withdrew it from her bodice, handing it to him with greater confidence this time and a slight smile of contrition. Alec accepted it with a gaze that assured her there were no hard feelings for her earlier doubt.

"I hate for you to have to sell your family heirloom," he mused aloud as he took it from her and sauntered over toward the stained-glass window to inspect it by the light. "I have a great many friends in the aristocracy who are obsessed with collecting such baubles. Who knows? For the sake of gallantry, even Drax or Rushford might keep it in trust for you—"

"No!"

He looked over in surprise.

"Forgive me, Alec, I know they are your friends, but they are not the sort of men a girl would like to be indebted to."

He raised an eyebrow.

"I am certain Lord Rushford hates me after I kicked him, anyway. Please—I don't want the whole world knowing how Mikhail threatened me or how my own family cast me off. I am . . . a rather private person, if you hadn't noticed. It was hard enough to share it all with you. I was only going to tell the Duke of Westland out of necessity. Please promise me you won't get anybody else involved."

"Well, that makes it more difficult, but . . . very well. If that's how you feel." That sturdy male pride gleamed in his eyes again. "I'm sure I am perfectly capable of handling this on my own, in any case."

"Thank you," she said in relief.

"Let's see what we've got here." He slipped the ruby out of its little leather pouch and took it between his fingers, holding it up to the light. "I'm told I have quite an eye for beautiful things." He sent her a suggestive half smile.

"Who told you that?"

"George."

"George who?"

"H.R.H. Prince of Wales. You know—" His brief glance brimmed with droll humor. "Prinny."

"The Regent?" she exclaimed, then quickly reminded herself to lower her voice while Alec chuckled. They were, after all, in a church. "You know the Regent?"

"Oh, sure. We've played cards on many occasions. Daresay I'm one of the few people who actually likes him."

She was still marveling at this revelation when the church door creaked open again. She glanced over nervously and saw more parishioners coming in. "We're going to have to leave soon. The service will be starting any minute. Well?" she prodded, unable to resist her impatience. "Any idea how much it might be worth?"

Alec did not answer; he had not moved.

Standing in profile to her below the stained-glass window, he continued scrutinizing the ruby by a single shaft of sunlight.

"Oh, dear," he murmured.

Becky did not like the sound of that. "What is it?"

Without explanation, he pivoted and walked out of the chapel into the brighter nave.

She followed, bewildered. "Alec?"

He still did not answer.

Ignoring the people taking their seats for the service, he walked over to one of the colorless windows and studied the jewel again for a long moment, his chiseled face etched with intense concentration.

"Alec, what's the matter?" she demanded.

Slowly lowering the ruby, he turned to her with a dazed look. "Uh, Becky—I'm not sure how to tell you this."

"Tell me what?" she exclaimed, her heart pounding.

He put the jewel back in her hand with an apologetic wince. "It's a fake."

CHAPTER
⚙ SEVEN ⚙

"*I*t can't be!"

"It is," Alec said, chagrined to have to be the one to tell her.

"But the Rose of Indra has been in my family for centuries!"

"Shh!" an old lady hushed them as the scant congregation rose and began singing the entrance hymn.

Alec took Becky's arm and led her out of the church. "It's not an uncommon situation," he explained in a low tone as he opened the heavy door for her. "One of your ancestors must have gotten into a scrape, sold the original for ready money, and then replaced it with this in hopes the family would never find out. Trust me, this sort of thing happens every day."

"But it's just not possible!" she insisted as they went back out into the dappled sunshine of the churchyard, the heavy door slowly creaking shut behind them, muffling the opening strains of a familiar hymn. "I'm sure you're wrong!"

"I know I'm right. I'm sorry, Becky. I know about jewels and such. I've been around the finer things my whole life, and that," he said emphatically, "is a fake. It's paste—a form of glass. If you were to hit it against something hard, it would shatter into bits."

"Well, we'll just see about that!" A blazing light came

into her eyes as she turned away, but he was too slow to stop her.

"Becky, don't—"

Bang!

She smashed it against the stone balustrade and cried out in shock as it crumbled into a few fractured pieces and a handful of strawberry-colored dust in her palm.

She stared at it in horror.

"Oh, Becky," Alec said wearily, setting his hands on his waist with a sigh. "I wish you wouldn't have done that." She really was a rash and impetuous creature, he thought. Not so unlike him.

As the sandy remains of the fake jewel sifted through her fingers, she lifted her stricken gaze to Alec, utterly at a loss.

"It wasn't entirely worthless," he informed her in a rueful tone. "Even as paste, we still could have sold the thing for twenty, thirty quid."

"Thirty quid?" she cried, her face ashen. "That's not enough to buy my house back! It's going to cost at least five thousand pounds!"

"No, but it would have been enough to get me into a respectable game of cards."

"*Cards?*" she gasped. "You intend to gamble for the money?"

He shrugged and held her in a blunt stare. "Got any better ideas?"

A short while later they were in a hackney coach, headed where, Becky neither knew nor cared. Her cause was lost already. She was sure of it.

She was ruined. She was broke, cast upon the charity of her ravisher. She could not get to Westland, and her only hope now of saving her village from Mikhail and his Cossack army was a rakehell gambler without any luck. She was doomed.

Outside the carriage window, London went high-stepping by with its usual crisp self-importance, but she could only gaze unseeingly out the carriage window, still numb to discover that the jewel she had been guarding with her life was just a bit of glass, exactly as the first jeweler had tried to tell her when she arrived in the Town.

So much for her inheritance. She felt like such a dimwit. Of course her kin would never have left her anything of real value. Who did she think she was fooling? Men like Mikhail always got away with their crimes. He was a prince, boyhood friend of the Czar. He had all the resources of her grandfather's title and fortune at his disposal, not to mention his own barbarian horde. She was no match for him, even with Alec's help.

"Becky?"

She realized he had been staring at her when he squeezed her shoulder in a gentle offering of comfort. "Are you all right? Talk to me. You're too quiet."

She shrugged. "It's ironic, isn't it? You pretend to be rich when you're not; I pretended to be a harlot to secure the food and shelter you offered; and now the Rose of Indra has turned out to be something it's not, as well." She started laughing dully, shaking her head. "Glass!"

"It's going to be all right, Becky. I won't let you down."

"Oh, Alec, I don't mean to sound ungrateful, I truly don't, but how can this mad plan possibly work—gambling for the money to buy my house back? At my grandfather's death the property and its three hundred acres were assessed at over five thousand pounds, and you said yourself you've been on a losing streak."

"There are ways. Strategy games that take more skill than luck."

"Like what?"

"Whist and vingt-et-un. Those weren't the games that

got me into trouble, you see." He hesitated. "It was faro. Hazard. Games of chance. And I—I could play cautiously. I usually don't," he admitted after a moment.

"Oh, God," she breathed, looking away in disbelief.

"Try to trust me, Becky. I know you're scared, but—try."

Staring out the coach window, she could feel his earnest gaze upon her. "It seems I have no choice."

Before long the carriage slowed to a halt. Alec jumped out first, helping Becky to descend.

"What is this place?" she murmured, shading her eyes against the noonday sun as she glanced up at the towering Palladian mansion at the edge of Green Park.

"Knight House." Behind them the hackney clattered away again, rolling off toward St. James's Street. "This is my eldest brother Robert's house. He is the Duke of Hawkscliffe. Nobody's home," he added to soothe the quick flash of alarm in her violet eyes, given his promise not to bring anyone else into their quest. "The whole clan's gone north to Hawkscliffe Hall for the summer. A blessed event is expected by the end of the month, Their Graces' second child. The other women all wanted to be there to help when the babe comes, so Jacinda and Lizzie have gone up to the castle with Rackford and Strathmore. Demon and Lucifer have also gone up to the castle with their wives."

She furrowed her brow. "Demon and Lucifer?"

"Sorry—Damien and Lucien, the twins."

"Oh. It's not very nice to call your brothers that, is it?"

He grinned. "Maybe not, but it fits."

"How come you're not with them?" she asked, slanting him a pointed glance.

"It's, ah, complicated."

She raised an eyebrow.

"Let's just say they're a little out of charity with me."

"Oh," she remarked, reluctantly restraining her female curiosity, much to his relief.

Walking her up to the stately front entrance of Knight House, Alec thought about his family gathered for the summer at the old ancestral pile, missing them with great affection. Most of all he hoped that Bel was doing all right. In many ways, the beautiful young duchess had become the heart of the family since Robert had married her a few years ago.

Alec did not mention it to Becky, but the doctors had voiced some concerns about Bel's second pregnancy. He did not know why. He only knew there was no way he was going to disturb them at a time like this. If he wrote to Robert to get advice about Becky's situation, Bel would be able to tell in a glance that something was preying on her husband's mind. She would no doubt manage to finagle the whole disturbing story out of Robert, and that could not be allowed. Nothing must upset her and risk her health or the babe's. In any case, Alec had no intention of drawing Robert's attention away from his wife's side at this critical time.

He could still contact the twins—well, easygoing Lucien, anyway. No-nonsense Damien was still disgruntled at him for coaxing a loan out of his heiress-bride, Miranda, a few months ago. Alec knew he shouldn't have done it, but he was desperate, and after all, he and Miranda had been great chums ever since the statuesque, raven-haired beauty had married into the family. But aside from having promised Becky that he would not involve anyone else, it was the thought of his wee nieces and nephews that forbade Alec from calling on his brothers.

It would be wrong to call their papas into action and risk their lives when his brothers had young children at home. No, Alec reflected, the heroic twins had already faced more than their share of peril in the war. If he got in over his head, then he would call in the cavalry, but not one bloody moment sooner. This was something that he had to do by himself. Baby brother was on his own.

He suddenly noticed that Becky seemed to be shrinking into her pelisse; she hung back with an overawed stare up at Knight House's soaring columns, haughty portico, and gleaming white facade. "Something wrong?"

"It's very grand, isn't it?" she murmured.

"That is the idea," he said wryly. Looking askance at her, he realized his plucky country lass was beginning to feel very much out of her element. He glanced again at the family showplace and did not need to wonder why.

The Town residence of the Hawkscliffe dukes had been built to intimidate all who entered, an opulent statement in stone of the family's pomp and power, from its fortresslike foundations to the crown of bronze goddesses posing here and there around the roof.

"What are we doing here, anyway?" She didn't look quite keen on going in.

Little did she know most girls of the ton would have killed for an invitation to Knight House, especially for a private tour on the arm of one of the Knight brothers.

"I daren't risk bringing you back to the Althorpe after what happened in the mews. Just in case there were any witnesses to my battle this morning, I don't want your cousin to be able to track you through me."

"Do you think he could?"

Alec shrugged. "I'm not taking any chances. My neighbors, as you noticed, are all young bucks. Can't bring a chit as pretty as you into that place without everybody noticing. Roger Manners is probably the only one who got a good look at you so far, and he's sensible enough to keep his mouth shut, but it's best to play it safe. Besides, if you're going to be staying with me for a while, we'll need some supplies."

"Like what?"

"Has anybody ever told you that you ask too many questions?" he asked lightly. "Come." Giving her hand a gentle squeeze, their fingers still firmly linked, he walked in without knocking, drawing Becky with him.

"Crikey," she breathed, ogling the white marble entrance hall and curved staircase that floated up to the first floor without any visible supports.

Alec turned at the sound of slow footsteps and spied gray-haired Mr. Walsh, the unsmiling Hawkscliffe butler, approaching at his usual funereal march. Mr. Walsh's nostrils flared at the sight of the family's scapegrace youngest son with yet another disheveled female, but Alec grinned.

"Good morning, Walshie!"

The butler honored him with a dutiful nod. "Lord Alec," he intoned, then bowed to Becky. "Miss."

"Good day, sir," Becky mumbled, slipping partly behind Alec in a sudden fit of shyness. Apparently his little battle-maiden was more frightened of the superior, frosty-eyed butler than she had been of the Cossacks. Recalling the bad luck she'd had with ducal butlers earlier today, Alec could understand why.

Mr. Walsh now eyed her with discreet suspicion and a stare that seemed to demand: Who might *you* be, on the arm of one of our young masters? And *where*, young lady, is your chaperon?

Harrumph, he seemed to say to himself before turning to Alec with arrogant precision. "How might I be of service, my lord?"

Alec cleared his throat. A distraction was needed to occupy this formidable old guardian of the doorway. "Will you, ah, have a spot of breakfast prepared for us in the morning room?"

Mr. Walsh pursed his lips and bowed. "Right away, sir."

"Excellent. Capital chap. Miss Ward: this way."

"He's terrifying," Becky whispered as they mounted the grand staircase side by side.

"No, he only pretends, trust me." He hurried her up to the third floor and showed her down the upstairs corridor, trying to remember which was Bel's dressing room. "You'll have him eating out of your hand within the hour."

"I don't know about that."

Hearing Mr. Walsh's footfalls echoing swiftly behind them, Alec gave an indignant growl under his breath. Becky glanced back worriedly at the butler, but Alec nodded to her to follow and marched on.

He stopped abruptly and turned around. "I say, old boy, are you following us?"

"Pray, forgive me, Lord Alec, but I have been asked specifically by His Grace to ensure that nothing should be taken from the house."

"Is that right?" Alec exclaimed. "My brother fears I might rob him and sell his goods for a few quid while he's away?"

"So it would seem, sir. Terribly sorry. Not 'rob,' to be sure. Perhaps 'borrow.' My lord has 'borrowed' things before."

Becky's eyebrows arched high as she glanced at Alec in question. He scowled.

"Quite."

"I'm very sorry, sir."

"Not at all, old boy. Not your fault. Simply doing your duty and all that."

Mr. Walsh raised an eyebrow at Alec's placating tone, instantly alerted to some sly business afoot. The old fellow had served the family for all of Alec's lifetime, after all; whatever tricks Alec had up his sleeve, old Walshie had seen them devised when he had been but a grinning boy, honing his charmer's slick devices to an art form over the years.

There was no getting past the man, hang it all.

"Might I have a word with you, Mr. Walsh?" Alec grasped the butler's bony elbow and took him aside, gesturing to Becky to wait.

"Indubitably, Lord Alec."

"Look here, old fellow," he said in a confidential tone. "This young lady currently finds herself in the direst of straits. I know what you're thinking, but trust me—she's not. She happens to be the granddaughter of an earl."

"Naturally, sir. And which earl might that be?"

Alec glowered at the old fellow's skepticism. "Talbot. But you are not to tell a soul, on your honor."

"Not even His Grace?"

"Especially not His Grace. No one," he said emphatically. "It's like this, old boy. The chit's got nothing but the clothes on her back, and as you can see, they are in tatters. She happens to be in considerable peril, and right now I'm all she's got."

"Oh, dear."

Alec frowned. "I'm doing my best to sort it all out for her, but in the meantime she's got nothing to wear, nothing to eat—"

"I say," Mr. Walsh interrupted, "is that your blood all over your shirtsleeve or someone else's, Lord Alec? What on earth happened?"

"Bit of a scuffle. Don't worry. It's just a scratch. I told you, she's in danger. There are rather . . . unpleasant individuals after the girl. She's got no one."

Mr. Walsh looked at Becky with new concern.

"I cannot imagine, surely, that either Robert or Bel would refuse this girl help, especially with all their running about after the poor."

"Well, you do have a point. If she is in peril . . ." He shook his head.

"I mean to take a few items of clothing for Miss Ward to wear until she has been restored to her home. You will not stand in the way, will you?"

Mr. Walsh hesitated, but only because he had his orders and was obsessive about his duty.

"Look at her, man," Alec urged him. "Is she not an angel?"

The butler glanced at Becky again, deliberating. "I assured His Grace that I would not allow any of your—pardon, sir—shenanigans, while he was away."

"No shenanigans!" Alec vowed, holding up his right hand. "It's not for me, it's for her. Robert would not turn away a poor young damsel in distress, and as for Bel, she's the size of a barn with the babe due."

"Sir," he chided.

"You know it's true. It'll be months before she can fit back into her gowns, and by then her whole wardrobe will be out of fashion, anyway. Have a heart, man. Where's the harm? We both know the duchess has got at least two rooms full of clothes—"

"Oh, very well," Walsh relented, pursing his lips. He glanced at Becky, a glimmer of softhearted sympathy peeping out from beneath his haughty facade, then he snorted. "I'll summon one of the maids to assist. This could be a rather large endeavor. Your young lady," he said pointedly, "is an utter mess."

In a struggle between pride and practicality, the latter won out in Becky's bosom as Alec, the maid, and Mr. Walsh all conspired to fill a fair-sized trunk for her with the duchess's borrowed clothing. Alec ignored the fact that a male had no business anywhere near an unmarried young lady in her chemise and brought his famed taste to bear in what looked beautiful on a woman.

Becky endured as best she could while the celebrated dandy thrust his discerning choices into her hands and threw others out of her reach. "No. Not that one, it's horrible. Try this, try that. No, not that color. Dreadful. Ah, better. Very smart. Now, that is very fine, indeed. . . ."

At last the trunk contained everything from stockings, shifts, and underthings to a silk wrap, kid leather slippers in three different hues, gloves, two wide-brimmed hats and a poke bonnet, a yellow parasol, four simple morning gowns, a few walking dresses, dinner dresses, promenade gowns, and two carriage dresses.

Still more luxury followed as several liveried footmen served them breakfast in the pale blue morning room. The white-wigged footmen marched through the tall white doors bringing coffee, tea, freshly squeezed orange juice and pastries, covered silver dishes containing sausage, beans, eggs, and warm toast with butter.

Dressed in a loose-fitting day-dress of sprigged muslin, Becky glanced at Alec. He had gotten rid of his bloodied shirt and coat and donned some clothes of his brother's, which fit well enough, but which he complained were "dull, dull, dull."

The Paragon Duke, as Alec informed her Hawkscliffe was nicknamed, apparently dressed too conservatively for his youngest brother's flashier style.

Now Alec, with a bored flick of his hand, directed the servants to put the food on the table instead of the sideboard. It was plain that he was thoroughly accustomed to this treatment, being waited on hand and foot.

Lord, Becky thought, *if I had lived like this all my life, I'd be spoiled, too.*

Maybe it wasn't "spoiled," after all, she mused as she gave the footman a quick smile of thanks; instead, perhaps it was a matter of being taught from the cradle to look at life and one's role in the world in a different way. Though half aristocrat herself, she was surprised to realize that she could get used to this. Usually she clung to the commoner's half of her nature, as well she might after her titled grandparents had rejected her, but there was something to be said for hedonism.

The meal did much to lift their spirits. Alec downed large quantities of food and coffee, and Becky found she had more of an appetite than she had expected.

"Who is that?" she asked at length, nodding to the portrait above the alabaster chimneypiece of a grand-looking lady with a mischievous glint in her dark eyes.

Alec paused, barely glancing at it. "That's Mother. She left when I was young." He resumed eating.

"Left?"

He shrugged. "Died. Whatever."

She was taken aback. "Well, which? Left or died?"

"Both. Left, then died." He wiped the corners of his fine mouth with his linen napkin and coolly inquired, "Do you really want to know or are you just asking?"

She furrowed her brow, regarding him with puzzlement. "I think I really want to know."

Alec poured himself another cup of coffee. "Quite a romantic tale," he said with breezy nonchalance. "When I was fourteen, she went racing off on some adventure with her paramour, the Marquess of Carnarthen. Her true love. He fathered two of my brothers—half brothers, technically. The twins."

Becky stared at him with her eyes like saucers.

"Mother and Lord Carnarthen ran away to France to rescue aristocratic children from the guillotine. They had quite a lot of friends in Paris who had been murdered by the mob. Many of the nobles' children had been taken into hiding by their servants and were unaccounted for. Mother felt it was her duty to help her slain friends' offspring, so she endeavored to locate them and bring them over to England."

There was something odd about his speech, as though he had memorized it by rote.

"Together they made a few trips back and forth across the Channel, bringing the children over on Carnarthen's ship. One day she never came back," he said frankly. "Got caught in her good work, it seems, and put before the French firing squad."

Becky gasped.

"Carnarthen had been dealing with the smugglers who let them come ashore in their port, and was too late in his attempt to rescue her."

"Good heavens!" She set down her fork and looked from Alec to the craftily smiling duchess on the wall. "I—I'm so sorry. I don't know what to say."

Alec looked at her intently. He did not look at all aggrieved, but surely the loss caused him profound pain.

"Don't you ever miss her?" Becky attempted in a soft tone.

"Not really," he replied.

She could only stare at him in startled confusion.

He twirled his fork with deft, idle fingers. "I hardly ever think of her at all." He paused and rested his chin on his hand. "Why should I? She didn't think of us."

Becky winced; Alec studied her as she lowered her gaze.

"How many brothers did you say you have, Alec?"

"Four, and one sister. Jacinda. Your age. She was only two when Mother left."

Becky took a steadying sip of tea. "I see."

He was watching her with a covert intensity that made her certain he wanted something very specific from her in response—almost as though he were testing her—but she was bound to fail because she did not know what it was he wanted her to say.

"You look shocked."

"I am."

"What do you think of my story?"

She shook her head guardedly. "You London folk are—different."

"You're not so put off about the marquess, are you?" he asked lightly, leaning back in his chair in a leisurely pose. "Because, I hate to say it, but the truth is we all have different fathers—except for the twins, who came as a matched set, obviously, and Robert and Jacinda, who are both his brats." He nodded at the portrait of a stiff, unhappy-looking man on the opposite wall.

THE EIGHTH DUKE OF HAWKSCLIFFE, the gold nameplate beneath it read.

"Poor bleeder," he continued, as though he were talking about someone else's family. He stared at the duke's portrait for a long moment. "Never said a word to me, but at least he had the decency to acknowledge us all as his own. Couldn't have borne with the scandal, don't you know."

She cleared her throat, half choking on her tea. "So, you're saying h-he wasn't your real father?" she asked ever so cautiously.

"No, poppet," he drawled. "My real father caught Mum's eye one night treading the boards at Drury Lane in the role of Hamlet."

Becky was not a fainting female, but if she were, this would have been a perfect moment to ask for smelling salts. "An—actor?"

"Yes." Alec's smile was sugared treachery. "Sir Phillip Preston Lawrence was his name. All the ladies were quite smitten with him while he was in his glory. I'm told I look just like him." He shrugged and sipped his coffee. "I wouldn't know. Never met the chap."

"I see." She dropped her stunned stare to her plate.

He laughed. "Now I've shocked you."

She looked at him uncertainly. "Are you bamming me with all of this?" She knew he loved to make jokes—

"Afraid not, Becky-love. It's all true," he said with a world-weary smile. "The whole ton knows about it. At least mine's better than Jack's. Jack's the second-born, you see—Mother's first indiscretion, and, Lord, it was a big one. She chose well when she decided to pay His Grace back after finding out about his mistress."

She sent him a questioning look, bracing herself with a wince.

"Jack's real father was an Irish prizefighter called the Killarney Crusher."

"Good God!" She quickly covered her mouth.

"At least Jackie inherited his father's fighting spirit. And a pair of fists like cannonballs—which was fortunate, because he needed them, you see, to constantly fight off all the lads at school who went around calling our dear mama the 'Hawkscliffe Harlot.'"

Becky let out a small sound of distress and closed her eyes for a second. Maybe Alec's life had not been as perfect as it looked at first glance.

He lounged in his chair, studying her with an expression of jaded amusement, but resentment shot like daggers from his eyes when he slanted another careless glance toward his mother's portrait. "You must admit it's charming how the lady got around. Quite picaresque. I can remember being nine or ten years old . . . I used to sit with her, you know, while she would get ready for her evenings out on the Town. Watch her putting on her makeup and her jewels, and telling me who would be at the party."

"You . . . were close to her."

"Close?" He paused, his stare far away. He shook his head, his long lashes veiling his eyes. "She was the sun and moon to me," he said softly after a moment. "I was her favorite." He sent her a whimsical half smile. "From the time I was knee-high, she used to call me her sunshine-boy. 'My little hero.'" He let out a low laugh and skimmed his fingertips restlessly across the white damask tablecloth. "I was her jester. Her confidante. If the duchess fancied herself an Aphrodite, I suppose I was just the little Cupid flying around to attend her whenever she was bored."

Becky just watched him, waiting. At length, her calm, open silence urged more detailed revelations from him.

"Jack used to kick me around and say I was attached to her apron strings," he admitted after a cautious moment, "but of course, Jack hated her." He shrugged. "Jack hated everyone. Still does. Not me. I felt important because of her. She would tell me things she couldn't tell anyone else. I was the only one who could cheer her up when Society gossip had made her cry, or when some man or other had disappointed her, or when she fought with her husband, or when her eldest son shouted at her to stop disgracing the family. She counted on me—and of course, she gave me everything I wanted. Bribes, I suppose, to ensure that at least one person in the family stayed on her side." He sent Becky a cynical smile.

She ached, gazing at him. The hidden anger in the depths of his dark blue eyes had emerged, and his smooth tone was edged with razor sharpness. So, he was angry at his dead mother, she realized. It was easy to understand why. From the way he described it, the duchess had treated him like a coddled pet while it amused her, heaped her adult problems on his tender child's heart, and then walked away from him without much difficulty when some new pleasure beckoned.

"She used to hug me tight and say, 'You're the only one who's ever really loved me, sunshine.' " His words trailed off and he was silent for a moment, then he added sardonically, "You were right. I guess I was spoiled. She bought me my first phaeton when I was twelve." He laughed again, and the sound was hollow.

"You must have been crushed when she died."

"Oh, no, I wasn't crushed, I was infuriated. I had told her not to go. It was too dangerous. But, as usual, Her Grace did whatever—and whomever—she fancied. To you, Georgiana: You were no coward. I'll say that for you." He toasted his mother's portrait with his coffee, but the edge of irony underlying his tone was as sharp as a duelist's sword.

Noting the pain in his blue eyes, so carefully hidden behind his rakish indifference—after all, he was an actor's son—Becky realized that even if Alec's adult mind had grasped the valor of his mother's tragic end, the child in him had never comprehended the betrayal. Here was a man who might never trust womankind as a species again.

Becky turned away for a moment from his bitter, unreachable smile and closed her eyes. If they were indeed undertaking this quest together, she realized she was going to have to treat him much more gently than she had previously thought. Behind that unflappable rogue facade, he was a more acutely sensitive creature than she had first assumed.

Indeed, it was that very sensitivity that made him such an attentive and incredible lover. From an obscenely early age, it seemed, he had been mastering the art of detecting the needs of a woman's heart and fulfilling them, just as he had done for her last night.

But how sad it was that his only notion of love was to consume or be consumed by the emptiness of another. There was no safety in that. If she thought of love in those terms, she, too, would have shunned it at all costs.

"Despite what you may think, Alec," she offered, gazing into her tea, "not all women are entirely out for themselves."

"Aren't they?" he asked pleasantly as he perused the

morning paper, vulnerability and fierce mistrust behind his casual glance.

"No." She felt herself getting angry at the scars the duchess had left behind, heroic end or no. She set her fork down abruptly and turned to him. "I am sorry," she forced out, "but I can assure you that in Buckley-on-the-Heath, if a mother of six young children had run off with her paramour, she would not be welcomed back."

"Really?" he murmured. He looked intrigued.

"Yes, Alec. Really."

He set the newspaper down and gave her a hard, probing look, shrewdness glinting in his gaze. Her anger seemed to please him. Some of the bitterness receded from his eyes, then he tossed the portrait a final cutting smile. "Hear that, Mother? Becky Ward does not approve."

A short while later, Alec left Becky to rest in one of the mansion's many extra bedchambers while he went off to make preparations for their departure from London.

They would leave by dawn tomorrow for the seaside town of Brighton.

This was not merely a matter of better guarding Becky, what with the Cossacks still combing the streets of London for her; but also, Alec's primary objective was to win at cards the needed funds to buy back her house for her, and for that he would need to get into some high-stakes games with the upper echelon of wealthy gamblers. With the Season over, the ton's richest players, along with the rest of the beau monde, were migrating to Brighton for the summer, just as they did every year.

In all likelihood, it would only be a matter of time before Kurkov showed up there as well, Alec mused, but if he played like he knew he could when he was in top form, if he used his bloody head instead of hurling himself recklessly into the arms of the goddess of Fortune, then, with a little luck, he'd be ready by the time the prince arrived.

For now, he was mainly relieved that Becky had agreed to the plan he had outlined. She seemed to have reconciled herself to his leadership. Her show of trust was deeply gratifying to Alec; it gave him back a small piece, somehow, of what he'd lost to Lady Campion.

Walking down the street, he felt invigorated at having joined her quest. His forward stare was firm. There was force and purpose in his stride. He needed to get his hands on some money before they left Town, but the first order of business was a scouting mission to the clubs for a bit of reconnaissance.

Know thy enemy.

He intended to put an ear to the ground at White's and Brooke's to listen for any interesting tidbits that might be floating about from the London gossip mill regarding the famous Russian war hero.

The walk was not long. Knight House lay a mere block away from the stretch of St. James's Street where England's most exclusive gentlemen's clubs were situated. It was a well-worn path that Alec and his brothers had trod innumerable times before, both sober and otherwise.

Phaetons and curricles passed; friends shouted out to him and waved as they went dashing by. Alec returned their hails and soon went marching into White's, where he was one of the acknowledged heirs to Brummel's famous bow window.

He sauntered from room to room like he owned the place, greeting his acquaintances here and there with his usual air of bored superiority and restless indifference. He asked a few questions, made a bit of idle conversation, and then checked the infamous betting book. There were two pages on Kurkov: one accepting wagers on whether the prince would take an English bride or import a Russian one, the other dedicated to bets on which party he would join, Tories or Whigs.

Interesting.

Alec was on his way out to try his luck at Brooke's when he spotted the portly Russian ambassador settling into one of the large leather club chairs. Count Lieven had a document box in one hand and a demitasse of coffee in the other.

Alec smiled slowly and then approached the shrewd and amiable man. They were somewhat acquainted, mainly through Countess Lieven, who had become one of the grande dames of Society during her husband's tenure as the Czar's ambassador to the Court of St. James.

Alec had always admired Lieven for his mild-mannered tolerance of his dragonlike wife. Only a diplomat of his finesse could have borne her haughtiness. Of course, to say so would have been social suicide. Countess Lieven was, after all, a patroness of Almack's.

Tall, elegant, and exceedingly blue-blooded, the countess came from a premiere Russian family and seemed to think she could have done a better job running both England and Russia herself than either the bumbling Regent or the wavering, nervous Czar. Wellington himself was said to fear the woman.

Alec avoided her when he could, treated her with the softest of kid gloves when he could not, and privately offered his sympathies to the lady's short, stout, long-suffering husband—especially since Prince Kurkov had come to Town. Lady Lieven had made the Russian prince's social success her cause célèbre from the moment Kurkov set foot in England. Alec feared she was a trifle infatuated with her countryman.

Her beloved brother was a military hero, and if she had one soft spot in her heart, it was for men in uniform. Count Lieven himself held the rank of general, though

Alec found it a little hard to picture the portly ambassador leading troops in his present dimensions. The count had cropped, thinning hair and a waddling gait, thanks to the rotundity of his person.

He had to exert a little effort at wedging himself into the club chair, but, this accomplished, Lieven dabbed at his sweating pate with a handkerchief. Meanwhile, his plum-colored waistcoat seemed to groan at the girth of the belly over which it was asked to stretch, the buttons holding on with all their might. But for all his size, the Russian had a jovial temperament, his affability matched only by the keenness of his wits.

"*Zdra'zhs-vu-tyay*, my lord ambassador," Alec greeted him with a bow.

"Ah, Lord Alec," he said brightly. "This is an unexpected pleasure."

Alec flashed a roguish grin, grateful for the few Russian phrases he had learned from his diplomat-cum-spy brother Lucien a few years ago for the purpose of charming a Guest Voucher to Almack's out of Countess Lieven for one of his less wealthy friends. "I see you are busy, sir, but I wondered if I might pick your brain for a moment for the sake of a wager."

"Ah, a wager. I hear you are very fond of them."

"Too fond, I fear."

They laughed.

"You are more expert than I at such things, Lord Alec," Lieven confessed. "Please, have a seat. How can I help you?"

He accepted the invitation, gracefully moving his coattails aside as he lowered himself into the chair beside the ambassador's. "Were you aware that at the present time there are two wagers in the betting book involving a certain countryman of yours?" he asked with a sly glint in his eyes.

"Ah, yes. Kurkov." Lieven's smile turned bland, the

twinkle in his eyes cooling considerably. "All the world is certainly abuzz with his exploits, aren't they?"

Alec nodded, hoping that Countess Lieven's devotion to the tall, good-looking prince might inspire her husband to give out a few private, unflattering details about the man. "I am trying to figure out how to lay my bets. You see, I always do my research."

"That is commendable."

"Well? Whig or Tory? What's it going to be?"

"Whig," Lieven said firmly.

"Really? You seem very sure."

"Because I am."

"The Talbot earls have always been Tories."

Lieven shook his head serenely. "That may be, but Kurkov will vote Whig, mark my words. To please the Czar," he added in a lower tone.

"I see. Very well, then," Alec said with a guarded smile. "What of his choice in brides? Russian or English?"

"English. That's where I'd put my money."

"Why?"

Lieven stared at him with a mild, worldly trace of resentment in the depths of his eyes. He leaned nearer. "Let me tell you a little something about the great Prince Kurkov, Lord Alec. He is much more popular in London right now than he is in St. Petersburg."

"Oh? I thought he was a great favorite of the court. Boyhood friend of the Czar and all that."

"Was, Lord Alec. Was," Lieven corrected him in a low tone.

"Aha," he murmured, regarding the ambassador intently. "Do tell."

"Well, it's just a bit of court gossip, but . . ." Lieven smiled and nodded graciously to some other club members who passed, then he continued speaking to Alec with his cunning eyes on the others, watching all. "It seems Kurkov overstepped his bounds with the emperor a few months ago. I was not there, but what I've heard is that in front of an entire banquet hall full of guests, not in anger, but quite coolly and matter-of-factly, mind you, Kurkov rebuked the Czar for mismanaging the war."

"*What?*"

"Oh, yes, particularly citing his youthful folly in allowing Bonaparte to dupe him during that brief period after Tilsit. Kurkov laid the blame directly on His Imperial Majesty for the French invasion and the burning of Moscow."

Alec let out a low whistle. "Damn me."

"One does not tell the Autocrat of all the Russians 'I told you so.' "

"But—if you will forgive me, my lord, I have no head for politics—didn't Kurkov rather have a point? If the Czar had not trusted Napoleon, the war might have been won with hundreds of thousands of lives spared on both sides."

Lieven shook his head discreetly, but his look led Alec to surmise he saw some truth in it himself. "That is not for me to answer. All I can tell you is that the emperor banished Kurkov to his country estate for six months after these spectacular remarks. Indeed, if not for their boyhood friendship, I daresay he would have been shipped off to work in the quarries of Siberia for his insolence."

"They say your Czar is magnanimous; it must be true," Alec murmured. "And so Prince Kurkov will take an English bride because he has disgraced himself in Russia. None of the great families would wish to make an alliance with an outcast?"

"Precisely."

"And he will turn Whig in the hopes of making amends with his master."

Lieven bowed his head.

"Most enlightening, my lord. I thank you." Alec paused. "Why do I get the feeling you are keeping a watchful eye on him?"

"Lord Alec, dear lad, I keep a watchful eye on everyone. Especially on a man who has my wife singing his praises."

Alec smiled in rueful sympathy. "The incident in question does not bother Lady Lieven?"

"Oh, heavens, no. On the contrary, she agrees with Kurkov's viewpoint and admires him all the more for his 'courage' in daring to say it aloud."

"Well." Alec lifted his eyebrows. "Her Ladyship is certainly admirable in knowing her own mind. You must be proud that your lady is so firm in the strength of her convictions."

Lieven laughed slowly, quietly, at his polite offering, and wagged a chubby finger at him. "Ah, Lord Alec, diplomacy lost an able man when you chose a career as a gambler. I mean it! I am a trained and worthy judge of men, and my instincts tell me you possess in spades that delicate understanding of human nature our field requires."

"Why, sir, I am greatly complimented," he responded in pleasant surprise.

"Did you never consider working for the Foreign Office, my boy?"

He shrugged. "We've already got one diplomat in the family."

"Ah, yes, how is Lord Lucien?"

"Quite well, as far as I know. I haven't seen him in a few weeks. . . ."

They chatted for a short while longer, then Alec thanked the count and left him to his work. Now that he had heard Lieven's theory that Kurkov would turn

Whig, he was even more interested to learn what he might find out at Brooke's.

White's was the bastion of the Tories, but Brooke's, the club where Alec had lost the greatest sums of his career, was the stronghold of the Whigs.

Alec was one of the few men in London welcome in both clubs because he had no politics himself, made himself agreeable wherever he went, and more important, had powerful brothers in both camps. In this regard, he did not mind being universally viewed as naught but their fun-loving younger brother. Access to both clubs got him into all the top games. Robert had defected to the Whigs a few years ago, and so for his sake Alec was welcome at Brooke's; but the twins were still loyal Tories, and for years Alec had been something of a fixture at White's.

Crossing the black-and-white entrance hall of Brooke's, he walked into the quiet morning room and was immediately puzzled to find it curiously dim, the curtains drawn against the cheery sunshine. The few elderly members that he spotted first in the gloom kept their voices to raspy murmurs.

Then he realized why. A cynical smile curved his lips as his gaze settled on the fashionable trio of his mates sprawled in the exclusive grouping of chaises and wing chairs in the center of the room, apparently convalescing from the previous night's revels.

Fort, Drax, and Rush were motionless and, Alec surmised, in agony. They had cold cloths over their eyes, soda water and a few ginger biscuits on the table in the center. The fourth chair, Alec's place, was vacant, only awaiting his return.

He could not resist tormenting them a little in sadistic, brotherly affection. Sauntering over undetected to the bank of windows, he threw open the drapes with a sudden motion. At once, violent shouts of protest erupted from the suffering party. Alec turned to face them in roguish amusement as Fort whipped the washcloth off his face as he let his feet drop indignantly from the ottoman. "Close those damned— Oh, it's you."

"Good morning, gentlemen." Alec greeted them with a loud clap that brought more exclamations of pain. He rubbed his hands together cheerfully. "Ready to tackle the day?"

"Cruel bastard!"

"For the love of heaven, Knight, shut those cursed blinds," Drax uttered with his forearm cast across his brow.

Alec laughed but relented slightly, letting the thick drapes fall back again over the nearest window.

"Last night's a bit of a fog, but I take it you caught your quarry after you went racing off into the rain," Fort mumbled. "I seem to recall that you didn't come back."

"No, I didn't." Alec prowled to the edge of their circle and rested his arms across the back of the nearest chair.

"We missed you," Rush said sweetly.

Alec tousled his friend's hair with an idle chuckle. "Rushie, m'boy, are you still drunk? You always turn so sentimental."

"Ow, don't make me laugh," Fort pleaded halfway between a wince and a grin. "My head is pounding."

"I hope the chit didn't hurt you too badly."

Alec chuckled suavely. "Not in any way that I minded."

"Vicious little minx. Oh, God, I'm never drinking again," Rush groaned. "Hand me one o' them biscuits."

"So, how was she?" Drax asked, nudging the plate of ginger biscuits toward Rush.

Three pairs of bloodshot eyes looked at Alec expectantly, awaiting his review on Becky's performance in bed. He stared back at them, the familiar question taking him off guard and, all of a sudden, sitting not at all well with him.

I saw for myself how you and your friends treat women. . . .

Just then the sound of clipped footfalls entering the room distracted him. Alec glanced over his shoulder and tensed as he spotted the Duke of Westland marching through the morning room with a leather folio in one hand and a folded newspaper tucked under his arm. Westland spared little more than a contemptuous glance at Alec and his cronies as he passed to the refreshment table and helped himself to coffee from the samovar.

Alec's heart began to pound as he realized this was the perfect opportunity to approach the duke. He did not intend to seek an audience with Westland in prosecuting Kurkov until after Talbot Old Hall was safely in Becky's possession; but given His Grace's outrage at their wager over Parthenia, it was clear that Alec had fences to mend if Westland was ever going to listen to him, let alone believe a word he said.

Here, at least, was a fleeting opportunity to make a friendly overture that might help matters when the time came. Surely, he thought, the passage of nearly a year should have lessened Westland's wrath, though it had not seemed to matter to the man that his daughter, like a pristine icicle, had preserved her virtue as securely as Excalibur in the cold, clammy hand of the Lady of the Lake.

Alec felt for Draxinger's thwarted tender for Parthenia when the earl looked at Westland with a great, heavy sigh and then sank back into the cushions, hiding his eyes beneath his forearm again. The earl's whole posture said, *"It's no use."*

"Excuse me, gentlemen," Alec murmured, gathering himself to make his move. "Anyone care for coffee, tea?" He did not wait for their answers, but walked away, his heart drumming faster.

The others watched with curious interest for a moment, then went back to nursing their heads and bemoaning their intemperance.

Alec sauntered over to Westland's side and made a show of fixing himself a cup of good strong breakfast tea. Westland eyed him askance with a dubious look, releasing the silver spigot of the coffee urn.

Alec offered him the sugar with a polite smile.

Westland stared skeptically at him, his steel-gray eyes flickering, but he picked up the tiny sugar tongs and accepted a few lumps with a faint snort of disdain.

"Hawkscliffe's little brother, isn't that right?"

"Indeed, Your Grace. Lord Alec Knight." He gave the noble peer a respectful bow.

"Thought so. You're the one who plagued my daughter a couple of years back. You and those other young popinjays." Westland glanced at Alec's friends and snorted. "Best thing for your lot is the press-gang," he muttered under his breath.

"Well, sir, I can scarcely argue that."

"Good day, Lord Alec." The imperious Whig magnate turned away. Alec knew he was dismissed when Westland looked past him and greeted another new arrival with a brisk nod. "Ah, Kurkov, good morning to you, sir."

"Westland," a cool, gravelly voice responded.

Alec froze, the hairs on his nape prickling with instinctive malice. He remembered that voice. A surge of violence flooded his veins as he heard the sound of boot heels striking swiftly over the hardwood floor, coming closer. He clenched his jaw, summoning up every drop of the actor's blood that flowed in his otherwise aristocratic veins. He must seize the moment. He might not get another chance like this to probe his enemy at close range.

"Forgive me, Westland," Kurkov said. "I fear I am a few minutes late for our meeting."

"Not at all, I'm early, actually."

Standing a few paces away from them, Alec had reason again to be grateful that he had put forth the effort to memorize those few Russian phrases.

He pivoted slowly, facing Becky's tormentor with a Machiavellian smile. *"Zdra'zhs-vu-tyay,"* he greeted the prince with a courtly bow.

Kurkov turned to him in astonishment.

Even Westland was impressed. "Good heavens," the duke murmured, his coffee cup halfway to his lips.

"It means 'good day,' Your Grace," Alec told Westland, turning on the full force of the high society snobbery that he had studied from Brummel and honed to an art form these ten years. He tilted his head back slightly in order to look down his nose at the prince, as though he owned the ton and knew it. "Won't you introduce me to your friend?"

CHAPTER
◌ EIGHT ◌

Mikhail was startled by the greeting in his mother tongue; indeed, enough so to jar him out of his dark thoughts. It was maddening to know that somewhere out there, at large, uncontrolled, was a very angry and tenacious young woman who had information that could send him to the gallows. Nevertheless, he had every confidence that his wayward cousin would soon be silenced—one way or the other.

His men were hungry for revenge, and rather than killing her, had talked of torturing Rebecca once they had her, until they made her reveal the identity of who had killed Pytor and Vasily. Cossacks had long memories. Though worry gnawed him, Mikhail refused to show any outward lapse in graciousness, especially in front of the duke, for he had made up his mind to take Westland's daughter to wife.

Meanwhile, the insolent blond-haired man regarded him expectantly, as though he believed they were equals. *Well, this one's very full of himself,* Mikhail thought in cynical amusement. He looked the tall, strapping Englishman over with a skeptical eye. He was about ten years younger than himself, with the air of a pampered, corn-fed stallion who knew he was damned handsome and lightning-fast around the track.

Westland, a gentleman in spite of himself, begrudgingly gave sway. "Prince Kurkov, this young rapscallion is called Lord Alec Knight. Beware of him," he added drily. "He is known for pulling pranks. Knight, this is Prince Mikhail Kurkov, heir to the Talbot earldom."

"Hm," the impudent fellow replied with an air of boredom. "How do you do." The fine head angled only slightly in a bow.

Mikhail just looked at him, unsure if he was offended or amused by this foreign creature, an English rakehell. They didn't have his kind in St. Petersburg, no more than they had an opposition party like the Whigs. There was decadence at the emperor's court, of course, but as the lowly serfs worked the nobles' lands, the nobles, in turn, were defined as the serfs of the Czar and had to fulfill their various civil functions.

No young Russian nobleman would have dared spend a whole day on the corner of a fine shopping street, for example, quizzing the young ladies through a monocle as they walked by, but here in London it was a common profession. Bond Street Loungers, they called them. Mikhail instantly suspected that this fine fellow had spent more than his share of lazy afternoons at such work.

Too bad, he thought. A damned waste. He was known for spotting military talent, and the Englishman had that sharp, cool, fearless eye he always looked for when handpicking worthwhile officers. "Lord Alec, is it?" Mikhail replied.

His smile was treacherously angelic. "Yes. Alexander— just like your celebrated Czar. Most people simply call me Alec."

"That's not all they call you," Westland said under his breath.

"His Grace is so frightfully droll."

"You speak Russian, Lord Alec?" Mikhail inquired.

"Gads, no. Just enough to impress the ladies," he drawled.

Westland snorted, but Mikhail succumbed to a small

laugh at the dandy's flamboyant insolence. "Are you a member of this club?"

"I only come for the gambling. Do you play, Highness?"

"A bit."

"Lord Alec must be let in everywhere, you see, whether he is suitable or not," Westland explained. "The Regent dotes on him, and his brother is the Duke of Hawkscliffe, whose latest bill I was telling you about earlier this morning."

"Bills, bills. I should hate to be a duke," the rake declared. "So much work! I'm more the grasshopper, myself. Dear Robert, now, he is a committed ant."

"I will let him know you said so." Westland folded his arms across his chest. "*Do* they still let you play here, Lord Alec? I've heard the golden boy has hit a bit of a losing streak."

"Win some, lose some, as they say, Your Grace. Just like in war. Or in politics."

"Or in your case, in amour, Lord Alec?" Westland riposted.

"Well, no, actually. That's the one game in which I never lose."

Mikhail laughed aloud at his tart quip. The fellow had panache. He supposed he probably shouldn't laugh when Westland harrumphed, but Lord Alec obviously did not purport to be a serious man, so why take him seriously? Mikhail welcomed the relief from his worries that the quick-witted jester had brought him. "Oh, come, it was a good hit, Westland," he taunted the scowling duke.

"Your Highness, I thank you," Lord Alec said to Mikhail with a bow, warming a bit from his initial show of frosty superiority, but there was a glint in his blue eyes that Mikhail was not sure he trusted.

Westland set his coffee cup aside. "Kurkov, we really

should be going. Today I've arranged to introduce you to the prime minister."

"Ah, old Cod-Liverpool!" said Lord Alec. "Easier to stomach if you hold your nose."

"Abominable boy. Don't encourage him," Westland fussed as Mikhail chuckled again. "Come, we mustn't be late."

"Dosvi`daniya," Alec called pleasantly as the two men walked away.

Kurkov gave him a casual salute and answered in kind, but Westland shot him a scowl. "Mind you stay away from my daughter."

"Far be it from me, Your Grace, to go where angels fear to tread."

"Rapscallion," Westland muttered.

Mikhail looked back sharply at his remark about Parthenia, but Alec's idle smile did not waver.

"Very interesting," he murmured to himself under his breath. Kurkov hadn't liked the Parthenia jest at all. When they had gone, Alec strolled back thoughtfully to his friends, his hands clasped behind his back.

"What do you want with dull old Westland?" Drax asked, sitting up just enough to take a sip of soda water.

"Oh, just amusing myself. A bit of sport. By the way, I'm leaving for Brighton tomorrow morning."

"Without us?" they cried.

"I'll see you there," he answered in a reasonable tone. "I'll be staying at my family's villa to the west of the town instead of bunking with you lads in the house on Black Lyon Street."

"What?" Fort exclaimed. "Not staying with us."

"What is going on?" Drax demanded.

"Yes, you're up to something!" Rush chimed in.

"I'm not 'up to' anything."

"Oh, yes, you are. Why the sudden change of plans?"

"This doesn't have anything to do with that girl from last night, does it?"

He evaded their questions—in other words, he lied to his closest friends for her.

He wished he could have trusted them, but he knew their reckless ways. One unguarded word while they were in their cups could bring disaster. Besides, he had promised Becky he would guard her secrets.

"I just need to relax for a few days. Is that so wrong? One can't get any blasted sleep being under the same roof as your lot."

"Another mood," Drax said sagely to the others.

"Well, I hope you get over it soon," Rush muttered. "You're no fun anymore."

"We'll call on you when we get into town," Fort offered.

Alec nodded. "Thanks, Danny."

Finally extricating himself from their company, he went back outside to continue his preparations for their trip, his protective instincts still on full alert after his encounter with Kurkov. When he saw the Cossacks positioned outside, a chill ran down his spine, but he was comforted by the fact that he had dispatched the two who had seen his face. To the best of his knowledge, the others had no idea who had killed their comrades.

At least not yet.

Definitely best to go to Brighton, he mused, starting down the street with his carefully honed nonchalance fixed in place. No Cossacks, no duns. Just the surf, the sea, and beautiful Becky—and plenty of well-heeled gamblers.

Collateral, he thought. He could not afford to sit down at the table in those high-stakes games until he first came up with some money to put in the kettle.

With that, he made a detour to Sotheby's famous auction house. Wincing a bit at the sacrifice, he arranged to sell off his treasured pair of Grecian urns and a few more pieces of his furniture. Thus, he said good-bye to his long-laboring effort to keep up appearances, knowing that once these items were gone, his apartment would be quite bare. Anyone who looked inside would realize he was in dun territory.

Oddly, that no longer mattered to him now the way it had just yesterday. The stakes were too high to bother with such things.

He conducted a few of the big, brawny auction-house workers to the Althorpe and oversaw the removal of his possessions, pocketing his cash in exchange. Then he packed his clothes for Brighton along with all the ammunition he had on hand to feed his pistols.

Lastly, he went over to the great bed, for this he had not sold. He picked up the blue robe Becky had worn last night and for a long moment stared pensively at the crimson mark from her shed innocence.

Despite her refusal, he was not sure that honor could be satisfied by anything less than marriage. *Becky,* he thought, slowly putting the proof of his misdeed away, *why don't you want me?*

The house was very quiet, and the guest chamber where Becky rested had wallpaper that made her feel as though she were drowsing in a summer garden. White afternoon light made the soft, clear colors glow: cream and lilac floral stripes, hints of muted blue, green, yellow, and rose in the flowered carpet. The modest four-poster, hewn from dark walnut, was draped with crisp white bed-hangings. It was a simple, cozy, unpretentious room, and Becky lay so still atop the woven coverlet that the listless weight of her body hardly rumpled the covers at all.

Her unbound hair spilled loosely over the pillow; she was comfortably clad in one of the young duchess's pretty day-gowns, a demure concoction of airy white-muslin simplicity, with loose sleeves to the elbow and cornflower-blue ribbon trimming around the square neckline, the high-waisted bodice, and the skirts.

She was waiting for Alec to come home.

In this afternoon idyll, her thoughts were not entirely serene, revolving, as they did, around her sworn protector and his half-frightening, half-thrilling vow to keep her safe. She found herself contemplating this unusual turn of events and trying to determine what it all meant.

What haunted her perhaps most of all was that breathtaking moment in the church when he had pledged himself to her defense like a knight in shining armor. He made her feel like a princess.

A very . . . wanton princess.

He had stepped forward to shoulder as much of her burden as he could, volunteering himself without hesitation; but the question in Becky's mind was, what, then, was her duty to Alec in return?

He clearly deemed himself responsible for her welfare as a result of what they had done together last night, but if that was the case, then didn't that also imply that she was responsible for him, in turn? It didn't seem at all fair that he should leap so gallantly into the breach to save her and get nothing in exchange but her thanks. Alec was right. Honor *was* involved here. Honor—duty—had compelled his offer of marriage, just as mulelike stubborn pride had triggered her rejection.

In hindsight, she wished she had not been so hasty in her refusal. Her being underage for another two and a half months had merely bought her some time, but before long, a real decision on the matter would have to be made. Gentleman that he was, Alec would probably let her change her mind without complaint, but what on earth would he think of her then?

She knew what he would think. No matter what she

said, if she changed her answer now, he would simply assume—cynically—that she had come to her senses, had taken note of his family's obvious wealth and position, and had suddenly remembered her own self-interest. In short, he would conclude she was just like every other female, in his view—only out for herself.

But that wasn't her reason for reconsidering his offer.

She was not sorry for what she had done with him last night—indeed, it was futile to deny that she would have very much liked to do it again—but having had some time to mull it over, she could see for herself that after the brazen intimacies they had shared, marriage was simply the right and decent thing to do.

Unfortunately, Alec did not want to marry her. He had offered, yes, but only out of honor; thus, she could not honorably accept. He had already put his life on the line to save hers, and that was more than anyone could ask. She was not going to commandeer his entire future as well.

Though he would probably accept a revised, sheepish yes instead of her current no, that did not mean he would be happy with their arrangement. No, tied down and domesticated against his will, rakehell Alec would soon begin to chafe against his bonds, and Becky mused uneasily on the knowledge that that would soon make her the object of his resentment. Lord, she thought with a shudder. Even ruin was better than that.

With his hedonist's low tolerance for boredom, it was easy to envision things going from bad to worse, the two of them living apart, she in Yorkshire while he dwelled in Town, resuming his former habits of chasing any empty pleasure. What deeper hell could there be for a wife wed to—worse, in love with—an untamed, gorgeous philanderer for a husband who could have any woman he fancied?

A man like that could leave a woman shattered. Becky

intended to spend her life with someone who genuinely wanted to be with her, in return: She deserved that.

Perhaps you should have thought of that last night, observed her conscience, where guilt had set in with a vengeance. There had to be some reasonable solution, but her heart told her that a marriage of duty would only lead to disaster. If, on the other hand, they could love each other . . .

A soft stirring in the room broke the surface of Becky's light rest. She opened her eyes slowly and found Alec staring at her, frozen in mid-motion as he attempted to cross the room stealthily.

"Oh—I'm sorry—I didn't mean to wake you," he said at once in a sheepish whisper. "I just came to, er, check on you. I was going to shut the blinds." He gestured vaguely at the windows, where the brilliant afternoon sun streamed in.

Becky gave him a languid smile and held out her hand to him. "It's all right. Leave them. I like the light. Come."

He obeyed.

"Checking on me, eh?" she murmured, rolling onto her side and watching him in womanly satisfaction as he walked around to the other side of the bed. "That's very sweet."

He had taken off his morning coat, and Becky's gaze moved with pleasure over the sleek lines of his slim waist in his dark, buttoned vest. His loose shirtsleeves of neat linen were cuffed tightly around his wrists.

"Yes, well, actually. About that . . ." He sat down on the edge of the bed at a respectful distance, half turning to her. "I've been wondering all morning if you're . . . well, if you're all right."

"Oh, I'm fine," she said with a reassuring smile, then shook her head with a trace of regret. "I'm just . . . so very sorry to have dragged you into all of this."

"Don't be." He reached over and took her hand.

Their joined hands rested on the smooth white coverlet between them.

"The truth is, I'm the one who's sorry," he said softly,
then lowered his head. "I've been doing quite a bit of
thinking this morning about some of the things you said."

"Really?" She came up onto one elbow and tilted her
head, studying him. "Which things?"

"Ah, your objection to the way my friends and I treat
women." He scratched his cheek and then flashed her a
quick, wry smile. "The fact that you assumed, based on
my manner, that I wouldn't care about your plight, that
I was only having fun. I suppose I do come across as
rather selfish now and then, and maybe sometimes I am,
but . . . I do care, Becky." He dropped his gaze. "I want
you to know that. Perhaps I give the impression of a
man no woman ought to trust too much, but for all that,
it's just a game."

She watched him in patient curiosity.

He shook his head. "I had no idea the kind of trouble
you were in. But I swear to you, if I had known——"

"Shh," she soothed, reaching out to caress his shoulder. "I already know."

He looked into her eyes. "You could have confided in
me."

"I realize that now. I feel a bit foolish, actually. Please
don't reproach yourself for me."

"It bothers me." He lowered his gaze, stroking her
hand with the pad of his thumb. "And I think it bothers
you, as well." He sent her a wary glance from beneath
his forelock and shrugged. "There's obviously a reason
you've refused me."

She paused. "My refusal quite surprised you," she remarked in a cautious tone.

"Well, yes," he averred. "Not to boast, but Society
girls have tried on numerous occasions to trap me in
matrimony. The thing of it is, they don't really know me

at all. All they see is this." He glanced around meaning-fully at the opulent ducal house. "External things. My family connections."

Becky furrowed her brow. "Are you implying they wouldn't still want you if they knew you better?"

He lifted his eyebrows and looked away. "You didn't."

"Alec."

"No, it's all right. Don't make excuses for me. If I had been the sort of man you could have readily trusted, you would still be a virgin. Instead, I've ruined you. I've learned to live with many sins, but I don't know how I'm going to live with that one." He searched the ceiling as though the answers might be written above. "I wish you'd marry me. It would make me feel a damned lot better, anyway."

"Look at me." Becky sat up as Alec reluctantly met her forceful gaze. She reached over and caressed his clean-shaved cheek, trying to chase away the brooding look in his eyes. "I don't regret what we did."

For a long moment he absorbed this, and slowly low-ered his lashes. At length, he heaved a sigh, his lips twist-ing in a sardonic half smile. "You scare me," he said flatly.

She smiled. "I know." Moving closer, she draped her arms around him, careful not to touch his bandaged cut, concealed beneath his shirtsleeve. "Fortunately, I've al-ready seen that you are heroically brave, Alec, so I trust you will not run away in terror of little old me."

"I'll try." He turned his face to press a little kiss into her palm and then got up restlessly, crossing to the bay of windows.

Becky watched him in affectionate silence.

"Whatever I am today, it's not what I intended to become," he said after a long pause, staring out the window. Then he let out a low snort of laughter and drawled, "Even such a jaded scoundrel as I had dreams of greatness at eighteen."

Becky gazed tenderly at him. "What was your dream, Alec?"

"I wanted to join the cavalry," he said in stark, quiet honesty, sending her a rueful smile over his shoulder. "Give Boney a thrashing."

She smiled back at him in fond warmth. It was all too easy to imagine him as a bold cavalry officer, swaggering out of the Horse Guards, too dashing to bear in that handsome uniform. Cavalry men were notoriously cocky, with a reputation for enjoying life to the full while it lasted; they tended to die gloriously, and young.

"So, why didn't you?"

"It was not to be." He turned toward her and leaned against the deep window frame. "Robert insisted I could not be spared for 'cannon fodder.' As head of the family, his word is usually law."

"He refused to buy you a commission?"

"Not exactly. It was . . . more than that. You see, Rob inherited his title at the age of seventeen. He's always been more father than brother to the rest of us. The dutiful sort. Starchy, ultraresponsible."

"What, then, did you two have a falling out?"

"Quite the contrary. One thing that resulted from my mother's defection was that it made us all band together with unusually fierce loyalty to one another. Well, Jack still has problems, but that's another story. The rest of us have always made quite a close-knit tribe." Alec shrugged. "As we boys grew into men, Jack went off to sea, the twins joined the army, and when it finally came my turn to do something with my life, Robert said that given the others' slim chances of survival, I must consider myself next in line for the dukedom. The nominal 'spare.' "

"Gracious."

"I know. Can you imagine me a duke?" He laughed

bleakly. "He said that if the others died, and if anything happened to him, as well, I'd be the only one left to watch over the family concerns. He was convinced— with good reason, perhaps—that our middle brothers would not be coming back alive. As mighty as the all-powerful Hawkscliffe appears, the big brother in him simply couldn't bear the thought of losing all of us after he had practically raised us himself. Starchy as he is, family has always come first for Rob." Alec shook his head slowly, his face half in light, half in shadow. "After all that he had done for us, I couldn't put him through that. So I put my shiny saber away and I stayed."

Becky was quiet for a long moment. "Your devotion to your family is to be admired."

He shrugged, brushing off his own valor. "As I said, I owe Rob a great deal. He was little more than a boy himself when our mother was lost, but he held our family together. He is the finest man I know," he said softly. Sauntering over to the round-backed armchair nearby, he sat, resting his elbows on his knees. He steeped his fingers and smiled idly, mysteries churning in his eyes behind his droll stare. "So, while my brothers went off to become heroes of the nation, I took to the easy life in Town and set out to become a London peacock."

"A peacock?" she echoed as a smile skimmed her lips.

He nodded in self-deprecating amusement and sat back in his chair, lounging in his luxurious way. "We Knight brothers, you see, are, as a rule, always the best at what we do, so, naturally, I had to be the best damned strutting cock there was."

"I see. And what did that entail?"

"Living fast and wild, playing hard, spending my winnings like water. Taking mad dares for no better reason than the moment's thrill. Seducing anything in skirts— well, never mind that. Launching into duels for any pin-prick to my honor."

"Really? You've been in duels?"

"They can't be avoided when you live that way. Oh, I've had my share of enemies, believe me."

"So, that's why you're such a good fighter."

"Don't praise me, *cherie*," he said dryly. "My ego, I'm told, is already larger than the moon." He rested his cheek on his fist, gazing at her. "But it seems I did succeed on rather a grand scale. Leader of the pack. Captain of all London rakehells, they called me. Oh, yes, I quite gloried in my celebrity for a while. Then the war ended, the heroes came home—"

"Your middle brothers all survived?"

"Yes, thankfully. I wasn't needed at all. Then Robert sired a son to carry on the family line . . . and ever since then, well, hell, I have no idea what I'm even here for." He let out a low snort and looked out the window. "Lord, why am I telling you all this?"

She got up and went to him, seating herself on his lap. She draped her arms around his neck and regarded him matter-of-factly.

Alec just looked at her, his cheek still resting on his fist. Though his tone of voice had remained as wryly nonchalant as ever, his expression now was a little apprehensive, and slightly glum.

She gave him a hug and then kissed his cheek. "You're so much more than just a London peacock, Alec Knight. For what it's worth, I think you're a fairly wonderful man."

"Mm." He considered this. "I warned you about complimenting me."

"Too bad. It's true."

"Fairly wonderful?"

"Yes."

"All right," he said slowly. "I'll take that."

She smiled at him, smoothing his golden forelock out

of his eyes, offering silent, uncomplicated affection. He seemed to relax gradually under her touch.

"My dear Alec," she offered at length, shaking her head. "Of course there's a reason you're here. You just haven't found it yet."

"Maybe I have," he answered, looking into her eyes with new, steamy intent. He wrapped his arm around her hip and pulled her more securely onto his lap.

They studied each other in a long, searching stare, until she quivered, resting her forehead against his. She closed her eyes. "Alec."

"Becky," he breathed.

She thrilled to the sensation of his hand climbing up her side. She shifted restlessly on his lap and tilted her head, offering her lips.

He cupped her nape. "God, I want you." He kissed her deeply, his other hand traveling up and down her back. She responded with a soft, eager moan, tightening her gentle hold around his neck.

Desire threatened to rage out of control in mere seconds. Alec stopped himself and pulled back, shaking his head. His eyes were closed; he wore a pained look on his face. "We can't do this anymore. You do realize that?"

"We can't kiss?" she protested, panting.

"Kiss . . . perhaps. But nothing more." As his eyes swept open, he held her in a tantalized stare.

"Why not?"

"Angel, don't tempt me." He caressed her lips with his fingertip, his gaze following his hand. "You are not mine. A man can be forgiven once for an error made in ignorance, but now that I know the truth, it would be wrong."

"It doesn't feel wrong," she whispered, but he merely hushed her, laying his finger gently over her lips.

He shook his head. She acquiesced, bowing her head obediently. For another moment or two his eyes glowed with the deep luster of sapphires. He licked his lips unconsciously, and Becky looked away, suppressing a groan.

The knowledge that their bond must be more than physical if it was to succeed helped bring her back to her senses. Their close association until their quest was done was going to be torment, but somehow she managed to rise from his lap and remove herself to the safer distance of the bed.

He smiled knowingly at her, sharing her frustration, then he reached into the breast pocket of his waistcoat. "This should cheer you up." He tossed over a thick wad of paper banknotes held together with a gold clip bearing his monogram.

"Good heavens, Alec! Where did you get all this?"

"Don't you worry your pretty head about it," he teased. "Everything's arranged for Brighton. We'll take a post chaise at midnight and get there in the morning. In the meantime, I'll see if I can't double that tonight at vingt-et-un."

"Where?"

"A gambling hell I know. I make a point of playing where the tables aren't rigged."

She sat up eagerly. "I shall come with you!"

"Oh, no, you shan't. A gambling hell is no place for a young lady."

"Neither is a bedroom with the captain of all London rakehells," she answered with a coy smile.

He attempted to give her a stern look. "You never did answer my original question, as I recall."

"What was it, Alec? I forget."

"I asked if you're all right," he said softly, looking into her eyes. "After last night, I mean."

She blushed—on cue, it would seem. "I—I think so. Why do you ask?"

"Losing one's virtue is no small thing. Oh, Becky, I wish

you would have told me. I would have done things . . . well, a little differently."

"You wouldn't have 'done things' at all, you mean."

"Well, that aside. I would have made it very, very special for you."

"It was," she murmured, her cheeks turning crimson. "You did."

He rose and came over to sit beside her on the bed. He put his arm around her. "Come here," he whispered, pressing a kiss to her hair. "Let me hold you."

She went to him gladly.

Their feet were on the floor, but they lay back slowly on the bed side by side, their embrace chaste despite the yearning that thrummed between them. Alec hugged her and played with her hair, offering all of the lover's comfort that a nervous ex-virgin could want.

"How's your arm feeling?" she ventured.

His answer was a male grunt of indifference.

"Alec?"

He glanced over at her in question.

"How did you lose yours?"

"My what?"

"Your virginity."

"Oh . . . that." He shrugged it off. "Can't remember."

"Liar," she whispered with a smile.

He coddled her with a playful growl. "What's this, does my curious girl want a naughty story?"

"Not fair!" she huffed, pouting at him. "You know how I lost *mine*."

He paused and stared pensively at her. "Well, if ever I should tell anyone, I suppose it should be you—considering." He brushed her hair behind her ear and took her into his arms again.

"You never told anyone?"

"Of course not, *cherie*. A gentleman never does—not when it matters, anyway. It's just . . ." His voice trailed off. She could feel the subtle tensing of his big body. "You don't really want to know this."

"Yes, I do. Why wouldn't I?"

"Well, for one thing, because I was a good deal younger than you are now." He stared up at the ceiling.

"How young?"

He closed his eyes. "Too young," he said.

"What of the girl? Was she young, too?"

"Who said anything about a girl?" he drawled.

Her eyes shot wide open. She sat up and turned to him in astonishment.

He laughed at her stunned look. "What, did you think I meant a boy? Nothing like that," he taunted in a silky tone. "No, it was a _lady_. A grown-up. A countess, actually."

Alec sighed and folded his arms behind his head with a show of idleness, but she sensed the same edge creeping back into his voice as when he had talked about his mother. "If you really want to know, I went home from Eton on holiday with a group of my schoolmates a million years ago. Half a dozen of us were invited to the country house of one of the lads in—well, it doesn't matter where. I was fifteen. It was miserable weather, so we all decided to play war indoors—with slingshots, of course. Boys enjoy causing each other maximum pain."

"Naturally."

"In the course of hunting the enemy through the family's wing, I wandered—rather unobservantly, I'm afraid—into Her Ladyship's bedchamber."

"Her Ladyship?"

"My friend's, ah, mother."

Becky's eyes widened farther.

"Beautiful woman. Twice my age and then some. I had, admittedly, been fascinated by her from the moment I set foot in the house. She smelled like flowers. Well, no one was in the room. The servants had given up trying to mind us. Given the chance, I lost interest in war immediately and seized the opportunity to investigate the domain of this ravishing, alien creature. I had found her dresser drawer full of silky, lacy underclothes when I suddenly heard someone coming. Adult voices. Ladies. I panicked. The voices came closer; the way out was blocked. Then I spied a big old wardrobe and I climbed right into it."

"Good Lord, Alec."

"That's when she came into the room. The countess, I mean." He shook his head. "I was trapped inside her wardrobe—but, Lord, what a view. I could hardly breathe as I watched her maid undressing her." Alec smiled, his expression remote. "It's still imprinted on my mind. She meant to take a nap before supper, but when her maid left, she lay on her bed, and she began to stroke herself. You asked," he said in a cool and reasonable tone at Becky's small cough of shock. "Shall I stop? I've shocked you. You do not wish to hear the rest—"

"No, it's all right," she forced out, struggling for equilibrium. "Go on."

"She must have heard me panting because she left off her solo pleasures and came over and opened the wardrobe door. Whereupon I tumbled out on my head."

"Oh—dear."

"I looked up at her and thought I was done for. Thought I'd be horsewhipped by her husband and sent home in shame to Robert, who would undoubtedly lecture me for a fortnight, but that was not what happened. No," he said slowly, "instead, she gave me a smile that turned my bones to jelly. She saw that I was hard, and she invited me to touch her."

Shocked to the core, Becky cleared her throat. "That was very wicked of her."

"Very." He shrugged. "I was still sprawled on the floor when she stepped across my body and touched my cheek, guiding my mouth to her mound." Alec cupped this location now on Becky through her skirts, his hard stare challenging her to stop him.

She held perfectly still, barely daring to breathe. His touch between her legs was warm, but the look in his eyes was cold, distant—as though this were some sort of test. As though he intended to tell her the very worst thing he could think of about himself to see if she ran away screaming.

Becky had no intention of letting him drive her away.

He had stood his ground to save her from the Cossacks, and if Alec's own demons were of the internal sort, she would stay by his side and take them on as boldly as he had fought her cousin's warriors.

Maybe then he'd see that not all females were like his selfish mother and the scandalous woman he was describing, and all the others, whoever they were, who had taught him to believe that love was some exquisite form of cruelty.

She ignored his claiming hand on her body, refusing to be rattled. "What did she do to you, sweetheart?"

Tell me how she hurt you.

"She clutched my head. She pulled me against her. Barely let me up for air." He faltered a little, seeing now, perhaps, that she had no intention of being scared off. "She made me kiss it. I . . . I did as she told me." His gaze sank, veiled behind dusky lashes. "Eventually, she went and locked the door. After I had made her come a few times, she let me enter her." He withdrew his possessive touch from between her thighs, then passed a hard, searching glance over her face, reading her reaction to his little tale.

Becky was tongue-tied, shaken, and a bit sorry she had asked, though she refused to let it show.

"I revile you," he said casually.

She shook her head. "No." She swallowed hard, hurting for him. "You're not the one to blame. All boys are curious at that age."

"Aye. Some more than others."

"Were you afraid of what was happening?"

"Yes. A little."

"What else were you feeling?" she whispered.

He shrugged, looking taken aback by the question. "I've no idea." He edged away from her a bit. "Can't recall. It was a long time ago."

Excuses.

"Lonely? Confused?" she prompted very gently. "You had lost your mother just the year before. Maybe all you really wanted that day was a little attention."

"Well, I certainly got that." He looked away.

"Come here, darling," She reached out to wrap her arms loosely around his shoulders. He resisted, his muscles tensing, but he did not brush her off. She stroked his clean-shaven cheek. "I'm so sorry, Alec."

"Sorry?" His low laugh rang hollow. "Why?"

"You know why." She kissed his cheek and then leaned her forehead against the hard line of his jaw. "That woman took advantage of your innocence."

"So?" He swallowed hard. "What happened to me is a boy's wet dream."

Becky shook her head, petting him with tender solace. "Maybe so, but you were still hurting. She should have left you alone, and you know it."

He pulled away. "Who cares."

"I do," Becky whispered.

Alec flinched at her soft answer. His heart was pounding thunderously. He was not quite sure what was happening to him. He sat on the edge of the bed and stared down numbly at his hands, suddenly concerned he had said too much. He felt horribly exposed and like he very much needed to get back in control. He only knew one way to do that.

"Come to me, sweeting," Becky murmured, lying back on the pure white bed, innocent-eyed. She held out her arms to welcome him, offering solace, kindness, he knew not what.

He stared at her for a long, searing moment, his pulse slamming in his arteries as he tried to decide if what she offered was heaven or hell.

She waited, so bravely willing to be hurt.

He went to her, and when he eased atop her, claiming her mouth in a bold, hot kiss that was almost rough, Alec already knew what he wanted.

She tried to stop him, tried to turn her face away to temper his sudden desperate need, but he blocked her escape, his kiss all the more insistent. Curling her hands around his shoulders, she briefly managed to dislodge him, but Alec was on fire.

"I want you," he growled, holding her down with his weight.

"You said we couldn't."

"I lied."

"Why are you doing this?" she whimpered in bewilderment. "Alec, hurting me won't change the past."

Her words eased some of the darkness from him. He stroked her thick sable hair, pushing it back from her face with his palm. "I'm not going to hurt you," he promised, kissing the corner of her plump, rosy mouth. "Not at all, my baby. Not at all."

"Alec, please, I know you're in pain." She tried to hold him. He wouldn't let her. "I only want to help you, to comfort you, sweetheart—"

"Then let me make you come," he whispered in a tone that even he knew sounded remote, maybe even frightening to a trusting young girl.

Becky searched his face in confusion. *"What?"*

"Shh," he answered, and then he stopped her words with a kiss. He tasted her in longing need, dizzying them both with the moist, silken glide of mouth on mouth.

Meanwhile, he soothed her with one wandering hand, laying claim to his territory all over again—rolling hills, lush valleys, fertile plains. She only quite realized what he was about when his fingers plucked at one ribbon garter beneath her skirts, skimming a velvet stretch of bare white thigh.

"Alec," she gasped out.

He kissed her again, gently, silencing her with his lips. He removed his hand from her limb just long enough to give her a reassuring caress on her hair.

"What the hell are you doing, Alec?" she demanded.

"Shh. You know you want this. You told me so just a little while ago."

"That was before you told me what that woman did to you!"

"What does it matter?"

"What does it matter?" she echoed in disbelief. She cupped his face, her fingers fever-hot against his cheek. "Alec, you don't have to do this to get me to care about you." She raked her fingers through his hair and clutched a handful of it, tugging just enough to get his attention.

He liked that.

"Listen to me. I'm not going to hurt you," she said. "You don't need to do this."

"Oh, yes, I do," he whispered as he went exploring again beneath those fields of white gauzy muslin. He knew just where to touch her. Her soft, warm, quivering body eased his pain, delighted him.

She moaned as he stroked her, her lashes fluttering closed as she struggled to fight it. She tried one more time to reach him, but her innocent will was fading as passion darkened the violet of her eyes. She clutched his shoulders and kissed his brow. "You can't buy me with pleasure, Alec."

"Can't I?" he murmured.

"Stop," she groaned, even as her hips arched in guilty pleading for more, taking his probing fingers in deeper.

Alec gave her what she craved, playing her smooth body like a quivering instrument.

"Oh, God, I can't resist you," she gasped out a few moments later, a confession purely drenched in the jungle steam of her core. He wanted to lick her.

"Why would you even try?" he whispered as softly as the wind. "Just enjoy it. Take what I give you."

"I don't understand."

"You will."

"What do you want?" she groaned, half despairing.

"Your surrender, my love. I must have it. Give it to me. Feed me with it. Put it in my mouth."

She finally seemed to understand, relaxing under him; finally, she decided to indulge him. Perhaps she had realized at last that he needed to do this to her; that she simply had to let him.

With yielding softness, she let her legs spread wider and brought her knees up loosely, cradling his head ever so lovingly between her hands as he descended.

"Oh, yes," she breathed, giving him exactly what he craved.

Alec was shaking with passion himself. He ripped the bodice of her dress in his feverish need to suck her tits. She helped to free them and put them in his mouth, watching hungrily. He moaned as he devoured them with shameless greed, each firm, round globe in turn; and barely satisfied, down he went, lower, kissing his way down her lovely body until his tongue danced lusty pirouettes upon her clit.

Becky was dripping, drenching his face and his hands with her body's glorious *yes*. She draped one leg over his shoulder, fucking his fingers and his tongue without a trace of inhibition. Alec was in heaven, worshiping her. He never felt more alive than those few precious, fleeting moments before he brought a woman to ecstasy. And this one, God knew, was wild. If ever a girl had been made just for him, it would be her. The fiery ardor of her response could have shattered his exquisite self-control. His swollen cock threatened to come bursting out of his clothes; but no.

He would not mount her, much as he might burn to. He had meant it when he said he would not put it in her again so long as she refused to marry him.

As she neared climax, his own pulse climbed.

"Oh, God, oh, Alec, my angel."

He could feel her hovering there on that airy precipice: She was right where he wanted her. With another smooth maneuver of his hand and a final slow stroke of his tongue, she plunged over the edge, writhing against his mouth, drenching his deeply buried fingers with the sweet, clear tide of her release.

"Holy Christ," she said after a very long moment's silence. Her lashes swept open; her violet gaze was fevered as she looked at him in spent and panting disbelief.

Alec closed his eyes like a man redeemed and laid his head on her trembling belly as he struggled to bring his own galloping drives under control.

She tangled her fingers weakly in his hair. "Oh, darling."

He reveled in her touch.

"Come here," she whispered.

He looked up warily at her.

She opened her arms again to him, just as she had at the start—undaunted.

He marveled.

Holding her stare in a kind of trance, he pushed up onto his knees between her legs and slowly wiped his mouth on his shirtsleeve. Then he came nearer and laid his head down on her chest, facing away from her.

She had nothing to say. No reproach. No head games. Not even a Lizzie-style lecture, not that he had ever even dreamed of doing this to Lizzie.

Lizzie, he had put on a pedestal, where he could never reach her, and more important, where she could never reach him. But this was Becky, who didn't run away at his evil little tricks the way Lizzie had; who not only had the power to reach him, but had somehow gotten inside of him.

"Now you understand," he said at length.

"Yes," she whispered. "Now I understand."

She wrapped her soft arms around him and kissed his head.

Slowly, as Becky caressed him with a world of patience and quiet acceptance the likes of which he'd never known, Alec felt the darkness leaving him bit by bit. By degrees. Her touch told him many things. Things he probably wouldn't have believed if she had tried to say it in words. He felt her fierce protectiveness over him. He felt her compassion. He felt the will in her to help him trust again.

And he realized that maybe his performance this afternoon had not been necessary after all.

Well, then. He smiled faintly against the delicate, tattered gauze of her white bodice. That made him all the more glad he had done it.

CHAPTER
∞ NINE ∞

"*B*ecky, would you please hurry up?" came Alec's third impatient call from the bottom of the grand marble staircase in Knight House.

"One minute—sorry!" Her heart fluttered with excitement as she peered into the mirror near the open door, seizing one last chance to make a hasty inspection of herself before going out on their evening's adventure to the gaming house.

After a leisurely day spent resting and then playing dress-up with Alec, she could barely believe her own transformation. The gown he had picked out for her and insisted she wear from Her Grace's borrowed collection was composed of white net over a sheath of pink satin, and trimmed with rows of dusky rose ribbon around the neckline, sleeves, and hem. It had a charming little bow tied in the front of the high waistline just beneath her bosom, but Becky's favorite part of the costume was the adorable toque of rich rose satin and white lace.

The large sweeping plume of white feathers were a bit of a nuisance, but she liked the way the hat framed her face, her dark curls swinging jauntily below it on the sides. She looked so elegant she almost scared herself. "You'll be fine," she whispered, making absolutely sure she had nothing in her teeth, then smoothing skirts.

"Hullo? Becky? I'm wasting away of old age down here!"

"Coming!" Hurrying out of the chamber, she tingled with self-consciousness. She was dressed like a duchess and looked like a fine London lady, but the only thing that stopped her from feeling like an utter fraud was the appreciative glow in Alec's eyes as his possessive gaze traveled over her.

"Highly acceptable, *cherie*," he purred as she hurried down the stairs, the banister slippery under her hand in the white satin gloves.

"Are you sure this cravat looks all right?" Her handsome escort frowned a bit as she joined him, handling the small knot of his white neckcloth gingerly.

"I told you it does. Well, I did my best."

Dressing him had been one of the most entertaining things she had ever done in her life, and she had earned that privilege because it seemed his valet had stormed out just last week in despair of ever receiving the back wages his master owed him. A very bad state of affairs for a London dandy.

"He'll be back," Alec had assured her with a grin. "Dressing me has made him a legend among his peers."

"You're so wonderfully modest," she had teased him.

"Thank you, Miss Ward. I do try."

Tonight he wore a formal black coat with clawhammer tails. The superb cut of the jacket accented the powerful breadth of his shoulders. Beneath it, his waistcoat was of snowy white silk. His lightweight wool trousers charcoal gray with a strap running under his elegant black shoes to keep them lying smooth and perfect down the front of his long-legged frame.

"You look thoroughly beautiful," she assured him, and it was true.

"Humph." His black chapeau-bras tucked flat beneath his arm, Alec was putting on his other white kid glove when he glanced up and watched her coming toward him.

The caress in his gaze reminded her of the fun he'd had, as well, lacing up her corset in back and rolling the white silk stockings slowly up her legs and ever so carefully fastening them to each garter belt.

"Don't careen so speedily, my dear. You'll throw yourself down the stairs. A lady *glides*."

"You'll catch me."

"Maybe," he drawled, his cobalt gaze softening. "Come here."

She obeyed, and quite tenderly he adjusted the angle of her hat.

She frowned as he smiled at her in fond amusement. "It just keeps flopping."

"Doesn't matter. You're charming." His pleasured gaze admired her, then he offered her his arm. "Shall we?"

She accepted with a blush, but still couldn't stop smiling. It had been a close contest, for he had almost forbidden her to come. While getting dressed, they had argued in the bedchamber.

"I can't take you with me to a gambling hell, Becky!" he had said while pulling on his trousers.

"Why not?"

"Respectable young ladies do not go into such places! Everyone will think you are my bit o' muslin!"

"Your what?"

"My ladybird. Kept woman. Mistress!"

"Really?" she had marveled, not half as appalled as she ought to have been at the notion. Then she shrugged it off entirely. Did he not yet grasp that she cared less than a fig what other people thought? "No matter. You will protect me," she had assured him cheerily.

"That's not the point." Alec had scowled. "Even married ladies only go to gambling hells when they're escorted by their *cavaliers servientes*—and that, provided only that they have finished having babies. They're usually women of a racy reputation to boot."

"What about their husbands?"

"Husbands?"

"Why don't their husbands take them to gambling hells?"

"Really, poppet." His worldly chuckle informed her that her question had been hopelessly naive. "Don't you know it is considered vulgar in the ton for a man and wife to be seen together overmuch? Besides, what man would bring the mother of his children to a gaming hell?"

"Vulgar for a man and wife to be seen having fun together?" She had stopped brushing her hair to squint at him in bafflement. "You aristocrats are so strange! Lace me up." She had turned her back to make him do her stays.

"No." He had captured her hands and wrapped his arms around her waist instead. "Call me sentimental, but I happen to like you sheltered. It's refreshing."

"Alec, you can't leave me here by myself again!" She had spun around, clutching his lapels. "Don't lock me in here all alone! Oh, please?"

"Such dramatics!" he had chided softly, but her pleas had finally won him over, except for one last, stern admonition: "Mind that you stay by my side at all times."

"I will! Oh, bless you!" She had hugged him excitedly and kissed his face ten times. "I will, I promise."

And so she was on her way to a gambling hell, posing as the ladybird of the captain of all London rakes. What Mama would've had to say about this, she did not care to entertain.

"Here," Alec said as they walked outside, nodding to

Mr. Walsh, who held the door for them. "I have something for you." As the butler shut the door behind them, Alec reached into his waistcoat and pulled out their stash of money, handing her some. "Put this in your reticule," he ordered.

"Do I get to play, too?" she asked, lighting up.

"No. That's for you in case of emergency. If for any reason we become separated or if anything happens to me, should we meet those Cossacks again, you are to buy a stagecoach ticket immediately to the town of Carlisle. From there you will go west to Hawkscliffe Hall. My family will help you, and Mr. Walsh can vouch for you if there is any question of your veracity."

His words brought back the ominous specter of danger that loomed over them, casting a shadow over Becky's lighthearted mood. It was hard to absorb that this man whom she'd met scarcely twenty-four hours ago was willingly putting his life on the line for her.

"Don't worry, nothing's going to happen. Just in case," he murmured as he put the coin-purse back into his pocket and then tucked her gloved hand in the crook of his arm. Patting it twice, he led her to his ducal brother's borrowed town-coach and handed her up into the opulent vehicle.

A moment later they were off.

It was about nine o'clock when they strolled up to the large, black-clad porter stationed outside the door of the gambling hell.

"Ah, Lord Alec. Good evenin', sir."

"Hullo, Tom. Busy night?"

"Fairly so, sir. I'm sure they will all make room for you at the tables, ha! Good luck to you, sir."

"Thanks, Tom. As you see, tonight I've brought my lucky charm." He gave Becky a rowdy squeeze as she clung fast to the crook of his arm.

As the man opened the door for them with a grin,

the noise from inside swelled and light spilled out onto the pavement. The porter tipped his hat politely to Becky as they passed him. "Miss."

Her heart beat faster as Alec led her into the gambling hell. It was a disreputable place, with elegant players like Alec rubbing shoulders with rough characters who looked slightly criminal. Excitement was palpable in the air, and Becky responded to its contagion, glancing all around her at the gaudy, red-carpeted salons and the startling *real* Cyprians with their rouged mouths and plunging necklines. She swallowed hard, unable to shake the thought of Mrs. Whithorn's scathing disapproval.

Sodom and Gomorrah, indeed, and her golden-haired guardian angel was leading her ever deeper into temptation.

Perhaps her uneasiness showed in her face, for Alec apparently sensed it. He gave her gloved hand another comforting pat where it rested on his arm.

"Relax, sweet. You're quite safe," he murmured, then gave a droll sigh. "For myself, on the other hand, I'm quite sure I'll be going to hell for bringing you here, if there was still any debate on the matter."

Becky just looked at him. There was no way she would have allowed him to come without her, considering all that she had at stake in his success. For all his generosity, she had yet to be solidly convinced that his risky plan would work. Also, given his aristocratic tendency toward extravagance, and her need to conserve their funds, she intended to watch him like a hawk; perhaps it was wrong to doubt him, however slightly, but all things considered, she had made a private decision not to let her hero get carried away at his second favorite pastime.

He gave her a wink, then tugged her onward.

She was glad she had left the floppy-feathered hat in

the carriage. She already felt self-conscious enough. As they sauntered through the smoky, noisy place where countless games were in progress, she was aware of the many people who stopped and looked at them as they walked past.

"What a beautiful pair," she heard someone say.

"She must be new."

"Wasn't he here the other night?"

Hearing the murmurs, feeling their scrutiny, Becky stayed close to him, but the sighing, staring females who ogled Alec as he walked by made her scowl.

"This way, sweet." When he placed his hand in the small of her back, she quivered slightly, but Alec's gaze was fixed on the cluster of crowded gaming tables ahead. A painted placard hanging from the ceiling proclaimed the mysterious message: DEALER STANDS ON ALL 17's.

Alec was glancing from one table to the other. "There." He nodded toward the first table on the left. "That's the one we want. Minimum wager's only a fiver."

"But you said we'd start with a hundred," she whispered.

"Yes, but first we've got to buy in."

Becky looked at him in question.

"Trust me. I've done this before." He caressed her while they waited for one of the seven stools at the "fiver" table to be vacated.

"So, this is vingt-et-un," she murmured, standing on tiptoe in an effort to see past the crowd around the table.

"Right. The object is to reach a total of twenty-one points without going over. Face cards are worth ten points, aces either one or eleven. In simplest terms, each player bets against the house on whether he or the dealer will have the better hand."

"Ah," she said sagely.

Alec chuckled at her mystified stare. "Hand's over. That fellow's leaving. Here we go."

She could sense his excitement rising as he moved forward and sat down on the stool that one of the gamblers, shaking his head over what Becky surmised was a defeat, had abandoned. As she came over to stand by Alec's shoulder, he smoothly produced a hundred guineas.

He put the money on the green baize table, and the dealer, a wizened old man, took it all. "Good evening, sir."

Alec nodded. A moment later the dealer slid a few stacks of chips toward Alec.

"The red's worth five guineas each, the white's worth one," he explained in a murmur. She looked on with rising interest while Alec exchanged a cordial smile with his fellow players.

"Gentlemen, lay your bets, please," the ancient dealer rasped.

Becky glanced around the table, noting that seven white circles about the size of a saucer were painted on the green velvet surface of the table, one in front of every player. Inside this circle, each player placed his chips.

"Don't touch anything," he told her in a low voice. "Once we put our wager in this circle—it's called the betting box—no one's allowed to touch it until the hand is over. Also, don't touch the cards."

"I won't," she quickly agreed.

Alec placed two red chips inside his betting box for an initial wager of ten guineas. When all of the other players had laid their bets as well, the dealer doled out the cards. Starting at his left, he made one pass around the table, laying all cards faceup; he dealt Alec a three and Becky noted that the dealer's own card was an eight.

"Do the suits matter?"

"No." Alec's anticipatory stare remained fixed on the

dealer, who was making another pass around the table, handing out a second card to all the players. Again the cards were dealt faceup.

Alec got another three.

"Is that good?" Becky whispered.

"Could be," he said, then nodded toward the dealer as the old man placed his own second card face down. "You see? Now none of us knows what the dealer's got in his hand. He's got that eight, but his second card could be anything. That's where the fun comes in." He glanced around at the other players' hands as he spoke.

"Fun? This is nerve-racking."

"No one's been dealt vingt-et-un," he commented under his breath.

"What happens next?"

"Each player takes his turn. You'll see."

She peered over his shoulder at the gamblers to his right who began taking their turns in succession. Her curious stare drew an answering leer from a sweaty fellow across the table whose scruffy jaw was badly in need of a shave. He lifted his flask in Becky's direction and toasted her with a harsh gulp of blue ruin.

Alec sent the man an icy look and pulled Becky onto his knee.

When his turn came around, he put another two red chips in the betting box and tapped the table casually with his fingertip. The dealer gave him a third card.

"A three again!" Becky exclaimed, then hastily stifled herself.

So, he had nine and he wanted twenty one. Two more red chips went into the betting box; again he summoned another card with a tap of his finger. This time it was a five.

Five plus nine: They were up to fourteen.

The other men around the table seemed to be holding their breaths as they watched him, but Alec, without a flicker of emotion on his face, placed another pair of red chips in the betting box and sought a fifth card.

Oh, please be a seven. They now had thirty guineas on this wager.

The dealer gave Alec his fifth and final card—a six.

Becky stared at it, crestfallen. They were short. They had only made twenty.

Then she heard one of the other men say to Alec, "Nicely done, sir," and she noticed the twinkle in his blue eyes as he amiably answered, "We'll see."

"I thought we wanted twenty-one," she whispered, turning to him.

"Yes, but we haven't gone over, and a five-card trick beats everything but vingt-et-un."

"Oh!"

As the other men took their turns, some fell short of twenty-one or even the twenty that Alec had gotten. Others went over—the term was going 'bust,' as Becky soon learned—and from these, the dealer immediately confiscated the chips they had wagered on the hand.

At last, in the final step of the game, the dealer revealed his facedown card—a ten, giving him a total of eighteen. He had to pay even money to one man who had slipped in with a nineteen, but Alec's five-card trick was a win that paid two to one.

"There you are, sir, well done, my lord," the dealer murmured, shoving two green chips and two more red ones toward Alec.

Becky stared at her rescuer in amazement. "You just won sixty pounds!"

He cast her an ever so slight, private smile. She realized he was jubilant within, though as cool as steel outwardly, like a proper gambler.

"I like this," she whispered, settling more comfortably onto his lap.

Alec nodded. "Everybody likes winning. They say it is an aphrodisiac," he murmured in her ear.

"What's that?" she asked innocently.

His laugh was low and very wicked. "I'll tell you later."

The dealer swept up all the cards and slid them under the bottom of the deck.

"Shouldn't he shuffle?" she inquired, but Alec was nuzzling the curve of her neck.

"Not until someone gets vingt-et-un. I like your hair like this," he purred, his warm breath tickling her earlobe. "It's very pretty." She had worn her hair pulled back from her face with a pair of combs, the back lifted off her neck, hanging in bouncy ringlets. Alec's lips explored while some of the players left the table and new ones took their places. Becky glanced nervously at them, biting her lip against the sizzling desire that he sent searing through her veins. "You look so innocent in pink. It just makes me want to debauch you. I love your neck."

"Behave, you scoundrel," she chided in a breathy whisper. "You need to concentrate."

"You are my muse, *cherie*. You inspire me."

"How much are those green chips worth?"

"Twenty-five." With that, he nudged one of the green chips into the betting box.

It was a steeper bet than they had started with last time, but Becky willed herself to trust him. The dealer again distributed two cards to all seven players, leaving his own second draw facedown. His faceup card was a four.

Alec had received a pair of sevens and was staring at them with a look of brooding intensity. "Are you superstitious, my girl?"

"A little, I suppose."

"Then give me a kiss for luck." He leaned his cheek toward her.

She smiled and obliged him, pressing a lingering kiss to his clean-shaved cheek.

Armed with her kiss, Alec slowly put the other green chip in the betting box and tapped the green tabletop twice. He stared at the dealer with a look of idle nonchalance, but sitting half on his lap, Becky could feel the tension thrumming through his body.

Cries of amazement erupted around the table before the third seven even hit the green velvet.

"A royale!"

"Damn me!"

"Ain't seen one of those in months!"

Alec exhaled slowly through his mouth.

"Three sevens, that's twenty-one!" she said, turning to him in excitement.

"You weren't fooling. You *are* lucky." He looked a little dazed as he glanced at her. "That kiss worked better than you know."

"A royale trumps everything, little missy," the middle-aged bald man beside Alec told her. "That's why it pays three to one!"

Her jaw dropped as she whipped around to face her rescuer again. "Alec! You just won a hundred and fifty pounds!"

The man beside them bought Alec a bumper.

As word of his "royale" traveled rapidly throughout the gaming hell, people began gathering around the table to watch him play; but Becky was a bit superstitious, and Alec's winning streak sent gooseflesh rising on her skin, as though someone had stepped on her grave. These sums were getting awfully large. She could barely believe he had won in one hand almost all that it cost to run the farm for a year. She swallowed hard, glancing nervously at the other players. Many of them were leav-

ing the game, but Alec showed no sign of quitting anytime soon.

Maybe he should, she thought. Why press their luck?

She was elated with his success, of course, and realized they still had far to go, but frankly, she was beginning to feel a trifle unnerved. As the stools again
changed ownership and the dealer added the used cards
once more to the bottom of the deck, she turned hesitantly to him.

"Perhaps we ought to quit while we're ahead."

"What, quit now?"

She nodded uneasily.

"Hell, no," he whispered. "Not a chance."

"Alec."

He ignored her, his gaze riveted on the card box. Now
that she noticed it, the fevered look in his eyes rather
scared her. It bolstered her decision to leave.

"I want to go now, Alec. I mean it. Let's get out of
here before we lose all that you just gained."

He shook his head. "Soon. Not yet."

"Why risk it? You've won over two hundred guineas
in less than twenty minutes—"

"Becky, I know what I'm doing!"

She blinked at his sharp tone.

"Sorry." He lowered his gaze. "I didn't mean that the
way it sounded." He cupped her cheek. "Sweetheart,
I'm doing this for you."

"Are you?" she asked quietly, staring hard into his
eyes.

He turned away with an impatient scowl.

She really could not argue with his success, so she held
her tongue and gave him the benefit of the doubt for one
more hand; but she swore to herself that if he lost their
winnings now, she was going to throttle the man.

As the dealer paid out their treble winnings, the hundred fifty quid he had won arrived in the form of one black chip and two more of the green. For their third hand of the night, Alec laid an initial wager that topped out the maximum this table allowed: the black chip worth a full hundred guineas.

Becky felt a little ill. "It's too much. We're going to lose it all."

"Child's play," Alec replied under his breath. "In Brighton, I'll be wagering many multiples of this. Relax. It's just beginner's nerves. Ignore it."

Becky took a deep breath, finally realizing the full extent of the trust she was going to have to place in him in order for this plan to work. A hundred pounds was a drop in the proverbial bucket compared to what they would need to regain Talbot Old Hall. He was right. In Brighton he would be betting thousands on each hand. Having lived very simply all her life, she was not sure her nerves could stand this, but Alec seemed perfectly composed.

She willed herself to have faith, and barely realized she was mentally reciting the Lord's Prayer as the dealer's nimble hands bestowed the requisite two cards on every player; on the first pass, Alec got the queen of hearts. Becky held her breath as the dealer came around again.

A worldly chuckle escaped his handsome lips as the queen found a partner in the ace of diamonds.

He sat back casually. "Vingt-et-un."

The crowd around the table cheered him wildly, but Becky stared at him, paling.

This was too uncanny. Obsessed as he was with honor, there was no way he'd ever cheat, but she knew what Mrs. Whithorn would have said. A man with this kind of luck must have surely made a deal with the Devil.

Alec raised one eyebrow and gave Becky an I-told-you-so glance.

She was unnerved, resisting the urge to bless herself with the sign of the cross as she eyed his perfect cards. "M-May we go now, please?"

"You must be joking."

"I'm in earnest, Alec!"

"Settle down," he said with a flicker of annoyance in his eyes. "I know what I'm doing."

Her temper flared. "Oh, really? Isn't this how you got yourself into that 'deep dark hole' you mentioned? Isn't this the reason half your furniture's gone? Forget this! I'm leaving." She got up abruptly from his lap. "I'll wait for you outside, if you can manage to pull yourself away anytime soon."

"Becky! Get back here! Becky, don't you dare walk out—"

She ignored his protest, her heart thumping as she exited, maneuvering through the admiring crowd that had gathered around to watch the famed Lord Alec Knight at play.

That—blackguard! she thought as she marched out of the salon, not stopping till she had reached the outdoors. The night had turned cool, but with ire heating her blood, she did not feel the chill. The black-clad porter stationed outside paid her no mind, conversing with another fellow as Becky paced back and forth beside the building.

She just knew Alec was going to come out empty-handed, and then she was going to find the nearest candle-snuffer and use it to clobber the rogue.

"Most stubborn creature I ever—chit's going to get herself killed!" Alec muttered angrily to himself under his breath, glancing in the direction in which his impossible charge had gone storming out. "Could you hurry, please?"

Hastily pushing his chips toward the dealer, he drummed his fingers on the green baize table while the old man counted out five black chips and two red, giving these to Alec. He tipped the dealer, in turn, and quickly strode over to the clerk's window, settling with the house to collect his winnings, a full five hundred guineas.

Then he was stalking out after her, triumphant over his success this night, yet gnawed at by the sobering realization that she might have a point. If he did not stay on his guard against himself, it would be distressingly easy to slip back into his old habits.

But bloody hell, he didn't need a mere slip of a girl telling him what to do, how to play his hand. Striding outside, he asked Tom the doorman if he had seen his girl.

The big man gestured to a white-clad figure waiting in the shadows. When Alec saw her bristling posture, he knew he was in trouble. Arms folded across her chest. Foot tapping slowly at the hem of her skirts. Cold, level stare. No, his demoiselle did not need to say a word to express the way she felt.

And so, pinned in her quelling glare, he resorted to the time-honored male trick of going immediately on the offensive. Marching across the street, he approached in an aggressive state of indignant masculine bluster.

"Don't you ever walk out on me again like that! Good God, you've got a horde of Cossacks after you—what if they had shown up while I was still inside?—and by the way, we do not happen to be in the best neighborhood!"

She stared stoically at him, unruffled by his rant. "I've heard about men like you, you know. Men who lose their fortunes in one night of gaming. There are stories of them all the time in the newspapers. They usually end up shooting themselves in the head. Is that what you want?"

"You really are the most incredibly ungrateful creature!" he exclaimed, throwing up his hands at his sides.

She thrust out her jaw, looking thoroughly obdurate. "How much did you lose?"

"Not a goddamn penny!" He reached into his pocket, and pulling out his billfold again, offered it insolently to her. "Here! Why don't you count it? You obviously don't trust me, so maybe I'm lying. Go on! It's all there."

She narrowed her eyes at him, making no move to confiscate the cash. "If you're not going to take this seriously, then maybe I *am* better off on my own. You said yourself that all you care about is pleasure, but we are not here so that you can have fun, Alec."

"Don't condescend to me. I know full well what is at stake."

"Do you? My village is depending on me—and I'm depending on you, as you promised I could."

"Do you want my help or not?"

They stared at each other in the darkness for a long, searing moment.

"God, what am I doing to you?" she whispered, shaking her head with a look of guilt. "Why didn't you just tell me flat out how dangerous gambling is for you?"

"What are you talking about?"

"It really is a problem for you, isn't it? Don't deny it. That was the deep, dark hole that you told me you fell into. And now—it's not enough that you're risking your life for me—now I see you're also risking yourself in a way that might be even worse."

"Oh, Becky." Feeling acutely self-conscious, Alec turned away and rubbed his face wearily. "I gave you my word you could count on me. Legion though my faults may be, I do not break my word."

She shook her head, staring at him. "I don't know

what to do. I need your help, but I fear this is asking too much of you. You haven't even seen what we're fighting for."

He looked straight at her. "Oh, yes, I have."

Her shoulders dropped as she held his gaze, realizing he was speaking about her.

"Becky." Alec went to her, resting his hands on her delicate shoulders. "Did it ever occur to you that I might need to help *you* just as badly as you need my help? Please," he said in a gentle tone. "Let me do something for once that actually matters. I was all right in there. I knew exactly what I was doing. That's the way gaming goes. We can quit for tonight since you've obviously had enough, but you have *got* to trust me."

He heard her sigh of distress; she was still for a moment.

"I'm sorry," she said at length, shaking her head. "You're right. I guess it was beginner's nerves, as you said. I'm just not used to this, Alec."

"You're not used to letting others help you, either, are you?" he countered softly.

"No," she admitted. "I usually find it easier just to do something myself, but this time . . ." She shrugged. "I can't."

"Well, I can. This is exactly what I'm good at. You don't have to be afraid," he whispered, pressing a kiss to her brow. "We're on the same side here. I will be careful. I promise."

"I'll watch out for you the best I can, all the same," she murmured, slipping her arms around his waist and laying her head on his chest. "Whatever happens, I won't let you fall back down into any deep, dark holes, Alec." She pulled back a bit and looked up into his eyes. "If I see any sign that you're losing control, I'm calling it off. I won't be responsible for harming you after you saved my life."

"You're not going to harm me, Becky. I'm a big boy."

"Yes, but gambling's the reason your family's angry at you, isn't it?"

"Well, yes," he admitted. *Indirectly.* But he had no intention of telling her about Lady Campion.

"You scared me in there, Alec."

"Well, you scared me, too, when you ran off," he answered, cupping her face in his hand. "How am I supposed to protect you if you won't stay put?"

"I had to get you out of there. It seemed the only way." Her intent stare as she studied him seemed to demand his complete honesty.

Faced with it, Alec felt something akin to pins and needles running throughout his whole body. "What's the matter? Why are you looking at me like that?" he murmured.

She shook her head. "I guess I'm still not totally convinced."

"Not convinced?" he exclaimed.

She shook her head with a look of contrition. "Sorry."

Letting out a startled huff of indignation, he released her from his embrace and paced a few feet away, scowling. He raked his hand through his hair, feeling restless and slightly trapped.

Bloody hell!

How was a rake to function when this hardheaded girl seemed to see right through his every move? He glanced over his shoulder at her. "Damn it, Becky, can't you give an inch?"

"If I did, wouldn't you take a mile?"

His eyes widened at her answer, then he let out an exasperated laugh and looked up at the night sky, wondering if he had gotten in too deeply over his head this time—not with those Russian blighters or the card games, but with this lovely, too-perceptive female.

After a long moment, he shook his head to himself

and let out a cynical sigh. Clearly it was useless trying to deceive her. "Very well, Miss Ward. You win. Yes, gambling can be a problem for me," he said crisply, his hands braced on his hips. "But I'll tell you something else. I am no fool."

"I never said you were—"

"I can control it," he interrupted fiercely. "For you."

She held his blazing stare.

"Don't underestimate me," he added. "I know full well what's at stake here."

Absorbing this, Becky nodded slowly—finally satisfied, it seemed. "Thank you—for explaining. I believe you now."

He scoffed, prickling all over with self-consciousness.

"I mean it, Alec. Thank you for your honesty."

He snorted and turned away, still scowling. "Let's go to Brighton, shall we?" he muttered. Not waiting for her answer, he whistled loudly for the carriage.

They arrived in Brighton by post chaise at sunrise.

Fortunately, Mr. Walsh had sent word ahead to the small staff at the Knight family's seaside villa to expect them. The postilion found the house without incident and proceeded to carry in their luggage, while Alec and Becky stood beside the yellow bounder, stretching after the ride of some three hours. After their tiff outside the gambling hell, the journey had been a trifle tense, but Alec was prepared to forget about it by now if Becky was.

"The springs on that thing were atrocious," he muttered, rubbing his neck and longing after his fine high-flyer phaeton, sold months ago to pay off some of his debts; but she paid him little mind, staring at a seagull that stood preening on the hitching post.

She turned to Alec, wide-eyed. "I can hear the ocean."

"Look behind you," he advised with a wry half smile.

She turned around slowly and gave a soft gasp, staring at the blue horizon visible between the buildings at the end of the street. "Oh!" she breathed. "Can we go and look at it, Alec?"

"Don't you want to go into the house first? Settle in?"

She was already on her way, walking toward the beach like a woman in a trance. Something in the set of her shoulders made him hang back, realizing she desired a few moments alone.

He followed at a respectful distance of some dozen paces, watching her and taking in the sun-splashed loveliness of Brighton's cobbled streets and neat, stuccoed town houses painted in pale colors.

Becky walked all the way down to the wooden railing that ran the length of the Promenade and stood staring at the water, her long dark tresses billowing slowly on the salt-tinged breeze.

Alec joined her at the picturesque railing and stood in silence beside her, studying the luminous pink and orange sunrise trimmed by purple eyelet clouds, with the promise of blue overhead. The sea was smoky green glass with a sluggish surf barely strong enough to curl itself into a wave at the shore; the pebble beach was a jumble of strewn confetti-stones, pink and orange, mottled white and blue-gray.

"So, this is sunrise," he whispered, then added cynically, "I usually sleep through it."

"It's so beautiful." Her face was illumined by the eastern glow, creamy skin, rosy cheeks.

Alec stared.

"I haven't seen the sea in years," she murmured. "Not since Mama and I moved away from Portsmouth."

He saw her touching the tiny seashell that she wore around a ribbon on her neck and knew she was thinking of her father; but he was taken utterly off guard when she slowly unfastened her treasured necklace and put it in his hand.

"Here," she said somberly. "I want you to have this."

"Becky, I can't—"

"Take it." She closed his fingers into a loose fist around her talisman. "Keep it with you."

"I don't understand," he whispered, searching her face with a gentle gaze. "This necklace means so much to you. Why are you giving it to me?"

"For luck," she offered, but her eyes told him it was much more than that. As she smiled wistfully at him, tendrils of her hair billowing on the breeze, Alec stepped closer, inexorably drawn to her. She held his hand. "After all, I won't always be able to be with you to give you my kiss for luck when you're gaming to raise the money for my house. You told me how most of these card parties are gentlemen-only events."

"Nor can we risk Kurkov finding out you're here."

"Now at least you'll have this." She smiled warmly at him as she cradled his closed fist between her hands; but distress lined her smooth forehead faintly as she gazed at him. "I shall worry about you so."

"Don't. I'll have you home very soon, my darling." He cupped her petal-soft cheek in his hand, bent his head and kissed her softly.

She sighed under the light caress of his lips and laid her hand on his chest. She seemed as happy as he was to leave their minor spat behind. Ending the kiss, Alec watched her open her eyes dreamily. She held his gaze with an innocent stare that seemed to reach right into his soul.

"Thank you," she whispered, her heart in her eyes— and her life in his hands. "Thank you for all of this."

Alec was shaken by the faith and trust that he knew she now placed in him by an act of will. A decision.

Narrowing his eyes against the light, he took her face

between his fingertips and gave her a reassuring smile, but his thoughts were fierce and warlike. He fairly trembled with his determination to make her proud. *My darling, you can thank me when it's over.* In grim silence he tucked her protectively under his arm, pressed a kiss to her head, and then showed her into the house.

While Becky unpacked her things, her heart light with the knowledge that her cousin and his men were many miles away and had no idea where she was, Alec visited Raggett's, Brighton's leading club for gentlemen, to procure invitations to a few private, high-stakes games.

When he returned at midday with news that he had now secured a seat in three upcoming contests, they dined alfresco in the walled garden beneath a striped open tent that the servants had erected. The table was elegantly set with a white damask tablecloth and gleaming silver. On that warm and pleasant afternoon, Becky was beginning to find Alec's flair for enjoying life contagious.

He related the local gossip that he had picked up at the club, and then they discussed a few practicalities. "Yes, the servants are a little scandalized, I fear, but don't worry about them," he confided. "They're loyal, and they're used to my 'shenanigans.' I've told them they are not to allow anyone to see you or to know that you are here." He took a sip of chilled white wine. "I gave them the excuse that I don't want Robert finding out I've brought my 'mistress' to the villa."

"Ah, very clever."

"By the way, I didn't tell the staff your real name—just in case any of them should spread gossip. I'm not taking any chances."

"Oh? What is my name to be?"

"Abby."

"Abby?"

He shrugged. "It's the first thing that popped into mind. From Aboukir, your middle name."

"Do I have a last name?" she asked with a wry smile as she plucked a grape from the bunch.

He blushed slightly and looked away. "Lawrence," he mumbled.

"Really?" She grinned, recalling that he had told her Preston-Lawrence was his real father's last name, the actor. "Miss Abby Lawrence, eh? Pleased to meet you."

He gave her a sardonic look.

"So, how long might it take you to win five thousand pounds?"

"Not long, I hope. Within a fortnight or so, if all goes well."

"Amazing." She could see how one could become addicted to such quick and easy profits. "Do you play tonight?"

"No," he replied with a sensuous note in his murmur. "Not tonight."

It made her blood burn.

For a long moment they were locked in a speculative, hungry stare. Becky felt her heart skip a beat. "We'll have to find some other way to amuse ourselves, then."

"I can think of one or two."

"I'm sure you can, my lord." She sent him the subtlest of wicked smiles and then lowered her gaze, savoring a dainty spoonful of her sugary lemon ice with fresh blueberries on top. "You know, the second time, they say, doesn't hurt at all."

"That is what they say," he purred. He took a drink of wine and licked his lips.

She flinched, staring at his lovely mouth. "Alec?"

"Yes, Becky?"

"When?" she whispered.

"Just as soon as you change your mind about marrying me," he replied, returning to his study of the racing odds printed in the sporting newspaper that he had been perusing.

"But—" Her voice broke off.

"Yes?" He glanced up with a sly look of nonchalance.

Becky frowned. "It's not as if I don't want to marry you. I know I'm compromised—even more so now. But . . ."

He lifted his eyebrows. "But I'm too much of a rake and you don't think I'll ever change."

His words startled her.

"I've heard that a few times before," he explained drily.

"Actually, that wasn't what I was going to say."

"Oh, very well. I'll bite. 'But' what, Becky-love?"

"As I told you in that little church, a woman has honor, too. Look at all you've done for me. You deserve to be happy. I, more than anyone else, must insist on your happiness. It's bad enough that I've tangled you up in all this trouble. I won't also drag you into a situation that might make you unhappy for the rest of your life. You don't want to get married. You are as free as the wind, that's clear. None of this was your fault. You don't deserve to be punished for your honor."

He looked away, pursed his lips, and then scratched his cheek. "Being married to you, Becky, would hardly rate as punishment."

She blushed red, her fluttering gaze cast downward. "You're only saying that to make me feel better."

"No, I'm saying that, obviously, because I want you in my bed."

She gasped and looked up, wide-eyed.

He flashed her one of his bone-melting, rogue-from-hell smiles.

Becky narrowed her eyes at him, recovering quickly, humor half concealed behind her stern look. Well, this fine rascal took a little too much enjoyment in shocking her, didn't he? It was his favorite way of changing the subject, she had noticed.

She looked away, taking another sip of white wine. *Yes*, she thought, *time to give him back a dose of his own medicine.*

"But Lord Alec," she said in her most demure tone, "there's nowhere I would rather *be* than in your bed."

Ha, she thought, hiding a grin at his startled look.

"Unfortunately," she continued sweetly, "I cannot go there with you until I can believe you actually *want* to marry me. If that should come to pass," she continued with a smoldering gaze, "then I will embrace it as my goal—my duty—nay, my *mission* as your lover and your mate—to make you forget every other woman you have ever known."

The look in his wide blue eyes plainly said, *Good God!*

Becky toasted him with her wine, just as he had taught her to do. Alec glanced away, looking utterly confounded and decidedly aroused by her words.

He abruptly cleared his throat. "Well, ah, isn't the garden nice this time of year?"

Becky stifled a laugh and let the subject go. She trusted she had made her point, and now she knew where he stood on the matter, too. If he could be happy married to her, then she could agree to the marriage, and they could lock themselves in his chamber and not come out again for a week.

With delicious awareness tingling in the air between them, they talked idly about nothing in particular, eventually subsiding into a companionable silence that was punctuated only by the occasional shriek of a seagull in the distance and the soft luffing of the tent's striped fabric in the sea breeze.

A honeybee hovered around the voluptuous bowl of fruit that adorned the center of the table while their second bottle of white wine sweated in the cooler. Becky gazed across the garden at the full-blown roses climbing up the back of the house: bright pink blooms and dark foliage against the creamy stucco, with the soaring dome of the azure sky arcing overhead. Alec lay back in his plump-cushioned wicker chaise and closed his eyes, reposing in all his sun-god glory.

She stared at him until he lifted his sandy lashes slowly again, as though sensing her rapt attention. He slipped her a lazy, knowing smile that sent her temperature climbing.

That night they were faced with the awkward question of sleeping arrangements. The villa had five bedrooms, but Alec wanted to be near her at night for the sake of her security. He was certainly taking his self-appointed role as her bodyguard seriously.

They resigned themselves without enthusiasm to two chambers across the hallway from each other—but then, peeking into the other bedrooms, they discovered the room with the summer bed.

"Oh, I forgot about this," Alec murmured, leaning next to her in the doorway.

"What a strange contraption," Becky remarked, studying it.

A silk canopy arched over the four tall bedposts, but instead of one large mattress beneath it, the bedstead was divided into two single beds, with an empty space about a foot wide separating them. This design allowed air to circulate better between the sleepers, thus keeping them cooler during hot summer nights. She supposed it was mostly intended for married couples who had gone past the first blush of passion to practicality.

Alec and she looked at it, then at each other.

With that, their choice of sleeping quarters was made. The summer bed provided an ideal arrangement for two people who desired close contact but were resolved to withstand the temptations of the flesh. At least in theory.

That night they stayed awake into the wee hours, talking, whispering, laughing in the darkness like children allowed the delicious treat of staying overnight at a favorite friend's house. Becky told him all about Talbot Old Hall, its priest-hole, minstrel's gallery, and resident ghost. She watched him pull his shirt off over his head in the heat, ball it up, and toss it onto the chair; as Alec reclined again on his too distant half of the summer bed, she tried not to gawk too much at his beautiful body, silvered by moonlight.

Instead, she went on to tell him of her village, describing each of the eight buildings on the square and most of the leading residents; Sam, the blacksmith; the Widow Harking, who ran the dame school; Mr. Bowers, who owned the local inn; and, of course, that sly pair, Sally the red-haired tavern wench, and Daisy, the yellow-haired milkmaid.

"Well, I should very much like to meet them," he drawled.

"Alexander, behave! That's it. I'm going to sleep." She shut her eyes determinedly, but she still kept smiling.

"Good night, Becky," Alec finally murmured, reaching across the space between them to touch her hand.

"Abby," she corrected in a whisper, opening her eyes again slowly to gaze at him.

"Abby," he conceded in a lazy tone. "Are you tired?"

"Mm."

"I'm not."

"Yes, you are. Go to sleep."

"I'll try."

Lying on her side, holding hands across the empty space between them, she gazed at him, and then smiled in the indigo shadows, feeling closer to him in that moment that she had to anyone in years. "Sweet dreams, lucky," she answered softly, having dubbed him thus, for it was only fair that he should get a nickname, too.

"Don't I get a kiss good night?" he whispered.

Her smile widened. "Do you really think it wise?"

"Wise, *cherie,* was never my specialty." He withdrew his hand from hers with a light parting squeeze. "Go to sleep."

Smiling blissfully, Becky let her heavy eyelids close and tried to. She was weary, true, her senses lulled by the music of the ocean pouring in through the open windows and the wonderful security of the strong man lying near her with a sword and pistol by his side; but after a moment or two the temptation was too great.

He looked over at her in the darkness as she rose and went to him, crossing the gap between them. In the next heartbeat she was in his arms. He pulled her atop him, her loose linen shift hitched up around her knees as she knelt astride him on all fours, kissing him with wild and tender passion.

Her hair swung down around him like a dark veil to shield their budding love from the many dangers of the harsh and jaded world. Alec's hands moved up and down her back, caressing her. He coaxed her tongue into his mouth; Becky tasted him with a longing sigh. As she stroked his broad shoulders, the splendor of his velvety smooth skin beguiled her lower.

She ended their kiss, lipped his perfect nose in naughty affection, and then eased downward over his body, covering his muscular chest in kisses. He petted her head, enjoying it. She skimmed her lips dreamily along the flowing lines and ridges of his sculpted belly. God, he really was outrageously well made. Alec played with her hair, the subtle pressure of his hands willing her to go lower still.

Dared she? Her heart pounded eagerly at the bold thought of returning the luscious favor that he had given her at Knight House. She wanted to, but she didn't know how. On the other hand, when she considered how insistent he had been about making her surrender to him, she knew she had to try. She had to show him that it was safe for him to lie back with her and simply receive pleasure, too.

His stomach was flat, but as she flirted with his navel, there was no escaping the demanding presence of his big, burgeoning hardness. It pulsated beside her cheek— and then throbbed beneath her hand. She heard Alec's breathing deepen as she caressed it through his thin, linen drawers.

Despite some kittenish fumbling, she managed to untie the drawstring. She reached tenderly inside and took him in her hand.

He let out a soft gasp. She felt him surge from hard and hot to steel rigidity as she wrapped her hand around his thick shaft. Then she placed a few exploratory kisses on the round, smooth head of his cock. The response that this elicited inflamed her. She suddenly knew what he wanted; she was all too happy to give. Parting her lips, she took him into her mouth.

His low, scratchy moan of bliss confirmed her theory about what to do; from there, her education quickened apace. After a few minutes of her kissing and fondling him, Alec moved up against the headboard and brushed her hair aside, avidly watching her pleasure him. "Ah, that's good, Becky. That's so good, little girl."

He stopped her only long enough to undress her, pulling her sheer white chemise off over her head. She went back at once to sucking his cock, quite obsessed with it.

"Come here," he ordered in a husky voice.

She licked her lips and let him tug her back up to him. He lay down flat on the bed again, turned her body until she was facing toward his feet, her knees planted in the mattress astraddle his face. His warm, smooth hands caressed the naked curves of her buttocks, then he guided her mouth back down again to his waiting erection.

"Hmm," Becky murmured, grasping him from this new angle.

She had barely begun paying homage once more to his wonderful body when his wet hungry kiss between her thighs made her nigh choke on the big, straining cock in her mouth; she then grasped the point of this exotic arrangement. Her eyes closed tightly. *Ahh.* Wicked, wonderful man.

He curled his hands around her thighs, gently pulling her deeper into his mouth. Becky could hardly bear it. How was she supposed to concentrate on what she had set out to do? She tried to protest, but he stopped her. This was something she had wanted to do just for him, but Alec wouldn't have it. No, he was Alec Knight, she thought with a certain degree of fond amusement, and no doubt deemed it a point of honor that any woman who got into bed with him must orgasm explosively. Preferably more than once.

And so they pleasured each other simultaneously.

Becky was in awe of his control. His skillful ministrations left her barely coherent, forgetful of what she had traveled south to do in the first place. Her hand clung weakly to his throbbing member, but her eyes were closed, her attention helplessly captivated by the way his clever tongue laved her. So generous.

Already aroused from exploring him, it only took minutes for Alec to bring her to climax. Becky whimpered and shuddered with release, arching her back. She could feel Alec's delight in her surrender. At last, the lusty fog in her head cleared a bit. She withdrew, moving back to her original position. Alec kissed her cheek and gave her a sultry, knowing smile.

He set her gently on the floor and moved to the edge

of the bed, offering himself to her, his muscled legs sprawled loosely. Becky lowered herself onto her knees between them.

Cupping her nape, Alec leaned down and kissed her softly before she resumed.

"You are so beautiful," he whispered, staring into her eyes. "You are the most beautiful person I have ever seen."

"Oh, Alec." She slipped her arm around his lean waist and tilted her head back to kiss him again, but their heaving passion soon overshadowed the moment's tenderness.

She curled her hand around him once more; and then she took him deeply into her mouth, nearly into her throat, stroking him with both hands and giving him her all. It did not take long to realize that her lover's awesome self-control also made it difficult for him to let go. Cast as audience instead of performer, the actor's son seemed to find his role as recipient a bit more threatening. She was beginning to understand that giving pleasure was a means of wielding power.

Becky moved slowly, patiently, not rushing him; she wanted his surrender, and she was willing to work for it.

"You're such an angel," he moaned, sinking back a bit to brace one hand behind him on the bed. The other remained tangled in her hair. She redoubled her efforts, feeling his control begin to fray at last. His lean hips bucked as his grip tightened ruthlessly on her hair. "Oh, Becky, don't stop, I'm going to come."

Her reply was little more than a lusty gurgle full of hearty assent. Her lips were chafed, her jaw aching. He was panting, thrusting into her mouth, the hot steel of him battering her tongue.

He tried to withdraw at the last second, but she held him fast, clasping his hip possessively. With a harsh groan, fairly a scream of pleasure, he suddenly spilled his seed down her throat, pressing desperately into her mouth. She drank it down wildly in one fiery gulp, reveling in the sharp, salty taste of him. He moaned, pulsating in her mouth again and again, though he had nothing left.

She was shaking, and so was Alec.

She felt his fingers go lax, all coiled in her tresses. He quivered violently when she finally relinquished his still-hard member with the slow lick of her aching lips.

"Oh, Becky," he panted. "That was quite a kiss good night." He fell back onto the mattress with a dazed sigh. "Un-bloody-believable."

She rose, glowing with her adoration of him. "I'd say you needed it."

He smiled, looking ravished—hair tousled, cheeks flushed. "Get over here, you."

"Who, me?" she murmured coyly as he captured her wrist and pulled her down beside him.

"Well, you have to marry me now, I'm afraid."

"Why?"

"Because, obviously, I'm going to need that for the rest of my natural life."

"Good reason," she drawled, giving him an arch look askance.

He laughed and wrapped his arms around her, locking his fingers so she couldn't escape. "Stay," he commanded, and kissed her on the nose.

She gazed tenderly at him for a long moment. "I could never imagine doing these things with anyone else but you, Alec."

"Then don't."

She kissed his cheek. Alec fairly purred with contentment as he held her, drowsing. Ten minutes passed, perhaps fifteen.

She was still mulling over his words and didn't realize

at first that he was already half asleep when she resumed the conversation where it had left off.

"I could promise that easily, if a similar promise were made to me, in return."

"Huh?"

"Oh, sorry, were you sleeping, darling?"

"No, what?" he mumbled, shifting a little and pulling the sheet over both of them. "What is it, sugarplum?"

She smiled at the pet name. "I just meant to say that . . . I could promise not to do these things with anyone else, ever, if somebody were to make the same sort of promise to me."

"Oh," he murmured noncommittally. "I . . . thought that's what you said." He let out a large yawn.

Becky just looked at him. Hardly the answer she had hoped for. Well, she would have to be naive to be surprised. A man did not become so expert in the erotic arts without years of practice. Aye, he had probably done this with more women than there were in all of Buckley-on-the-Heath. The realization left her a bit peeved, but even more than that, it made her wonder about the effects such intemperance might have had on his heart. Could he even love, or had he grown too jaded?

She refused to believe the latter. Still, it hurt to see that, even now, after what they had just done, he couldn't really let his guard down.

Lowering her gaze to hide her disappointment, Becky pulled away and got up, slipping her chemise back on over her head. Then she watched Alec retying the drawstring of his loose linen drawers.

"Well, good night, then," she said.

"Wait, where are you going?" He captured a handful of her shift's white muslin to detain her.

She pointed to her side of the summer bed.

"Come back, sweeting. Lie with me awhile."

After a moment's consideration, she accepted the invitation and lay down in his welcoming arms; she rested her head in the crook of his neck. He held her, stroking her hair.

They were silent for a time.

"If we did marry, Alec . . ." she whispered hesitantly at length.

"Yes?"

"*Could* you be faithful to someone like me?"

His hand stopped its gentle petting. "Someone like you? What do you mean? Someone beautiful and kind and good and extremely, ah, talented?"

"You're avoiding the question." She moved up to face him, bracing her elbow on his pillow. She propped her cheek on one hand while she drew little figures on his chest with the other. "Could you be faithful or not?"

"Well . . ." Alec eyed her uneasily. "If that sort of thing is important to you, yes. I suppose."

Her light touch stopped; he surely felt her stiffen. "How could it not be important?"

He shrugged, his tone turning even more careful. "To plenty of people, it's not. Trust me," he added under his breath. "I should know."

Well, damn. Though a bit let down, Becky felt too close to him right now to get angry at him. She knew perfectly well he was a bona fide London rakehell. At least he was listening. At least he was telling the truth, being painfully honest, not making empty promises. She took that for a sign of respect and a degree of genuine affection. It was only when he turned on the charm that she knew she had to worry.

She chose her next words carefully. "It always makes me very happy to see married couples where the people actually love each other."

"Yes, well, that's probably ideal," he conceded. "Unfortunately, some of us aren't very good at that sort of thing."

She turned and gazed at him intently. "I don't believe that of you."

He looked at her in sudden inspiration. "Is that the real reason you refused me?" he blurted out in an abrupt exclamation, as though thunderstruck. "Because you wish to marry for love?"

Becky's eyebrows lifted in startled amusement. Then she snorted. "Genius!" she exclaimed, picked up the extra pillow, and clomped him in the head with it.

He let out a loud, bold laugh and tackled her, rolling her onto her back. "You think you're smart, little miss?"

"Smarter than you."

"Is that right?"

For a second, as his lips lingered inches above hers, she thought he was going to kiss her senseless for her jolly assault, but instead he stared at her. Becky touched his face, pained to realize that until this moment, he had believed deep down that she had refused his offer of marriage because he thought she found him wanting. Her ardent ministrations this night, along with her admission of a desire to marry for love had helped to correct his mistake. She caressed his cheek gently for a moment—and then his eyes suddenly flared with mischief. Planting a kiss on her cheek, he proceeded to tickle her until she shrieked with laughter.

She fought back as well as she could, but in the end she had to flee him, scampering back to her side of the summer bed. "You are a very bad man! Stay over there!" she ordered between gasps of laughter. "I mean it. Don't follow me!"

"All right," he mumbled, his eyes sparkling as he watched her slide under the light coverlet and snuggle down into her bed. "Good night, princess."

In answer, she blew him a kiss from across the gap between them.

CHAPTER
∞ TEN ∞

*H*er eyes weren't actually violet.

They were changeable blue, with navy rims around the irises and tiny flecks of white, but the soft lavender bars like wheel-spokes fanning out from her big black pupils were what made them so unique.

Such details obsessed Alec as the days progressed. These fine distinctions seemed to hold momentous weight. He studied her with a naturalist's eye and a lover's fascination, like some rapt scientist who had discovered a never-before-beheld species.

As to the true color of her mesmerizing eyes, he had discovered this particular Becky fact one afternoon when he had plucked a sprig of sea lavender and tucked it behind her ear while she lay with her head resting on his lap, reading a highly sensational Gothic novel to him and doing all the voices.

He had tickled her chin with the flower until she smacked his hand away; then, laughing softly, he used the delicate bloom to adorn her sable hair—another rich topic for his contemplation. Thick and silky, curly in humidity, fast-growing; perfectly matched to her lovely eyebrows. Her long lashes, on the other hand, were a shade blacker. He could picture her precisely with his eyes closed. He could hear her laughter in his dreams.

Something strange was happening to the captain of all London rakehells.

The next fortnight represented, in point of fact, the most time Alec had ever spent with one female. He had often liked to say in his flip manner that he fell in and out of love as frequently as Beau Brummel changed his linen. But his passing fancies had never felt like this.

There was something very solid about the girl, though she stood only five-foot-something and weighed less than nine stone. He had never found so much to admire, so many treasures of character all dwelling within one woman: kindness, courage, and common sense; humor, cleverness, warmth, lush sensuality. He had even grown to enjoy her occasional flashes of stubbornness.

Her independent streak perplexed him; her lack of trust toward the world redoubled his desire to protect her and, above all, to be worthy of the trust she had placed in him.

Invitations for various summer social events around Brighton began arriving in a steady stream, but Alec declined most of them, too busy, he told himself, with his efforts to amass the five thousand pounds they needed for her house. But the truth was, the balls and routs and levees simply did not tempt him when he could be alone at home with his darling demoiselle.

Well, it would have been inconsiderate to leave her by herself too much, he reasoned, considering all the uncertainty she was feeling about her situation. Like him, she was not a natural loner. He took pleasure in keeping her entertained and in deepening his quest for knowledge in the field of Becky-ology.

They spent lazy, sun-drenched days together and warm, starry nights. Since Kurkov was not yet in Brighton, he deemed it safe to take her out for a change of scenery, as long as they avoided being spotted by members of the ton. There was no doubt that if Alec Knight were seen escorting a young lady, the gossip would be flying in the blink of an eye. The less the outer world knew of them, the safer she would be.

Besides, he rather liked keeping her to himself. Not in a way that would cage her, of course, but, as damned foolish as it sounded even to him, he felt as though, inside the villa and behind the high walls of the garden, Becky and he had founded their own private world.

Not even Lizzie had put him under this spell. No, Rebecca Aboukir Ward was not like anyone else he knew. One never could anticipate what bizarre little countrified opinion might come out of her mouth. She astonished him; delighted him; tickled the soft spots where, to his surprise, it turned out there were still a few chinks left in his jaded armor. He simply liked the girl and couldn't get enough of her company.

His friends had come to Brighton, but Alec hid her presence at the villa even from them. He knew they wouldn't understand. They claimed he was acting damn eccentric of late, but at least he was no longer in a "mood." No, for possibly the first time in his thirty-one years, Alec Knight was genuinely happy—unthreatened— and himself.

They went for long walks on the beach behind the villa and picnicked there as well, tossing bread crumbs to the gulls and spotting other waterbirds; a big blue kingfisher and a ghost-gray heron sleeping on one leg. One cloudless afternoon, he hired a pair of hack horses and took her riding out to look at prospects of Arundel Castle and some cliffs that overlooked the sea.

They had shared a light repast on a windy promontory that towered above the ocean and then became caught up in impassioned kisses, lying in each other's arms on the soft green turf that edged the lonely lookout point.

Each night, he went to the club or one of the few honest gaming hells and brought home his winnings to her—for which he was rewarded richly. Indeed, their amorous encounters continued almost daily, similar in adventurousness to the ones that had already occurred. The lady relished lovers' play almost as much as he did, and Alec found her nearly impossible to resist.

Sometimes, when that smoldering light came into her eyes, when her lips curved with that particular sensuous smile, when she brushed past him in sinuous invitation, seemingly so innocent, her luscious body whispered to his male senses, *"Touch me. Take me. Come."* She wanted him inside of her, but what she hungered for most of all was his love. He could see it in her beautiful eyes. She was waiting, knowing, biding her time. He fought it, he barely knew why. Somehow he held back, though he burned for her.

The night they had exchanged back-rubs had nearly been their undoing. He knew it was a bad idea, but saying no had never been his forte. One thing led to another, and soon he was in her arms, Becky writhing under him. Her body had begged for him, her pleading whispers in his ear driving him insane; Alec had been literally inches away from breaking his promise to them both, when he finally tore himself away from her by sheer dint of will and instead flung himself bodily into the cold, dark sea.

There had been a time when, cynic that he was, he would have suspected that her kisses were doled out based on how many shiny gold guineas he brought home, but no more. Not with Becky. Other women, yes, but Becky wasn't like that.

Sometimes he came back with more, sometimes less. Only twice did he return home empty-handed, but at least he wasn't in the red. Now and then at the tables he touched his fob-pocket where he kept her talisman, the little seashell; and then he remembered to quit while he was ahead, no matter how his fellow players complained.

Together Becky and he watched the sum of his winnings rise from one thousand, two thousand, three. Alec did not say so aloud, but no one was more relieved than he to see that his plan was actually working.

And so time passed, as it was wont to do, and the outer world kept turning.

One invitation that Alec quickly agreed to attend was Countess Lieven's ball. The wife of the Russian ambassador had put all of her formidable social support behind her countryman, so Kurkov was certain to be in attendance. Alec was determined to have the five thousand amassed by the night of the ball. He would approach the prince that night, he decided. Provided he could temporarily set aside his desire to run the man through, Alec intended to charm the hell out of the Russian nobleman until he had convinced Kurkov that they were all but brothers. Then he would persuade the prince to sell him Talbot Old Hall.

In the meantime, he watched the newspapers from London for any mention of the two dead Cossacks in the mews. If the law was coming after him, he wanted as much advance warning as possible, but he finally concluded that Kurkov must have kept the matter quiet somehow, considering the prince's own culpability in what had happened. No mention of the incident ever appeared in the *Times* or the *Post* or even the scandal sheets, whose authors knew everything. They were veritable Delphic oracles, those anonymous fiends; what they couldn't confirm, they concocted.

Early in the third week of their stay at Brighton (the pot stood at four thousand pounds), Mr. Walsh forwarded a letter to Alec that had arrived at Knight House.

It was from Robert, telling Alec that Bel was delivered of a healthy baby girl.

Becky came running at the sound of his gleeful whoop. "Alec, what is it?" she cried.

He told her, missing his family bitterly all of a sudden. "Mr. Walsh writes that both my sister-in-law and the babe are doing well. God, Robert must be beside himself—a daughter!"

She joined in his enthusiasm. "That's wonderful! What will they name her?"

"Lady Katherine Penelope Knight. I can't believe it," he murmured, staring into space. "A new baby. Another niece! At last, little Pippa will finally have a girl-cousin instead of all boys."

"You must be so happy for them." Becky hugged him. Reading his face, she guessed his thoughts. "Oh, my darling, don't worry, I'm sure you'll see them soon."

He returned her embrace. "I can't wait for them to meet you. My brothers and their wives—and the children. I must warn you, those little beasties will steal your heart."

"I'm sure they're not beasties, Alec."

"No, they're good," he admitted softly, smiling as he held her. And then Alec had what was possibly the most astonishing realization of his entire life. He dared not even utter it aloud—perhaps he had gone mad—but he suddenly felt it would be a fine thing to be a papa someday himself instead of merely Uncle Alec, favorite jester, patsy, and all-around climbing tree of the Knight children.

Good God, he thought with a shiver, half dread, half wild anticipation. *What has this girl done to me?*

"Is something wrong?" Becky asked, pulling back with a frown when she felt him tremble.

He had to think about the question. Slowly, it all became clear.

"No, nothing," he whispered, gazing into those magnificent eyes. Capturing her beloved face between his hands, he kissed her with sudden aching ardor. For, ready or not, scared out of his wits, Alec Knight knew he was in love.

His arm had healed, but a scar remained.

Becky had tended the wound daily, cleaning it, putting salve on it, changing bandages. She wished she could regret the fact that he would carry a scar for the rest of his life from his battle with the Cossacks in the mews, but despite herself, she took a certain satisfaction in knowing that he would bear the mark of saving her forever.

He had gone back to his usual regimen of sporting practice with the top Brighton fencing master and the young bucks' favorite local boxing coach, an ex-prizefighter. He insisted on keeping himself in top form—especially now, when her safety depended on his skill. Not that Becky was complaining about her sporting gentleman. His muscular physique was a thing of beauty to behold. The man made her womb ache.

She had had strange thoughts about him ever since the news had come the day before yesterday about his brother's infant daughter. She couldn't stop wondering what a child from the two of them would have looked like. Blue eyes. Brown hair or blond?

Ah, well. She'd probably never know.

She felt so tenuous, falling for him more deeply every day, yet still fretfully uncertain about whether their affair was really leading to anything more permanent. The more she cared about him, the greater the hurt he could inflict if he did not return her feelings. She dared not speak of them to him. She feared he was not ready; he would only run.

Instead, she found other ways to tell him how she felt. Actions spoke louder than words, anyway. Small things. Thoughtful gestures. She did not think her little kindnesses went unnoticed. Most of all, she told him with her kisses and the exuberance with which she gave herself in his arms. She knew by now that she was indeed more than just a whim to Alec; of that, there was no doubt. But actor and chameleon that he was, it was difficult to tell how much he really cared.

She didn't want to get her hopes up falsely. She already had enough troubles without adding a broken heart to it as well.

That night, she worked patiently by candlelight on a gift for the newborn child, little Lady Katherine. While Alec was out playing cards for the cause, Becky commenced knitting a pair of tiny pink booties with white ribbon trim and the baby's initials on the side. She had given great consideration to her gift. A duke's daughter with lords and ladies as uncles and aunts was sure to need nothing under the sun, but Mama had always said that a handmade gift meant more. For her part, she was happy merely to have a new project with which to occupy her hands while Alec was out gambling, for she worried so.

Till now, she had spent the nerve-racking nights, while he was out, writing up her official account of Mikhail's dark deeds that fateful night in Yorkshire. The authorities were sure to ask for it. Best to have it ready right away so they could arrest the brute all the more quickly when the time came. Thoughts of her tormentor passed away, giving place instead to those that brought a secret smile to her lips.

Alexander.

Her thoughts strayed to the wonderful times they had shared in the midst of all this uncertainty. Her knitting needles clicking, she smiled to recall the afternoon he had taught her a few simple card games. The playing cards kept blowing away, the wind making havoc of their fun. On another occasion a few nights ago, she awoke in a panic from another bad dream about the Russian pris-

oner in the gatehouse and his murder on the moors. Alec
had comforted her and let her sleep the rest of the night
in his arms.

But her favorite memory of all was the night they had
found the astronomy book on the parlor bookshelf.
They traipsed out to the beach with blankets and wine,
hunting constellations. What they found instead was
something just as silent as the stars, but even more mysterious. It had not been an occasion of wild desire nor
even one illumined by his roguish mischief. As they had
shared the warmth of their bodies, sitting huddled beneath the blanket, deciphering the orderly patterns of
the stars, she sensed the power of the bond that had
been born between them, alive, aglow. Perhaps he felt it,
too, for Alec had fallen silent by her side, his arm around
her. The rocky beach had been uncomfortable, but neither of them complained. She remembered his touch,
brushing her blowing hair out of her eyes. She remembered his hand outstretched to the heavens as he pointed
swiftly to a shooting star. It disappeared too quickly for
her to make a wish, but with Alec beside her, she could
think of nothing else to want. . . .

By the time he sauntered in that night at half past
three, Becky had fallen asleep with her knitting. Alec
leaned down, smiling, and woke her with a light kiss on
the cheek.

"Hullo, lovely."

She stirred, coming awake to find his cobalt eyes shining with sharp brilliance. He gave her a cocky little smile
and tossed down 750 pounds on the table where she had
set her yarn.

Becky looked up at him in openmouthed awe. "You
did it," she breathed. "It's done. You've won all the
money!"

"That's right," he drawled.

She was out of her chair in a heartbeat, leaping into his arms and jumping up and down. They celebrated with triumphant laughter, gleeful exuberant kisses, and French champagne—the same vintage they had drunk together that first night at the Althorpe. They had been saving it for just this occasion. The next step was for Alec to convince Mikhail to sell him Talbot Old Hall, but there was time enough to think of that in a day or two, when Countess Lieven's ball was nearer. For now, they relished his victory.

She knew how much it meant to him. He was exultant, sweeping her into a waltz right there in the parlor, sans music.

"I'll have you back at home in no time!" he had declared.

But as Becky smiled at him, she wondered . . . would the Hall still feel like home if Alec was not with her?

The next morning, Alec slept in past noon after his late night. Eager for him to get up but not having the heart to wake him from his well-earned rest, Becky decided to amuse herself with her favorite hobby and donned an apron, intent on honoring her hero with one of her prize puddings.

Bending near the kitchen fireplace, presently, with its familiar collection of spits and clockwork smoke-jacks, she prodded the breakfast cooking embers back into a worthy blaze, then put two cauldrons of water on to boil, hanging them from sturdy fire-cranes.

Straightening up again, she wiped the perspiration off her brow. The kitchen was already sweltering between the hearth fire and the usual heat of a July afternoon. She took off the sheer fichu that she had tucked into the low neckline of her borrowed morning gown and fanned herself with it a bit. Familiar with a kitchen's heat, she had already put modesty aside to a quite risqué degree,

going without stockings, petticoat, or stays. All she wore
under the pretty, simple round-gown of almond-blossom
pink muslin was a fresh chemise and a pair of sandals.

Summer sunshine warmed the big terra-cotta floor
tiles and sparkled on the copper pots hanging from the
ceiling rack. Becky took down the drying pudding cloth
hanging from a hook on the rustic oak mantel, spread it
out, and dropped it gently into the water of the larger
pot, maneuvering it with a wooden spoon so it floated at
the top.

This done, she went to the thick beech worktable in
the center of the kitchen, surveying her gathered ingredients and the array of necessary bowls and utensils that
she had assembled. Flour, sugar, butter, three eggs, a
quart of milk, a few spices, peaches, and almonds. Caster
sugar and sack wine for the sticky sweet wine sauce.

She was busily combining flour, a dash of salt, and
four spoonfuls of sugar when her sleeping prince awoke
and made his first appearance of the day.

"Well, well, how very domestic."

She looked over in surprise to find Alec leaning in the
doorway, his arms folded across his chest and a look of
amusement on his handsome face.

"Good morning!" she said brightly, delighted that her
main source of companionship—and entertainment—
had finally arrived.

He covered a mild yawn, smartly dressed to pay a casual call on England's future king later this afternoon.
Becky was a trifle jealous to know that he and his friends
were expected at Brighton Pavilion today to pay their
respects to the Regent. Alec wore a dark green coat for
the occasion, fawn pantaloons that hugged his manly
form in all the right places, and gleaming black Hessian
boots. His black cravat made him look particularly rakish; Becky kept her dreamy sigh to herself.

"What in heaven's name are you doing?" he asked, sauntering into the kitchen.

"Preparing you a special treat," she answered cheerfully as he stopped across the table from her, leaned over it and gave her a kiss, purring, "Hullo."

Gazing into each other's eyes, they exchanged a smile, then Alec pulled out the bench and sat down heavily, propping his elbow on the table. He leaned his cheek in his hand and watched her in restless silence.

"Something on your mind?" she asked.

"You're beautiful."

She eyed him with a suspicious smile. "Your breakfast is still sitting in the plate-warmer. Shall I get it for you? Coffee?"

"Nothing yet, sweet creature. Do proceed. Quite fascinating business. Cooking, you call it?" He dipped his finger into the caster sugar, touching it to his tongue. When he reached to do it again, she tapped his arm.

"Stop that," she scolded playfully. "Most unmannerly."

"What?" he protested with his big, blue eyes widening.

"Don't give me that look. Go and see if the water's boiling yet."

"Yes, ma'am," he muttered. He heaved himself up from the bench, glancing at her with a naughty sparkle in his eyes as he went over to inspect the cauldron. Lord, the kitchen suddenly felt even hotter. She sent him a sultry smile, acutely aware of him, and then exchanged her wooden spoon for a paring knife. She began cutting the peaches into bite-sized morsels.

"I would say this looks like a simmer rather than a boil to me, but what the devil do I know?"

"Thanks. I'll take your word for it."

He drifted up behind her and slipped his hands

around her waist. "Is this *supposed* to be making me hot for you?" he asked by her ear.

"Alexander, behave," she whispered breathlessly, though she didn't mean it at all. She felt his hardness stirring against the curve of her backside.

"I have been behaving," he murmured plaintively, his touch ever so coaxing. "I've been good. You know I have." His hands traveled down to her hips, and she realized his kneading fingers clutched at her skirts, lifting them slowly. "I'm so hungry for you, Becky—"

"Here. Eat this." Trembling, she reached up slowly over her shoulder and fed him a morsel of juicy peach.

He accepted it, capturing her fingertips in his mouth as well. He let her skirts fall again on one side as he reached for a piece of peach to feed to her. He rubbed it against her lips, teasing her with it, before he let her have it. Becky closed her eyes and savored it, summery sweetness dripping down her throat.

When she opened her eyes again, aching with desire for him, Alec was staring at her, looking transfixed and a little in pain. He reached for her again, but she stopped him gently, laying her fingertip on the center of his lovely chest.

"Patience."

"You know I have none." He let out a large sigh as he got his libido back under control. "Well, what's next, then?" He peered into the bowl of egg whites as she picked it up, wrinkling his nose. "My pugilism coach makes me drink this stuff. Swears by it."

"Now, we simply beat the eggs . . . and combine the wet ingredients with the dry." She efficiently whisked the eggs to an airy lightness, added milk, then stirred in the flour mixture, and finally added a few drops of rose water. The result was a nice smooth batter. As she dumped the almonds and fruit into the mixture, Alec nimbly grabbed a piece of peach from the lot, but instead of popping it into his lovely mouth, he pressed it against her neck, shocking her.

As she gasped, her work interrupted, he bent his head and licked the juice that rolled down the curve of her neck. "Mmm, God, Becky. You have no idea how good you taste," he murmured with a low groan.

"Alec . . ."

"Just kiss me once before I lose my mind," he whispered, taking her face between his hands. She did, opening her mouth in welcome to his tongue's ardent incursion. He pressed her back against the table, the length of his muscled body hot and eager against her. His peach-flavored kiss intoxicated her, but at last she managed to tear herself away, holding him weakly at arm's length.

"Let me get this boiling and then we can play."

"Forget the damned pudding."

"But I made it for you," she said softly, a little wounded.

Her small pout shook him out of passion's trance enough to remember his manners. "You really know exactly how to melt me, don't you? Those eyes . . . Well, go on, then. There's something I have to talk to you about."

"What is it?"

He nodded toward her cooking. "Finish up first."

She withdrew from his embrace with a curious glance. "I only need a moment."

Alec looked on in silence as she returned to check the cauldron, intrigued by his cryptic words. The water was bubbling along at a rolling boil. She fished the now heated pudding cloth out of the water with her wooden spoon, let the excess water drip from it, then brought it over to the table and laid it flat, sprinkling it generously with flour. She spread the prepared pudding cloth into a large bowl and then carefully poured the batter into it. Gathering up all the corners and edges of the pudding cloth, she tied them into a loose sack, securing the top with a length of kitchen string.

"In you go," she said to her creation, lowering the sack gingerly into the boiling cauldron. She put the lid on it with a small gap to let the excess steam escape. "Now then, my dear man." Turning back to him, she walked toward him slowly, enjoying his smoldering stare, which traveled over her. She took off her flour-streaked apron, wiped off her hands, and then coyly turned over the kitchen hourglass. "I'm all yours. What did you want to discuss?"

"You," he purred, drawing her into his arms. Kissing her hungrily, he lifted her up onto the edge of the big beech worktable with a playful growl. Not far away sprawled the mess she had made with her cooking, but Becky didn't care. She gave herself up to the splendid thrill of Alec kissing her senseless.

With one arm slung around his neck, the other braced behind her, she reclined partly, with him leaning over her, his compact hips between her thighs.

"What about me?" she panted as he tore his mouth away from hers several minutes later.

"Becky, I want you—"

"Oh, Alec, I want you, too," she breathed with a lusty quiver of anticipation. She leaned forward eagerly to kiss him again, but he stopped her.

"You didn't let me finish. I want you," he repeated, taking a deep breath, "to marry me."

Becky blinked, taken entirely off guard. Then her heart began pounding impossibly fast. "Pardon?"

Alec pulled back and cleared his throat as Becky sat up in shock.

She let out a wild exclamation and clapped her hand over her mouth when he went down on one knee.

Round eyed and holding her breath, she watched him in pure joy-crazed incredulity as he took off the gold-

and-onyx pinky ring he always wore, the one bearing his family crest.

"Miss Ward . . ." He licked his lips nervously, offering the ring in both hands. "Will you be my wife?"

She couldn't even speak.

He attempted, gingerly, to explain himself, but immediately faltered, at a most un-Alec-like loss for words. The chiseled planes and angles of his sculpted face were taut, his eyes blue shimmering pools of emotion. She read determination there, but also vulnerability. He might have run from love a thousand times before, but this time—for her—he held his ground.

"We can be wed after your birthday, in Buckley-on-the-Heath, if you desire. That's one advantage of being a mere younger son. You can marry without all the ducal pomp and circumstance—and just so you know, we will not starve," he added hastily, his cheeks flushing. "My brother will reinstate my portion of our family's income once we're wed. I haven't written to him yet, but as I said before, family comes first for Robert. He will not impose my punishment on you, when I'm the one who made him cross. And this ring is, er, for you to wear just for now," he explained, floundering a little. "I shall get you a proper one soon. I didn't think you would want me to divert any of our winnings from buying back the house—"

"Oh, Alec," she forced out in sheer wonder, finding her voice at last. "My darling—it's perfect." She sprang off the table into his arms; he quickly stood to catch her.

Her feet did not even touch the floor as she clung to him, swiftly kissing his cheek again and again in trembling emotion. Somehow she stopped herself, taking his face between her hands. "Are you sure this is what you really want?"

"I've never been more sure of anything." He set her back gently on the table and searched her face with glowing determination in his eyes. "Becky, for the first time in my life, I feel I'm seeing clearly. I know that this is right—what we have. Everything that used to seem so important is mere tinsel to me now. You're what's important. This . . . happiness we've found. It's real. That's all I know."

Her voice failed her. As Alec gazed at her, leonine amusement crept into his shining eyes at her speechless state of distraught joy. He cupped her face. "Do you even know how wonderful you are?" he asked tenderly.

She could not answer.

"Shall I tell you? I'm not sure I even have the words. I look at you and—can barely find my tongue." He shook his head, stroking her hair slowly. "I love your eyes. Your walk, your smile, your laugh. Your frankness, your independence—God, I admire that—your courage, your spirit. I love the way you believe in yourself. I love your strength of will, and your loyalty to the ones you care about."

Can this be happening? She felt a bit dizzy.

His caressing gaze deepened as it traveled gently over her face, and then a wicked half smile tugged at one corner of his mouth. He leaned down lower and stared into her eyes with a flicker of roguery in his own. "And do you know what I especially love, Becky-girl?"

She shook her head, mute with trembling amazement.

He caressed her face with his knuckle. "The way your cheeks turn pink every time I look at you."

They did so now, much to her tender embarrassment. Lifting a hand to her cheek, she bit her lip, her heart fluttering at the things he had said.

"This is much more than a whim to me now or even a matter of honor. You do know that, don't you? You are silent," he added worriedly, searching her face.

Barely able to speak past the lump in her throat, she blinked away the threat of tears. "No one's ever said such beautiful things to me before." She lowered her head. "I—I haven't truly mattered to anyone in a very long time, Alec."

"Well, you more than matter to me."

She lifted her gaze and met his tender stare.

"Becky, you mean the world to me," he said. "If anything happened to you, I'd be destroyed."

"I feel the same for you," she whispered, grasping his forearms. She almost said she loved him, but she feared it might still be too much. He had not said those actual words, after all. Somehow, she held back.

His cobalt gaze caressed her. "You are a jewel, Becky." Leaning nearer, he kissed her forehead. "There's no one like you in the whole wide world. I've searched. I know." He pulled back and stared nakedly into her eyes. "So, will you marry me or not, girl? Put a chap out of his misery—"

"Yes," she whispered with a catch in her voice as tears overtook her. She threw her arms around his neck and hugged him hard. "There's nothing I want more in all the world."

They held each other in trembling joy, and then Alec pulled back a small space, glancing into her eyes. "Give me your hand."

She did, and he slipped his signet ring on the ring-finger of her left hand. They smiled ruefully at each other, seeing how big it was on her.

"Not to worry. I've already thought of that." He pulled one of her white silk hair ribbons out of his pocket and proceeded to thread it through the gap, weaving it carefully around and around until the ring was secured on her finger.

She stared at it, then lifted her gaze to meet his with a tremulous, beaming smile.

Alec took her face between his hands and gave her a kiss that halted time. Aye, she was sure the sand stopped falling through the hourglass.

Returning the kiss fervently, she gripped the lapels of his coat and pulled him closer, kissing her princely betrothed for all she was worth. "Make love to me, Alec," she gasped when he finally tore his mouth away. "There's no reason now why we should not."

"Yes?" he purred with a discreet inquiring smile.

"Mm." She pushed his tailcoat off his shoulders. "How much time is left on the hourglass?"

He glanced at it. "Enough." Then he loosened his cravat.

She stroked his chest, savoring the thin silk of his waistcoat under her palm. With one arm slung around his neck, the other braced behind her, she reclined partly, with Alec leaning over her, his compact hips between her thighs. "Hurry. I need you."

"I think . . . I'd rather do a little cooking first." With a devilish half smile, he pushed her down gently all the way onto her back on the table and reached for the caster sugar.

"The door's open—"

"It's all right," he whispered. "I told the servants to stay away." He sprinkled a pinch of sugar onto her chest and then licked it off with playful little flicks of his tongue.

Becky closed her eyes, writhing with needy pleasure beneath him. As he kissed her, his clever hands wandered, unfastening with smooth expertise the few copper hooks and eyes at the front closure of her bodice. His touch warm and ever so persuasive, he pulled the tiny sleeves down a bit and freed her breasts. His eyes glowed as he straightened up, staring down at them.

"I think we require . . . a pinch of cinnamon."

She laughed dazedly, putting out her tongue for a taste as he sprinkled her with sugar and cinnamon, from her throat to the valley between her breasts. Becky clutched his head as he lipped her chest, rubbed the tip of his nose in white powdery sugar with a playful growl. Then he licked her clean. She reveled in his devouring, feeling scrumptious and sticky delicious.

He lifted his head from kissing her chest, his face flushed, his mouth bee-stung from tasting her. His golden forelock, tousled from her feverish petting, hung over his smoldering eyes. He threw it back with a toss of his head, his skin gleaming in the heat.

"Now for the milk." He reached across her for the small bowl of milk that she had used in her cooking. He held it over her and spilled out the remaining droplets from it onto her breasts. His mouth swooped down upon her nipples; he suckled her with wild, urgent hunger.

She closed her eyes, transported. "Oh, Alec."

When the milk was gone, he rubbed his face in the valley between her breasts. "Becky, I need you. Let me love you, sweeting. Are you ready for me?"

I've been ready for a fortnight. She gasped aloud when he thrust his hand beneath her skirts and stroked her teeming wetness, deftly penetrating her with two fingers. Becky groaned and arched her back, reveling in his exploratory touch.

God, she had needed this—and more. She needed him.

He withdrew his hand from beneath her skirts, gazing at her in tender possessiveness. He gently slipped her sandals off, caressing her feet. "You are the sweetest, prettiest thing," he whispered. "Becky?"

"Yes?"

"I'm going to make love to you now."

"Oh, yes, Alec. Please."

He quickly unbuttoned his falls and freed himself, lifting her skirts. Breathy moans escaped them both as he slowly slid himself inside her.

He was motionless for a moment, his eyes closed, the sunlight dancing on his dusky lashes. He licked his lips, taking in the experience through every atom, as was his way. Her knees were bent, her heels resting on the table's edge.

"No pain?"

"None," she murmured dreamily.

"Good." He gripped her hips, his questing cock foraging more deeply into her body's wet welcome. She groaned, sweating in the heat; standing between her legs, he took her there on the kitchen table.

Becky gave herself without reservation.

It felt so different from the first time. None of the anxiety, the fear of the unknown. No exhaustion. No strange-feeling condom between them, but Alec's smooth, slick member, bathed in her juices. She could feel his every blissful pulsation, every quiver of muscle as he stood between her thighs; every pass, in and out, of the firm ridge around the head of his cock, where he was most sensitive.

"I love being inside you," he groaned.

"Kiss me," she whispered.

He bent over her and obeyed. She smiled as she tasted the sugar-and-cinnamon flavor on his tongue. Alec captured both her hands and pinned her down against the table, linking his fingers tenderly through hers.

A few minutes later he went suddenly still as he sometimes did when his desire threatened to run away with him. He ended the kiss, steadied himself with a slow, deep breath, and released her hands, straightening up again. Instead, he grasped her hips, not moving, simply, for a long moment, staring down at her in the midst of their beautiful joining.

His hard, steamy breathing heated her throat as he wrapped his arms around her and held her more tightly. Their pace quickened, his thrusts deepening. Becky gritted her teeth until a cry of anguished delight wrenched from her lips. Each sumptuous stroke was divine, but as Alec's lusty passion climbed, the pounding force of his loving began to bruise her spine against the hardwood table. The whole piece of furniture shook as he claimed her; a wooden bowl went jolting off the edge and fell loudly to the floor, rolling away across the clay tiles.

"Darling, wait," she gasped out, laughing at the commotion.

He waited, though impatience blazed in his blue eyes.

She sat up, wrapping her legs around him, and he was content again. "Yes," he breathed, holding her closer.

She moved with him as she balanced with one hand behind her, the other clinging to his big, hard shoulder. He kissed her, one arm hooked roguishly around her waist. He tore his mouth away with a breathless order: "Look into my eyes."

She did, holding his storm-tossed stare as he clenched his jaw, clutching her bottom. She could feel his control hanging by a thread, as was her own. "Alec."

"Yes." He dropped his head back. "Oh, God—Becky!"

They climaxed together with loud, ragged cries of release, their sweating, straining bodies entwined. She was awash in the most primal of pleasures as he filled her with his virility, flooding her womb with one massive pulsation after another. His essence mingled with her own. She heard his shaky exhalation; he rested his head dazedly atop hers for a moment.

Utterly spent, she laid back on the hard beech table and held out her arms to welcome him to her. With his only somewhat-slackened erection still nestled inside her, Alec laid his head on her chest. She wrapped her arms around his broad shoulders, hugged him tenderly, and kissed his sweaty forehead.

"You were right," she said after a moment. "The second time is even better."

"Wait until you try the third."

She let out a breathless little laugh, too sated even to open her eyes.

"You smell like cinnamon," he mumbled.

"The pudding!" she suddenly exclaimed. Whipping her head around to glance at the hourglass, she saw the time had expired. "Up, up! Get off! I have to save our pudding."

Alec released her and got out of the way, startled. She brushed down her skirts, jumped off the table, and rushed to the hearth, her open bodice flapping. She did her best to hold it closed and grabbed a towel to guard her hand from the heat. She swung the creaking fire-crane out of the hearth while Alec fastened his trousers again and tucked in his shirt.

"Ahem—excuse me—my lord?"

They both looked over toward the open door. The stout, aproned housekeeper spoke from behind the corner of the hallway to avoid any possibility of seeing things she oughtn't see.

"Er, what is it?" Alec called, quickly smoothing his tousled hair.

"Milord has a visitor," she informed him from behind the corner.

"I'll be right there—thank you."

"Yes, sir." The floorboards creaked out in the corridor as the housekeeper hurried off, no doubt scandalized.

Alec sent Becky a guarded look.

"It's sure to be Fort and the lads. I told them I would meet them at the Pavilion. They never listen." He shook his head with an irked look. "Stay out of sight till I get rid of them, would you? No need to risk them seeing you and endangering you with their carelessness. I'll be right back."

Becky gave him a wide-eyed nod, blew him a kiss, and

then refastened her bodice with a blush. "I'll just—see to the pudding."

Alec winked at her with a lingering twinkle in his eyes after their impassioned interlude. Then he took a deep breath, adjusted his clothes, and marched slowly toward the foyer.

Some men smoked opium. Others drank gin. A few—poor blighters—became ensnared in the thrill of high-stakes card play.

Alec was addicted to Becky.

And he looked forward to indulging, practicing, and nurturing his new habit daily, for the rest of his life. *I am engaged,* he thought in wonder, marveling, his heart light. His brothers would never believe it.

Successfully completing the first phase of their quest had infused him with new confidence in his own abilities. Marrying her was the right and honorable thing to do, and he was glad his stubborn lady had finally agreed to it, but it was more than that.

For the first time in his life, he felt he could make a go of a serious relationship with a woman. For the first time in his life he was ready to commit to it—but he told himself it was best not to think about it overmuch lest he lose his nerve. The idea would still take a bit of getting used to. Nevertheless, nothing could pierce his state of postcoital bliss.

He floated more than walked out to the foyer, a thoroughly satisfied man. The housekeeper stood near the bottom of the stairs and pointed up to the first-story drawing room with an uneasy look. Alec nodded and climbed the staircase.

As he strolled to the doorway, it belatedly struck him that his raucous friends were unusually quiet. When he stepped into the drawing room, he stopped in his tracks at the sight of the visitor who waited for him.

"Darling!" Lady Campion turned away from her idle study of the small framed watercolors on the wall and greeted him with a practiced smile. She held up her gloved hands coyly, presenting herself. "Surprise!"

Alec felt the blood turn to ice in his veins as the flush of lovemaking drained from his face. For a second he was utterly disoriented. And then a dangerous, churning wave of dark emotion rose within him.

What the hell was she doing here?

"Why, you rogue, aren't you happy to see me?" she asked with playful indignation, cocking her whip hand on one lean hip.

Alec lost his voice.

If, in the past, running into the baroness at social functions had caused him mild embarrassment and uncomfortable sensations of guilty distaste, the sight of her now, under the circumstances, filled him with dread. If she learned about Becky—or worse, far worse, if Becky learned about her . . .

Alec swallowed hard, realizing, like a man cornered by a hungry tigress, he must make no sudden movements or he would be shredded limb from limb. His attachment to Becky, his need for her, had engendered this horrible Achilles' heel. He must protect it. He must get Eva out of here. Pacifying her just a little, he recalled, was the swiftest way to get rid of her. Whatever happened, he must not arouse her suspicions.

Eva Campion had been unnaturally possessive over Alec from the day she first gained a measure of control over him through her gold. As many times and in as many ways as he had tried to tell her it was over between them, she just kept coming back every few months. Alec knew she would not take kindly to seeing her favorite hired stallion betrothed, of all things, to a beautiful girl so much younger and lovelier than she.

Indeed, if Eva found out about Becky, everyone in

Society would also know within the hour, including Mikhail Kurkov. As for his future bride, Alec could not bear to think what she would say if she found out the truth. Especially now. Like this. She would probably retract her acceptance of his proposal. He would lose her.

He swallowed hard, able to do nothing with Eva standing there, staring expectantly at him, but to pray that Becky obeyed his orders in wifely fashion and stayed out of sight. Damn it, he should have told her while he'd had the chance. His conscience had plagued him to confess his past arrangement with the baroness—indeed, he knew that he would have to, in time—but he was already up to his eyeballs in complications right now. It had been more than he was ready to take on.

His main reaction, however, as he looked at Eva, standing in the parlor as if she owned it—as if she owned *him*—was cold anger.

Get her out of here before she ruins everything.

He was outraged that this snake dared invade his and Becky's little private Eden, their holy ground. Lady Campion was poisonous.

Alec knew that better than most.

"To what do I owe this honor, my lady?" he asked in a wary drawl.

"Well! That's not a very nice welcome for an old friend." She glided over and presented one rouged, knife-hilt cheek for him to kiss.

Alec turned away, bristling with hostility. "Oh, so cruel darling?" she chided with a knowing smile and a hard gleam in her coal-black eyes. She tapped him lightly with her folded fan. "You know you've missed me. Why aren't you staying in Black Lion Street with your idiotic friends?"

He sent her a warning glance from under his lashes.

"Ah, in a mood again, are you? I should have known. You're so cute when you're grouchy." She pinched him playfully.

"What do you want?"

"The same thing I always want, darling. You!" she said with a bright, trilling laugh. "You're going to the Lieven ball, of course? I need an escort. You may come by to pick me up at nine."

He clenched his jaw and propped his hands on his waist, studying the carpet designs and willing himself not to throw her out bodily. "I thought you had a new— friend."

"Oh, young Jason?" She gave a worldly little wave of her fan and sighed. "No. He was just a . . . snack. You, on the other hand, my lovely Lord Alec—" She flung herself down into the deep-cushioned sofa and put her feet up on the ottoman, heels crossed. "You are a connoisseur's feast."

Arching her back with a sinuous motion, she stretched like an expensive and pampered pet cat, then smiled at him and patted the spot on the sofa beside her.

Alec shook his head in answer to her invitation, slowly folding his arms across his chest.

She frowned. "Come over here. You *owe* me."

He lifted his chin. "I paid that debt, as you'll recall."

"It's paid when *I* say it's paid, darling. Come, haven't you missed me just a little?"

Why did she talk to him as though he were a baby or a favorite lapdog? How had he borne it all those weeks when he had been, for all intents and purposes, her sex slave? But then, he thought grimly, a man could withstand quite a lot when thugs working for a low-life East End moneylender threatened to cut off his balls.

"I hear you're winning again," she remarked with a glint in her dark eyes.

He watched her, on his guard, trying to listen to the far end of the house, where he hoped to God that Becky was engrossed in the task of whatever had to be done next to her pudding. "A bit."

"Oh." Eva gave him a rouged pout. "I guess that means you don't need me anymore."

He sent her a chilly smile. "Guess not."

She got up from the sofa and sauntered toward him, folding her thin arms across her waist. "You know, I have the oddest feeling that you're up to something, Alec."

He raised an eyebrow.

"Nobody sees you, except at the tables. You play as cautiously as an old granny now, they say." She shook her head. "That's not like you. They say you always quit without giving the other players a chance to win back any of their losses."

"So, you've been checking up on me again. You know I hate that, Eva."

"It's only because I care."

He narrowed his eyes in warning. How dare she claim to care about him after the way she had used him? Now that he knew what real caring was, her imitation of it sickened him. He turned away. Facing the empty fireplace, he ignored the insipid china figurines that adorned the white mantelpiece; instead, his gaze homed in on the gaudy Poseidon cup, an oversized porcelain goblet encrusted with countless tiny seashells.

It was kept on display beneath a bell jar to protect it from dust and careless hands, for it was so delicate. So easily broken, all of those little pink seashells held on with mere glue. It had to be kept under glass, he thought, for such fragile things could not withstand the callousness of the world. . . .

He closed his eyes as a tremor moved through him. *Oh, God,* how would Becky take the news when she learned he had been the ton's most celebrated gigolo, and that everybody knew it except her? She would feel betrayed, she'd feel a fool. She would despise him. She—who had come to him a virgin.

"I've heard the most horrible rumor that you've turned into a monk," Eva announced, breaking into his thoughts. "I know it sounds impossible, but that is what they're saying!" she averred at Alec's scowling glance. "Not a single one of my lady friends has enjoyed your company in weeks, and I know you hardly ever resort to whores. So, what's afoot?"

He took a cool glance at the wall clock. "Dear me, I'm due to see the Regent in ten minutes. Sorry to cut this visit short, my lady, but I really must go."

"Not until you tell me what's going on, you rogue. You might be able to fool everyone else with your actor's instincts, but I know you far too well."

"You don't know me at all, Eva," he answered quietly. "You never have."

She tilted her head. "Have you taken a mistress?"

Alec felt his patience running razor thin. "Either way, I don't think that's any of your business."

"My business? Darling, keeping track of who's sleeping with whom is a national sport! And you—darling—well, if sex is our sport, then you are our Gentleman Jackson, reigning champion—"

"Do shut up!"

"Ah, there's that spark," she whispered, sidling up to him. "You were so cold, I feared it had been extinguished . . . perhaps from overuse." She had always loved baiting him. Especially when he was tied up. It was a familiar game. The angrier she could make him, the more aroused she got. "What's that I smell on you?" she whispered, moving around him, taking a whiff. "Smells like come, you naughty boy. Who have you been fucking?"

His tolerance snapped. He recoiled from her touch.

"Get the hell out of here! I don't want you anymore, Eva! Don't you understand that?"

"What the hell," she demanded, setting her gloved hand slowly on her hip, "has gotten into you?"

"I have," replied a voice from the doorway behind him.

Becky's voice, cool and even.

Alec flinched, and then his eyes drifted closed with a look of pain. *God, no. Why?*

Too late. He lowered his head slowly as he felt his heart crumble. . . .

CHAPTER
~ ELEVEN ~

Becky leaned in the doorway, still rosy from Alec's ravishing, and barefoot, her sandals dangling from her
hand. She had left her pudding to cool and had headed
for the bedchamber to clean herself up a bit after their
oven-hot, sugarcoated lovemaking. Tiptoeing up the
stairs outside the drawing room, mindful of Alec's warning not to let herself be seen, she had heard a trill of
sparkling feminine laughter and stopped in her tracks,
frowning over her shoulder in the direction from which
it had come. A girl who intended to marry the erstwhile
captain of all London rakehells, after all, had to be
ready for anything. *That doesn't sound like his friends,*
she had thought.

Well, then. Who was it?

Stunned by the fierce territorial instinct that flooded
her veins, she had gone to investigate. What little she
had heard of their conversation, she could make scant
sense of and dared not try, lest she leap to some very
bad, erroneous assumptions about her betrothed of less
than an hour. That was no way to start their life together. Best to let Alec explain this to her himself. What
she saw, by contrast, she liked even less.

His visitor was a slim brunette dressed in yellow.
Becky had arrived in time to see the woman hanging all
over him, though he held himself aloof from her as best
he could. She was a glamorous-looking creature a few

years older than he, and the diamond-studded bracelets she wore over her high, yellow gloves screamed obscene wealth. Her hair was short and chic, her features patrician, but her cosmetics could not hide a complexion roughened by dissipation.

The lady's coiffed head whipped around toward the doorway when Becky spoke up; now, her brown, empty eyes narrowed.

The second their gazes locked, Becky felt an instant overwhelming hostility that raised the hackles on her nape. "Won't you introduce me to our guest, my lord?" she managed to ask in a tone that passed for politeness, folding her arms across her chest. She kept her chin high.

The woman recovered her artificial smile as Alec slowly turned around.

"Oh, you naughty, naughty boy," the woman chided him in an airy tone. "So, this is what you've been hiding. Now I see why you've been trying to get rid of me ever since I walked in the door." She slanted Becky a superior look and beckoned her in. "Well, come here, girl. Let us have a look at you."

"Leave her alone, Eva," Alec growled in a low tone fraught with hellfire.

Becky, far from intimidated by this "Eva" woman, summoned up an equally false, sugary smile, and accepted the invitation, sauntering proudly into the drawing room. Her heart was pounding and she barely knew where her own brazenness came from, but she could sense Alec's seething anger and was more than willing to enter the fray on his behalf. As a gentleman, after all, there was not much he could do against a female.

"Why, she's lovely," Eva told Alec with a doting smile and little hateful sparks flying from her eyes. "Of course, you always did have an eye for beauty. Wherever did you find her, darling? The gutter?"

"Actually, it was Lord Draxinger's doorstep," Becky said sweetly, noting that Alec's fists were clenched.

"Really?" Eva nodded to Alec. "Spirit, too. Enough to give some cheek to her betters. I'm impressed."

"Leave us—Abby," Alec forced out, his face pale, his mouth taut. His murderous stare was fixed on Eva, and his use of her alias alerted Becky to the fact that this woman could be dangerous.

But if Alec thought that she would leave him alone with this harpy, he still did not know the stuff that she was made of. She was nothing if not loyal.

"Abby, is it? But of course. What a common little name." Eva let out another peal of brittle laughter that jangled like broken glass. "So, you have taken a mistress. Just as I suspected. You see? You cannot lie to me, darling. I know you too well."

"Oh, I am not his mistress, ma'am," Becky informed the lady with an angelic smile. "I am his fiancée."

"Damn it, Becky," he muttered under his breath at her bold revelation, but then horror at his own blunder flashed across his face.

"Becky?" Eva echoed. "I thought her name was Abby."

Becky glanced uneasily at Alec, realizing this woman must have truly rattled him for him to have made such a slip.

"Her name is none of your concern," he informed her, taking a menacing step toward the lady. "Go, Eva. You are on thin ice."

"Isn't the Regent waiting for you? Why don't you run along and let little Precious and I have a nice long chat about all of your exciting skills." She turned to Becky with a *tsk tsk* full of hollow sympathy. "Poor little thing. Is that what he told you—that he'd marry you? For shame, Alec, you heartless cad! This is a new low even for you."

"She's telling the truth, Eva," he replied darkly. "Would you like an invitation to the wedding?"

Eva stared at him for a long moment. Smug as she was, she looked seriously shaken by his announcement. "Well!" she said at last, choking on her words a bit. "I certainly hope she knows what she's getting into. What kind of slut you really are."

At that, Becky reached for the long wooden pole used for opening and shutting the blinds on the high, arched windows, visions of candlesnuffers dancing in her head, but Alec saw her fingers graze it and shook his head sternly at her. She lowered her hand again with a scowl.

"I hope at the very least that you've told her about us," Eva taunted him. "Or do you prefer that she find out from Society's gossips?"

Becky glanced at Alec in question, though she was hardly inclined to believe a word out of that harpy's painted mouth. He met her gaze at last. His expression was thoroughly remote; his eyes were the blue of storm-tossed seas. "Excuse us, please. Wait for me upstairs."

She was taken aback by his request. "You want *me* to leave?"

He nodded, then jerked his head toward the door. "Go."

She just stood there, staring at him in embarrassed confusion. "Why should I be the one to go? Tell *her* to leave—"

"Damn it, just do as I say for once!" he yelled at her so loudly that she jumped, her eyes widening in bewilderment.

"Oh, trouble in paradise, darlings?"

When Becky lingered a moment longer, angry, embarrassed by his outburst at her, and loath to abandon the field to a woman who was either an enemy, a very formidable rival, or both, Eva seized the opportunity to stick Alec with another verbal dagger. "Ask him how he paid back Mr. Dunmire, precious. Then you'll see why I call him a slut. Because he is one—and damned good at it."

"You bitch," he spat.

"Alec?" Becky whispered.

He turned to her. "What are you still doing here?"

His baleful glower and Eva's bright burst of laughter combined to unnerve her. Becky looked from one to the other, feeling unsure and outnumbered all of a sudden. These two might be well-matched as foes—or as something else that she didn't want to think about—but it was obvious that she was in deep over her head.

Still taken aback by his harsh tone, she stared at him for a second in wounded reproach, then pivoted and left the room on legs that shook beneath her.

Distraught as he was over the question of how much Becky had heard, Alec could not believe he had slipped and used her real name in front of Eva. He was sickened by his blunder, allowing Eva to get to him.

This was no time to start making careless mistakes. The potential threat in his misstep now made it necessary for him to take some harsh, desperate, and possibly very ugly measures to repair the damage and ensure Becky's safety.

Eva watched her rush out of the room, then turned to him with a look of condescending boredom. "You can't be serious."

He just looked at her, still deciding how far he was willing to go to protect his future bride.

"You truly mean to marry her?"

Certainly, he was prepared to lie.

"It's unavoidable," he said. Because he was a gentleman, and because she had saved his neck once, he gave the baroness one last chance to back away from danger unscathed. He made one last effort at diplomacy, though deep down he knew from experience that brute force was all she understood.

"Is she breeding?" she murmured suddenly. "Ah, so, that's why you've been so assiduous in your efforts at the tables." She tapped her folded fan thoughtfully against her chin. "You wanted to play, and now you must pay. Is that it?"

"I'm afraid so."

"Oh, it's too rich. Imagine! The captain of all London rakehells, to be a papa! And now you need money, don't you, darling?" She moved closer, fingering the lapel of his coat. "How much? Maybe I can help."

"I don't want your help, Eva." He grasped her wrist and plucked her hand off him. "All I want is your silence on the matter."

"Why?"

"Well . . . because the young lady has a number of very protective menfolk in her family who will come after me if they find out I bedded her well before the ring was on her finger. It would be most inconvenient to have to kill them."

Her painted lips quirked in a smile. "Yes, one ought not to kill one's in-laws, as much as one might like to."

"Exactly." He set his revulsion aside to lift her gloved hand to his lips, then kissed it. "I knew you'd understand."

Eva looked slightly mollified, but she had never been one to let opportunity pass her by. "Not so fast, my stallion." She reached down boldly between his legs and cupped him through his clothes. "If you want my silence, it'll cost you." She caressed his cock. "God, I've missed you in my bed."

Staring at her in taut anger, Alec tried to tolerate it, but he could not—not after today and the sublime lovemaking he had shared with Becky. His smooth mask of manipulation slipped as he broke away from her.

"God, you disgust me," he ground out, turning his back to her as his heart pounded. He didn't think he could get hard for her even if he wanted to. "I feel nothing for you but revulsion."

He sensed her anger leap and heard it in her voice. "Strange, you found me quite attractive when you needed someone to pay off your debts. Then again, I knew you were only using me, you whore. Well, then, it seems all bets are off. What is her name, anyway, Becky or Abby?"

When Alec turned to her, his only answer was a hand around her throat as he shoved her hard against the wall. "Her name is none of your concern," he whispered ferociously, holding her pinned there.

Real fear flooded Eva's eyes as she dangled upon her toes, grasping at his hand while he squeezed just enough to show her how easily he could cut off her air.

"You're—mad!" she gasped out.

"No. Quite the contrary. The game has changed, Eva," he said, "and this time I make the rules. Do you understand?"

She choked, her face turning a fashionable shade of purplish scarlet.

"I tried to reason with you, but you always have to play your little games," he said. "You may not value her life or mine, but what of your own?"

"Put—me—down!"

"Listen carefully. You never saw her. You're good at keeping secrets. You've got plenty of them yourself. If you tell anyone you saw her here—if you breathe a word about that girl or the two of us to any living soul—I swear I will hunt you down and kill you, Eva," he said slowly. "No jest. I know where you go. I know where you live. I still have a key to your town house, as you'll recall. If you mention her presence here to anyone, I will come after you and cut your throat. And I won't think twice about it."

She fought him, trying to kick at him.

He was impervious.

"Let me go! You're—bluffing. What of your fine honor?"

"She means more to me than honor."

"You'd hang—for murder!"

"If anything happened to her, I would welcome the gallows. Don't try me, Eva. Not unless you want to die."

It was difficult to tell beneath the thick white rice-powder that coated her skin, but the red in her face was giving way now to purplish blue. She clawed at his wrist like a feral cat.

Alec tightened his grip ever so slightly. "You really don't seem to be getting the message. Perhaps I should just squeeze a bit harder, kill you now, and dump your body in the sea?"

"No! No!" she finally choked out, struggling to shake her head negatively. "I won't—tell—anyone!"

"Good. You see?" He dropped her. She slumped against the wall, protecting her reddened throat with both hands. "That wasn't so difficult."

She scanned his face with the most genuine look of fear that he had ever seen in her eyes.

"Get out," he finished in an icy tone.

She fled, slipping past him and darting to the door. Without another word she was gone.

Alec cracked his knuckles. Unpleasant that, but he trusted he had made his point.

He raked his hands slowly through his hair, a bit stunned that he had done it, but refusing to wonder how threatening to murder a woman corresponded with chivalry. But he was past such nicety of feeling. He'd make a deal with the Devil himself to keep Becky safe.

Taking a deep breath, he struggled to calm the beastly rage in his breast, then stalked out of the room where the despised scent of Eva's French perfume still lingered.

Becky had heard the whole thing, leaning in the deep shadows of midday with her back to the wall of the corridor, her arms folded across her chest. She had seen Eva rush out, looking shaken, and now Alec prowled out, also going past without noticing her there.

She marveled to see that he immediately headed for the exit as well. It seemed he had no intention of seeking her out to explain what in blazes had just happened in there. "Unavoidable?" she flung out when he reached the top of the stairs. "Our marriage is unavoidable? That's what you said."

He stopped, stiffening. He turned around slowly, the look in his eyes so painfully guarded, all those steely defenses locked back into place. "You know I had to say that."

Becky pushed away from the wall and approached cautiously. "Would you really murder her in cold blood?"

He considered the question for a moment, then shook his head slowly. "I don't know. Possibly. The important thing is that she believes I would. If you'll excuse me, I have to go. The Regent is expecting me."

Becky followed doggedly but kept a safe distance. "Are you quite all right, Alec?"

"Fine. You?" he clipped out like an automaton.

"I'm not fine," she informed him. "I'm still trying to figure out if you wanted me out of there simply to protect me or to stop me from finding out whatever it is that you've been hiding from me."

Reaching the foyer, he took his black top hat from the wall-hook and lifted his walking stick from the corner stand, scrupulously avoiding her gaze. She was only a few steps behind him.

"You can't ignore me, Alec. We need to talk about this. Who was she, and who is that man she mentioned, Mr. Dunmire?"

He put his hat on and walked past her to the door. "I have to go." His voice was devoid of emotion.

"Nonsense, this is more important." She reached for his arm, but he pulled away roughly.

"Don't touch me. Just—let me go."

"Alec," she pleaded, though she obediently released him. "Can't you even look at me?"

When he turned and stared at her for a second, Becky marveled at the tortured look in his eyes. "Alec," she murmured, searching his face. She touched his arm; he brushed her off.

"It would be folly to keep the Regent waiting." Faltering, he gave her a stiff bow and retreated.

"Alec?" She followed him again. "Alec, don't you dare leave!"

Becky gasped at the door's slam: He was gone.

His stomach was in knots, but Alec strove to put the incident aside for the moment and tried to focus on the company at hand. Drax had already asked him what was the matter, and Fort was regarding him with worry. Alec offered nothing. His heart, his hopes, were crushed. If Becky hadn't figured it out yet, innocent as she was, she soon would. The girl was no fool.

Perhaps it would have been better if he had just let Dunmire's thugs kill him a year and a half ago, when he had been unable to pay back the loan. Instead, he had proved himself the Hawkscliffe Harlot's son and sold himself for gold to a woman he had come to despise.

A sense of doom had settled over him. His arrangement with the baroness had cost him Lizzie, and now he knew it would cost him Becky, too. Yet this fresh wound was somehow worse than all the ones before. Even worse than the ancient wound of losing his mother. Worse than losing Lizzie's blind devotion. He had never known love, but with Becky, he had come close.

It was no use.

Well, he thought, lacerating himself with his own black humor, that had certainly been the shortest-lived betrothal in the world. Sweet while it lasted. He dreaded the thought of going back to the house. Again he strove to put it all out of his mind. Amid the noise of pounding hammers and the rough, busy zigzag of handsaws, the party of gentlemen marveled at the metamorphosis that Mr. Nash's army of carpenters and craftsmen were steadily working over the Regent's Marine Pavilion.

They had paid their respects to His Royal Highness and had been warmly received; the corpulent Regent, so dashing in younger days, still had a soft spot in his heart for the band of handsome young rogues who still lived the Don Juan fantasy that had eluded him with the passage of years. Their audience with the future king was brief, however.

Poor royal George was harried by the inescapable, everyday matters of state—what little of it, anyway, that his ministers entrusted to him. He bid the young men to have a look around the Pavilion to observe his famed architect's magic, and so they did just that.

With the brim of his top hat shading his eyes from the full sunshine, Alec sauntered around the grounds with his friends and a few other hangers-on. He kept to the back of their party, distracted, saying little in response to his friends' exclamations of surprise at the whimsical construction.

The building really was astonishing. The neoclassical mansion by Henry Holland was being steadily transformed into an exotic Oriental palace. The domed Roman portico still stood in the front center, dignified as Tacitus, but now it was flanked on both sides by shocking minarets. Even Alec, for all his imagination, could not decide if this *thing* the Regent was building would be a delight in the end or a monstrosity. At the moment, he frankly didn't give a damn.

If there was one bright spot in the depths of his despondency, it was that he had managed to learn the fate of the real Rose of Indra. That had been his true reason for coming here in the first place. Before disaster had struck, he had thought it would make a splendid wedding gift for his bride.

Alec had asked the Regent privately if he had ever heard anything about the Talbot jewel. To his fascination, His Royal Highness, with a boyish sparkle in his eyes, craftily revealed that he not only knew of the famous ruby: He owned it.

"I bought it, oh, thirty years ago from old Lord Talbot, lately deceased," the obese "Prinny" had confided to him, wheezing with exertion as they promenaded down the garish pink Long Gallery. "I was going to present it to a, er, lady friend, but, you see, we had a falling out, so I kept it for my own collection. Why do you ask, dear boy?"

Alec had been evasive, but that bit of information was well worth tucking away in the back of his mind.

"I hear you are winning again, by the by. Will you be entering the annual whist tournament?" the Regent added with a knowing look askance.

Alec had forced a rueful smile, strolling beside him with his hands clasped behind his back. "I fear not, sire. Too rich for my blood. The entry fee this year is, what, ten thousand pounds?"

"Your friend Draxinger tells me he has bought in."

"That's because Parthenia Westland asked him to play," Alec murmured confidentially. "We are to pretend, however, that my Lord Draxinger has no particular attachment to that lady whatsoever."

"Ah, I see." Prinny looked pleased at being included in the Society gossip.

"Do you plan to join in the game, sire?"

"Indubitably. Pity it's only whist, though. Dreadfully dull. Give me faro, hazard. "

Alec had laughed politely at the Regent's eager mention of the games that had been his own nemesis.

At present, his attention ambled back to the foreman explaining the workmen's various projects. "Over there, my lords can see the kitchens, which are complete. Here we're building the banqueting hall, and on the other end they're working on the music room." The foreman's voice trailed off as something in the distance caught his eye.

Furrowing his brow, Alec turned and followed his glance. At once his eyes narrowed and he felt a sudden chill in the warm afternoon. A black traveling chariot trimmed in silver was wheeling around the crescent-shaped road that banded the Pavilion's front garden. It was drawn by six black horses with white plumes on their heads and surrounded by an escort of mounted Cossack guards in full regalia.

Kurkov.

So, the reprieve was over. Their enemy had finally come, arriving right on schedule for the Lieven ball tomorrow night. Making a damned showy entrance, at that. Alec's heart began to pound fiercely.

Becky.

He had to go to her. Warn her. Make sure she stayed out of sight. He did not know how he would face her, but that mattered less than his overwhelming need to keep her safe.

He did not even try to explain himself to his friends, but clipped out a curt farewell and excused himself abruptly, striding off across the sculpted grounds.

"Alec?" Fort called.

"Knight, where are you going?" Rush demanded.

He didn't answer; he didn't even look back.

Jumping up into his hired phaeton, he urged the pair of cherry bays into motion; a moment later the light, fast carriage went barreling down the street, the horses' hooves clattering over the cobblestones. He knew his hasty exit would seem entirely bizarre to his companions, but there would be time for apologies later. It was a grim enough matter to ponder what Becky would have to say to him when he walked through that door.

Becky had *nothing* to say to him.

No, Alec was the one who had blasted well better start talking, so far as she was concerned, and an apology for the callous way he had walked out earlier was only the start of what she wanted to hear.

Before all of this had happened, she had meant to continue on with her day as usual. Wash up in the kitchen. Make the sauce for the pudding. Work some more on her knitting for the babe. But after that conflagration, she did none of this.

Moments after his desertion, she had walked up to their bedchamber, hurt and dazed, and sat down on a chair in a state of astonishment.

She couldn't believe that he had *left* in the middle of the crisis between them, more concerned, apparently, with keeping up appearances before the Regent than mending the huge tear in their hours-old betrothal. She knew the supposed urgency of his visit to the Pavilion was just an excuse.

He had shut her out.

Becky clenched her jaw and fumed, glaring at the summer bed, twisting his signet ring angrily on her finger, half tempted to take it off, but that seemed too harsh, too definite a rejection. She did not want an end to their affection, but if he did not tell her what this deep dark secret of his was, then she was going to have to reconsider marrying him at all.

Whoever Mr. Dunmire was, whatever Lady Campion had meant by her tirade, lacking Alec's explanation, her mind conjured up all sorts of ominous possibilities that she assured herself were probably worse than the truth. He was Alec, after all. He was a wonderful person and she loved him. How bad could it be?

But in spite of herself, the gnawing fear that had set in shook her faith to its foundations. Had she not told him *her* entire story weeks ago, when they had sat together in that little church? She had taken the risk of trusting him, so why couldn't he do the same? It hurt to think that he had been deliberately keeping secrets from her all this time. As much as he had urged her again and again to trust him at the start of their alliance, now she was beginning to wonder if maybe she shouldn't have.

All she knew for certain was that she did *not* like being kept in the dark.

Listening constantly for the sound of his return, she fought not to let her fears run away with her and ordered herself again to await his explanation.

At last, she heard his carriage come clattering back down the lane. A few minutes later, Alec came into the room.

She looked at him coolly over her steepled fingers, her elbows resting on the chair's arms, her legs crossed. She held him in an unblinking stare. With a subtle blanch, he dropped his gaze and ventured cautiously into the room, taking off his jacket.

"I'm back."

"So I see."

He glanced over guardedly at her cool tone, putting his coat down on the bed. He kept a safe distance and leaned against one of the bedposts a few feet away. He folded his arms across his chest. As he studied the carpet, she could almost see him casting about for any neutral topic. She offered nothing, but with considerable satisfaction let the villain squirm.

From beneath his dusky lashes, Alec's searching gaze was hopeful, ginger, conciliatory; but the trace of stubbornness that hardened the angles of his jaw suggested he was still unprepared to explain himself.

We'll just see about that.

"Kurkov's come to town," he announced, treading carefully. "You're going to have to be mindful again about staying out of sight."

"Fine."

He licked his lips and dropped his chin, his forelock falling into his eyes. "How much did you hear?"

"Not enough to make sense of it."

The scoundrel had the nerve to look relieved. He ventured forward and went down on one knee before her chair, laying his hand on her forearm. "Don't let her ruin what we have, Becky. Please. She has no hold over me. She had no right to come here. You're everything to me—"

"Charm won't work this time, Alec." She withdrew her wrist from his light grasp and folded her arms across her middle. "I want answers. Real ones."

He stiffened, rose, and turned away, pacing over to the window. Resting his hands on the sill, he gazed unseeingly at the sunny cobbled street below. "What happened between Eva and me is a closed chapter of my life, Becky. One I wish neither to return to nor discuss."

She fixed him in a quelling stare, tamping down frustration. Sometimes he was the most magnificent warrior she had ever seen, the dreamiest lover she could imagine; and then there were moments like this, when he shut her out so completely. "Alec, why don't you just tell me what it is and get it over with?"

Turning from the window, he narrowed his eyes in agitation. "If you simply would have listened to me and stayed away as I had asked, all of this could have been avoided."

"So, it's my fault?" she exclaimed, shooting to her feet. "You said it was your friends who had come calling, but when I walked past, instead I heard you talking to a woman! What was I supposed to think?"

"Oh, so that's why you jeopardized everything?" He leaned his hips back against the windowsill, his arms still folded across his chest. "For a bout of female jealousy?"

Her jaw dropped. "You are unbelievable!" She took a step toward him. "You are not going to manipulate me, Alec. Stop trying to twist everything around as if I've done something wrong, just so you don't have to tell me what's really going on!"

He fell silent. He dropped his gaze, but his roiling scowl made her wonder if he even realized what he had been doing. After a second he turned back to the window and stared out of it, stubbornness solidifying before her very eyes. "Eva's a wicked person, and I've been wicked, too, at times. But I've left it behind me, I'm not going to crawl, and you're just going to have to accept my apology if you want us to be together."

Becky stared at him in astonishment, then shook her head and stalked out of the room, banging the door shut behind her.

What a miserable state of affairs.

By some miracle, he had been spared. Becky had not heard enough specifics to piece the sordid tale together—which left Alec in the untenable position of having to tell her the whole story himself. He couldn't do it. He was too ashamed. Afraid he'd lose her if she knew. Gambler though he was, what they'd found together was too precious to risk.

Unfortunately, over the next day and a half he began to see that he ran an equal risk of losing her if he did *not* speak up, go to her, spill his guts. He was not even sure if they were still engaged or not, and frankly was afraid to ask.

With every passing hour that he deliberated over what to do, keeping his distance, his frustrated thoughts churning in circular motion—*yes, no, tell her, keep your mouth shut*—he could feel their magic slipping through his fingers.

She had obviously made up her mind not to ask him for explanations anymore. Nor did she utter another word of reproach—she didn't need to. Her silent treatment said it all. Obviously she had no intention of budging from her position, despite his vague hope that she might realize it was too awful to discuss and let it go. Her tenacious resolve to know the full truth was palpable in the air. It filled the house. Through walls and stairs and ceilings, he could feel her waiting, waiting for him to come to her, open his heart and speak his piece. But, God, what was he going to say? How could he even find the words? And even if she was miraculously willing to forgive him, Alec was not sure she should.

With every hour that he refused to confess, she grew more distant, increasingly withdrawn. He despaired, damned if he did and damned if he didn't. The only thing that he *could* do was brace for the loss as best he could by pulling back from Becky, in return.

In the final hours leading up to the Lieven ball, they lived like strangers under the same roof. It was awful. Soon, if all went according to plan, he would hand over the deed to her precious Talbot Old Hall, maybe within a few days, and then what? he wondered, brooding as he finished dressing for the ball. It would be easy for her to get rid of him once he had fulfilled his oath to help her. At last, they would be . . . even.

They could go their separate ways without remorse. The thought darkened his mood even further.

Before long Alec was sauntering through the crowded ballroom with Fort and Draxinger in tow. The fashionable four were only three tonight: Rushford had cried off with a headache that still persisted from last night's overindulgence in drink.

Hundreds of winking candles glittered in the grand chandeliers inside the large and commodious assembly rooms where Countess Lieven, wife of the Russian ambassador and leading hostess of the ton, was giving one of her inimitable balls.

There were large arched windows and a row of high white pilasters against the pea-green walls. In the gallery overlooking the ballroom, the musicians serenaded the throng with a dainty air. Plumed heads bobbed in time with the melody; jewels twinkled on highbred throats, earlobes, and fingers. The dancers wove through the elegant figures of a country dance, the ladies' gowns a swirling flower garden of pale pinks and whites, soft yellows and blues, greens and violets. Partnering them, a few of the gentlemen stood out in dashing military dress-uniforms, but the majority were clothed like him— though perhaps not quite so impeccably.

He was, after all, still Alec Knight.

His white-gloved hands elegantly clasped behind his back, Alec, in formal black superfine and white silk brocade waistcoat, strolled with his friends through the assembly rooms, nodding here and there to his acquaintances throughout the ton.

"Lady Jersey, you look radiant," he complimented the Almack's patroness with a bow. She blushed like a girl at his offering and tapped his arm coyly with her fan. He might need her later, he thought, along with other influential hostesses, if he managed to keep his bride. If she stayed with him, he would use all his skill to launch her in Society like a princess. Lord, he'd make her a sensation. Not that a stalwart soul like Becky gave a fig for such things.

For now, he kept an eye out for his quarry.

"I still don't see why you had to go dashing off like that from the Pavilion," Draxinger was muttering indignantly. "It was quite bad form to leave us all standing there like dunces left to wonder where the devil you were off to."

"You do seem strange of late, Alec. Are you sure everything is all right?"

"Everything's grand, Fort," he muttered, still thinking about the quartet of Cossacks he had seen posted outside, around Kurkov's showy equipage.

"Drax—look!" Fort said with a sly smile, nodding to the distant refreshment table. "There's Lady Parthenia."

The earl stopped in his tracks at the sight of her radiant figure, and then suddenly remembered to act bored. He lifted his quizzing glass nonchalantly to his eye and inspected Westland's daughter from a safe distance. "Lud, have you ever seen such a big nose?"

"Right," Alec muttered.

"Methinks, old Draxie, doth protest too much," Fort said under his breath as he and Alec exchanged a wry glance.

"Oh, leave me alone," Drax huffed.

They chuckled at his discomfiture and moved on, paying their respects to their host, Count Lieven.

"Ah, Lord Alec! I hear you're winning again," the stout Russian murmured as they shook hands. "By the way, have you heard? My prediction was right. Kurkov has joined the Whigs."

"Well done, sir!" he exclaimed amiably. "You have

won me twenty quid. Remind me to buy you a drink when we're back in London."

He laughed.

Hm, Alec mused as they moved on, mingling in Society. If Lieven had been right on the first wager—Whig or Tory—what if he was right about the other? There had been discussion of an English bride versus a Russian import. Lieven had opined that Kurkov would choose the former. He might seek a Whiggish alliance.

Alec suddenly looked at Parthenia Westland. She was fluttering her fan and talking excitedly behind it to another girl, but her gaze trailed after someone in the crowd. He frowned and followed the line of Parthenia's stare.

Kurkov.

Oh, bloody hell. Alec's pulse quickened to an ominous drumbeat as his stare homed in on his enemy. Kurkov was in full-dress uniform, gold sash, epaulets, and all. Alec curled his lip, wondering if the famous Russian war hero had been courting Westland's daughter all this time. He wouldn't put it past him. He only hoped that Parthenia's icicle nature had held firm against such a formidable suitor. She was the sort of girl who would marry to please her father, and no doubt Westland liked the idea of a son-in-law who had grown up with the Czar and could do things for the party.

Well, he thought, old Westland might judge him and Drax and their friends a lot of "surly jackanapes," but he doubted the duke would have looked favorably upon Kurkov as a possible son-in-law if he knew about the murder on the moors and the threat of rape on Becky— not to mention the harem of concubines whom Kurkov had boasted all received his harsh regimen of "training."

Something had to be done.

Alec took Fort aside while Drax stood speaking to a lady—or rather, to the chest of a lady—whose fleshy bosoms threatened to come bursting out of her bodice. Alec looked at them in startlement, then lowered his head discreetly by his friend's ear.

"Fort, take Drax over to talk to Parthenia."

"Why?"

"Their foolishness has gone on long enough. If he loses her, he'll never forgive himself. Flirt with her yourself if it's the only way to get him to leave off his stupid affectations."

"You do it. Nobody cares when I flirt with them."

"Daniel, my lad." Alec chuckled and clapped his trusty, fellow younger-son on the arm. "You are pure sterling. Never mind that, I'll be along in a moment. There's a lady over here I have to talk to," he said meaningfully.

"Ah," Fort replied with a knowing nod, scanning the crowd discreetly to try to see who he meant.

Alec hated lying to his mates, but if he told them the truth, they would have leaped into the fray, and there was no way he was risking them against the prince's Cossacks. His brothers would have been another matter. His brothers could have wiped out a Cossack regiment in time for nuncheon, but his friends were not warriors, just good, solid chaps and high-spirited Corinthians.

As Fort steered Drax toward Parthenia, Alec hoped his friend finally left off with the games and realized his window of opportunity to win the girl he really loved could be closing fast. Ice-princess or no, Parthenia did not deserve to be hurt by Kurkov's impending doom. After all, once he had Talbot Old Hall in his possession, he and Becky would move on to the task of bringing the prince to justice.

Lifting a fresh drink from the tray of a passing footman, Alec put on a cool half smile and approached Prince Kurkov with an air of rakish ease. Fortunately, he must have made an impression on the prince that day at

Brooke's Club, for Kurkov greeted him with instant recognition.

"Ah. Lord Alexei. Good to see you again."

"Likewise, Your Highness." Alec clinked glasses cordially with the man. *"Zdra'zhs-vu-tyay."*

"Spa'sibo bolshoi," Kurkov said with a throaty chuckle.

Alec tilted his head. "I beg your pardon?"

"Drop the *bolshoi*. It means grand, large, eh, formality," he explained. "There's a new phrase for you."

"Aha." Alec laughed, relieved. For a second there he had thought the man had already seen through his false friendship, but he'd been mistaken, thank God. He endeavored a quick change of subject. "So, Your Highness, what do you think of Brighton?"

"Enjoyable."

"Have you seen the Regent's building project?" he asked with a confidential air, turning on the old Alec charm.

Kurkov made a face, stern and soldierly, and then shook his head in baffled scorn over the strange goings-on over at the Pavilion.

Alec laughed softly. "Ah, yes, on the subject of property, that reminds me. I was referred to you, sir, to query after a hunting lodge that you own, I am told." He clasped his hands idly behind him. "My friends and I have been speaking for some time about going in together on the purchase of a hunting box, but we have not been able to find anything large enough to suit us. We were talking about it at the tables just the other night, and someone suggested you might have a place for sale—in Yorkshire?"

"Did they?" he asked. Alec held his breath as a glimmer of suspicion snaked ever-so-faintly through the depths of Kurkov's cold gray eyes, but then the man shrugged it off. "Yes, I do have an old hunting lodge in Yorkshire. But it is not for sale."

Alec drew breath to try to finesse the prince to change his mind, but Kurkov continued before he could speak.

"It is a pity I did not learn of your interest sooner, Lord Alec, for I would have instructed my solicitor to accept any reasonable offer. I have no use for the place myself. Unfortunately, a certain very determined young lady coaxed me into staking the property in the annual whist drive."

Alec's eyes widened with shock, which he quickly masked. "The—whist drive?" he asked in a slightly strangled tone.

"Yes." Kurkov took a sip of his rum punch. "Lady Parthenia Westland is on the charitable committee that organized the game."

"But isn't the entry fee . . . ten thousand pounds?" he forced out, reeling and making a herculean effort to hide his shock.

"Indeed," Kurkov agreed drily, observing his astonishment at the sum. "They've doubled the entry fee since last year, I'm told, which is why they are permitting players to stake such things as property, carriages, jewels and the like, as long as the total value is equal to ten thousand pounds. It is no wonder they put Parthenia in charge of enrolling players," he added. "That fair creature is not easy to deny. But . . . it is for a good cause."

"Navy widows and children," Alec echoed, instantly thinking of one particular navy brat who was very dear to him, indeed.

Kurkov smiled cynically. "I was referring to Parthenia herself."

Alec managed a smile and then dropped his gaze, his heart pounding. Good God, this was a catastrophe! Ten thousand pounds was double the sum they had, besides which, only about twelve hours remained before the

deadline ended to buy into the game. He didn't even
know if there was a single seat left in the tournament at
this late date, as it only allowed for thirty-two players.

"Well—enjoy your evening, Highness."

Kurkov nodded politely and Alec started to turn away
when an all-too-familiar voice stopped him.

"Alec—*darling*!" Eva suddenly blocked his retreat.
The baroness pinned him a brief, hostile glance before
fixing her sultry smile on Kurkov. "You must introduce
me to your friend."

His blood ran cold as Kurkov's answering glance traveled over Eva with open interest. Alec thought he might
be sick.

Of course, recalling Eva's penchant for brute force, it
was no wonder she had been drawn over to meet the big
Russian, especially when he was a newcomer and she
had already had her way with most of the men of the
ton. Her desire for an introduction was also, no doubt,
intended to get back at him for the ugly scene at the villa
yesterday. He might have threatened her life, but it was
not as though he could do anything to her in the middle
of a crowded ballroom. This was her chance to rub it in
his face.

Alec pursed his lips and looked from her to Kurkov,
on the very horns of an agonized dilemma. He hated in-
troducing them when Eva was the only one who could
connect him to Becky-Abby to Kurkov.

On the other hand, Eva did not know that Kurkov
sought the girl. And to refuse to introduce them would
only have alerted the baroness's opportunistic instincts.
It would be fatal to let her scent advantage. Best not to
cue her in to the fact that she held anything of interest to
Kurkov other than the shapely contents of her gown.

It seemed he had no choice.

"Lady Campion, allow me to present Prince Mikhail

Kurkov. Your Highness, this is Eva, Baroness Campion." *Brute force, meet decadent corruption.*

"*Enchanté,* madame," the prince said, bowing low over her gloved hand in Continental fashion.

"How very gallant," she purred, enjoying the gesture, but sparing a coldly reproachful, aye, a punishing glance, at Alec when Kurkov's head was bowed.

He stared back at her coldly, loath to leave the two of them together, but the whist drive deadline was fast approaching. He could only hope that, lustily engrossed in each other, Kurkov and Eva would not waste time on conversation. If they bothered to speak at all, the subject of Becky was unlikely to come up, and besides, Eva would not soon forget his threat to keep her mouth shut.

Neither paid him any mind as Alec took leave of them with a muttered farewell. In a moment he was on his way out the assembly rooms, striding swiftly across the marble floor of the columned foyer, his focus on the problem at hand.

'Sblood, it had taken him three weeks to amass the five thousands pounds it should have taken to buy Talbot Old Hall. Where the hell was he supposed to come up with another five thousand before tomorrow noon?

Outside the villa, a dog was barking somewhere nearby, and a big gibbous moon hung over the sea. Becky sat in the first-floor parlor, where the house was coolest. With the windows open and the curtains blowing listlessly, she sat curled on the sofa with her feet tucked under her, sipping lemonade and waiting for Alec to return from the Lieven ball.

Though still seething over his secrecy, she waited up for his return. Knowing that tonight he faced Mikhail, she was anxious to see him back safely and to know the outcome. She pulled the candle closer and endeavored again to concentrate on the book that Alec had put in her hands some time ago, before they had quarreled. He had said she must try it, for it had been written by a friend of his, called Byron. Perhaps she was not able to give it her full attention, considering the jangled state of her nerves, but from what she could glean, it seemed as though this Lord Byron fellow had an even bigger chip on his shoulder against the female race than Alec did.

Her thoughts wandered away again from the sly remarks of Byron's cheeky Don Juan to the problem of her own exasperating paramour.

Really, where was he? The ticking wall clock read half past two. Surely the ball was over by now, so where was the rogue? And with whom?

She shifted uncomfortably in her seat, scowling to think of him surrounded by elegant ladies in ball gowns, a dozen copies of Lady Campion, all fawning on him, no doubt. Blast it, this vexing jealousy only added insult to injury. Who would have guessed she would turn out to be such a possessive woman over her man?

But that was just the problem.

She did not know whether Alec was still hers or not. Obviously she did not mean as much to him as she had thought she did, or he would have talked to her by now. She hated giving him the silent treatment, but she knew it was vital not to back down. And yet . . .

She *missed* him.

Oh, maybe this fight between them wasn't worth it, she thought, fretting as she raked her hand through her hair, staring into the flickering candle. It was foolish to alienate her protector and provider. What right did she have to ask anything of him when he was the one keeping her alive?

On the other hand, to capitulate merely for self-preservation would have been manipulative, dishonest, and low. No, she did trust Alec that much. Whatever conflict might simmer between them, she knew for certain he would never throw her to the wolves just because, in his view, she was being a "headache."

An odd sound outside the window suddenly snared her attention. Becky looked over warily, jolted from her thoughts.

Already jumpy with the thought of the Cossacks having arrived in Brighton, her heart began to pound. She told herself she was being silly.

Mikhail's men had no idea where she was. But even though she was at odds with Alec, she felt safer when he was here. The servants were hardly going to protect her, after all. No, in fact, they had gone to bed.

There it was again! She wasn't imagining it! A crackling sound—as though someone were shuffling about in the shrubberies just outside the window. Blanching, she quickly blew out the candle to hide herself in the darkness.

She unfolded her legs from beneath her and got up from the couch, silently taking the long, heavy pistol out of the slim drawer in the sofa table. She had loaded the weapon earlier simply to make herself feel more secure while he was gone. She had not dreamed she might actually have to use it.

Fortunately, she knew how, thanks to her inquisitive country childhood and the kindly gamekeeper on the estate, who had let her join in when the village boys clamored around him, begging him to teach them how to shoot. She ended up despising guns in the end, when she had seen what they could do to poor little game birds and rabbits, but she still knew how to use one when she was backed into a corner.

Stalking silently toward the window, she held the weapon in both hands, pointed at the ceiling. Her father would have been proud, she thought, as she set her back against the wall beside the window and gathered herself:

With a sudden lunge, she shoved the curtains away and aimed out the window.

No one there.

She scanned, sweeping the front area with the muzzle of her weapon. All was clear—until she saw the large black figure running along the wall, slipping around to the back of the house.

A chill ran down her spine. She suddenly remembered the kitchen door that led out to the garden. Had she locked it?

I can't remember.

She had seen one figure outside, but there could be more. With no other option than to defend herself and her home territory, she ran to the kitchen at the back of the house. If the trespasser came through the back door, she could take him by surprise.

She crouched under the kitchen window and listened.

There was definitely someone out there. She heard movement, low breathing. An able man could have scaled the high garden wall. She swallowed hard as her pulse escalated. *Oh, Alec, if only you were here.*

The audacity! She heard the intruder lay hold of the doorknob and twist it.

Damn! She had been sure she locked it three times over. Of course, she had kept going outside for air because the house had been uncomfortably warm and stuffy tonight. . . .

Gliding through the darkness, Becky brought up her weapon and blocked the hallway, her pistol aimed at the intruder's heart. "Don't move or I'll put a hole in you."

"Boney's balls—don't shoot!" The tall broad-shouldered man lifted his hands into the air. "I'm unarmed."

The voice sounded vaguely familiar.

"Who's there?" she demanded, reaching around the corner for the wall candle in the hallway. Lifting the taper, she gasped in recognition—and so did the intruder.

"You!" the black-haired man cried, narrowing his eyes at her. Lord Rushford blanched and quickly shielded his groin. "Please—for the sake of my family line, don't!"

Becky stared at him sardonically. "Nice to see you again, too, my lord."

"It *is* you, isn't it? I say! That little bird from Draxinger's doorstep? Though much improved—"

Rushford sobered as Becky cocked the pistol in response to his lecherous stare trailing over her body. He suddenly remembered his manners. "Er, sorry."

"Alec will be home in a bit," she said coolly. "You may address me as Miss Ward." She lowered her pistol with caution. "What the devil are you doing creeping around the house that way?"

"Nothing! I was only looking for Knight," he said defensively.

"Poppycock. Why not announce yourself? Are you trying to get yourself killed? What are you doing here at this hour?"

"What am I doing here? What are *you* doing here?" he exclaimed.

"What do you think?" she retorted in a dull tone.

"Oh! So you and Knight are . . ."

She raised an eyebrow, waiting.

"Together?" he finished delicately.

"Something like that."

Rushford paused gingerly. "May I please put my arms down now, Miss Ward?"

She gave the pistol a dismissive wave. "Suit yourself. I'm still waiting to hear why you were creeping around the garden."

"If you must know, I came to have a look around because Knight has been acting damned strange lately. I knew he was hiding something!" He eyed her in suspicion. "Now I see I was right. When I realized we were all supposed to go to the Lieven ball tonight, I cried off, thinking I'd come over here and see what I could find out. But I certainly wasn't expecting to find you here."

"Well, you might as well come in and wait for him, then. That's all I've been doing, waiting—but no grabbing," she ordered, emphasizing her point with a thrust of the pistol in his direction.

"No—no grabbing. Of course, never," he agreed, the soul of obedience.

"Do you want a drink?" Becky asked none too politely as they walked back into the parlor. She relit the candle, then went to the liquor cabinet. "I know I could use one." Her hands were still a bit shaky after the scare.

"Please." Rushford came over to her side and commenced investigating the available liquors until his gaze lit upon her left hand. "What's this?"

Becky sent him a questioning look askance.

Rushford took hold of her wrist and lifted it, examining her hand. "My God, this is serious!" He looked askance at her. "Why are you wearing Alec's ring?" he demanded before releasing her warily.

She, too, glanced down at the oversized gold-and-onyx ring on her finger and let out a great, rueful sigh. "Oh, Lord Rushford, at the moment, I hardly know myself."

"What's that supposed to mean?"

She shrugged as she gazed at him and shook her head, at a loss.

He eyed her with new interest and then poured them both a sherry. "There there. Don't be troubled, my dear," he murmured sympathetically. "Call me Nick." He handed her the sherry with a sly and highly intrigued smile. "Whatever the blackguard's done, why don't we sit down and you can tell me all about it?"

CHAPTER
⤜ TWELVE ⤛

*A*lec came in wearily at four A.M., annoyed with the world. He had succeeded in grabbing the last open seat in the whist tournament, but he couldn't help scowling. His only option now was to win. To beat all the best gamblers in England. If he lost, not only would Becky never see the inside of Talbot Old Hall again, but he, too, would be homeless.

Having plunked down the five thousand he had already won gambling, he had been forced to make up the other half of the entry fee by staking everything of value he had left as collateral—his beloved bachelor rooms at the Althorpe and all his remaining furniture, including his legendary bed.

Ah, well. In for a penny, in for a pound.

In hindsight, he supposed he could have sold his home from the start in order to buy the Hall from Kurkov, but before this time in Brighton, living with Becky each day, such a sacrifice would have been incomprehensible to him. *Selfish bastard. Ah, well,* he thought with a sigh. He must really be ready for marriage at last, because giving his all for her sake was becoming second nature to him now, despite the fact that, these days, the cherished recipient of his efforts was out of charity with him.

Still brooding on the worrisome memory of those heated glances he had witnessed between Lady Campion and Prince Kurkov, Alec trudged into the house, decidedly in a mood. It had just occurred to him with a twinge of guilt that he had abandoned Fort and Drax again without a word at the Lieven ball, when he suddenly heard low laughter coming from somewhere upstairs.

He stopped, drew his eyebrows together and frowned.

Following the sound, Alec tracked it to the dining room. Stepping into the doorway, he discovered its source: Becky and Rushford sitting cozily together at the dining table, drinking coffee, chatting like old friends, and eating pudding.

His pudding.

"Well, look who's here," Rushford said with a cocky and rather accusatory glower, sitting back in his chair at the head of the table.

"My thoughts exactly," Alec muttered, meeting his stare.

"If it isn't the man of secrets himself."

"I thought you were recovering from intemperance," Alec answered guardedly.

"You, old boy, have got some explaining to do," Rush countered.

Becky dabbed at her lips with her napkin and glanced uneasily from her visitor to Alec. "Would you like some pudding?" she spoke up, hoping, it would seem, to head off fisticuffs.

"Yes," Rush drawled. "We saved you some. Though it wasn't easy. Miss Ward is *very* talented in the kitchen."

As his rich, titled, good-looking friend sent Becky a conspiratorial smile, Alec flinched, pulsating with possessive jealousy. "Indeed, she is."

He sauntered toward them warily, bristling.

"Who knew cooking could be so much fun?" Rush taunted him with a knowing grin.

The bastard.

Becky dropped her gaze, fighting a slightly wicked smile.

Alec glowered. How dare the two of them make sport of him? Reaching Becky's side, he leaned down to greet his lady with a territorial kiss, but she turned her face away. He caught only the corner of her mouth. From the side of her eye she shot him a haughty glance.

"And where have you been?" she asked coolly. "The ball was over hours ago."

Alec straightened up again, suddenly grasping the cause of this chilly reception. A glance at the wall clock reminded him that it was now past four in the morning. *Oh, bloody hell.* God only knew what she thought.

The hour was very late, and she still had no answers about Lady Campion. Having no firm information to go on, she had no reason not to suspect the worst. But if Becky-love thought it possible that he had been out to this late hour in the company of another lady, then how far might she have gone in flirting with Rushford, the famous stealer of mistresses?

"Nick, old boy, a word, if you please?" Alec asked coolly.

"Certainly," Rush shot back with a reproachful stare. "Miss Ward, if you will pardon me?" he said to Becky, clearly having rolled out his best manners for her.

Quite a change from when they had first met on Draxinger's doorstep, Alec thought cynically, unhappy to know that his friend could be a formidable rival when he chose. Becky dismissed the future marquess with a ladylike nod. Rushford rose and bowed to her before exiting, while Alec stood simmering beside her chair. He gestured to Rush to go ahead of him toward the drawing room across the hallway.

When Rush walked past him, Alec, still bristling, reached his hand into the moist bread pudding and tore off a small handful, shoving it defiantly into his mouth as he held Becky's mutinous stare.

She narrowed her eyes at him.

When Alec strode into the drawing room, he did not mince words. "Hands off, Rushford. This one's mine."

Rush raised his thick black eyebrows and then laughed at him, shaking his head. "Don't be a jackass, Alec. I'm not making a play for your lady. Calm down."

"She is to be my wife!"

"Not if you don't tell her the truth about Eva," he said flatly.

Alec's face drained. "What did you tell her?"

"Nothing. You have my loyalty, of course. God knows the girl's been trying to get it out of me all night, but no damned way am I getting in the middle of that. She told me all about the two of you, though," he added.

Alec set his hands on his waist. "Oh, did she?"

"I can be a very understanding listener."

"When you're trying to get a female into bed."

"Not this time. Of course, if you don't want her, then that's another—"

"I want her!"

Rush raised his eyebrows. "You might try telling her that, then, because she's not sure what you feel for her."

Alec turned away restlessly, his jaw set at a stubborn angle, for he did not need Rushford telling him how Becky was feeling.

"What the hell is the matter with you?" his friend persisted. "Good God, man, you're engaged to be married! How could you keep something like that from us? We are your friends! At least I thought we were. I knew you had something up your sleeve, but—perdition, a fiancée?"

"I couldn't tell you!"

"Why?"

"Because she is in danger!" he finally exclaimed, fed up with bearing it all on his own shoulders. "Someone's trying to kill the girl, Rushford. Did she mention that?"

"No," he answered, shaking his head in amazement.

"The situation is very serious. I've been hiding her here with me to keep her safe. That's why she was on Drax's doorstep that night," he explained. "She wasn't a harlot, she was on the run. She got caught in the storm. She had nowhere else to go."

Rush took a step toward him with an angry expression. "Who could harm that sweet creature?"

Alec shook his head. "I didn't tell you, and I'm still not sure I can, because I cannot risk anybody being careless. Not when her life is at stake."

"So, that's why you've been acting so bloody bizarre."

Alec shrugged. He didn't think he had been acting all that strange.

"Damn me," Rush marveled. "If that's true, all the more reason why you need us—me and Drax and Fort. You should know by now you can count on us."

Alec stared at him. "Can I?"

"Aye! For your sake, and hers. If that darling lady is in danger, you must allow us to help you protect her."

"You must not speak of her to anyone."

"Of course!"

"Very well." Alec nodded ruefully. "I could use someone to watch my back."

"Whatever you need." Rushford clapped him on his scarred arm and nodded.

"Come by with Fort and Drax tomorrow noon and I'll explain."

"Done. I'll be on my way. You two will no doubt want to be alone. By the way, a word of warning: She's rather furious at you at the moment. I'd tread lightly if I were you. Tell her about Eva, Alec. She isn't Lizzie Carlisle. This girl can take it."

Alec frowned, not appreciating being told how to handle his woman, but Rush never shrank from speaking his mind. "Don't drive her away like you've done with all the rest. I'm telling you as your friend, this girl is the best thing that ever happened to you."

"I know," he admitted under his breath.

"Whatever you do, don't set her off," Rush added with a twinkle of roguery in his eyes. "Chit's got a kick like a racehorse, trust me."

Alec smiled wryly, and Rushford took his leave.

After shrugging out of his formal black tailcoat, Alec headed back toward the dining room to see Becky, but she appeared first, prowling into the drawing room. He stared hungrily at her as she passed him, going restlessly to pour herself a sherry, pure poetry in motion in a low-cut evening gown of scarlet satin that clung to her generous curves.

"Lord Rushford's gone, then?"

"Don't weep, *cherie*. He'll be back tomorrow," he taunted gently as he tossed his coat across a nearby chair's back. "Though I don't think there'll be any pudding left for him by then." He sauntered toward her, pinning her in his heated stare. "Not a single bite."

She sipped her sherry with a guarded pout, thwarted desire crackling in the air between them after a few days of pent-up frustration.

"Pretty gown," he purred, looking her over boldly as he passed behind her. "What's the occasion?"

Becky turned with a quelling stare. "I had hoped we would be celebrating having gotten the Hall back from Mikhail. So? What happened?"

"All in good time, my dear. First, tell me. Are you wearing that pretty frock for me or for Rushford?"

She snorted. "I was in my night rail when he came

sneaking around the villa. It was the first thing I grabbed from my dressing room and one of the few things I can put on without the maid. She's sleeping."

"Rushford saw you in your night rail?" Alec checked his exasperation, clenching his jaw. "Don't you know he is one of the most notorious roués in the ton?"

"Even more notorious than you, Lord Alec?" she asked innocently.

He narrowed his eyes in warning.

Staring at each other in seething hostility and mutual lust, they circled like prizefighters warming up in the ring.

"Why are you home so late?" she demanded. "Tell me where you've been. Or am I not allowed to know that, either? Am I supposed to just take your word for it?"

He knew that he had brought this on himself, that his silence and secrets had jolted her trust in him, but at the moment, he could only shake his head. "You know, it's very strange that you tell me to trust you, when it seems you don't trust me."

She set her glass down with a flushed glance. "I've been worried sick!"

"Worried? Or jealous again?" he asked mildly.

"You're the one who's jealous! Where were you? What happened with Mikhail?"

"What happened with Rushford?"

"Nothing! He came looking for you. I let him keep me company."

"Is that all you let him do?" he demanded, hooking an arm around her waist as she turned her back to him.

"Don't be a fool."

"Do you think this little game of yours is amusing?" he whispered by her ear as he pulled her against him, holding her captive around her waist. "That's how duels get started, *cherie*."

He felt her tremble. "I didn't do anything wrong."

"He wants you, you know." Alec skimmed the curve of her neck with his lips. "And do you know what else, Becky-love?" he whispered. "So do I."

"Let go of me, you brute." She pushed her elbow against his chest, but he did not release her. Her struggle, in point of fact, was not very convincing. "I have no idea where you've been all these hours—or with whom! Was that horrible woman at the ball? I swear, if you were with her, Alec—"

He cut off her question with a hard, claiming kiss, turning her partly in his arms. "I wasn't with anyone," he ground out, taking her hand and pressing it to his hardening cock. "I already told you I'm yours. You see? And you're mine. You seem to need reminding."

"Oh, what's the matter, love?" she retorted in a breathy whisper. "Silly male jealousy?" Her gleaming eyes mocked him, dared him, flung down a sensuous challenge.

Alec shook his head with a narrow, simmering smile. Such fight. Such spirit. Her fire filled him with dark delight. *Impertinent vixen.* He cupped her nape in a soft but masterful hold and drew her nearer, staring hotly at her lush, rosy lips. "Don't forget who you belong to."

He kissed her again, roughly, and her soft groan with his tongue in her mouth, opened wide for him in eager reception, told him all that he needed to know. He caressed her face, trying to temper his wild need for her; they both paused, took a breath, and then simply tore into each other like starved people at a feast.

Alec's hands were shaking like those of an untried youth. He touched her everywhere, greedily. He stroked rosy satin; he wanted white skin. He tore her lovely bodice in his haste to get his hand on her breasts while she flew through the buttons of his waistcoat, dragging the vest off his shoulders.

He plucked the pins out of her upswept hair and brought it tumbling down, letting it spill luxuriously through his fingers like so many strands of sable silk. Then he knelt before her, hungrily sucking on each of her rigid nipples. She hugged his head to her bosom, tangling her fingers in his hair. She tugged his white shirt off over his head a few moments later, and then, bare-chested, he pulled her down onto the floor with him, fierce and reckless in his haste. Becky kept pace with him as no woman ever had.

Both of them on their knees, Alec bent her over the long silk chaise, lifted her skirts, and took her from behind with quick, hard thrusts.

She arched her back and urged him on; he grasped her hips and quickened the pace, simply ravishing her in raw, mind-numbing bliss without a word between them. His cock was enormous sliding into her, a lancer's pike, a frigate's mast. He'd never been so hard in his life. Caressing her round bottom, he trailed his fingers up her back and grasped the silken rope of her hair, dragging her head back gently, just hard enough to make sure she knew who was in charge. She groaned in helpless pleasure, submitting to his mastery, perhaps despite herself.

He closed his eyes, savoring the velvet wetness of her dripping core. As he stroked the warm, supple curves of her back, his whole body tingled with celestial sensation. "Ah, Becky." He wrapped his arm around her thin waist and rained steamy kisses on her back, her nape, her shoulders. He told her with his body, with his proprietary hold, as his fingers dug into the soft flesh of her hips; he told her with every deep stroke, buried in her to the hilt; and even with the light teeth marks that he left on her tender shoulder; that under no circumstances was he letting her back out of this marriage. *"You're mine,"* he whispered.

She groaned his name, quivering violently as his middle fingertip played ever so lightly over her pebble-hard center. "Oh, yes, Alec. Don't stop."

"No, Becky, never."

She carried him away with her when the hot wave of her release crashed through her nubile body, making her shudder and grind against him, her backside slapping wildly against his groin. Her skin damp with sweat.

Alec buried his face in her hair and followed her blindly into oblivion. A few final pumping heaves of his hips lunging into her, and he was flung out in another world, where there was only this woman and pleasure and sweet darkness.

"Becky," he breathed as she quieted in his arms. He could barely open his eyes, but as a bead of sweat rolled down his cheek, his embrace around her slim waist gradually changed from one of dominance to chastened affection. Still inside her, he nuzzled the sweet shoulder that moments ago he had covered in love bites. "Ah, angel. You are miraculous." She let out a quivery little sigh as he withdrew. "Are you all right?"

She nodded, suddenly turning shy after their wild mating. Alec smiled, taking in her crimson blush. She was just too adorable, he thought, besotted.

"Come here." He fixed her torn dress a bit, fastened his trousers, and glanced warily into her eyes. "Do you want to talk now?"

She lifted her eyebrows, searching his gaze. "Do you?"

Alec gave her a somber, wordless nod. Maybe if he stopped running from his demons and instead looked them straight in the eyes, the past would lose some of its terrible power over him. Yes, it was time to have done with it, and face the consequences.

Becky cupped his face in her hand and then nestled her cheek against his, her long lashes dusting his skin. "Whatever it is, Alec, we'll get through it together."

He wrapped his arms around her and closed his eyes, praying as he held her that these were not just pretty words. Then he stood, lifting her with him.

She clasped her hands behind his neck and held his stare as he carried her slowly upstairs to the summer bed.

"I had grown used to winning. Winning . . . well, it was who I was. But about a year and a half ago, you see, I hit a losing streak at the tables. A rather . . . spectacular losing streak."

A short while later Alec began his confession. His low murmur reached Becky from the shadows on his side of the summer bed. They had changed into their nightclothes and assumed their respective sides of the separated bed, which had already served as the intimate setting for so many whispered conversations.

Moonlight filled the room; a slight breeze stirred the curtains. Becky turned onto her side and stared at his muscled silhouette.

"Faro and hazard," he said with a low sigh. "Games of chance were my poison. There's no strategy to it. Just put your money down and see what happens. Those were the kinds of games I loved to win."

"Why?"

"I don't know. It made me feel . . . Singled out by fate. Beloved by the goddess of fortune. Chosen. I guess that sounds absurd." The pillow rustled as he shook his head, staring up at the canopy above them. "But if it made me feel uniquely blessed to win, then losing, as you may imagine, made me feel cursed. I kept thinking I could turn it all around—as if I were being tested. I refused to give up. One more throw of the dice, one more hand at cards. I became fixated on regaining my golden status."

"Why did it all hold such appeal?" she asked softly.

He considered the question. "I guess it took my mind off other things."

"Like what?"

"Well, for instance," he said hesitantly, "like how I could have everything and still not be happy. More and more of everything could still not . . ."

"Fill the emptiness?" she asked softly.

He turned his head and just stared at her for a moment. Slowly, somberly, he nodded.

"Go on."

Lying back again, he stared up at the canopy with his arms folded under his head. "The longer I hung in there, trying to turn it around, the worse it seemed to get. It was a disaster taking shape, but still, I refused to admit defeat. Robert warned me a few times that I was getting into dangerous territory, but I didn't listen. Finally, he cut me off in an effort to force me to quit. He had no other choice, really. It was for my own good—but I did not intend to take that lying down. Instead, I made a few discreet inquiries about taking out a bank loan to cover my expenses until my luck returned. Bad idea, yes, I know. In any case, the reputable moneylenders around Town heard that I had been cut off. Without Robert's backing, they wouldn't grant me a farthing. And then things got really . . . interesting."

"What happened?"

"Some of my creditors caught wind of my situation and came banging on my door. I had borrowed all I could from my friends; I owed them all. I couldn't bring myself to ask for another penny. Even a ruined gambler's got his pride. I was so angry at myself, so disgusted," he said, his voice thickening. "I had bailiffs lying in wait for me to drag me off to debtor's prison, and I knew Robert was going to leave me there, because he had told me so. He feared that was the only way I was ever going to learn."

Becky listened in silence.

"Well, I knew that if I allowed myself to be locked up, it would be the end of Lord Alec Knight, captain of all London rakehells," he said cynically. "It was bad enough to have inexplicably become a loser overnight, but debtor's prison would have made me a social outcast to boot. Ton life can be damned shallow, God knows, but it's the only sort of life I've ever known. I wasn't thinking clearly," he admitted in the darkness. "And so I went off and did something . . . incredibly stupid."

"What was that?" she murmured.

"I took a loan from Mr. Dunmire." He rolled onto his side and propped his cheek in his hand, his elbow resting across his pillow. His eyes glimmered in the silvery moon-glow. "He's a sort of underworld businessman, part criminal. He owns half a dozen crooked gambling hells throughout the East End. Brothels. Low pubs that usually feature cockfight pits. He's got an army of black-legs who prey off the Fancy. I knew it could be suicide to deal with him, but as the only honorable option that remained held, shall we say, limited appeal, I signed on the bottom line."

"Oh, Alec." She shivered, remembering all those gamblers whose fates were printed in the newspapers, blowing their brains out or hanging themselves, after having chased ruin to the end of the line. Such exits were reported as customary, unsentimental, matter-of-fact. Acts of honor. For, when a proud gentleman had disgraced himself beyond recovery at the tables, self-slaughter was viewed as the only way to answer the disgrace he had brought down on himself.

"But still, I refused to give up hope," Alec said. "The loan's rate of interest was outrageous, but I was absolutely certain that my luck *must* turn around sometime. Well, once I had the money from Dunmire, I paid down a few of my debts and got rid of the bailiffs, but

by the time the first payment on the loan came due . . ."
He shook his head. "I couldn't pay."

"Oh, no," she said softly, wincing as she held his gaze.

"Dunmire wasted no time in sending his thugs out
after me. They pounced on me one night when I was on
my way home from a party, foxed and alone. I did my
best to ward them off, but I was in no condition. . . . If I
had been sober, I'm sure I could have taken them on,
but, well, to be perfectly frank, I was bloody drunk.
They got the best of me. Slammed my damned head
against the ground until I saw double, and then one of
them jumped on the lower part of my leg and broke it—
as a warning."

"Oh, sweetheart." She got up and crossed the gap between them, sitting on the side of his bed. She searched
his face in astonished concern.

He sat up against the headboard, shirtless, one knee
bent. "I wish I could tell you that I held my ground
boldly, but that wasn't exactly the case." His lips twisted
as he met her questioning gaze. "Having barely managed to limp away from them with my life, and quite defenseless after the condition in which they had left me, I
hid at Knight House—at least, for a few weeks, while I
was mending. I didn't even tell my family what was really going on. I told them it had happened during a
drunken wager with my friends. They believed me and,
considering my injuries, they called for a doctor and
took me in." He took her hand, lowering his gaze. "It
didn't take long for Dunmire's thugs to find me. I was
sitting on the terrace one evening playing chess with
Miss Carlisle when they came up to the fence and told
me I couldn't hide in there forever, and that when I came
out again, I was a dead man. By that time, of course, I
had missed several more payments."

She petted his shoulder in pained sympathy.

"Unfortunately, Lizzie had heard the whole thing.

You remember, I told you about her—lady's companion to my sister."

Becky nodded.

"I had been hiding it from everyone, but she was right there, so of course, she found out. She questioned me about it, and she had been so kind to me, looking after me while I was on crutches, that I just couldn't lie to her. I finally broke down and told her the truth, but I made her swear not to tell the others. Do you know what she did for me?"

She shook her head.

Alec was pale, the fine planes and chiseled angles of his face taut with sorrow. "She took out her dowry that her father had left her and—she gave it to me to pay back Dunmire."

Becky rested her hand on his forearm. She couldn't help feeling a tiny bit threatened by his past bond with Miss Carlisle—or Lady Strathmore, since her marriage, as Alec had also told her. She wished she could have known Alec all her life, as Lizzie had. On the other hand, she was grateful that he had had a friend like Lizzie when he needed one most. "She must have loved you very much," she said wistfully.

"Almost as much as I despised myself," he answered in a low tone. He paused. "The truth is she never really knew me. Not like you do. She was in love with an image of me that she had made up in her own head. She finally came to understand that, because what she later found with Dev was real by comparison. In any case, her generosity that day thoroughly humbled me. Lizzie comes from modest origins, you see—the money she was offering me represented her entire future. At first I took it. Because she insisted. And because my back was to the wall—I thought I had no choice. But on the way to Dunmire's office, I realized I couldn't possibly go through with it. I couldn't have lived with myself.

Instead . . ." His voice dropped to a pained whisper. "I told the driver to take me to Lady Campion's house."

Becky studied him apprehensively. He touched her arm for a moment, took a deep breath, and then visibly forced himself to continue. "Eva . . . is a widow with a fortune of her own. She can do what she likes, when she likes. With whom she likes. She had been trying to lure me into her bed for years, but I never . . . I had heard things about her. The sort of things she likes. I never . . . We made a bargain."

"I see." The short, whispered words rushed from her on an exhalation, as though someone had punched her in the stomach, or perhaps stuck a dagger in her heart. She dropped her gaze. Outwardly she sat very still, but inwardly she was reeling, for she grasped what Alec was about to tell her before he actually said it.

He swallowed hard, a trifle pale; but with a look of stony resolve, he forced himself to be done with it, and Becky closed her eyes as he said the words. "Eva paid off Dunmire in exchange for my services in her bed."

She sat very still, one arm hugged tightly across her waist. She was appalled, indeed, shaken to the core.

"Our liaison went on for over a year. She refused to pay Dunmire off all at once because she so enjoyed the power she had acquired over me. She flaunted it in front of all the world; she enjoyed testing how far she could push me."

"How could your family let you do this?" Becky uttered, trembling.

"They did not know how serious my situation was, and I was unwilling to involve them further in circumstances that had been brought on purely by my own folly. I could not bear for their opinion of me to sink any lower." He swallowed hard. "I was merely relieved not to be in prison, and Dunmire was satisfied. As for Society, some were scandalized—I lost a portion of my invitations around Town—but in general the ton allowed me to carry it off as naught but a lark, a rakish prank. I brazened it out as a sort of jest, all the while knowing poor loyal Lizzie had been crushed. She viewed what I had done as a pure betrayal. My 'jest' had all but destroyed her, at least until Dev came along."

"Oh, Alec."

"Do you know what the worst thing is that I did, though?"

She glanced at him in alarm, her face pale. *It gets worse?*

"When I saw Dev and Lizzie falling in love, I tried to win her back. I tried to take that away from her, too—unthinkingly, selfishly." He paused. "I even asked her to marry me."

Becky flinched with mingled jealousy and pain at all these bewildering revelations. "You really loved her?"

He was silent for a long moment. "I did not feel for her what I feel for you. Lizzie is a sweet girl who will always be dear to me, but in my selfishness, my main reason for proposing was abject fear that if she chose Dev, there would be no one left in the world who could ever love me. But then I met you. And it occurred to me that maybe it's not getting but giving that's the answer."

Becky met his stare with a pang of guarded tenderness. Blue shadows from the moonlight sculpted his face as he searched her eyes. "When I saw you that first night and mistook you for a whore, I felt . . . drawn to you. I felt that I could help someone like you and that . . . you wouldn't judge me. That you'd understand what it was like. I didn't know you were innocent. Becky, God's truth, I'd forgotten what innocence was."

She flinched at the pain underlying his whisper and dropped her gaze.

"Being with you, I've had the chance to give to another person as I've never done before, and no matter what you might have to say about all that I've told you, I'll always be grateful to you for letting me help, and trusting me to take care of you. It's meant more to me than you know. You've given me the chance to feel pride again in who I am." He looked away. "In any case, I was honestly going to tell you all of this once our business with Kurkov was done. I didn't want to shake your faith in me: It would only leave you frightened about my ability to save you. And . . . I was frightened, too. That I would lose you." He eyed her askance with great caution. "Have I?"

Becky wanted to weep.

She stared at him for a second and then lowered her head, laying her hands on her lap. She struggled to know what to say. Her emotions were in chaos. Anger at the situation. Hurt and shock.

Alec waited, his soul naked before her—utterly vulnerable.

She shut her eyes, wanting to withdraw, to nurse her own bruised emotions after what he had told her; but she was the one who had insisted on hearing all this, and now that he had willingly exposed his throat, she knew that if she cut him, he would never trust her again.

Nor should he.

She saw she had a choice. Either she could vent her anger and ensure he'd never open up to her again or rise above it, move past it somehow to be there for him in this moment when he needed her most. She took a deep breath and let it out, and then she looked at him. Her gaze trailed over to his finely chiseled face, wary of that potent male beauty he had used to survive.

"I'm sorry," he said, stark grief in his blue eyes. "You don't have to marry me if you don't want to anymore. I'll understand."

She flinched, her fears whispering to her to flee while she still had the chance. A woman would have to be mad to risk joining her life to a man who could do such rash, intemperate things. But in the silence, as she struggled with herself, Becky chose not to listen to her fears. It was emptiness that had driven Alec to do those things, not a true reflection of who he really was. Emptiness that she could heal. No, hurting him now would be worse than anything Alec had done.

Her decision to reach out to him was made.

Lifting his tense hand from where it rested on the bed, Becky bent her head, closed her eyes, and slowly kissed it. She heard his unsteady inhalation as her tears fell upon his hand. She kissed his big thick knuckles again and again, soothingly, every moment strengthening her will and her resolve to reach deep within herself to show him love.

The love he had never known.

"Oh, my darling," she whispered, lifting her sorrowful gaze to his once more, "you did the best you could do at the time."

He breathed her name.

Holding his stare through a blur of tears, she saw he looked astounded by her reaction. She put his hand against her cheek and pressed another kiss into his palm. "I don't care about the past, Alec," she whispered in fierce loyalty. "I want you to forgive yourself for this."

He swallowed hard and shook his head. "I cannot possibly, unless you forgive me, too."

"It's not my place to bestow forgiveness or withhold it. You did not wrong me. You didn't even know me then."

He gazed at her as though he could not believe this was happening.

"Look at the choice you made under those terrible circumstances. You sacrificed yourself and your pride rather than take advantage of Miss Carlisle. You really care about people, Alec. That's part of what makes you so beautiful."

He took back his hand from her light hold and glanced away, looking shaken. "I don't understand."

She cast about for a means to explain. "Has Miss Carlisle forgiven you?"

"Yes. She's happy now with Dev," he said guardedly.

"Has your family forgiven you?"

"Of course they have. They—" He stopped suddenly, as though hearing his own words for the first time, realizing it. "They . . . love me."

She gave him a tremulous smile through her tears and nodded. "You see?" she whispered. "You've put everything to right as best you can, so why should you continue to punish yourself?"

He had no answer.

"Do you remember when we were under the awning that first night—when I threatened to brain you with the candlesnuffer? Remember? You thought I was a—a prostitute."

His faint smile at the reminder of her makeshift weapon faded at the term; almost with a flinch, he nodded.

"What if I *had* been?" she asked candidly. "Think back to that night, my darling. How kind you were, the compassion you showed me. The dignity and gentleness with which you treated me. Though you thought me a mere harlot, you ordered the best dinner in the city for me. You opened your home to me. You didn't have to do any of that. Your friends certainly wouldn't have bothered. Why would you go to such lengths for a mere street girl?"

"Because . . . I knew that whatever had befallen you, that you were a good person and wouldn't have chosen that life unless there was no other way."

She nodded slowly.

He absorbed this and lowered his head.

"But your kindness to me didn't stop there, Alec. Such

pains you took to soothe my fears and make me smile, remember? And then . . ." She took his hand once more and held it between both of hers. "You made love to me so tenderly." She petted his hand, remembering that night all over again.

From beneath his forelock, he sent her a swift glance full of anguished heat.

"You were not just a man taking a woman home that night to have his way with her," she murmured. "You were a Good Samaritan to me—and the next day, you proved to be my knight in shining armor, as well. You saved my life. You offered to marry me when you realized my innocence—even though I had deceived you. You may never have gotten to ride with Wellington's cavalry, Alec, but to me, you are the stuff heroes are made of."

"Me?" he whispered.

"Yes," she answered, wanting to take him into her arms, but she waited, for there was much more to say, so much to make him understand. "You claim you're some sort of selfish scoundrel, but that's not what I see." Her own feelings for him, though lately tangled, emerged ever more clearly as she talked it out. "You have continually risked yourself for me . . . in profound ways. Fighting the blasted Cossacks, for goodness sake. The armies of Europe are afraid of them! Bringing me here in spite of possibly angering your family—I know how much they mean to you. Making sure that I was safe and fed and even clothed." She stroked each one of his fingers, tracing them lightly, her gaze following her hand. "Gambling night after night to help me get my home back and save my village, despite the fact that this gambling is the very enemy that was so deadly to you in the past. All the while, you've asked nothing of me in return—except to trust you." She lifted her head and looked straight at him. "Is that not the very soul of chivalry? Don't you think a man like that deserves to be forgiven?"

He was staring at the far wall with his mouth pursed in a taut line, but when he looked at her with over-whelming emotion churning in his eyes, Becky moved into his embrace.

They held each other tightly. Her silver-tongued lover couldn't even speak. He wrapped her in his arms and clung to her as though the hour of redemption were at hand.

Alec closed his eyes, burying his face in her long tresses. "Oh, God, whatever I've done for you, it's noth-ing compared to what I would do," he choked out barely audibly. "Becky—I would die for you."

She stroked his golden hair, shaking her head. "No. Don't even say that. I need you alive, and I want you to be happy, Alec, at peace with yourself, not tearing your-self apart for a past you cannot change, and certainly not afraid of losing my love. It would take someone a great deal mightier than Lady Campion to destroy what we have." She lifted her head from his shoulder and looked into his eyes, cupping his face tenderly. "You're a good man, and I love you."

Stunned silence filled the room at her simple state-ment.

Beyond the window, the ocean soughed.

Alec, staring at her, looked as dazed by her words as a man who'd been thrown from a horse. "You love me?" The question slipped out softly. His big blue eyes looked so lonely and wistful that they brought fresh tears to her own.

She cupped his cheek. "More than words could say, my darling."

He stared into her eyes, clearly struggling for a re-sponse.

With a fond smile through her tears, she shook her

head. "It's all right, my sweet," she said, ruefully, lowering her hand from his face. "You don't have to say it back until you're ready."

"I'm sorry."

"No. You have nothing to be sorry for." She pushed his hair out of his eyes. "You've been through a lot where love's concerned. All I ask is that you let *me* continue to say it. Can you live with that?"

He searched her face with a faint uncertain glimmer of a smile. The man was plainly mystified. "A—all right."

"Good. Do you want to hear it again?"

"I'm . . . not sure."

"Let's try and see what happens." She leaned closer and kissed his brow. "I love you, sweetheart." She trailed soft fluttering kisses across his forehead, his eyelids, his nose. "I love you, Alexander Knight."

When she stopped, his breath quickening, he dragged his eyes open slowly and stared into hers. "Show me," he whispered in the darkness.

"How?"

His gaze dropped to her lips. "Make love to me."

Becky raised an eyebrow.

Alec licked his lips and waited intensely to see what she would do, that edge of challenge, that you-can't-reach-me look threatening to darken the depths of his eyes once again.

She smiled.

He was insatiable, but her stare was tender as she moved astride his lap without argument. His wounds would heal in time. If for now his fear required proof of her love before he could believe, she would give it. If his emptiness demanded her surrender in order to be filled, then she would yield. Her core was still damp from their exertions in the drawing room. With glittering eyes and trembling hands, Alec freed his thick straining phallus once more and lifted her chemise as she straddled him, entering her slowly.

She quivered at his warm hands clamped atop her thighs, pulling her down onto his rigid shaft. As before, her willing submission ignited something wild in him, just as his passion set her soul on fire.

They had made love less than an hour ago, but she was happy to give herself again if that was what it took to make him see that he was safe in her arms. He would not be used or exploited; he would not be abandoned or betrayed. If he needed her surrender in order to feel like a man again after the shattering blow to his pride of having to sell himself as a rich woman's plaything, then she would yield gladly and give Alec full control.

He took it hungrily, savoring her body's welcome with a lusty look of intoxication, but a moment later he rolled her onto her back across the bed and simply took her. Took what he wanted. No love play, no teasing games. He was hot and hard between her legs, urgent and commanding, with quick, deep thrusts.

His bare chest crashed against her with every stroke; his harsh breathing rasped at her ear. Becky winced with slight discomfort at his primal roughness but did not dream of stopping him. It was bliss to give herself this way: body and mind, completely, heart and soul. Her hands glided up and down his smooth, rippling sides in unwavering assurance; she opened herself to his plundering without regret.

She was fascinated by the way he ravished her now, the deepest, truest Alec revealed beneath his glittering charm and many masks—a man starved for love. Oh, yes, she had begun to understand how his mysterious mind worked.

He needed this.

She wrapped her legs around him. Rising up onto his hands over her, his hips pumped fiercely as he took his pleasure of her. With a ragged murmur, he asked if she wanted to come again. She shook her head, breathless. *This is all for you.*

He lowered his lashes and accepted the gift.

After a time, he gripped her harder, holding her under him just the way he wanted her. He clutched her breast in his hand. "Oh, God, Becky!" he gasped harshly, then went rigid in her arms, seizing his climax with thunderous force. His groan was long and strange and faded to a whisper.

There was no sound, then, but his panting as he lay heavily atop her.

She stroked his back and cradled his head in the crook of her neck. "I love you," she whispered.

"Even now?" he asked in a husky murmur.

"Always."

He pressed up onto his elbows and lowered his head, kissing her with rich, drowning depth, his body still sheathed in hers. Ending his wholly possessive kiss, he withdrew from inside her and moved lower, laying his head on her chest with a shaky exhalation.

"I don't understand," he said.

"You will."

Becky savored him, petting him and wishing she could shield him from the world with her love.

"You really are a very gentle girl."

She smiled softly at his pensive murmur but said nothing.

Alec splayed his hand across her belly, staring thoughtfully at it. After a moment, he lifted his head and looked into her eyes. "Are you still going to marry me?"

"Do you still want me?"

His eyebrows rose in surprise as he sat up and stared at her. "Want you? Good God, Becky, you're the only woman I've ever met who could keep me in line."

She gave him a wry smile, but her eyes beamed with

joy at his answer. "You're not so difficult. A challenge, but . . . worth it."

He flashed one of his brilliant, rakish smiles and scooped her onto his lap.

Becky wrapped her arms around his neck and gazed, smiling, into his eyes. "Of course I still want to marry you. You're the only man who could ever make me truly happy."

"Me?" he whispered, staring at her with the fragile bud of true, deep trust only now beginning to unfurl in the depths of his eyes.

She trailed her fingertips down his cheek. "Yes, my darling. You."

He pressed a soft kiss to her lips.

"No more secrets between us, Alec. Promise me that," she pleaded, pulling back a small space. "I know if you give me your word, you'll never break it."

"My darling wife, I could refuse you nothing."

She smiled, blushing at his tender endearment. Of course it was not official yet, not until they said their vows, but it was only a matter of time.

"You have my word," he whispered as he gifted her with another kiss. "No more secrets between us, ever."

CHAPTER
∽ THIRTEEN ∾

Reborn.

Alec awoke the next morning filled with new fire to protect Becky and restore her to her home.

He left the house early before she awoke to scout out the situation with Westland in anticipation of the next phase of their mission—revealing Kurkov's crimes to the authorities.

Before they had gone to sleep last night, he had filled her in about her cousin putting the Hall up for the whist drive and how he had gotten into the contest himself, staking his rooms at the Althorpe on the game. She had been moved by his willingness to sacrifice his home to try to win back hers, but after last night, God's truth, it was the least he could do. They were in this now together, all the way.

As he drove through Brighton in his hired phaeton, he couldn't get her face out of his mind. Not that he wished to. The sweetness of her violet eyes gazing at him as he had taken her by storm.

She said she loves me.

His brain could not stop marveling on it. Lovers had said those three sweetly treacherous words to him in the past, in their effort to own him, but he had believed none of them.

He believed Becky.

No one had ever been so abundantly kind to him. So

patient with him. Accepted him so completely. No one had ever believed so much in his essential worth, least of all himself.

He had crossed a line with her last night that he had never ventured past before, a place beyond which there could be no turning back. He had gone willingly, drawn past the fear; she had lured him out of his dark familiar world into this strange new country, and it was like awakening in another world.

It all looked the same, streets and houses, sky and trees, but the strong gold light of dawn struck every surface at a new angle, bringing everything into sharp focus. The earth seemed newly cleaned as after a hard rain, and there was a smell of true freedom in the air.

Though in one sense he was in a state of blissful bewilderment, he felt better equipped than ever before to deal with whatever came his way. He had only set out last night to tell her the truth because he owed her that, she deserved it; he had not expected fair Becky to deal the demons of his old self-doubt a deathblow. But apparently she had.

He had long wanted to change, but for the first time in ages, he felt as if the power to do so was in his hands. At last, his destiny was his own to control: No longer was he subject to the bidding of Robert or the rest of his elder brothers, not Lady Luck nor Lady Campion, nor even his own compulsions. The reins were in his hands now.

Somehow Becky had given him back to himself.

He wondered what she thought today of his inability to repeat those three dangerous words back to her. The last thing he wanted was to hurt her. He had been afraid as he sat there faltering last night that she would get angry at him, but instead, she had smiled tenderly.

He did not know why those words were so difficult for him, but his voice locked down in their presence, as though he alone knew that they comprised some black magic spell that, if uttered, would summon Mephistopheles.

Mephistopheles apparently didn't scare Becky Ward. Alec was beginning to wonder if anything did. How she surprised him over and over again with her strength.

For a few minutes this morning, in wonder and reverence, he had watched her while she slept, trying to comprehend what made her so beautiful, what made her so brave. He had seen in her eyes the pain that his confession had caused her, and he had watched her triumph over it. Courageous, dauntless female. She inspired him.

Could it be love, in fact, this fierce, tangled burning in his chest? But he had always believed the poets when they said love was all sweet breezes and gentle brooks. Deadly dull, he had always thought it sounded.

What he felt for Becky was more like a firestorm inside him, a primal certainty that he would burn down the world if it threatened her. This "love" of which the poets sang bore little resemblance to the violent ardor that he felt for her.

In any case, he recalled again her urging him to forgive himself for the error of his ways, and though the idea intrigued him, it was a damned lot easier said than done. Perhaps when he had accomplished what he had set out to do and put the deed to Talbot Old Hall in her hands, and was satisfied that she was permanently safe, maybe then he could do as she asked.

Maybe then he would deserve it.

By the time he returned to the villa from his morning's reconnaissance for the noon meeting with his friends, his mood had darkened after what he had seen: Cossacks, still posted discreetly outside the Westland town house.

He was glad he had kept a distance, for Kurkov was still apparently monitoring all comings and goings from the duke's home. Though out of uniform, Kurkov's men had stood out to Alec's practiced eye.

Large, rough, non-British-looking men loitering here and there, trying to look inconspicuous, might have been able to blend in back in London, but Brighton was less crowded and more refined. The Cossacks were watching the house from all four corners, but when the duke's carriage pulled away, two of them had followed in a plain covered carriage, while the others held their posts.

Such dogged persistence sent a chill down Alec's spine. He supposed Kurkov was going out of his mind, knowing Becky was still at large, still possessed of information that could nail his coffin shut. If the prince was going to those lengths, then it was entirely possible he had also bribed a servant within the Westland household to spy for him, Alec mused. Such practices were easy enough to arrange. He recalled an incident a few years ago at Knight House when an underbutler had been dismissed for tampering with Robert's mail. The chap had been reading letters from the duke's political associates among the Whigs and reporting his findings to unnamed persons in the Tory party. Once the insolent cur had gotten the science down of using steam to pry off the wax seals, he even helped himself to reading a few love letters written to their sister Jacinda, from her countless beaux.

In any case, Kurkov's resourcefulness made matters all the more difficult for Alec and Becky. Not only was the Duke of Westland unlikely to take either of them seriously, having already determined that Becky was an afflicted madwoman and Alec a scoundrel, but it now seemed impossible to reach His Grace at all without Kurkov discovering them first and heading them off at the pass.

Perhaps there was someone else whom they could

bring their case to instead of Westland, Alec mused as he strode back into the villa. Count Lieven, the Russian ambassador? He was a powerful man and certainly seemed to bear his mighty countryman no love. . . .

These thoughts swirled through his mind as he told Becky what he had found, both of them waiting for his friends to arrive.

All of a sudden the front door flew open. Draxinger appeared, looking tempest-tossed. "Alec! Calamity! I must speak to you at once! It is Parthenia!"

Alec strode into the hall to meet him while Rush and Fort followed Draxinger in. "What is it?"

Drax gripped Alec's arms, searching his face wildly. "I spoke to her last night at the ball—me and Fort. Do you know what she said?"

"No. I've no idea. What?"

Drax swallowed hard. "She told me—to my face!—that she intends to accept another man's offer of marriage. She taunted me with it. It took me half an hour to get her to say who it was!"

"Prince Kurkov?" Alec asked with a wince.

The earl gasped. "How did you know?"

"Gentlemen," Alec said wryly, sweeping a gesture toward the drawing room. "Won't you please come in?"

Draxinger nodded, looking stricken, and made his way up the stairs in a daze. Alec watched with a wry twinge of lingering jealousy as Rushford greeted Becky warmly and bowed to kiss her hand. "Miss Ward, you look even lovelier than yesterday."

She gave him a smile of thanks, but then noticed Alec's stare and discreetly blew him a playful kiss before going upstairs behind Rushford.

Fort was the last to go up, but he harrumphed at Alec as he passed him at the foot of the stairs.

"Is it true you're getting married?" he demanded.

Alec nodded, chagrined now to have been caught

keeping still more secrets, this time from his friends. "Aye, Daniel, it's true."

Fort stared at him, marveling. "But, *why*?"

Alec laughed quietly, clapped him on the shoulder, and turned Fort toward the stairs. "Come and meet her and you'll know why, my friend. She is the most wonderful creature."

"You could have told us!" he muttered with a scowl.

"And give you a chance to talk me out of it?" Alec asked in amusement.

"Precisely! Looks like our fun's over. Ah, well. Congratulations, anyway." Fort succumbed to a rueful smile and headed for the drawing room.

As he watched his best friend trudging up the stairs, Alec couldn't help feeling like a bit of a heel for having kept them in the dark. Well, hell, his friends had never been known for their discretion. On the other hand, he had no choice but to trust them now. Somebody had to guard Becky, after all, while he was in the whist drive.

He joined them in the drawing room and spent the next hour explaining their quest to regain Talbot Old Hall and to bring Kurkov to justice. The latter part of their discussion nearly sent Drax into a fit of apoplexy.

"We must warn Parthenia! She cannot be permitted to marry this fiend! I'll call him out! Yes! That's it! I'll cut him down on the field of honor!"

"Don't be daft," Rushford drawled.

"Lord Draxinger, it's not just that Mikhail is a renowned warrior himself," Becky spoke up. "He uses all those Cossacks to carry out his dirty work for him. Mikhail doesn't waste his time with duels. He'd just as likely have you killed before the hour of the duel arrived."

Drax cursed. "Well, we've got to do *something*."

"We will warn Parthenia—after the whist drive," Alec said pointedly.

"Why not now? She'll be at the ladies' sea-bathing beach in a quarter hour—"

"You know her schedule?" Fort cried. "What is happening around here?"

Rush chuckled. "Oh, leave him alone, Fort."

Drax turned red, neither confirming nor denying the obvious.

"The main thing is Parthenia is not in danger yet."

"At least not till she marries Mikhail," Becky added under her breath.

"Nevertheless, it would put my mind greatly at ease if I could talk to her about it," Drax said.

"You mustn't yet," Becky murmured, shaking her head.

"Besides, Parthenia won't see you, remember?" Rush reminded him.

"Oh, right," Drax said, crestfallen. "She hates me. I forgot."

"And so does her father," Fort offered drily.

"Try to get ahold of yourself, Drax. You see, this is why I was so hesitant to tell you all this!" Alec exclaimed. "We cannot have any overreactions. Parthenia's pride might end up bruised when her suitor is exposed as a felon, but if you don't guard your tongues, Becky could end up dead."

"I could do it," she volunteered suddenly. "I could warn her."

They all looked at her, taken aback.

Folding her arms across her chest, Becky leaned her hip against the sofa's scrolled arm. "Not even Mikhail with all his guile and all his soldiers can get into the ladies' sea-bathing beach," she said, looking from man to man with a frank demeanor. "I could go there and talk with Parthenia secretly, inside one of the bathing machines. Tell her what's afoot. No one need even see us conversing."

"Why, she could, at that," Drax murmured.

"Absolutely not," Alec said flatly.

"Why?" Becky countered. "If all of you are taking so much trouble for my sake, then it's only right that I should help. Besides, this is easy. I could do it in a trice. It's not as if Mikhail or his men can come anywhere near there. The ladies' beach is private for the sake of the swimmers' modesty. Women only."

"Well, yes and no," Fort interrupted.

Becky looked at him in question.

Fort hesitated, his expression turning sheepish. "Up the hill from the ladies' beach there happens to be a lookout point where, if you'll pardon my saying so, any interested young man with a telescope can see, uh, everything."

Her eyes widened. "Really?"

Alec scratched his cheek as his friends and he exchanged guilty glances.

"Yes, but we could go up there and if we find any fellows spying through telescopes, we could shove them down their throats," Drax suggested in growing conviction.

"Or toss them over the cliff," Rushford cheerfully agreed.

"I see what you're getting at and it all *sounds* easy enough," Alec conceded, "but if we tell Parthenia the truth about Kurkov, what if she slips and lets him realize that she's on to him? Then she could be in real danger—and so could Becky."

"I needn't tell her everything," Becky said in a reasonable tone. "Just enough to put her on her guard."

"Won't she recognize you?"

"I doubt it. If we were in Buckley-on-the-Heath, then she would probably remember me, but out of that setting, she won't be able to place me."

"Can she be trusted, Drax?" Alec asked, turning

soberly to the earl. "Can Parthenia keep her mouth shut if we warn her to keep Kurkov at arm's length for the time being?"

"Absolutely. I will vouch for her. Parthenia is not some vapid ninny. She's an intelligent young woman. And besides," he added wryly, "if she can keep me guessing about her true feelings when we've known each other for years, then I trust she can jolly well hide her emotions from *him.*"

"I agree." Becky stood with firm confidence. "It's the best solution. Not only can we warn Lady Parthenia to keep a distance from my cousin, but if we get her on our side, we can also go through her to make sure her father reads my report at the exact moment when it's most advantageous for us that he do so. Westland will listen to Parthenia before he'll listen to any of us. But I won't tell her enough to make her terrified of Mikhail. He must perceive no change in her outward demeanor or he will become suspicious."

"This could work," Rush murmured, nodding.

"I still don't like it," Alec grumbled.

Becky looked at him frankly. "I can do this."

Pride in her washed through his heart in a fierce but troubled wave. He searched her eyes uneasily. "You don't have to put yourself on the line."

"You have," she countered, holding his gaze for a moment longer before she turned away, pacing in thought. "It's the simplest solution. I'll make an extra copy of my report and arrange for Parthenia to get it. If the servants are inspecting the mail, as you suspect, then we can send my papers disguised as something else—something innocuous. A delivery from the laundress or the modiste shop. She's got to know ahead of time to look for it, though, so it doesn't end up in the wrong hands. This way, Parthenia can intercept it from whatever spy Mikhail might have put in her household, and make sure it gets to her father."

"Well, don't tell her that one of her servants might be against her," Drax declared. "The Westlands won't tolerate that sort of thing for a second. If I know them, they'll turn the household upside-down at once to root out the evildoer—they may even summon the constable— and then Kurkov will know something's afoot."

"Agreed," Alec said, nodding as he rested his hands on his waist. "We can't make any sudden moves with that blackguard. At least not until I've got the deed to the Hall in my hand and we're ready for him. We don't want to set him off prematurely or alert him to what's coming. A man with that much power, fortune, connections—he's slippery. We've got to get him right where we want him."

"Well, then," Rush said. "That's settled."

Becky sent him a challenging glance. "Alec?"

Searching her eyes, he relented with a reluctant nod. "Very well. You speak to Parthenia and we'll keep watch. And if we see any Cossacks—"

"Or men with telescopes," Fort chimed in.

"We'll distract 'em," Drax finished.

"They'd better hope that's all we do," Alec murmured, cracking his knuckles.

The bathing machines, colorfully painted, looked like tiny striped houses atop wagon wheels. The only males present on the ladies' beach were little boys of eight or nine, too young to care if they glimpsed a bit of ankle. Their job was to handle the huge, gentle draft horses used for backing the bathing machines into the water.

A lady desirous of sea bathing for her health and pleasure would climb up into one of these miniature buildings; the bathing machine would then be wheeled down into the water to its axles, saving the passenger inside from the discomfort of crossing the rocky shingle and being buffeted by the waves at the shoreline. When it had reached a depth of two or three feet, the little door would open and the lady would appear again in her long modest swimming costume and bathing cap. Helpless and blinking like a newborn kitten in the sunshine, she would mince her way down the small ladder with the help of the "dippers," two large peasant matrons in wide-brimmed hats who were stationed in the water like docking posts, set to assist the shrieking Lady of Quality into the chilly, salty waves.

Becky watched the process intently as she crossed the rocky beach to the water's edge, pebbles crunching under every step. She did not personally intend to use one of the silly contraptions, trusting that her own two legs would serve perfectly well to convey her into the water. Her face was concealed by a deep-brimmed poke bonnet, and for a bathing costume she wore a lightweight green pelisse over a thin, modest morning gown of fawn-colored calico. It was loose-fitting enough to allow easy movement, high-necked and long-sleeved to protect her skin from the sun.

Glancing up at the distant cliff top with a vague scowl, she took off her bonnet and pelisse and threw them on the ground for later. The water would be very cold and she would need the easy, sleeveless coat to put on over her wet clothes once her mission was accomplished. Squinting against the sun, she paused to take off her borrowed half boots of soft kid. Impertinent gulls bickered over a dead crab nearby: Becky wrinkled her nose and looked away.

Water swirled and foamed around her legs, brushing her with slimy bits of seaweed as she waded into the indolent surf, which was busily polishing the stones bright, rolling them up and back ceaselessly over the layer of sand beneath. The breeze played with the long single plait of her hair as she searched the waves for Parthenia Westland, trying not to get caught up in the sheer beauty of the sea. It mesmerized her, the watery realm of her birth; she drew strength from it surrounding her.

Becky gasped a little, reaching freezing-cold water up to her waist, but she noted that the dippers had their hands full today—literally. There were probably fifty swimmers frolicking in the shallows, with five bathing machines continually bringing more. Seeing so many girls her own age laughing and swimming together in the waves, she could not help but feel sad for a moment, thinking of all that she had missed out on, thanks to her grandfather's unyielding grudge against Mama. It was bad enough to have been denied things like parties and pretty dresses, but she wished she could have at least found a few suitable companions of her own rank.

No point in fretting about it now. She shrugged it off. Her teeth chattered a little as she scanned the crowd of sea bathers again, shading her eyes from the sun. There! Parthenia Westland. She fought an irreverent smile at the elegant lady's current state of soggy bedragglement. *Good.* Now all she had to do was wait for the right moment.

Becky dove into the water and swam casually in Parthenia's direction. The sunshine, the movement, and the brisk chill of the sea greatly refreshed her. The initial bite of the cold passed; Becky enjoyed herself, keeping one eye on her quarry.

Earlier, out of earshot of Lord Draxinger, she had asked Alec, the master socialite, how he suggested gaining Parthenia's ear long enough to make her listen.

"Simple. Charm her."

"How?"

"I always find it safest to go for their vanity," he had said dryly. He then helped her to design a simple but convincing cock-and-bull story to help frame the information in a way best suited to gain Parthenia's cooperation. "I don't care what Drax says," Alec had confided in a low tone as they walked ahead of the others to the carriage. "She's an arrogant creature. Whatever you do, don't come across as if you think yourself her equal, or she won't listen to a word you say."

"Ingratiate myself?" Becky had asked ruefully.

"Just this once," he answered, giving her a quick, roguish kiss. "If you can stand it."

Well, if she had to lie a bit for now, she thought, so be it. The whole truth would come out in due time.

She spent a few minutes floating on her back, the skirts of her morning dress spreading out over the low waves that rocked her gently. Arms out by her sides, she gazed up at the puffy white cloud-towers with the sky behind them as blue as Alec's eyes.

She was still amazed to learn that he had put up his rooms at the Althorpe for her. If he lost in the whist drive, he would be as destitute and homeless as she. What they would do in that case, she did not care to consider. But he seemed different today somehow. Very much in command.

Suddenly, she came to attention and thrust her musing thoughts aside, seeing Parthenia making her way back to one of the bathing machines. *Perfect.* Becky pushed off the bottom and casually swam toward it as well. When the duke's daughter climbed up the ladder, assisted by the dippers, Becky was right behind her. Once inside the wobbly contraption, she quickly pulled the little door shut and locked it.

"I say!" Parthenia exclaimed, pausing in her task of drying her ear with a towel. "Madam, what are you doing? This is a private bathing machine!"

"Lady Parthenia, I must speak to you on a matter of the greatest urgency." Becky tugged the string that rang the bell that in turn signaled the boy to lead the horse back to the shoreline.

"Who are you?" she demanded in mingled hauteur and alarm.

"A friend."

"No friend of mine. I've never seen you before in my life. What is the meaning of this intrusion? Explain yourself at once!"

Well, at least she doesn't recognize me, Becky thought. "We've little time. I come to you with a warning, my lady. I fear you may be in danger."

"Danger? What on earth . . . ? What kind of danger?"

"The danger of public humiliation—and of possibly making the greatest mistake of your life!" The theatrical hint of melodrama with which she purposely imbued her words won her Parthenia's complete attention.

Alec, the actor's son, would have been proud, she thought.

Becky sat down on the bench across from Parthenia as the bathing machine lurched slowly toward the shore. "My lady, I am a navy orphan," Becky said, keeping to the story the two of them had concocted. "You have benefited me and my poor mother and all my little brothers and sisters in the past with your charitable work through the whist drive."

"Have I?"

"Oh, yes—and your efforts have made you our bene-factress. We pray for you every night around our humble dinner table, all my . . . seven younger brothers and sisters and I, and our poor, sick, old mother."

"Oh—that's very sweet," she conceded, somewhat mollified.

"Naturally, after all the good you've done us, I would not see you come to harm for all the world. I should not even be here. It could cost me my living, but my mother said we owed it to you, to warn you of the peril you are in." Becky feigned a nervous glance around and then lowered her voice. "You see, my lady, I am in domestic service in the household of a very important gentleman in the government."

"Whig?"

"Tory. A noble lord, associated with the Foreign Office."

"I see." She immediately detected the wheels turning in Parthenia's mind as she tried to guess who the fictional Tory lord might be.

"I overheard my master and some of his associates discussing some very unpleasant matters about—" Becky now dropped her voice to a whisper. "Prince Mikhail Kurkov."

Parthenia's right eyebrow arched. "Really."

"I should never eavesdrop on my employer's conversations, I'm sure, but while I was, er, dusting in the hall, I heard my employer speaking in his study with certain gentlemen from the Foreign Office, saying they have located some sort of mysterious blot upon Prince Kurkov's name—back in Russia," she added hastily. "London Society has not yet learned of it, but they will."

"What sort of blot?" Parthenia asked skeptically, but she had begun to look worried.

Excellent, Becky thought. She was taking the bait. Perhaps Parthenia had noticed during their courtship that there was something altogether untrustworthy about Mikhail.

"I do not know, my lady. I did not wish to be impertinent. But it sounded serious, and I must confess I thought of you at once. Forgive me, I mean no presumption. I had seen you and the prince promenading so beautifully on the Steyne, and the scandal sheets have suggested that an alliance between yourselves might soon be announced."

"You should not be reading scandal sheets, Miss . . . ?"

"Abby, my lady. Just call me Abby."

"If you are fortunate enough to have learnt to read, Abby, you should seek to elevate yourself by studying worthier reading material."

"Of course, ma'am, sorry," Becky mumbled, swallowing her impatience.

Parthenia looked away with a troubled frown. "I wish you could tell me more," she mumbled, plainly wondering what sort of dirt the Tories might have on her fiancé. She turned to Becky again. "Perhaps it was something that happened during the war? Money troubles?" Then her eyebrows drew together. "Not something regarding another lady, I hope?"

"I do not know for certain, but from the way they were talking, my lady, I—I fear it may be even more serious than that."

"Really?" she breathed, wide-eyed.

Becky nodded with great sincerity. "After all you've done for me and my family, I felt it my duty to warn you, as you can see, that my lady might wish to delay in accepting the prince's suit until his past misdeeds have come to light."

Parthenia frowned and shook her head. "Papa says never trust a Tory. Perhaps they are only trying to blacken Mikhail's name since he has joined the Whigs. They're jealous!"

"They have an eyewitness. A person of considerable credibility," Becky added, unable to resist. "I wish I could have heard more, but the housekeeper nearly caught me, ah, snooping."

"I see." Parthenia's eyes narrowed in thought. "Abby, you did the right thing by coming to me."

"Oh, thank you, my lady."

"Even if it all proves false, it is better to be safe than sorry. Still, I do wish we had more information."

"Perhaps there's a way. . . ." Becky feigned hesitation.

"I did see my master put some papers away in a locked drawer. I believe they pertain to the case. I did not see them myself. . . ."

Parthenia leaned closer. "Abby," she said, "perhaps you could get to those papers. Just for a look. What say you? You see, the prince has asked my father's permission to marry me!"

"Oh! Oh, dear. In that case . . ." Becky paused, and then delivered the coup de grâce with a look of increasing worry. "Lady Parthenia, do you think it's possible the Tories are deliberately planning to conceal the facts about Prince Kurkov's misdeeds until you have married him, only waiting to spring out the truth of his infamy once the match is sealed? For by doing so, they could cause your noble father great embarrassment."

Parthenia paled. "Oh, they would do that. Yes! As a leader of the Whigs, Papa has long been a thorn in their side. Well," she declared, "if Mikhail has secrets to hide, he shan't take Papa and me down with him!" Parthenia leaned closer and gripped Becky's shoulder intensely, quite startling her.

Well, perhaps Lord Draxinger was right. Perhaps all that frostiness was just for show.

"Abby," Parthenia said shrewdly, "can you get me those papers?"

"Oh, dear me . . . I do not know if I dare."

The duke's daughter lifted her chin. "It doesn't matter if you are dismissed from your post. Who wants to work for a cranky old Tory, anyway? When this has all been sorted out, you shall come and work for me! Yes, I'll even let you train to become lady's maid if you like," she announced with great magnanimity.

"Oh, my goodness, ma'am, you are even more generous than I had known!" Laughing up her sleeve, Becky feigned heartfelt gratitude, but she was happy to let

Parthenia think it had all been her own idea. "I will do it!" she said boldly. "But in the meantime, pray you, my lady, do not reveal to His Highness that you have any reason to doubt him."

"No?"

"No, for if he is innocent, then you may lose him. No one likes to be doubted by the person he or she loves, my lady." Her own words brought back a flush of pride in how she had handled the situation with Alec last night, choosing to rise above her doubts to trust him. His amazed reaction had made it all worthwhile.

"You're right." Parthenia nodded, looking energized by this exciting bit of intrigue. "I shall keep my doubts under my bonnet and withhold judgment until you've brought me those papers and I've read them for myself."

"Very wise, ma'am." Becky nodded reverently. "Considering this could be viewed as theft—"

"Theft? No! We're only going to borrow them, after all." Parthenia actually smiled. "You'll put them back after I've read them, won't you?"

"Oh, yes, my lady. Still, perhaps it would be best not to let anyone else see the papers, just to be safe. I shall send them to you disguised as something else. A delivery from the modiste shop, perhaps?"

"Good idea. But, Abby, I will have to show them to Papa. If Mikhail is hiding something, my father must be told of it. He always knows what to do."

"Very well, ma'am. If you read the papers and take them directly to His Grace, then I can return to retrieve them from you and put them back into the drawer before they're even missed."

"Just so. Why, I should be glad to have a maid as clever as you, Abby. You are much out of the common way."

"Thank you, my lady." She fought a smile and bowed her head.

"You needn't thank me. It is I who should thank you," Parthenia declared. "It would be very vexing to have announced an alliance between the prince and me only to have some unpleasant information come out. I should have to break off the engagement then, and I would hate it if all the world supposed Mikhail has broken my heart—for he could not!"

"You are . . . not in love with him?" Becky asked gingerly, careful to keep a humble posture.

"Pshaw, no. I've only encouraged him to please Papa. The truth is, I love another," she confessed with a wry smile, letting her guard down in light of their little conspiracy. "Unfortunately, he does not return my affections."

"Are you sure of that, my lady?" Becky asked with a twinkle in her eyes.

Parthenia sighed and nodded wistfully as the bathing machine lurched up onto the rocky shore. "Quite. You know, Abby, good breeding aside, there are some gentlemen in this world that you just want to punch in the nose."

Becky nodded, biting back laughter, and suddenly very glad she had knocked Draxinger's tooth loose. "Oh, my lady, I know exactly what you mean."

CHAPTER
∞ FOURTEEN ∞

*T*he opening of the whist drive was held on the fair-grounds outside of town to accommodate the throng along with their countless carriages and hundreds of horses. Bathed in dazzling afternoon sunshine, the mood was festive, part horse race, part church social. Eight tables for the first round were set up beneath the huge open tent, which had several points atop it and was gaily striped.

There had been an alarming moment when the children running all over the grounds like little heathens kicking a ball amongst themselves, a spaniel barking at their heels, had dislodged the rope tying the tent down. One corner of the fanciful structure almost collapsed, thanks to their antics. Parthenia Westland nearly had an apoplectic fit, but fortunately, the mishap occurred before the card game had started, and thanks to a few servants with quick reflexes, disaster was averted.

Now round one was well under way, and the duke's daughter had gone back to serving refreshments to the Quality along with the rest of the charitable ladies, all sporting superior smiles and large, elaborate, flower-laden hats.

Safely removed to the outer fringes of the festivities, and guarded by Rush and Fort, Becky paced endlessly as she waited for the outcome, her stomach a flutter of nerves. Alec had tried to forbid her to come today, but nothing could have induced her to stay at home.

Every woman had her limits of what she could endure, and Becky was near the edge of hers. He had finally relented when she promised to keep a distance of at least three hundred yards. Alec had also bade Fort and Rush to keep the Cossacks in constant view. Mikhail was under the big tent playing cards with the other thirty-one gamblers, but the Cossacks were in sight, keeping watch on the crowd that surrounded the players.

Becky had worn a deep-brimmed poke bonnet draped by a veil of light blue lace as an added means of concealing her identity, with a final added line of camouflage in the form of her parasol.

While Alec and Lord Draxinger tried their luck in the first round, she waited in suspense that was equal parts hope and dread. She hated the feeling of being so powerless, but she knew it was all in Alec's hands now. For their plan to succeed, Mikhail only had to be eliminated at some point along the way, but Alec had to win. If—or rather, *when*—he did so, she corrected herself, he would not only be in possession of her house, but would also have won for himself a fortune that was almost beyond her imagining.

The grand prize of 320,000 pounds was a fortune of staggering proportions. The winning pair of players would split the pot, taking home 160,000 pounds each, minus, of course, the ten percent that would be deducted for charity. The victors would be feted at the Winners' Ball when the whole thing was over.

Becky knew Alec had been nervous leading up to the start of the tournament. He had barely slept last night, up pacing and sitting in the garden, smoking cigarillos; he barely touched his breakfast, though he'd guzzled a pot of strong coffee. Though he obviously appreciated her efforts to encourage him, he had remained distracted. Loath as he was to forgive himself for his past, it was as though he had placed his own full worth as a human being on the outcome of the whist drive, and Becky knew that was a dangerous state of affairs.

He had become, however, intensely focused going into the game. She remembered that come-hell-or-high-water look on his face this morning, with a fierce, cool glint in his eyes similar to the one she'd seen during his bloody fight against the Cossacks.

Oh, what if he is eliminated? What if someone else wins the Hall?

Pacing through the overgrown grass, she could do naught but wait. She couldn't help feeling a trifle suspicious about Mikhail's decision to use the Hall as collateral. *Why?* Perhaps a guilty conscience made him eager to be rid of it—though she doubted it. He had stated flatly that the Tudor style was not to his taste. But maybe, Becky mused, as impossible as it sounded, maybe Mikhail did not *have* ten thousand pounds. . . .

The brief toot of a horn broke into her thoughts, coming from somewhere under the shady tent. She turned to Fort in question.

"That signals the end of round one," he murmured.

Becky laid her hand vaguely over her thumping heart and gripped the handle of her parasol hard as she waited for the results.

Whist had a rather staid reputation for a card game and was so simple, fundamentally, that even a novice like Becky had no trouble understanding how it was played. As Alec had told her, a good memory gave a player a distinct advantage.

At each of the eight tables in round one, four players sat in two fixed partnerships, the partners facing each other. Partners were assigned at random and were changed after each hand. A full deck was used, and the man designated as dealer dealt each player thirteen cards, facedown.

Starting with the man to the dealer's left, the game moved clockwise, each player throwing down one card. The other players would have to match by throwing down a card of the same suit. It was called a "trick" when each of the four players had thrown down a card; there were thus thirteen tricks in a game. Whoever had thrown down the highest-valued card of the trump suit won the trick, and a point was awarded to the winning team. Because it was a tournament, the trump suits were always designated in advance, per traditional rules: For the first deal, it was hearts; second, diamonds; third, spades; and lastly, clubs.

Clubs would not be played during round one, however, for there would only be three deals. Whoever had the most points at the end of the deal won the hand. The team that won the best of three hands would progress to round two, where there would only be sixteen players seated at four tables.

The losers who had been eliminated after round one had to sign away their funds at the master of ceremonies' table before filing out of the roped-off playing area and exiting under a garlanded arched trellis, to the applause of all for their generous contribution. It was a very quick way to lose an enormous sum of money. Becky watched breathlessly for Alec as the first-round losers emerged while the crowd applauded them.

Alec had not appeared.

"He's made it!" she breathed when the last man passed under the arch and gave a good-natured wave to the audience.

"Drax stayed in, too," Fort murmured.

"So did Kurkov," Rush said grimly.

She sucked in her breath and turned away swiftly as two of her cousin's Cossack warriors stalked around the edge of the distant crowd and, with weapons jangling, went to check on their horses. Alec's friends concealed her until they passed. Then the three of them exchanged grim glances.

Meanwhile, beneath the tent, the remaining sixteen men played in silent concentration. Though the time dragged, it was barely half an hour before a second toot of the horn sounded and round two was also done.

Just as before, the team at each table who had won the best of three deals would progress to round three, with only *eight* players at *two* tables.

Round three was to take place tomorrow night, and would no doubt be a raucous affair, for the gentlemen only, to be hosted by the Duke of Norfolk at nearby Arundel Castle, where Becky and Alec had ridden out one afternoon some time ago on hired hack horses.

Instead of the fairly speedy best out of three hands, the remaining players in round three would probably be at it half the night, for they would be playing "long whist," in which each game was nine points.

Finally, on the following night, the Regent would host the fourth and final round of the annual Brighton whist drive aboard the opulent royal yacht, anchored some distance offshore. In the final round there would be only one table. Four players. Two teams. This last stage of the tournament would be the most difficult and grueling of all, for a win in the final round could not be declared until one team had gained a five-point lead over their opponents.

"Prince of whales," Rush murmured as the future king waddled out from under the tent, squeezing his royal girth through the arched trellis and then giving his beloved Brightonians a gentlemanly bow. They cheered him madly, for unlike the rest of the country, the people of Brighton adored their royal patron.

"Oh, he's not so bad, is he?" Becky answered, smiling

ruefully as "Prinny" reveled in the adulation for a few moments longer.

At last the future king trudged off with his attendants, leaving the rest of the vanquished to file out as before. The crowd applauded the rich losers' generosity once again.

Becky held her breath, counting each man in the short queue coming out of the tent, but no Alec. "He's still in!" she whispered, her heart pounding wildly. *Lucky.*

"Told you he'd do it," Fort said with a smile.

"Lord Draxinger's held on, as well," Becky answered.

"And so has Kurkov," Lord Rushford repeated, his stare on the distant tent.

Some fifteen minutes later Alec and Drax strode out together. They spotted them on the crest of the hill where they waited and headed toward them.

From across the meadow Alec flashed her a small grin, the afternoon sun shining on his golden hair, and gossamer-winged butterflies zigzagging across his path.

"Those blackguards," Rush murmured, shaking his head sardonically. "There'll be no living with them now."

As Alec came closer, he held up a small piece of paper in his hand, waving it.

"What's that he's showing us?" Becky asked.

"His ticket to round three," Fort drawled, watching his friends with an affectionate smile spreading over his face.

The very next night, heavy brass torchères lit the manly space of the great hall at Arundel Castle.

Ducal ancestors stared down proudly from their portraits in gilded frames, sharing the creamy walls with the Great Masters and a frieze bearing the various colorful coats of arms associated with the family. Overhead, a coffered ceiling was paneled in warm ruddy oak diamonds. On one wall, massive Norman arches housed the window bays; opposite them, a towering white chimney-piece slanted all the way up to the ceiling and posed a setting for yet another display of a coat of arms.

The long spacious hall easily accommodated the two gaming tables left in round three, along with several dozen spectators.

The Regent had come for a while but left early. Meanwhile, the other gentlemen staved off hunger with an array of sandwiches, but the late hour and the quantities of liquor being consumed had exalted them to a rowdy joviality that, in Alec's view, bordered on bad form.

Most of the men were preoccupied in laying side wagers amongst themselves on which team would win at each of the two tables. Alec was tempted to tell their audience to shut the devil up. The noise was distracting his thrice-damned partner—but not him.

No man in the great hall craved victory more than Alec did. He had already made up his mind he was not walking out of here a loser.

Staving off bleary fatigue, he held on grimly to his concentration, keeping everyone's cards filed away neatly in his head. His luck was with him.

As one who appreciated irony, Alec could not fail to see a certain humor upon finding himself randomly paired with Kurkov as his partner for round three. How the goddess Fortuna loved to play her little jokes.

Though Alec's real goal was to destroy the prince; and though Kurkov, in turn, would have happily run him through if he had known that Alec was the one protecting Becky—the very man who had cut down two of his Cossack warriors—for now the two of them were forced to work together to reach nine points before their opponents did.

At the next table, Drax's partner was no less unpleasant than Alec's own, the dissolute and disfigured nabob,

Colonel Tallant. A hard, wiry man in his fifties, Tallant wore a black patch on one eye above a cheek scored by the slash of a saber, gotten supposedly in some cavalry charge, though Alec could just have easily believed that Tallant had incurred the scar doing highway robbery.

On the one occasion that Alec had ever spoken to the colonel, Tallant had revolted him with his bragging of all the tigers he had shot in the forests of India, even baby ones. *What did those tigers ever do to you?* Alec had nearly asked him.

In any case, Drax and the colonel were pulling ahead of the esteemed MP and the upstart grandson of a Birmingham coal factor who looked rather dapper with his monocle fixed in his right eye as he inspected his cards. Drax, for his part, was wearing his lucky hat with a brim that cast a shadow over his face, helping to conceal his expression.

Between hands, Alec lifted his head, stretched a bit, and spotted Count Lieven. He started to greet the ambassador, but noticed that Lieven was engrossed in a note that a servant had brought him. Alec watched intently as the count folded up the note with a tense look and put it in his pocket, unaware that he was being observed. He then stood and hurried out of the room, thanking his host on the way out.

Lieven did not return.

It was two A.M. before a win was achieved. Drax and Tallant at the other table claimed the victor's laurels; ten minutes later Mikhail and Alec tasted triumph. His heart pounding, his smile tentative after such a long bout of intense effort, he rose from the table and shook the losers' hands, rather stiff after six hours of play.

Tallant was exuberant, like he could smell a kill. Kurkov puffed out his chest and broke out with a cigar.

"Well played, Alexei," he rumbled, landing an easy blow on Alec's shoulder, a smile slashing his dark beard.

"Good luck in round four," he added with a ruthless glint of humor in his gray eyes. "Of course, I'll kill you if I have to."

"Likewise, Your Highness," Alec answered in a silky tone, more pleased by the prospect than his enemy knew.

"Do you know something, Mikhail?" Eva asked, regarding the great hard beast in cynical amusement. "You are the first Russian I ever fucked. Isn't that nice?"

He merely grunted.

Paying her little mind, Mikhail lay staring at the sea, brooding and smoking a cheroot much later that night while Eva played with his short beard and raked her fingers through the fur on his chest.

"Give me that." To get his full attention, she borrowed his cheroot and took a puff from it, blowing an expert smoke ring.

"That's very impressive," he remarked, watching her. "Are you sure you don't have any Cossack blood?"

She laughed.

Mikhail took the small thin cigar back from her with only the trace of a smile.

Dawn was drawing near, but it was still gray outside Lady Campion's little yellow pastel summerhouse. Far off on the ocean's horizon the sun showed only a flat glimmering line. They could see it from her bedroom window, indeed, from her curtained bed where the two of them had spent all night battling for supremacy, nearly tearing each other apart as they struggled to determine who was going to be in control of this affair.

When Mikhail had come back from Arundel Castle, victorious after round three of the whist drive, Eva brushed off the news that he had been paired with Alec Knight and then playfully offered her new lover his reward. He accepted, and their rough contest had begun.

It was rare to find a man who could give back to her as good as he got, and in the end, to Eva's amazement, Mikhail had won. She had teeth marks and bruises all over her body and felt, in all, as though she had been ravished by the big bad wolf of fairy-tale fame. Extraordinary, but she quite believed she was smitten. Her Russian beast was not like any other lover she had ever known. A man completely beyond her control. A man who could force *her* to obey. Put her in her place. She might chafe under his domination, but she knew it was exactly what she needed.

In short, the baroness had made up her mind to keep him. She had been alone long enough, playing games and chasing pleasure. The change in Alec, her former plaything, his new discovery of love, he and his little Precious, had made Eva fear the future in a way she never had before. She had brooded on it for days after finding out he was engaged, and after receiving his threat. For the first time in her life she faced the fear that had gnawed at her for longer than she cared to admit: that she was really going to end up old, shriveled, and alone.

But now she had found her perfect mate.

All she had to do was strip Mikhail of his silly plan to marry Parthenia Westland and replace the chit with herself as his bride. She was tired of always being the mistress. She wanted to be the wife—and she licked her lips over gaining the title "Princess," as well. That would be a fine feather in her cap—a cap she had now privately set at Mikhail Kurkov. She was eager to endear herself for the added reason that if she could secure his affection, then she could make her ruthless prince punish that male whore for daring to threaten her. What gall he had, after all that she had done for him! She had saved his bloody worthless life, and in return, Alec Knight had scorned her. Well, he would learn sooner or later that *Hell hath no fury*. . . .

Still, after his quite terrifying threat, Eva dared not cross Alec outright yet, nor reveal to anyone the existence of his precious little ladybird. Instead, she kept her eyes and ears open for some way that she could safely strike back at the ingrate. Most of all, her grudge festered over the way he had humiliated her, causing her to flee the house like a frightened ninny—she, Eva Campion!—who had taken such pleasure in mastering him. That was what stung most of all.

When Alec had thrown her against the wall and menaced her, Eva had seen in his eyes how much he hated her. She had realized in shock that after all she had gleefully done to him, she had real reason to fear this man.

But soon she would have Mikhail to protect her, and then she could do what she liked. Oh, yes, she would pay that pretty bastard back somehow, as well as that hateful young beauty now warming his bed. Fiancée, indeed.

God, someone ought to throw vitriol on that pretty face and then see if the chit could still snare herself a Knight brother. Becky—Abby—whatever the hell her name was, Eva thought with an inward sneer.

When a discreet knock sounded on the door, Mikhail got up abruptly, tossing her aside. Eva scowled at the offhand treatment.

Mikhail hitched his trousers up and prowled to the door. When he opened it, she heard but could not understand his low-toned exchange with the leader of his six huge warriors stationed outside her house.

Turning onto her side with a sulky stare, she rested her face on her hand.

Mikhail shut the door and stalked back toward the bed, his closed expression more remote than ever. He seemed restless and agitated. Indeed, in the few short days of their acquaintance, she had often noticed this dark mood of his beneath his outward indifference. It fascinated her.

"What is it, Misha?"

"Nothing," he rumbled, sitting on the edge of her bed. He laid his hand appreciatively on the curve of her naked hip.

"What did your men want?"

"To see if I had any further orders before the changing of the guard."

"Why do you need so many bodyguards, anyway?"

"To protect me from women like you," he said, clapping her soundly on the rear end and causing her to squeal.

"You mean old hairy monster, Kurkov!" she scolded, then sat up and gazed deeply into his steely eyes. She could see the dark thoughts churning in his brain. "You look troubled." It took considerable courage, but she lifted her hand and caressed his head. "Why don't you tell Eva what is wrong? Maybe I can help."

"Help me?"

"Yes," she answered, lifting her chin. "Don't underestimate me, darling. Men have done so in the past, to their folly."

Mikhail considered her words and chewed upon her offer, studying her.

He could not help but smile faintly at this she-wolf he had found. If Lady Parthenia was ice, Eva Campion was pure deadly fire. She was the most enticing female he had ever encountered, and if she possessed a single inhibition, he had yet to find it. She had started as a mere distraction for him, a bit of recreation to take his mind off his missing cousin as well as the worrisome fact that he had not had any communication from his co-conspirators back in Russia for some weeks.

But now as he dragged her across his lap, he knew he

had found a possible ally. Unlike most people, including Parthenia and all fourteen of his concubines at home, this scheming harlot understood him. He raked his hand in uneasy but possessive affection through her short, dark curls, which he had already tousled thoroughly. He owned her, he knew, every inch.

Eva closed her dark eyes, reveling in his touch. Her eager submission pleased him, hard won as it had been. "Tell me your troubles, Mikhail," she murmured. "I only wish to serve you."

His eyes flickered with gratification, and he felt his loins grow heavy yet again with want of her. He still didn't trust the bitch, but at least now he was satisfied he could control her. "Shall I?" he whispered more to himself than to her.

"Yes." She dragged her eyes open and stared into his. "Let me prove myself worthy of you."

Mikhail considered her offer cautiously. Perhaps she could be of use. God knew, nothing else had worked so far. He had men scouring London and Brighton for the girl, men posted along the main routes back to Yorkshire, men watching the Westlands' house around the clock, but no one had seen hide nor hair of Rebecca Ward. This had led Mikhail to suspect that someone must be hiding her. Perhaps this single, crafty woman could succeed where all his men had failed.

As a fixed presence in the ton and a woman privy to the rich mine of Society women's gossip, the baroness no doubt had means of learning secrets that he could not tap into. Perhaps she could learn for him who might be hiding the girl, or at least find some new lead for him to follow in his maddeningly fruitless hunt for her.

Confiding in a woman was a risk he would not normally take, but Rebecca had been missing for nearly a month now and he was getting downright nervous. Besides, he needn't tell Eva everything. He could tell her just enough to give her the scent, and then let her track the quarry by her own devices.

"Perhaps there is something you could do for me."

"Name it," she whispered, straddling his lap with her arms wrapped around his neck.

"When my grandfather died, I was made the guardian of a young cousin of mine, an orphaned girl of about twenty. Well, the foolish chit rebelled at having been placed under my authority; until I came along, her caretakers had let her run wild. When I tried to impose some discipline, she threw a tantrum and ran away." Mikhail spilled her off his lap and got up to crush out the stump of his finished cheroot. "I don't know where she is or who may have her," he said while Eva watched his every move. "I suspect she is entirely ruined by now. She had little money when she left, and her youth and beauty would have made her easy prey."

Eva flinched at the words "her youth and beauty." The fleeting jealousy she betrayed amused Mikhail, but since he wanted her help, he gave her a soothing glance.

"For myself, I don't give a damn what becomes of Rebecca at this point," he lied. "What concerns me is that the girl has shown a nasty habit of going around telling lies about me."

"Really?" she murmured.

"Yes. Lies of a most shocking and serious nature. Enough to cause me considerable trouble unless she is brought to heel. Unfortunately, my men have had no success in finding her to date. She was last spotted in London a few weeks ago. Since then, it's as if she's simply vanished."

"Perhaps she's dead."

"No. I have a man in London keeping an eye on the obituaries for just that possibility, but so far, nothing."

"Have you contacted her close friends?"

"She has none that I know of. She knew no one outside her village. I think it's possible she may have fled to one of my grandfather's old cronies for help, using the Talbot name to gain entry."

"Someone in Society?" Eva murmured, intrigued.

"Yes. She could be with anyone, saying any manner of filth against me. I have been restricted from making inquiries myself because of," he said delicately, "the situation with Lady Parthenia."

"Right." Slipping into her red silk dressing gown, Eva tied it and went to him. "Perhaps I can help you find her." She tilted her head a bit, studying him with a distinct, wicked gleam in the depths of her coal-black eyes. "What does she look like?"

"Well, as I said, she is about twenty years old. About this high." He held his hand up to about the level of his breastbone. "Shapely girl, quite pretty. She has wavy, dark hair to her waist and bluish-colored eyes."

"Why, she sounds beautiful," Eva said sourly, then eyed him skeptically. "Are you quite sure she ran away because of your . . . discipline, Mikhail?"

"What are you implying?" he demanded with an indignant lift of his chin.

She just smiled at him like a cat with cream. "Oh, nothing. So, what is this ravishing young thing's name?" She turned to put out the nearby candle as the dawn's light grew.

"Rebecca. Rebecca Ward. She more commonly goes by Becky."

For a fleeting second Eva went very still. "There wouldn't happen to be . . . any other names she goes by?"

He shook his head. "None that I know of."

"Aha."

"You will make a few discreet inquiries among the ton? Subtlety is paramount, *loobeemaya*."

"Why, yes. And I suspect I can produce her for you

like a—a magician pulling a rabbit out of a hat!" she exclaimed in a sinister purr. "But first I have just one small condition, if I am to give you my help."

"Now, why am I not surprised?" Mikhail murmured. He could not help smiling, bewitched by her scheming when he probably should have been outraged. She was as brazen as she was beautiful. "What is this condition I must grant you, Baroness?"

She slipped her arms around his neck and offered up a coy smile, flames in her eyes. "If I find her for you, then you must forget Parthenia Westland and marry me."

He put her hand against his cock. "Find her for me, and I'll let you have this again."

"We'll see."

They exchanged a slightly diabolical smile, and then Mikhail turned and got dressed. "I'm leaving," he said. "I require sleep before the final round of the whist drive tonight. Some wicked sorceress kept me awake half the bloody night."

With the wheels in her mind already turning, Eva folded her arms beneath her breasts and gave him a wary nod of farewell as he slipped out of her chamber and went marching off with his private army.

How delightful! she thought in wicked anticipation, tickled by her extreme good fortune. No wonder Knight had looked so queasy when she demanded an introduction to Mikhail at the ball. Mikhail was searching for this Becky girl, and Alec was the one trying to conceal her. Well! It seemed now that she could kill two birds with one stone—revenge on Alec, and an act of fealty that would show Mikhail what an excellent pairing the two of them made.

She was not naive enough to believe Mikhail's obviously whitewashed version of the story concerning his cousin. Men were men. No doubt he had behaved inappropriately with the young beauty, driving her to run away.

But, given her own less than pristine past, Eva frankly didn't care. She required revenge on Alec Knight and she wanted to be a princess. She was bent on marrying Mikhail, and when she delivered little Precious to him by the end of the whist drive, accomplishing for him what he and all his Cossacks had been unable to do, he would have to see that they belonged together.

Oh, yes, she mused with a sly smile curving her lips, *I'll wear that jeweled tiara soon.* Alec would be at the final round of the whist drive with Mikhail, nowhere on hand to protect the girl.

Tonight.

As sunset faded to indigo twilight, a final burning-vivid pink streak on the western horizon refused to be extinguished by the encroaching night. Stars peeked out from their secret places in the great dome of the firmament, like the eyes of innumerable cupids come to spy on the match they had made.

Alec and Becky stood together on the beach, staring in silence at the ocean. In moments, she knew, he must go. He was dressed in formal black-and-white attire to visit the Regent's yacht; to show her certainty that they would have much to celebrate when he returned, Becky had donned an evening gown of pale jade-colored silk, the picture of elegant simplicity.

Lord Draxinger stood some twenty yards away, restlessly skipping stones into the waves as he waited for Alec to go with him to the final round of the whist drive. Fort and Rush stood at a respectful distance near the foot of the garden, waiting to escort Becky back to the villa. They had been assigned to protect her again while Alec and Drax went off to battle.

No more than a quarter hour ago Becky's deposition

had been dispatched to Parthenia, tucked away in a slim bandbox from one of the local modiste's shops. The duke's daughter would be receiving the "delivery" momentarily, and if all went according to plan, Westland should be reading Becky's testimony while Mikhail was playing cards on the Regent's yacht—separated from his Cossacks, trapped out at sea, and unable to get away. Becky had strongly suggested in her dispatch to Westland that His Grace rouse the local constabulary and have men waiting on the docks to arrest the prince the moment he stepped off Prinny's yacht.

She was confident that was how it would happen.

Alec had his doubts.

Down the beach, Drax waved to get his attention and pointed to his fob watch.

Alec sent him an answering gesture. "I have to go," he murmured.

They turned to each other.

"Well, then. I suppose this is it," Becky replied, mustering up a brave smile despite her raw nerves. She rested both of her hands in Alec's white-gloved ones.

He shook his head, staring at her, then he raised her hands to his lips and kissed both of them in turn. "You look so beautiful," he said softly. "You make it hard to leave."

She smiled, looking deeply into his eyes. She saw courage there, and steadfastness, despite his edgy impatience to have the thing done. Though his words were sweet, his face was set with grim resolve.

She lifted her hand and cupped his tense jaw. "Alec, I want you to know that whatever happens tonight, it won't change the way I feel about you."

"Er, yes. About that . . ." He moved closer and enfolded her in his arms, then pressed a lingering kiss to her brow. "Since we promised no more secrets, there's something I should probably tell you."

She tilted her head back and searched his deep blue eyes worriedly. "What is it, my love?" How troubled he looked, she thought with growing uneasiness.

"Becky." He took a deep breath and let it out. "There's a small but real possibility that I won't be . . . coming back."

She furrowed her brow. "What? What do you mean?"

"If I lose at the tables tonight," he said slowly, his tender gaze hardening, "I shall kill Kurkov while I have him out there on the boat."

Her eyes widened. "Alec!"

"It's the simplest way. He won't have all his damned Cossacks on hand to protect him—"

"No!" She backed away from him, aghast. "Alec, you mustn't! The Regent is always surrounded by soldiers and bodyguards, is he not? They'll arrest you! You could be killed—"

"Becky, if your cousin wins tonight, he'll be unstoppable, and we'll have nothing. If I should fail to win your house back for you, at least by doing this I shall have made sure for once and for all that you won't be in any more danger. With Kurkov dead, the Cossacks will have no further cause to chase you. Without his orders, their main concern will be getting back to Russia."

She shook her head dazedly. "Alec, this is madness! No! I will not hear of it! If they don't kill you on the spot, they'll send you straight to the hangman—"

"I cannot leave this undone. Don't you understand that by now?" he exclaimed. "Whatever the cost, I gave you my word I'd see this through to the end, and I will. I must. Becky." He reached for her. "Try to understand."

She pulled away, her face ashen. "What does anything matter if I lose you?" she cried.

For a long moment, they held each other in a searing stare.

"I know why you're saying this," she forced out shakily. "You just don't want to have to face me if you lose, but that's what I'm trying to tell you, Alec—you're what matters—not the house, not the money!" She cast about for words. "When we started all of this, getting my home back was paramount, because—well, because it's the only place I ever belonged. But that's changed since I found you. I belong with *you*. Alec, please don't run from me now by doing something so outrageously rash—"

"God, Becky." He turned away with an angry exhalation, raking his hand through his hair. "I'm not running from you," he said in a taut voice.

"Aren't you?" She reached out and touched his arm pleadingly, trying to make him look at her. "Alec, I promise I'm not going to stop loving you if you lose tonight. That's what you're really afraid of, isn't it? Didn't you hear what I just said? Whatever happens tonight, it won't change the way I feel about you. Even if you do lose, we'll still have each other, and that's worth more than all the houses and fortunes in the world."

He slanted her a guarded look askance. "No, Becky, what matters is your safety. One way or the other, the nightmare you've suffered through will all be over by morning." He lifted his hand and cupped her cheek ever so gently. "If I have to kill him, so be it. You will be safe, and that's all that matters to me."

It was fortunate that he steadied her, for a wave of sickening dizziness washed over her as it sank in that her attempts to reason with him were having no effect. His mind was made up, and no one could be as stubborn as Alec Knight when he had settled on a thing. "Be strong for me, Becky. I need you to be strong for me now." He stared hard into her stricken, welling eyes.

No words came. Her world was reeling.

"I've already made the arrangements for you if the

worst should come to pass. If I do not return, you are to marry either Rushford or Fort."

"*What?*"

"It's your choice. Don't argue, Becky—you could be with child even now. I won't have you left pregnant and husbandless, nor my babe raised without a father. I've already discussed it with the lads, and either of them will take good care of you. They've both given me their word that if there is a child, they will care for it and raise it as their own. You must go along with the pretense, for my sake. Promise me. I don't want a child of mine being raised as I was, with the whole world knowing he's a bastard."

She just stared at him, shattered by what he was suggesting. How could he speak so calmly of his own death? Of their never seeing each other again? Of her giving birth to a son or daughter who would never know their real father?

Somehow she strove to scrape her wits together in a desperate effort to dissuade him. "Alec—please. You mustn't do this. You mustn't even speak of it. Put it out of your mind! I need you with me."

He looked away. "I knew I shouldn't have told you."

"Of course you should." She realized in astonishment that he was only telling her this at all because of his oath to keep no more secrets. His blasted word of honor, that might now be the death of him. *Her fault.* If it weren't for that promise, he'd have left her in the dark.

She thrust the shocking thought aside and struggled to focus on the problem at hand, her whole body shaking. She couldn't let him do this. "Haven't I been saying from the start that I would not have you give your life for me? I've already got one man's blood on my hands—"

"I do this freely," he ground out, then his jaw clenched as he struggled for calm. He took her face gently between his hands and kissed her forehead. "You've got to trust me, my sweetest darling. Trust me now to take care of you. It's for the best. There is no other way."

"Of course there is! Mikhail will be arrested when he gets off the boat!"

He pulled back angrily, releasing her. "You have so much faith in Westland? He's a bloody politician, for one thing! For another, he's been duped by Kurkov before."

"But when he reads my report, he'll understand—"

"What if he doesn't believe it? This is no time for your naïveté! What if he calls for some long endless bureaucratic investigation? You could be dead while we wait for justice. I'm tired of waiting, risking you day after day! What if Westland ignores your report altogether? Sweeps it under the carpet? What if he chooses to protect his new protégé? After all, it's your word against Kurkov's, and though you may be a goddess to me, why should anyone outside ourselves take the word of a Yorkshire lass over that of a war hero, a prince, the darling of the Whigs, bosom friend of the Czar?"

"Oh, my God." She stepped back from him, covering her mouth with her hands for a moment. "You always knew it would come down to this, didn't you? You just didn't want to tell me."

Alec stared at her. "Don't hate me," he whispered. "I only want to deserve you."

She saw there was no getting through to him. Her whole body was shaking as she lowered her hands to her sides. "Go. Do what you have to do," she said bitterly, tears burning in her eyes. "But if you kill him, Alec—if you throw your life away tonight—throw away *our* life together, then know that you're doing it for yourself, not for me. I never wanted this. All I wanted was to love you."

He winced and then lowered his gaze, shaking his head slowly. "I swore on my honor that I would protect you, and that's what I'm going to do. Now, kiss me good-bye."

"No!" She took a step backward. "You're not leaving until we've sorted this out!"

"Oh, Becky." He pinned her in a final searing stare, as though committing her face to memory for all time. His chiseled face was taut, and a fierce blue light shone in his eyes. Without another word, he pulled away from her, pivoted, and began walking away.

"Alec!"

He just kept going.

"Don't do this to me, Alec, I beg you. You're all I have," she choked out, taking a step after him, barely noticing Rush and Fort approaching from behind her.

As Alec reached Draxinger on the beach, she turned her panicked efforts toward the earl. "Lord Draxinger, don't let him do it!"

Drax glanced back at her anguished shout, his face grim, but he said nothing.

"Alec, wait! She lunged after them, but Fort and Rush caught her by her arms.

"Don't, Becky," Rush soothed her. "It's hard enough for him already."

"You knew!" she exclaimed, turning on his friends with tears burning in her eyes. "You knew, and yet you let him go?"

"There was no talking him out of it," Fort said, his face taut and pale.

"We would do the same thing in his place," Rushford stated.

"You're all mad! He could die! Don't you even care?"

"He can win this, Becky. Let him do what he must."

"No!" She fought them. "Alec!" she screamed after him. "Don't do this, I'm begging you! Come back to me!" He just kept going, and fury struck her wild grief like a lightning bolt. "Damn your pride!" she flung at his retreating back. "You'd rather die than admit you love me, wouldn't you? Don't you leave me, you bastard! I'll never forgive you if you do this, Alec—please! You're all I've got!" Her pitiful cries had brought a faint glint of tears to her captors' eyes, but neither of them would bend.

"Come inside, Becky. Let him go."

"Never. I'll never let him go—not for either of you!" She wrenched her arms free of their hold and, sobbing, ran into the house.

CHAPTER
✽ FIFTEEN ✽

*T*he Regent's yacht was breathtaking in its opulence, containing every luxury a man could want on land or sea, but Alec barely noticed. The players took their places on each side of the square table, partners facing across from each other, and drew straws for the first deal. Norfolk himself, their host from the third round, held the straws in his lordly fist. To Alec's relief, he and Drax were made partners, while Prince Kurkov and Colonel Tallant had been paired.

Tallant drew the shortest straw and claimed the honor of the opening deal. Alec was displeased. The seat to the dealer's left was not a happy place to be. It meant he must lead with the opening trick, and everyone knew that the players to take their turn after him had the advantage over him. Worse, Kurkov sat to his left, ensuring that the prince would have the advantage over him for most of the game, except when it was the Russian's turn to lead. At least it fell to Alec to shuffle, which he did with nimble alacrity, then he handed the cards across the table to Drax, who gave him a confident nod, cut the deck, and gave it to the dealer, in accordance with the ancient rules and traditions of the game. The opening trump suit, as usual, was hearts.

"Shall we?" the tiger-slayer rasped, sweeping their company with his scimitar glance. Then Tallant proceeded to flash out thirteen cards facedown to each man at the table.

The spectators throughout the yacht's flamboyant saloon leaned in, watching the players' faces. Their side bets would be flying all night as some of them struggled to recoup the ten thousand they had lost upon being eliminated in the earlier rounds.

As he picked up his cards, Alec did his best to put the echo of Becky's piteous cries out of his mind so to focus on the game. His heart bled within him behind his cool facade, but he had done all that he could do.

His jaw clenched as he thrust his own suffering aside and evaluated his opening hand without expression. *Not bad.* Not a perfect deal, but one that he could work with. . . .

The great contest began.

By the seventh trick, Alec and Drax were a solid three points in the lead, but in the eighth, Tallant rallied with the queen of diamonds, claiming the trick. The ninth brought the lead back to Alec. He tossed out his strongest card, the ten of hearts, and took the point, for no one had anything to beat it. By the end of the first deal, he and Drax were one point ahead, their seven tricks beating Kurkov and Tallant's six.

Frustratingly, the rest of the night progressed that way, the two teams racing neck and neck. Neither could quite pull ahead to the five-point lead necessary to win.

Each time one gained a point, the other soon matched it. Sometimes they were dead even, sometimes one pulled a point or two ahead, but it was not long before the other caught up with tenacious will. It was not until after midnight that Alec and Drax's lead widened to two points, but at this rate, Alec was beginning to wonder if the game would ever end.

They got up for a stretch at one A.M.

Alec splashed his face and asked for tea with sugar, while Drax used the loo. Strolling around on deck to stretch his legs, Alec gazed up at the graceful sails of the yacht and thought about a little girl who'd once had a navy warship for a nursery. Obviously, her courage had been forged early. Extraordinary.

She was so damned . . . extraordinary.

He gave his brain a break from the extreme concentration, merely staring over the rails at the waves streaming out in white-crested ripples. Again, he thought of Becky and her enraged parting words, that if he risked his neck tonight by killing Kurkov, he would be doing it for himself, not for her. He had brushed it off as absurd when she said it, but maybe there was some truth to it, after all. 'Sblood, if he failed her now, he did not know how he would ever look her in the eye again—let alone look in the mirror. Death seemed at least *slightly* preferable to going back to Becky empty-handed after they had come so far. . . .

The pain he'd caused her tonight agonized him, but he shook his head to himself. He could not afford this distraction. The game wasn't over yet.

Revived by the coolness of the night sea air, he left the rails and wandered restlessly toward the fo'c'sle, where he heard Kurkov vaunting affably to his listeners that he would crush the two of them before dawn peeked over the misty horizon.

We'll see, Alec thought, his brooding gaze fixed on the prince, though he remained unnoticed in the shadows. Kurkov's angular face and narrow beard looked ghoulish by the orange glimmer of a nearby torch, and Alec realized it was true—he *wanted* to kill Kurkov, aye, so badly he could taste it. Punish the blackguard for the things he had said and done to Becky. Terrifying her. Sending his Cossack hunting dogs after her. Kurkov had struck her, half strangled her, threatened to rape her, by God. The blackguard deserved a slow and painful death. *Patience.* All in good time. For now, he watched the prince down a few swigs of vodka, and knew that would make him sleepy, unalert.

Walking back to the table, Alec's stare homed in on the carving knife next to the roast beef on the sideboard, where footmen offered the gentlemen elaborate refreshments. The weapon would be in easy reach if he had need of it.

Drax and he exchanged a hard look. Alec nodded.

On they played.

The boat rocked gently; the candles burned low. So many deals went around and around that the cycle passed through hearts, diamonds, spades, and clubs again four times over.

Around two o'clock the Regent gave up quietly fussing about his gout and went to bed in his gilded stateroom, leaving a few of his raffish royal brothers to play host. The raucous royal dukes poured another round of brandy and upped their wagers, never mind that most of them were practically as penniless as Alec.

In a state of grim resolve, Alec sat down to the fourth hour of whist, took a deep breath, and accepted his turn to deal the cards.

Again . . .

Shaken up and confused, Parthenia waited in thin-lipped silence, her arms folded across her chest, as her father sat at his huge desk in the library rereading the terrifying account that had arrived this evening tucked inside the bandbox. She had intercepted it from her maid and opened it personally, as she and the woman who called herself Abby had planned.

After reading it herself, Parthenia had realized that the dark-haired girl's name wasn't Abby at all. She had been duped as to the young lady's real identity, but to her chagrin, Parthenia now understood why. She had heard people whisper about her on occasion, complaining of her pride, saying she gave herself supercilious airs. Even Lord Draxinger had once called her arrogant. Parthenia could not reproach Miss Rebecca Ward for tricking her. Clearly, the girl had needed some way—any way—to make her listen, and so "Abby" had appealed to her vanity as a benefactress of the poor.

Parthenia had learned a bit of a lesson in it; moreover, Miss Ward's ruse had worked. Parthenia had stalked into her father's library, pulled him away from his umpteenth late night reading of Voltaire and commanded his full attention, telling him of their strange meeting at the bathing machine.

The duke had squinted at her over his reading spectacles as though she were making it all up, but then Parthenia handed him the report with shaking hands and demanded he read it immediately.

After his first pass, Westland scoffed at the story those pages told. Parthenia made him read it again. Ten minutes later the duke set the last page down, took off his spectacles, and rubbed his eyes wearily with one hand.

"Well?" she asked nervously, warming her arms with her palms in the eerie chill that had taken hold of her at the thought that she had been courted by a killer. "What do you think?"

Her father braced his cheek on his knuckles and stared intently at the candle flame. "I do not know, daughter. I am at a loss! It could be a trick. Kurkov has enemies, as do all powerful men. I certainly do."

"No enemy has ever accused you of torturing a man, secretly holding him prisoner in an outbuilding, and then shooting him in the back, Papa!"

"But the prince told me himself that his young cousin was unstable. Such things often run in great families. Remember, she tried to break into our house. . . ." His voice trailed off uncertainly, his expression darkening. "But perhaps there was another reason for that."

"Of course, Papa. She was trying to get you to listen. It's all so clear now! Do you really think these pages read like the ramblings of a lunatic? The writing is logical, perfectly lucid. I assure you that the person I spoke to at the ladies' beach was as sane as you and I."

They stared at each other with the grim prospect hanging ominously upon the air between them. Both contemplated the unnerving thought that they had hosted many times a murderer in their house—a murderer so bent on hiding his crime that he would hire one of their own servants to spy on them, if what Miss Ward claimed was true.

For the great majority of the time, aristocrats went about their business blissfully unaware of how much they depended moment by moment upon the silent horde of servants that attended to their needs around the clock. To think that one of those servants might mean them harm struck dread in their hearts.

"I'm afraid it's even worse than that." Parthenia walked over to his desk and blew out the candle. "If you don't believe these pages, perhaps you'll believe your own eyes. Papa, come over to the window," she murmured, moving the curtain aside.

Westland groped his way through the darkness until he had found his way to her side.

"Miss Ward's report said we're being watched," she whispered. "Look and see for yourself." She pointed toward the leafy back corner outside of their house.

Her father's eyes narrowed. Parthenia heard his low intake of breath as he made out the large black silhouette of a male figure loitering in the shadows beneath the trees.

"They're all around the perimeter of the house. I've already checked. It's true, Papa. Mikhail's not only spying on us through one of our domestics, he's also got us under guard."

"Damn him!" Westland breathed, turning to scan in the other direction. There, too, he found the skulking shape of a lurker in the darkness. He let the curtain fall and pulled her away from the window. "Oh, Parthenia, I am so sorry," he uttered, leaning against the back of a nearby wing chair to steady himself. "It would seem the prince has been manipulating me for weeks—and I pushed you toward him."

"It's all right, Father." She clutched his arm, instinctively huddling near him for protection, for if they had been in this danger without even knowing it, who could say what would happen now that they were aware of Mikhail's scrutiny?

"How could I have been so bloody stupid?"

"Never mind that, Papa. I never really cared for Mikhail, anyway. I was only letting him court me to please you."

"You were?" he asked abruptly.

"Oh, Father, my heart has always belonged to Lord Draxinger."

"What?" he cried.

A sudden pounding knock on the distant front door reached them in the library.

Parthenia glanced toward it with a gulp, wide-eyed in the dark. "Who can that be at this hour?"

"I do not know," her father murmured, moving in front of her. "I will go and see who it is."

"Let the butler get it!"

"He could be the one who's spying on us," he reminded her coolly.

"Well, then, I'm coming with you."

"No, Parthenia, stay back. I will handle this."

Her heart pounding, she ignored his order with a willful scowl and followed her sire at a cautious distance as he made his way toward the entrance hall.

"Westland! Westland, open up!"

Parthenia saw her father wave off the butler with a suspicious glance. The duke went personally to the front door. He laid his hand on the knob while the person outside continued knocking.

"Westland! I must speak to you at once!"

Her father threw the door open abruptly.

"Westland!" Count Lieven exclaimed, his fleshy face illumined by the lanterns flanking the front door. The Russian ambassador was visibly taken aback to find the duke answering his own door.

"Come in, what is it?" Parthenia heard her father say.

"Your Grace, we crave a moment of your time." Out of breath and dabbing at his sweaty, bald pate, Count Lieven stepped inside with another man, unknown to Parthenia. "We have come with dire news."

"Regarding?"

"Your protégé, Kurkov," Lieven said grimly. "I'm just back from London. Can you tell me where he is?"

Eva glided into the Cossacks' midst with a feline smile, dressed in her dark riding habit with a tall-brimmed hat and a long riding crop. They stared at her intrusion, halting in their tasks, some roasting their dinners over the fireplace, others cleaning their saddles.

"Does anyone speak English?" she inquired, whisking the train of her riding habit gracefully around her. "Right, then. *Parlez-vous français?*"

One of the men stood. Eva drew in her breath, eyeing the great iron hulk. "My my." *So many men, so little time.*

"I speak French," the Cossack officer said to her in that tongue, drying his hands on a small towel.

"And you are?"

"I am Sergei, the sergeant of this company. How may I help you, my lady? His Highness is at the whist drive—"

"Yes, well, if you gentlemen will come with me, we will fetch him a little present. Interested?"

Sergei stared at her with a sudden flare of excitement in his eyes. "You've found the girl?"

"I may know where she is."

Immediately, he ordered his men to their horses. Within ten minutes they were on their mounts and riding to the Knight family's neat stuccoed house by the beach.

Eva's heart raced as she reined in with Sergei beside her. "There," she murmured, nodding at the darkened villa.

"You are sure?"

She nodded with a knowing half smile.

Sergei gave an order to his men. At once they were off their horses, drawing their weapons, creeping stealthily toward the house. Eva stayed back, watching in breathless excitement.

In the wavering moonlight, she could see Mikhail's men testing windows and doors. One scaled a rose trellis silently, mounting to the second story window. Everywhere, they were swarming the house—and for a moment Eva's heart quaked as she wondered if she had gone too far this time.

Suddenly, shots rang out—shouts broke through the night—an opening volley and return fire. She turned her face away with a frightened gasp as someone screamed.

Eva steadied her horse as Mikhail's men stormed the villa.

"May I stay, Father?" Parthenia asked, relighting the candles in the library, into which Westland had shown Count Lieven and the mysterious stranger that the Russian ambassador had brought with him.

The duke glanced at Lieven in question.

He nodded and quickly beckoned Parthenia to take a seat. "This concerns her, too, I'm afraid, if the rumors about their coming engagement are true. Lady Parthenia, Your Grace, allow me to present my associate, Alyosha Nelyudov, who arrived just last night from St. Petersburg."

Introductions went around.

Nelyudov was a trim, unassuming man of about forty, with very correct manners, short, curly hair of a reddish-brown hue, a rather pale complexion, and piercing black eyes behind his scholarly spectacles. He did not look at all like Parthenia's idea of a killer spy, but that, she supposed, was the point. Count Lieven termed Mr. Nelyudov a secret agent of the Czar. He spoke a dozen languages, was versed in the laws of most of the countries of Europe, and had been sent on a special assignment to England to retrieve Prince Mikhail Kurkov, who was wanted, he revealed, for his involvement in a conspiracy to overthrow the Czar.

Nelyudov pushed away from the wall where he had been leaning and prowled restlessly through the library. In a cool, soft-spoken voice, he explained: "An associate of mine, Dmitry Maximov, was one of the first of our agents to uncover the plot. The conspiracy was formed by some fourscore of our highest-ranking military officers. Their intention was to abduct the emperor and use their authority in the army to seize power."

Parthenia gasped at the mere suggestion of such treachery.

"Much of the army rather despises the Czar, I'm afraid," Count Lieven interjected with an apologetic look.

"When we began arresting suspects back in Russia, Kurkov's name came up. It seemed he was using his trip to England to claim his British inheritance as his alibi. With the cooperation of your government, we put a halt on his funds to trip him up a bit. We also sent Maximov to follow Kurkov to England and quietly investigate his degree of involvement. Dmitry sent us a dispatch from Calais before crossing the Channel," Nelyudov said. "He has not been heard from since."

Parthenia and her father exchanged an uneasy glance. At her sire's nod, she picked up the report from Miss Ward and handed it to Mr. Nelyudov. "I think we may know what became of your colleague, sir. I am very sorry. This letter just arrived."

Count Lieven frowned, scanning it over his shoulder as Nelyudov skimmed the top page by candlelight. The two Russians exchanged hard glances and a few low murmurs in their native tongue.

Lieven took the report from him and quickly glanced through it. "She is a brave young woman for coming forward. Few dare to cross the prince." He turned to Westland. "We must secure this witness. She is in great danger. Do you know where she can be found?"

"I have no idea," the duke started, but Parthenia cleared her throat, interrupting.

"She is with Lord Alec Knight."

"Parthenia!" Westland exclaimed. "Where does it say that?"

She took the final page of the report sheepishly out of her pocket, unfolding it from a neat square. She handed it to Mr. Nelyudov. "I didn't think it prudent to show you that page, Father."

"Oh, really?" he replied, raising one eyebrow.

"I was afraid you wouldn't pay any attention if you knew Lord Alec was involved."

The duke snorted. "Count Lieven is more right than he knows. We must see to Miss Ward's safety ourselves if that rogue is all she's got for protection. By Jove, who's going to protect the chit from *him*?" he grumbled.

"Nelyudov and I have already contacted the nearby garrison," Lieven said hurriedly. "A company of your British dragoons based here in Brighton have agreed to help us arrest Kurkov and his men. They are assembling even now."

"Yes, well, as I've said, he's on the Regent's yacht at this moment," Westland told them.

Count Lieven nodded. "Good. We can have our men in position, and take him at the docks."

"No," Nelyudov said. "Not by the waterfront. It's too risky. He could too easily lay hold of a boat and slip away. Better to ambush him at the hotel where he's staying. Box him in."

They nodded as this sounded a logical strategem.

Nelyudov glanced at the wall clock. "I must go. I'll have to meet with the captain of dragoons to discuss our plan and make sure our men are in position."

"Poor Mikhail," Parthenia couldn't help murmuring, overwhelmed by his crime. Not just murder, but treason, as well! It was difficult to believe it was all happening. "What will happen to him, Count Lieven?"

"It's possible the Czar may spare his life, due to their boyhood friendship. In that case, he'll probably be given the usual sentence—to spend the rest of his life working the mines in Siberia."

She shuddered and dropped her gaze.

"My dear duke," the ambassador continued, "if you are so inclined, we may go together to fetch the girl."

"I'm coming with you!" Parthenia said at once, rising to her feet. "Oh, please don't protest, Father! Lord Alec is at the whist drive, too. Miss Ward will be alone, and no doubt frightened. I'm the one she contacted. I should be there."

"Another young lady's presence might help to reassure her," Lieven agreed with a nod.

"Only if we bring adequate protection." Westland took Parthenia's hand. "I've put my dear girl in enough danger already with this fiend."

Parthenia gave him a rueful smile, then glanced at the Russians. "Perhaps one of you gentlemen might have a suggestion on what is to be done about the Cossacks stationed outside."

Nelyudov turned, his fiery stare homing in on her with lethal, sudden attention. "Cossacks? Here?"

Her father nodded. "Aye, four of them. One posted at each corner of my dashed house."

Stalking toward the door, Nelyudov withdrew a large, curved, savage-looking knife from a sheath concealed beneath his dark coat. "I will deal with them."

"Alone?" Parthenia murmured, her eyes widening as the Czar's agent slipped out silently.

"Egads," Westland said under his breath. "Best take pains not to cross that fellow, what?"

"Nelyudov," Lieven said softly, "is the best we've got."

The game stretched into the wee hours of the night.

The two teams' scores climbed into the seventies, eighties, nineties, and even past one hundred, but still, neither had acquired the necessary five point lead.

Up four points, Drax and Alec nearly tasted victory,

only to fall behind again as their opponents edged up alongside them, matched and then overtook them by one point. The grueling length of the game, however, the infuriating disappointment of nearly winning and then seeing it slip through their fingers, had begun to take its toll.

The score was now 123 to 122, in Kurkov and Colonel Tallant's favor. This damned game was never going to end Alec thought. He feared he and his partner were becoming a trifle demoralized.

All he knew was that if he looked anywhere near as bad as the others did by now, Eva Campion herself wouldn't have bedded him. The four of them were a bleary, sweaty, stinky, rumpled, haggard, groggy mess, with bloodshot eyes, slouched postures, and armpit circles darkening their clothes.

He shifted in his seat, his rear end sore from too much sitting. But what alarmed him most was that after so many hours of play, it became harder to remember clearly which cards in each suit had already been played. Each new hand began to run together with the last in his brain. His only solace was knowing that the others were in no better shape than he.

Most of their audience fared even worse, the previously raucous royal dukes now asleep on every piece of gilt velvet furniture in the grand saloon. Others were strewn, snoring, around the floor with cushions under their heads and the Persian carpet for a bed. A few had napped already and arisen again to watch the ongoing play.

Alec had switched from tea to coffee in the hopes it would do a better job of keeping him sharp.

And then, sometime around five A.M., eight hours into the game, a mysterious thing happened.

Drax shuffled; Alec cut the cards and handed them to Kurkov.

"Your deal."

The Russian yawned and took them.

Rubbing the back of his neck, Alec waited for Kurkov to finish giving them all thirteen cards, then picked his hand up wearily—and blinked.

At first he thought he was having an hallucination brought on by fatigue.

But though he squeezed his burning eyes shut for a second, the vision did not change.

Holy Mother, he thought, hastily masking his incredulity. It seemed his former mistress, Lady Luck, had come back one last time to say good-bye forever, but perhaps sorry for her faithlessness, had left him with one last golden kiss.

Kurkov had just dealt Alec the hand of a lifetime.

Hearts were trump yet again, and Alec held no less than seven of them, including the queen, king, and ace. He had three high diamonds, as well—jack, queen, and ace—along with the eight. Of the other suits, he held just one of each, the jack of clubs and one lousy card, the three of spades. He'd get rid of it, and then, if he used his head, he'd be in control of this game.

Immediately, his pulse began to pound, renewed vigor pouring through his veins. *Come on. This is it.* He straightened up slowly in his chair. Lifted his chin. *For Becky.* If he could win, then he need not kill Kurkov tonight. He could deal with him later, and Becky and he could still have a shot at a future together.

The stare he gave Drax alerted his friend that something was afoot. He lowered his lashes again, concealing his wild eagerness.

This time he was going in for the kill.

Since Kurkov had dealt the hand, it fell to Drax to lead. Naturally, the earl chose one of his strongest cards with which to open the round.

Ace of spades.

Nicely done, he thought.

Tallant tossed down the two and Alec immediately got rid of the three of spades. Kurkov offered up the seven, and the trick went to Drax.

Alec gave him a narrow smile.

Tallant stuck with spades, no doubt thought he'd deal a crushing blow with the king, but Alec, out of spades, had no choice but to play the trump suit of hearts. *Hm, a calculated risk.* Willing to chance it that Kurkov still had a spade left, he played the lowest card he had in the trump suit. Two of hearts.

Irritation flicked over the prince's face. Kurkov smirked and tossed down the nine of spades.

Whew. Next it was his turn to lead the trick. Time to show them who was master of this table. He looked at them matter-of-factly.

Ace of hearts. That should flush a few more hearts out of the woodwork.

Drax lifted his pale-colored eyebrows, amusement beginning to dance in his ice-blue eyes.

Alec's expression was serene.

The five, four, and eight of hearts followed. His ace clobbered them. Alec took the trick.

They now had three tricks. The fourth began with Kurkov, his chance to come booming out of the gate with another big card.

Ace of clubs.

Drax bowed out with the three of clubs. Tallant supported his partner with the six. Alec frowned, but his jack of clubs could not beat Kurkov's ace.

At least now his hand would be composed only of the diamonds and the trump hearts. Very strong. *Hope you enjoyed taking that point, Your Highness, for you shan't get another out of me.*

Again came Drax's turn to lead. He must have divined Alec's strategy, for he opened the trick with the eight of spades, setting Alec up to trump. Tallant followed in the suit of spades with the five, but Alec, having none, put down the king of hearts.

When Kurkov followed with the two of diamonds, it meant that the prince was also out of spades. He might still have had a heart in his hand, but nothing high enough to beat Alec's king, so Alec held onto his hearts for use later. He still wasn't worried, having yet another high trump card, the queen.

Still, the other team was crafty. He and Drax would have to be careful.

Sixth trick; Tallant's lead. The other team played the suit of clubs. Alec had none and took the trick, king and all, with his mighty little three of hearts. A bit nerve-racking, but he was having fun.

Seventh trick; Alec's lead. Noting that only the four of diamonds had been played so far, and seeing the high ones safely nestled in his hand, he didn't even resort to hearts this time. Instead, he took the trick with his ace of diamonds.

They had now claimed six of the tricks of this hand to Kurkov's one, and the prince was beginning to look nervous.

If there was any question left, they turned a corner in the eighth trick, when Kurkov led with what was apparently his strongest card, the jack of hearts. *Not bad, not bad,* Alec mused, watching as his friend followed suit with the ten. Couldn't beat a jack, of course. Tallant contributed the nine of hearts.

Alec let them agonize for a moment, then, with a half smile, set down the queen of hearts. He had been paying close attention and now knew that he held the only hearts left in play. Unbeatable advantage. Kurkov leaned his mouth against his fist; Alec noticed that the prince's left eye began twitching.

If only Becky could see this!

The next few hands rolled out swiftly, but the upshot was that while Alec's hand favored hearts, Drax obviously held a lot of diamonds, and Kurkov clubs, leaving Tallant with a useless mix of middling cards. All of them could feel the one-eyed nabob seething.

Drax won the ninth with the king of diamonds, but Alec still had the queen of that suit and used it to claim the tenth.

Across the table from him now, he could see sweat running down his partner's face. Drax was flushed and boyishly tousled. The sight of him reminded Alec of their days back at Eton. The inseparable four back then had made a winning crew team.

Eleventh trick: his seven of hearts cleaned up.

Twelfth: with a mere six, Alec put the rest to bed, his heart pounding.

And in the final trick, the thirteenth, the last card on which everything counted, without which they must fall back into endless hours of neck-and-neck frustration, Drax led off with the queen of spades. He stared at Alec after he had thrown it down.

Tallant cursed, casting the jack of spades away.

Alec gingerly put down the jack of diamonds and slid it away from him.

Kurkov muttered a curse in Russian and ended with the ten of clubs.

Drax proclaimed victory with a barbaric yell, both he and Alec on their feet, reaching for each other across the table, embracing heartily.

The next thing they knew, their audience had woken up and they were being carried on the shoulders of the men who had come to watch the game. Champagne burst out everywhere. The thunderous cheering awoke the Regent, who came out swaddled in his satin dressing gown to congratulate them.

But the greatest victory of all was the moment Alec

had so long waited for, when he finally held the deed to Talbot Old Hall in his hands.

Waiting beside the table as Kurkov completed the paperwork, signing the house over to him, he accepted the scrolled document with a certain measure of awe. He had actually done it. His heart soared; he couldn't wait to give it to Becky.

Drax cleared his throat at Alec's silence, offering his hand to Kurkov with perfect gentility, despite their rivalry for Lady Parthenia's affections. "Well played, Your Highness," the earl said. His nudge jarred Alec out of his wonderment with a silent reminder that it was still too soon to let Kurkov realize anything was amiss. All must appear normal for just a little while longer. Though it seemed like too much luck to hope for in one night, Westland still might be waiting on the docks with the constabulary ready to take the prince into custody when they got back.

Kurkov shook Drax's hand with a visible twinge of reluctance. "Not well enough, obviously." Then he turned to Alec, his gray eyes narrowing. "Alexei, your famous luck seems to have returned just in time."

"So it has."

Alec held Kurkov's icy gaze without flinching, but as he dutifully shook his hand, he gave an inward shudder to think of how close he had come to plunging a carving knife in the man's chest. He would have enjoyed doing it, too, except for the consequences.

No matter. Soon Kurkov would belong to the authorities, and once they had him behind bars, Alec intended to pay the prince a visit in his cell. Then they were going to have a little talk about his threats against Becky. But that moment was still well in the future. For now, he would take no such reckless chances.

Kurkov released his hand and excused himself with a

cynical snort, as though he only wondered now why he had wasted his time on all this.

With a gleam of cold satisfaction in his eyes, Alec watched the war hero pivot with martial precision and go prowling off to nurse his defeat with a flask of vodka.

Drax and he looked at each other in discreet relief.

Mikhail had had his fill of English company for one night.

It vexed him to no end that he himself had dealt the insufferable Alec Knight his astonishing winning hand. Mikhail hated losing, even if he could afford the loss. As for that ratty old farm, well, the rogue was welcome to it. For his part, he was glad to be rid of the cursed, haunted, crumbling pile. How devastated his little bitch of a cousin would be when she found out she had been kicked out of her home for good. The thought pleased him greatly.

Having demolished the old gatehouse to destroy any lingering evidence of Dmitry Maximov's imprisonment there, and having ordered his Cossacks to bury the corpse on the heath in a place where no one would ever find it, Mikhail was not worried in the slightest about new occupants taking up residence in the place, especially not a thoughtless pleasure-seeker like Alec Knight.

Still, smarting from defeat at the hands of that impertinent coxcomb, he was bloody glad to set foot on solid ground again, and gladder still to spy Sergei standing on the torchlit dock waiting for him. Through the wet gray mist of dawn, Mikhail could just make out the comforting shape of his waiting carriage. He was exhausted, a little dry-mouthed from drinking all night, and eager to return to his rooms at the luxurious hotel. He could well use a few hours of sleep, and then, perhaps, when he was rested, he would call for Eva and nurse his wounded vanity a bit—as long as the West-lands didn't find out.

As his top man strode down the wooden-planked dock to meet him, Mikhail smirked in the direction of the winning pair some distance away. The two rakehells were being cheered all over again as they stepped off one of the small rowboats conveying the Regent's guests from the graceful yacht back to dry land.

"Don't look so eager, Sergei," he said sardonically as his top Cossack bowed. "I lost by the skin of my teeth."

"No matter, sire. I have an even better prize for you." Sergei flashed a quick, fierce smile. "We've got the girl."

Mikhail drew in his breath swiftly, violence flaring to life in his eyes. *"Where?"*

"We're holding her in a secret place outside of town. Come, sire. I will take you to her."

Racing home in the flashy equipage he had won, a showy, dark blue coach with gilt trim and six white horses, Alec stood on the driver's box handling the ribbons while Drax hung on for dear life beside him, laughing uproariously and still swigging champagne.

"The springs on this thing are better than those on my curricle!"

Alec barely nodded, paying his foxed whist partner little mind. Most of his eager attention was fixed on his destination: the villa. Careening through the misty dawn at breakneck speed, he could not make the horses gallop fast enough to carry him to Becky. Oh, when he laid eyes on her again, he was going to catch her up in his arms, twirl her around in a circle, and give her the biggest kiss the world had ever seen. He could not wait to see her face when he put the deed to the Hall in her hands.

As the coach clattered noisily over the cobblestones

only a block away from the villa, one thought made Alec frown, and that was the fact that, just as he had suspected, Westland had not been inspired enough by Becky's testimony to send police to the docks to arrest Kurkov, as she had hoped.

Well, perhaps he had not read it yet, Alec thought. Perhaps Westland still needed more convincing.

In any case, now that she had officially reported the crime, Alec intended to remove her to a safer distance until Kurkov was shackled and caged. Perhaps he'd take her all the way to Hawkscliffe Hall to meet his family while the authorities finished the job of bringing the blackguard to justice. He had wanted to move her earlier, but she refused to leave his side.

As they went barreling around the final corner to the villa, Draxinger's laughter stopped abruptly.

Alec felt his innards turn to ice.

It was barely six A.M., but the street outside his house ahead was filled with a throng of neighbors and onlookers milling about with grim faces, a few constables urging everyone to go back to their homes. Half a dozen carriages were parked willy-nilly in the street.

"Oh, Jesus," Drax breathed, turning waxy white.

Windows were broken, the front door hung open, and lights burned on every floor. Black smoke wafted out of an upper window, as though they had just managed to put out a fire. Numb with dread, his stomach churning queasily, Alec halted the coach and jumped down on legs that felt rubbery. *This can't be happening.* In spiraling horror, he ran through the crowd, hearing small snippets of low-toned conversation that turned his blood to ice.

"—two men killed inside—"

The neighbors fell silent when they saw him coming.

"Sir, you can't go in there," said a constable, blocking his path.

Alec shook off the man's hold violently. "I live there! What's happened?"

"Draxinger!" a tense, feminine voice shouted.

"Parthenia?" Drax uttered as the duke's daughter ran to them. "What are you doing here? What's happened?"

"Officer, let them pass," she ordered the policeman. "Oh, Piers. Lord Alec." She shook her head. "They've taken Miss Ward."

Alec was already running into the house. His mind a whirl of pure horror and fear, he paused on the threshold to scan the scene frantically.

Everywhere bustling constables hunted for clues. Alec smelled charred carpet and then saw a trail of blood on the hardwood floor. He spotted Westland and Count Lieven, too, angrily giving orders, but he ignored them, his gaze homing in on the surgeon bent over a motionless figure on the ground.

Fort.

No. Ashen-faced, Alec walked to his fallen friend's side. "Is he alive?" he choked out.

"Barely," the surgeon said, not looking up from his work. "He's lucky they left 'im for dead. Lift him," he ordered his assistants. The burly young medics heaved Alec's unconscious best friend onto a stretcher and took him away.

Alec's mind reeled.

"Knight," a deep voice called weakly.

"Rushford!" He raced into the next room and flung himself down on his knees by Rush's side. The future marquess was also bloodied, his arm and head bandaged, one eye blackened.

The doctor attending him searched his black bag for laudanum.

Rush clutched his arm. His dark eyes were glazed with fear and pain. "I'm so sorry, Alec," he forced out weakly with a hard swallow. "They took her. We tried to stop them. There were too many. It was—Eva. She led them here."

Murder leaped into Alec's eyes.

"Come, my lord. We must take you to hospital."

Alec struggled to absorb the news of Eva's treachery as Rush was placed on a stretcher and taken away.

The room was spinning. "Somebody send for my brothers," he ordered blindly. By God, together, the lot of them would unleash hell on Kurkov for what he had done. Through swirling fury, he felt someone shaking his shoulder hard.

"Alec, do you hear me?"

His chest heaving, he turned to find Draxinger searching his face anxiously. Parthenia clung to the earl's arm.

"We have to find her!" Alec wrenched out, then his voice dropped to a fierce but agonized whisper. "Oh, God—I've let her down. I've failed her—so badly, Drax. I've got to find her—" He couldn't have won the whist and Talbot Old Hall with it only to lose Becky herself.

"Alec, listen to me! You can't go out looking for her. You've got to *stay here*," Drax said emphatically. "They will contact you. They'll have to."

Never had Alec been so grateful for his friend's cool-headed nature, for Drax's steadiness at the critical moment helped reel him back from the brink of mindless fury.

"Why?" he demanded in a hellish tone.

"Parthenia, tell him."

With a surge of will, Alec seized back his equilibrium and listened with excruciating attention as Parthenia quickly explained about Nelyudov's mission and the charge of treason hanging over Kurkov's head.

"Then, you're right," he whispered when she had finished. "Kurkov does need her alive. She's his only bargaining chip." *Thank God.* He shut his eyes briefly, struggling to sort it all out despite the chaotic fury pounding in his temples.

If Eva had led the Cossacks here, then Kurkov would soon know it was he who had been helping, hiding, protecting Becky all along, that it was he who had killed two of his men. As soon as the prince knew the truth, Alec had no doubt Kurkov would want his blood.

A trade.

Yes, he thought, flicking his eyes open, with fiendish zeal taking hold of him. He would offer up his own life in exchange for Becky's release. He would die in her place without thinking twice. It was far better than living, knowing he had failed her.

CHAPTER
∽ SIXTEEN ∽

*F*ear had tangled her sense of direction, but Becky believed that the old abandoned cottage where they had brought her lay in the same remote countryside where Alec and she had gone horseback riding on that pleasant day more than a fortnight ago.

That day seemed now to belong to another life, another person.

For hours her whole existence had been demarcated by the broken stone walls and crumbling mortar of the ruined cottage, half reclaimed by vines and weeds. For how many years the place had lain untouched, she could not guess. It had not even been scavenged by the poor; it felt like a place cursed.

Around it, the light woods resounded with morning birdsong. From where Becky sat, her back aching, her hands bound with coarse rope, she could see through the glassless, gaping window, a large crow standing on a squat tree trunk amid some daisies and other scraggly wildflowers. The bird's raucous cawing grated on her nerves, already worn raw. Beyond the stump where it perched, a winding dirt road led down the steep hill through the shady woods. Faintly, very faintly, she could hear the rhythmic pounding of the surf.

The room where she was being held contained nothing but a rough, rotting table and a long bench in somewhat better condition for having been pushed up against the wall. Beneath her feet the cracked flagstones lay covered in dust; a large brown spider went scuttling by. Above her, through the great hole that gaped in the roof, the sky had changed from dawn's thick gray to luminous heaven-blue, like Alec's eyes.

The thought of him gave her strength and at the same time threatened to undo her cool composure. Her tears had ended. Enough hours had passed to harden her terror into cold, stoic rage.

But beneath it, behind her outer impassivity, she was worried sick about Alec, and about Fort and Rush, as well. The latter pair had fought so bravely against the Cossacks, to no avail. Becky had given herself up when she saw they were going to be killed.

As to Alec's fate, she could only agonize, not knowing what had become of him. Was he alive or dead? Had he killed Mikhail on the boat, as planned? Had he been arrested or killed in turn by the Regent's guards? She could not allow herself to contemplate the possibility that he was dead.

No, it weakened and rattled her too much, and right now she needed all of her strength and all of her wits to hold her own against the madwoman tormenting her.

Becky now knew how the mouse felt when the cat caught it, crippled it, and played with it before having it for supper.

"It's not nice to go around telling lies about your guardian, dear Becky."

"I never told a single lie about Mikhail. He's the liar."

Crack!

Lady Campion dealt her another cutting blow across the face with her riding crop. "I detest children who tell lies."

Becky refused to be bowed. "I am not a child."

"Yes, you are. You're just a pretty young thing, aren't you? So, so pretty. Do you know what this is, Becky, my girl?" she purred, holding up a glass vial of some thick clear liquid.

Becky closed her eyes for a second. "No."

"Oil of vitriol. A concentrated form of sulfuric acid. There are vitriol attacks in London all the time. A vial like this is thrown at someone, leaving them blinded, you see, burned, and horribly disfigured. Watch." Roughly, Eva tore part of the sleeve off Becky's gown and brought the remnant over to the table. She put a drop of vitriol on the cloth, and very soon the acid ate a hole right through it. "Imagine what it could do to this lovely complexion," she murmured, trailing her gloved fingertip down Becky's cheek. "I wonder if our beautiful Alec would still want you with your face melted. I'm afraid not, because, well, just between us girls, he is rather shallow, isn't he?"

Becky glared at her but refused either to flinch or to beg for mercy.

Suddenly, the sound of galloping hoofbeats could be heard approaching up the dirt road.

"Ah!" Lady Campion put the stopper back in the vial of acid and glided over to the window. "He's come!" The baroness turned to Becky with a spiteful gleam in her dark eyes. "Now you're in real trouble."

When the baroness hurried out to greet her lover, pulling the thick weathered door shut behind her, Becky drooped forward on the hard bench, trying to rally herself to face Mikhail. Her heart pounded with sickening force. Her shoulders ached from having her arms bound behind her. Parched with thirst and coated in dust from the road, she was bleary with exhaustion and woozy from Lady Campion's gleeful abuse.

She heard Mikhail's voice and pulled deeper into herself, remembering in terror his long-standing threat of rape. The door banged open and there he stood, huge and hard-eyed and every inch as terrifying as she remembered him. She swallowed hard. Mikhail prowled into the room, looking her over as though she were a valued bit of merchandise. Becky flinched when he grasped her chin, lifting her face.

He inspected it, took note of the welt on her cheek, and then turned his icy stare on Eva. "What have you done to her?"

A chill ran down Becky's spine as she picked up the note of danger in his voice. The baroness, unfortunately for her, had not yet learned to recognize the subtle signs of his displeasure.

Her tone blithe, she was still preening over having found Becky for him. "Yes, well, she was a little obtuse, so I decided to soften her up for you a bit."

Mikhail's swift backhand sent her reeling. "How dare you strike my blood kin?" he thundered at her as she fell back against the broken wall.

"But—Mikhail!" Eva's face turned ghastly white, her eyes dark and staring. She bore the red imprint from his blow on her cheek, along with a look of utter disbelief.

"Get out of here," he growled. "Go and fetch me Alec Knight."

He's still alive!

"Bring him here—alone. Tell him we have her, and that if he wants to see her alive again, he will surrender himself immediately. I don't like being humiliated."

"Oh, Lady Campion, don't," Becky uttered, though she knew it would only bring her more pain. "They'll kill him! I know he threatened you, but surely you know he didn't mean it. Alec would never hurt a woman. If you ever cared for him at all—"

"Silence!" Mikhail roared at Becky. "You, go!" he ordered the baroness.

Lady Campion staggered to her feet and inched toward the door with a look of lingering bewilderment. To her credit, she attempted to stand up to him. "Mikhail, I got you the girl," she pointed out. "Don't be reckless! Isn't it enough that your brutes already cut down Nick Rushford and Daniel Fortescue?"

"I'll be the one to say when it's enough." He rose and stalked over to her. She stepped back, cowering. "Eva, you will see this through. After all, you're the one who started it, didn't you? You got yourself in over your head, and now you will do as I say. Unless you want to hang for kidnapping, I suggest you do as you're told. Bring him. Alone."

She fled.

A moment later the baroness streaked past the window on horseback. She had no sooner gone off on her mission than Mikhail closed the moldering door and pivoted to face Becky, who was seated on the long wooden bench with her hands tied behind her back.

He lowered his chin as he walked toward her; his gray eyes gleamed with brutal pleasure. "Now, then, little cousin. You and I have some unfinished business to attend to." He grasped a handful of her hair and pulled her head back, then touched her bruised lips with the pad of his thumb. "So fair," he crooned.

Becky's face drained. His steely touch made resistance futile as Mikhail pushed her back slowly, inexorably, until she was lying on the bench, shaking with fear.

"I told you I'd teach you a lesson you'd never forget. You've had this coming for a long time."

She began fighting him, struggling to escape his rough taunting attempts to kiss her, but when he reached down to unfasten his breeches, terror overflowed Becky's mind. "No! Mikhail, don't. Oh God, please—" she wrenched out. "Wait—I beg you!"

He wrapped his hand around her throat in a warning grip. "Shut up and spread your damned legs. You spread them for him, didn't you?"

"That's what I'm trying to tell you." She cast about

for some means to deter him. "Lord Alec—he gave me the French disease!"

He paused warily, studying her with scorn.

"You know his reputation as a libertine!" She forced herself to hold his stare, praying he'd believe her.

Mikhail's lips curled in a sneer. He left his breeches fastened, but Becky's relief was short-lived, for he continued to hold her down. Instead, he reached for his pistol.

"Fine. Have it your way."

Oh, no. Now he was simply going to shoot her.

But to her bewilderment, he unloaded the gun with a cruel smile, spilling out the metal ball onto the table. It rolled away, plopping onto the floor, where it stopped in a crack between the flagstones.

"No matter," he whispered, lifting the side of the gun to her lips. "Kiss it," he ordered.

She jerked away uneasily as he rubbed the gun against her mouth. Her heart pounded, then she gasped as he pressed it between her legs, warming the cold steel of the long hard muzzle against her inner thigh. Becky's eyes widened with revulsion as she realized what he intended. She screamed and fought him with wild violence, trying to kick the weapon out of his hand. Mikhail laughed and slammed her back down onto the bench in a supine position. "Shh, lie still. You're only making it worse for yourself."

Their struggle was so fierce, her horror so encompassing, that she barely noticed the rider who arrived. Mikhail was laughing, trying to force the gun inside her when a frantic knock rattled the moltering door.

"Your Highness! A word, sire! I implore you!"

"What is it?" Mikhail barked.

Urgent words in Russian followed. The tone was dire, but the only word she recognized was "Westland."

She had no idea what the Cossack had said; all of her

awareness had contracted into the small circle of terror
that centered around Mikhail and his horrific, degrad-
ing assault. She was not even aware that she was crying.
Instinct had taken over, and all she could focus on was
the need to fight him off.

But then, after whatever magical words the Cossack
had uttered, Mikhail let her go, cautiously lowering his
hand from her throat. Becky had been reduced, however, to such primitive fury that she snarled and kicked
at him again as he withdrew.

He turned and slapped her across the face. "Sit
down!"

Already unbalanced, Becky pitched back against the
stone wall and banged her head so hard that she fell
onto the bench, knocked out cold.

"Nelyudov has come?" Mikhail echoed ominously.

"We didn't realize it at first. He went in too quickly. It
was dark."

"Westland received him?"

"Yes, Your Highness. They spoke for some time, and
Lady Parthenia was with them. The Westlands must
have discovered our presence somehow, because Nelyudov came out after us. He killed Boris and Yuri, and
captured Vlad, but I got away."

"There is only one reason the Czar would send his top
assassin after me," Mikhail murmured, recalling the
lack of communication from his co-conspirators back in
Russia. His heart began to pound. He suddenly felt a trifle ill, but managed to maintain a veneer of calm. "The
plot has been discovered."

"It's worse than that, sir. Nelyudov had called up the
local garrison to seize you. After he attacked us at
the Westlands', I went to the hotel, thinking you'd be
there after the card game. They had at least twenty dragoons, heavily armed, waiting there to ambush you."

"Damn it!" Mikhail punched the door, bloodying his knuckles. He felt as though the walls were closing in on him. "That little bitch in the next room must have gotten to the Westlands' somehow, despite all our efforts. Alec Knight probably helped her." He stared coldly at his men. "This is your doing. You were supposed to find her and stop her before any of this happened. You've failed me." He walked away from them, his temples throbbing.

His remaining Cossacks exchanged uneasy looks.

"I will question Rebecca myself to learn how much she's told them." He examined the broken skin of his knuckles. "Well, then, it would seem the game has ended," he said in a cool tone after a moment.

"Sire, we are not far from the sea! Why wait for Lady Campion and the Englishman to return when there's still time to escape? We can go now. It would be a small matter to get our hands on a boat and be gone before they discover us."

"Run?" Mikhail hated the prospect of retreat, nor did he know where he could go. If his treasonous plot had been discovered, what country would receive him? "It is a boon that at least we have the girl," he mused aloud. "She may be our only point of leverage. Of course, we'll soon have Alec Knight, as well, and Eva. We can kill them one by one if Nelyudov or anyone else tries to lay hold of us."

"Your Highness swore that we could have the man who killed our comrades when we found him," Sergei grumbled in a surly tone.

"How dare you speak out of turn? I'll give you your orders and you will follow them!"

"Our brothers must be avenged!"

Mikhail heaved a snarling sort of sigh and turned away. *Perfect.* The last thing he needed right now was an insurrection among his Cossacks. Without his men's loyalty, he knew he was doomed. "Very well. When Lady Campion brings Alec Knight, you may kill him. But indulge me, won't you, and at least do it slowly. It will be a pleasure to hear that cocky bastard beg for his life."

"Gladly, sire. We thank you."

"Stay here and guard the girl." Mikhail began walking away. "Escape may already be impossible if Nelyudov has blockaded the bay. I'll be right back. I shall go and have a look."

"Yes, Your Highness."

Mikhail followed the footpath through the woods for about two hundred yards, until he came out to a treeless, grassy promontory with a broad view of the sea. The towering cliff face dropped off to the pounding surf far below. There was no sandy beach, just jagged rocks jutting up from rough water.

Resting his foot on a rugged gray outcropping of rock, Mikhail stared out to sea, his eyes narrowed against the sun's glitter on the waves. He clenched his jaw and shook his head, spying two formidable warships of the Royal Navy on the horizon. He swallowed hard. Just as he feared. Nelyudov was too shrewd to have overlooked the task of blocking his escape route.

The ships were moving into position to intercept any small boat that tried to slip past them and to blow any craft out of the water that did not heed the order to turn back. His fist clenched at his side. *Too late.* No getting away now, unless he used his hostage.

With a low growl, he shrugged off intimations of doom, left the cliff side, and went striding back to the ruined cottage to interrogate his little cousin. He needed to find out how much she had told Westland, and he was happy to beat it out of her if he had to.

* * *

When Eva showed up at the villa, the authorities had immediately moved in to arrest her for her role in the abduction, but Alec shoved them back almost savagely, knowing the baroness was the only one who could lead him to Becky.

One look into Eva's eyes told Alec that this time she knew she had gotten in over her head. Perhaps she understood now why he had been driven to threaten her life, for though she gave him Kurkov's message to come alone and unarmed, she tried in a lower tone to dissuade him from going.

"They will kill you."

"They can try," he had said, immediately swinging up onto his horse. Knowing that this summons would come, he had already ordered a groom to saddle the massive thoroughbred hunter that he had won in the whist drive.

Eva had flinched. For her part, she did not seem to relish the idea of going back to that madman, but having already implicated herself by choosing to aid the outlaw, she had no choice.

Alec's final words had been a terse command to Nelyudov not to attempt to follow him or to interfere, for Kurkov had said he would kill Becky if Alec did not come alone. Eva had then mounted up again to show him the way, and they were off, thundering out of town.

Swift as eagles, they rode now through the woods, their galloping horses sweeping over the dusty ground. Alec could think of nothing but Becky, her safety, her well-being. Until he saw her with his own eyes, he would know no peace. He did not expect that Kurkov would let her go once he gave himself up, but at least when he arrived, he would have a chance to fight for her. Somehow, he would get her out of there. If it cost him the last breath in his body, he would find a way.

Motioning to him, Eva pointed wordlessly to a small dirt road that branched off to the right ahead. Choked with weeds, it wended its way up a steep hill as the woods thickened. His face taut and coated with traces of dust, Alec guided his horse into the sharp turn.

The baroness, however, kept riding down the main road. She glanced anxiously over her shoulder as their paths split. Alec headed up the hill; but Eva, ever the survivor, galloped on toward the next harbor town, seizing her one chance to escape.

Alec clucked to his horse, squeezed its sides with his calves, and forged on grimly alone.

As Becky opened her eyes, coming to after several minutes, the room still wove unsteadily. The door was closed. Mikhail was gone. At last she had been left alone.

It all came flooding back in a rush. Alec was on his way, and when he got here, they were going to kill him. Cold fear gripped her. She had to escape.

Struggling to sit upright again, she carefully bent forward, stretching her shoulders painfully until she could step through the circle of her bound wrists. Lifting her hands in front of her, she seized the rope-end between her teeth, hurrying to work the knot free, but her gaze was riveted on the unloaded pistol Mikhail had left behind. The bullet had rolled away, but she saw exactly where it lay in the dust.

She could hear the men in the next room arguing. She had no idea what they were fighting about, but she heard several repetitions of a word that sounded like "*Nelyudov.*" She did not know what it meant, nor did she care. Her sole concern was escaping before Alec walked into this trap. Freeing herself was the only way she could be of help to him. Hope climbed.

At last she cast off the ropes and retrieved the pistol

and bullet, handling both with disgust, considering the use Mikhail had tried to make of the former. She dropped the silver ball back into the muzzle and checked the powder. Gingerly lifting Lady Campion's abandoned vial of acid for extra protection, she moved silently toward the open window.

The door suddenly banged open. She whirled as Mikhail saw her heading for the window and cursed.

She menaced him with the pistol. "Stay back!"

"It isn't loaded."

"It is now."

"Ah, so you can't make a proper curtsy but you know how to load a gun. It figures. Well, I hope you're a good shot because you've only got one bullet. Do you think you can hit me?"

She cocked the pistol. "Don't try me."

"You've been a great deal of trouble to me, Rebecca. I hear that you managed to get to Westland. Don't bother denying it. They're after me now, and it's all your fault."

Mikhail barked out an order to his men. At once the Cossacks filed into the room. He gestured at Becky, who stood with her back to the wall with the open window. Uneasily, she watched the soldiers surround her in a loose U-shaped formation, but her thoughts flew. If the Duke of Westland had taken action based on her report—if the authorities were now after Mikhail, as he claimed—then she was no longer just a prisoner. She was a hostage, and they needed her alive.

The prince muttered another command, and the Cossacks started closing in on her slowly. Becky surmised he had ordered them to take her weapon. She swung the pistol from left to right, trying to hold all of them off at once.

"You're very happy to sacrifice their lives, aren't you?" she challenged her cousin, her eyes on his men. "Why don't you try to take my weapon yourself and see what it gets you?" Still pointing the gun from one Cossack to the other, she backed up against the low wall.

The nearness of escape was bitterly tantalizing, but she feared that the awkward motion of climbing out the window would give the Cossacks an easy chance to grab her, and if she ran, she already knew they had no qualms about shooting people in the back.

She heard, then, swift hoofbeats approaching as a rider galloped up the hill and into the clearing where the cottage stood.

"Aha," Mikhail murmured, lifting his chin with a cutting smile and a glimmer of cruel anticipation in his eyes. "Here comes your hero, riding to your rescue. The fool."

"Alec, stay back!" she yelled over her shoulder out the window behind her. Becky's heart beat faster, but she dared not take her eyes off the Cossacks in order to turn and look.

"Becky!"

Out of the corner of her eye she saw him through the window as he swung down off his horse and strode boldly toward the cottage.

Mikhail just shook his head cynically at Alec's courage. "Seize him. And bring him in here first. I'd like a word with our lucky gambler before he dies."

"Mikhail, please," Becky begged him. "He had nothing to do with this. He didn't know anything. It was all my doing—" Her words broke off as she heard the scuffle erupt in the next room. "Alec!"

In the next moment, the Cossacks dragged him into the room and threw him to the floor. A few could not resist the opportunity to kick him in the ribs when he was down. Alec let out a grunt of pain, holding his middle.

His black leather riding breeches and knee boots were coated in dust from the road, but his state of undress attested to the haste with which he had responded to

Mikhail's summons, for he wore no waistcoat, jacket, or cravat, only a loose white shirt—and no weapon.

On his hands and knees before her, surrounded by five towering Cossacks, he slowly lifted his gaze, meeting hers. Becky could not utter a word—could barely breathe as they stared at each other for a fleeting second with a world of emotion between them.

Beneath his tousled, sun-streaked forelock, Alec's eyes, now dark blue, were stormy with tortured love.

"Get up," Mikhail bit out.

As Alec climbed warily to his feet, he scanned Becky with an assessing glance. The dark cast in his expression sharpened as he took in her torn dress and the welt on her cheek, but pride gathered in his eyes when he noted the weapon she had managed to commandeer. Standing to his full height, he squared his broad shoulders and lifted his left chin, looking, for all the world, she thought, like Prince Charming from the fairy-tales, taken prisoner and battered, but far from bowed.

Her heart raced as she cast about for a solution. His very nearness gave her new courage. He veiled the treacherous glint in his eyes beneath his dusky lashes, but he seemed to be swiftly mulling over some way to get them both out of there. He smiled at her with discreet pride, glancing meaningfully at the pistol in her right hand. But then his gaze homed in on the vial of acid in her left.

"Where is Eva?" Mikhail demanded in a jaundiced tone.

"Ah, sorry, Kurkov. Your lady has abandoned you. I can't imagine why."

His cocky drawl almost made Becky smile. How did he do it? How did he lift her heart even now? But when she looked at him in awe, only one thought came to mind.

I love you so, so much. She couldn't believe he was really here.

"Your insolence, Knight, is unadvised under the circumstances."

"I had a feeling you'd be a sore loser. Did you hear, Becky? I won the whist drive for you."

"Oh, Alec," she breathed, staring at him. "I knew you would."

"Kill him," Mikhail snarled to his men.

"Stop!" Becky shouted, and then she pressed the pistol to her own head with a shaky gulp. "Don't anybody move! If you hurt him, I swear, I'll pull the trigger and you won't have a hostage to bargain with."

Her announcement seemed to take them all aback. Even Alec looked startled. He knitted his eyebrows, clearly not liking this move.

She could see no other way.

"I said get away from him," she reiterated coldly.

The Cossacks glanced at Mikhail for instruction, for their fate, too, rested on using Becky as a hostage, since, after all, they planned on killing Alec. The prince hesitated, then called off his dogs with a curt nod.

"Put the gun down, Rebecca," Mikhail ordered her as the Cossacks reluctantly backed up, giving Alec a bit of room.

All but one—the ugly, bearded one behind him who seemed more interested in revenge than survival. With a curse, the Cossack drew a knife and reached to grab Alec's shoulder, as though he intended on cutting his throat, but as they grappled momentarily, Alec met Becky's gaze and then sent a forceful nod at the vial of acid in her hand.

She nodded, flicked off the lid, and hurled it at the Cossack as Alec ducked.

The vial of acid hit the Cossack in the face, and spilled all over him. The man let out a bloodcurdling howl and dropped his weapon, lifting his hands to his face and eyes. As he went running blindly out of the room, Alec swooped down and grabbed the weapon he had dropped and in an instant was slashing out with it.

The Cossacks swarmed him, but Alec held his own, stealing a sword for his right hand and shifting the dagger to his left. He fought in all directions at once. Embattled with the man in front of him, he did not see the one behind him draw his weapon.

Without hesitation, Becky aimed the pistol at the man's chest and fired. He dropped to his knees and fell dead with a gurgle

"You little bitch," Mikhail spat at her.

"Becky, get out of here!" Alec shouted, parrying a brutal thrust. "Take my horse and go!"

"I won't leave you here alone—"

"Go!" he roared furiously at her.

When one of the Cossacks pointed a gun at her, Becky gasped and dove out of the low window behind her. The bullet slammed into the stone wall, spraying dust. She raced toward Alec's huge, unfamiliar horse and spooked it in her haste.

"Damn it," she whispered, recalling the trouble she'd had the last time she tried to steal a horse. How could she leave him behind? But he was her protector and he had given her an order. He had demonstrated his prowess as a warrior before. . . .

While the sound of blades clashing filled the cottage behind her, Becky laid hold of the hunter's bridle. Mounting the huge thoroughbred was another matter, however. She struggled to lift her foot up into the high stirrup. "Damn it!"

The horse was just too tall. Recalling the tree stump where she had seen the crow cawing earlier, she quickly led the hunter over to it, but she was too late.

Though only one minute had passed, Mikhail came bursting out of the cottage's broken door. "Oh, I've had it with you," he said, and came after her.

He waved his arms wildly as he moved toward her, deliberately spooking the horse. Becky lost her grip on the leather reins as the animal rebelled. She had no choice but to turn and run.

"You're a dead woman. Do you hear me? If I'm going down, I'm taking you with me!"

Terror overtaking her, Becky fled, tearing down the narrow footpath through the woods. Her chest heaved frantically. The world spiraled. She ran as fast as she could in her kid slippers, feeling every sharp rock and breaking twigs beneath her feet. She tripped on a fallen log but kept going, pausing only to wrench her skirts free when they caught on a stubborn branch. The delicate silk tore. She kept going, her chest heaving.

Mikhail was not far behind her. His bellow sent a chill like ice down her spine.

"Rebeccaaaaaa!"

Ferocious protectiveness burned through Alec's veins as he battled the three remaining Cossacks at one time. Parry, thrust, turn, parry, riposte. He had never fought like this before in his life. Something had taken over: A power flowed through him. He surrendered to it, moving with the rhythm of the fight. It all came with ease; he no longer felt the injuries he had sustained when they had leaped on him. He paid no mind to his quivering muscles and the sweat that poured down his face. There was no way he was going to lose. The greater part of his attention, however, had fled outside with Becky.

She needed him.

Kurkov had gone after her, and Alec knew now that her cousin wanted her blood. His foes were tiring. It was time to finish them off, and Alec did so without mercy for what they had done to his friends.

He struck the first man hard in the sword arm, laying it open to the bone, then ran him through. He freed his weapon from the dying man's rib cage as another man sliced at him; Alec ducked the blow and struck back with a hacking blow to his neck, nearly taking his head off. The third man looked at him, aghast.

Alec moved toward him. The Cossack tried to run. Alec nimbly blocked his exit and forced him to fight. In moments the last Cossack sank to his knees with a yelp of pain that dwindled to a gasp. Alec twisted the blade in his gut, his jaw clenched.

Withdrawing his sword, he wiped blood and entrails off the blade on another corpse's uniform, took the dead man's pistol, then jumped out of the low window to save Becky from Mikhail.

Chasing the sound of the prince's deep, mad bellows, Alec raced into the woods, following the narrow footpath.

Still propelled forward by her wild momentum from running down the hill, Becky burst out of the woods and nearly went barreling headlong over a cliff. She stopped herself with a gasp, flinging herself to her knees to stop her fall.

The sea sprawled out before her with the blinding morning sun straight ahead, nearly level with the promontory. *I know this place,* she thought, taken off guard by sudden, fleeting wonder, sweet memory flooding her mind.

This was the very spot where Alec and she had picnicked weeks ago . . . and exchanged deep, longing kisses as they rolled around together on the soft green turf.

Then she heard low, cold laughter behind her and scrambled dizzily to her feet. When she turned around, Mikhail was only about twelve feet away with a sword in his hand.

"Oh," he said richly, "I've been waiting for this."

She looked over her shoulder at the drop-off behind her. In front of her, her murderous cousin approached, brandishing his weapon.

"You know, Rebecca, you never should have tried to fight me back in Yorkshire. You should have simply submitted to my authority, and none of this need ever have happened. Look at what you've done. All of us are ruined for it. All because of you. Dmitry Maximov—dead. Your fault. I did not intend to kill him. You forced me to."

"I don't believe you," she said in a shaky voice.

"It's true. I meant to keep him for a hostage, as with you, but it's too late for that now. It's too late for all of us. All you had to do was yield to me, but you were too . . . damned . . . stubborn. And now my future, the hope of Russia, some of my best men, your own worthless life, and even your precious Lord Alec, all of us done for. All . . . dead."

"Not quite, Kurkov."

Becky drew in her breath; Mikhail turned with a grunt of astonishment to find Alec alive, coming cautiously out of the woods.

"My lady at this moment is wishing, I think, for a candlesnuffer to aim at your head, Highness. Unfortunately, all I've got is a pistol." Alec brought the gun up and leveled it between Mikhail's eyes. "Becky, sweet," he said softly, "turn away."

He cocked the gun. Becky obeyed, but just before she did, she saw Mikhail lift his chin in steely arrogance, bracing himself for the bullet.

"*Dosvi`daniya,* Highness."

Click.

Nothing happened. *No bullet!* Becky gasped and peeked through her fingers as Alec scowled.

"Bloody hell."

Mikhail let out a gloating laugh. *"En garde,"* he growled, then swiped at Alec with a massive chop of his blade.

Their battle exploded.

Becky got out of the way, keeping her distance from the cliff's edge, but she could hardly bear to watch the shattering blows they exchanged, both men hacking at each other with relentless speed and savagery. The climbing sun flashed on their swords, which whirled and churned and twisted like the revolving blades of some razor-sharp metal windmill. The harsh rasp of both men's labored breathing filled the air, Mikhail's brute power matched with Alec's precision, speed, and agility.

The moments stretched like years while the surf went on endlessly pounding the rocks below.

Jump and heave, topple and lunge, they dueled back and forth across the promontory, their spurs tearing into soft green turf and laying bare the soil beneath. With a sudden leaping thrust, Mikhail attacked; Becky gasped; Alec let out a swift, furious yell as the blade pierced his left shoulder—the same side that had been wounded barely a month ago.

"Son of a bitch!" he spat as he backed away to regroup.

Mikhail wiped the sweat off his forehead with his sleeve and smiled.

Becky, on the verge of panic, gazed at Alec. Having already spent a good deal of his strength fighting the Cossacks, now he was hurt and Mikhail was not. When he glanced down at his wound, which was bleeding freely, it crossed her mind to go running back up to the cottage to find some bullets for that empty pistol, just in case, but before she could move, Alec lifted his head again, his stare homing in on Mikhail. As Becky watched, a subtle transformation came over his face, as though he reached deeply into himself to summon forth some terrible new strength.

He shrugged off the wound and swept his sword up gracefully into a salute, upright before his face. Then he lowered it to an angle aimed at Mikhail's heart. And he advanced.

Staring at him, Becky did not know where the fury had come from that he now unleashed, but Mikhail was no match for it. Driving him back with a relentless advance in perfect form, Alec slowly backed Mikhail to the cliff's edge, parried a hit aimed at his throat, and then lunged, running Mikhail through with his deadly lightning-fast riposte, a snarl on his beautiful face. In that moment, with his blue eyes blazing and the golden sun burnishing his hair, he was a warrior archangel bent on casting down the demon from the edge of heaven.

Mikhail let out a throaty scream, dropped his weapon and gripped Alec's blade. Alec gave him a shove; Mikhail threw himself sideways, trying to avoid going over the cliff, but he was too late. He was falling—

And then Becky screamed as Mikhail grabbed hold of Alec's ankle on his way down, pulling his vanquisher down with him.

"No!" She fled to the edge of the cliff.

Alec let out a bellow of pain as he caught himself on a rock about two feet over the edge. The wrench to his injured shoulder was surely agony, but at least he had staved off the fate that now claimed Mikhail.

Becky stared past Alec over the drop-off as her cousin went plunging downward, arms and legs flailing, to smash against the jagged rocks far, far below. She flinched when he hit, but in an instant she was lying on her stomach on the turf, reaching both hands down to Alec.

"Take hold!"

"Get back!" he gasped out.

"Alec, take my hand! I'll pull you up!"

"You can't. I'm too heavy."

"Grab hold of me, Alec! I won't let you fall!"

"It's too dangerous. It's my shoulder. Becky, I can't pull myself up."

"Don't you let go! Alec, you're slipping! Take my hand!"

"No—I'll pull you down with me," he panted.

"No, you won't. Come on, sweeting. Reach out to me. I'm not letting you go!"

"I can't. Becky," he groaned. "I love you."

"Oh, Alec, I love you, too." Tears leaped into her eyes as she hung over the side of the cliff, reaching her hand out toward him. Her fingertips could nearly graze his bruised, cut knuckles.

"I love you," he repeated through gritted teeth, "and don't you ever forget it."

"Then take my hand, Alec. Please. Let me pull you up."

"You're not strong enough."

"Yes, I am! Do it, damn you! Alec, I need you with me. Don't you see that?" she wrenched out. "I don't want to live without you! If you don't let me help you, you're going to fall."

"Bloody hell," he whispered, then flicked a grim glance over her face. Wetting his lips, he braced himself to try. "A-All right." Wincing, he clung to the rock with his right arm and tentatively stretched out his left to her.

Her hair blowing in the updraft of wind rushing up the rock face, Becky inched closer to the edge and gripped his forearm with both hands, anchoring her toes in the turf. His fingers dug into her elbow. He let out an anguished growl as she pulled with all her might on his hurt arm.

"Come on! Don't give up, Alec. Climb!" She felt herself slipping forward but refused to budge. Better that she should go over the cliff with him than lose her hold on him.

"I'm hurting you," he panted, noting her grimace of pain.

"No, it's just—your ring. It's biting into my finger a little."

"You're still wearing it?" he panted in surprise, sweat pouring down his face.

"Of course I'm still wearing it. I never want to take it off! I told you nothing could ever change my love for you and I—meant it!" Gritting her teeth, she dragged him upward with a burst of wild strength that came from she knew not where.

Alec suddenly found a toehold in the rock face on which to brace himself.

"Steady . . ."

A bead of perspiration ran down Becky's face; her back strained; her every muscle trembled. Alec exerted even greater effort.

"That's it—you've got it . . ."

Rising slightly, inch by precarious inch, with Becky holding onto him for dear life, he was finally able to get his knee wedged atop the rock he had been clinging to.

With a sudden heave, he thrust himself up over the edge and pitched forward, landing on top of her.

They both just stayed like that, panting with exhaustion, but alive.

Safe.

At last.

Together.

"You all right?"

"Yes, you?"

He nodded, raising himself onto his elbows. He took her face between his hands and gazed down at her. "You just saved my life, you little hellion."

Flat on her back beneath him in the soft grass, she had barely caught her breath as she wrapped her arms around him. "Then I guess we're finally even."

Without warning, Alec bent his head and kissed her, hard. His mouth slanted over hers in fierce, claiming need. Becky returned the passionate onslaught of his kisses eagerly, tightening her hold around his neck.

"Oh, God," he breathed at length, resting his brow against her cheek. "I thought I'd lost you." He smoothed her hair behind her ear with a hand that trembled, and then pressed a kiss to her brow. "Are you sure you're all right? Did he hurt you?"

"I'm all right," she assured him. "You came to my rescue in time. Just like I knew you would."

"This is all my fault. I shouldn't have slipped that day in front of Eva. If I hadn't used your real name, she would never have—"

"Shh," Becky cut him off, laying her finger over his lips. "It's over now. He's gone, and you were magnificent. Besides," she added as Alec kissed the finger with which she had silenced him, "I'm pretty hardy, if you haven't noticed."

"I've noticed," he replied. "It's one of your most adorable qualities. Becky," he added, staring earnestly at her, "I love you."

"Oh, Alec, I love you, too." She gave him a tremulous smile and then hugged him. He sat up, taking her with him. They sat holding each other tight, on the edge of the cliff where they had picnicked all those weeks ago.

"What of Fort and Rush?"

"They're going to be all right."

"Oh, thank God. They fought so bravely, Alec, but there was nothing they could do."

"I know." He squeezed his eyes shut and pressed a kiss to her cheek. "Becky?"

"Yes, my darling?"

"I love you," he murmured, again, almost inaudibly. Now that he had made up his mind to tell her so, he couldn't seem to stop saying it. "I never thought I could love anyone like this." Though he sounded shaken by the force of his emotion, there was an indefinable note in his voice that she had never heard before, a new ring of solid steel that had been forged in him by all of this. "I'm going to take such good care of you," he whispered fiercely as he kissed her forehead. "I'm never letting you out of my sight again. I hope you don't mind."

"That sounds grand." She sniffled and pulled back from his embrace just far enough to look into his deep blue eyes, so filled with protectiveness and soulful longing. She caressed his face. "My Alec."

He nodded mutely, pressing her palm over his heart.

She searched his blazing eyes then gently wiped a streak of dirt off his cheek. "What is it, my love? You look like you might burst if you don't say what's on your mind."

"It's just—Becky—I'm a different man because of you—you changed me—and you weren't even trying to."

She cupped his cheek with a flood of overwhelming tenderness toward him rushing through her. "All I know is that I love the man you are. You've stood by me with such loyalty and gallantry and courage. Look at all you've done. You've won the whist drive, saved me, *and* beat Mikhail and all of his Cossacks . . . and in the process, won my heart forever."

He swallowed hard and smiled at her a trifle self-consciously.

"My good sir Knight," she declared with a faint mist

of tears in her eyes, "you have got a real talent for saving the day."

"I'm glad you think so," he replied as his wry smile slowly grew. "Because we both know you saved me, as well, and I'm not talking about any damned cliff."

With a shining smile Becky wrapped her arms around him and kissed his curving lips. Alec eased her back down onto the grass with extreme gentleness, cradling her head in his hand. His deep, masterful kisses made her head swirl, but then a sudden snuffling sound startled them both.

Their glances met with a large equine muzzle curiously investigating Alec's shoulder. They laughed, and the Irish hunter let out a snort.

"Do you think he's trying to tell us something?" Becky asked, glancing at Alec with a twinkle in her eyes.

He nodded reluctantly and captured the dangling reins, sending Becky a rueful smile askance. "He's right. We had better be going. There are a lot of people who are going to be awfully glad to see you."

A short while later they were riding together on his tall, liver-brown hunter, winding their way back down the hill through the woods. Alec had set Becky on the horse's withers and held her securely around the waist, keeping the powerful thoroughbred to a sedate walk.

After the ordeal of her abduction, he sought to soothe her with the pleasant topic of the fortune he had made. Now that she was safe, he could begin to think about all the ways the two of them could enjoy it for the rest of their lives.

"He's a nice horse." She patted the animal's neck. "What are you going to call him?"

"Whatever you want. Wait till you see our new carriage. I won all sorts of pretty things for you," he teased gently, nuzzling her ear. "Sapphire earrings, a castle in

France, a famous racehorse, part ownership of a merchant vessel, a tea plantation somewhere in the East Indies . . ."

"Alec, someone's coming!" she whispered, still a bit on edge.

He harkened to the distance as the thoroughbred pricked up its tapered ears. As soon as they left the weed-choked drive, Alec spotted Nelyudov and his force of some twenty dragoons storming up the main road.

They reined in as Alec hailed him.

"This is the Russian agent I told you about, my dear. Mr. Nelyudov. The chap I asked not to follow me," he added pointedly.

"Where is Kurkov?" the Czar's agent cried.

"He's dead."

Alec quickly told them what had happened.

Nelyudov looked at him with new respect. "You killed them all?"

The dragoons exchanged astonished looks and admiring murmurs.

"Lady Campion got away, however. She went that way." Alec pointed down the road. "Aside from being an accomplice to kidnapping, she may know something of Kurkov's plot, considering how he took her into his confidence on the matter of Becky."

The Russian nodded. "I will get the details of Kurkov's death from you later."

"As you wish," Alec said.

Nelyudov signaled to his men, and the riders took leave of them, thundering on down the road in pursuit of the baroness.

When Alec and Becky returned to the ransacked villa, they found Westland and Count Lieven still waiting anxiously. Everyone crowded around and made much of them. Drax was there, and Parthenia, too, along with more dragoons and a few local constables.

"You've brought her back!" the ambassador cried, kissing Becky's hand before she could even get down off the horse. "Oh, my dear, without you, we'd never have gotten to the bottom of Kurkov's perfidy! You and Lord Alec have done our emperor a monumental service—and I don't mind saying the Czar does not forget his friends."

"Let me through, Lieven. I owe this sweet young lady an apology," the great Duke of Westland said in front of everyone. Helping Becky down off Alec's horse, he bowed before her, taking both of her hands in his own. "My dear child, can you ever forgive me? My servants should have shown you in to see me that fateful day that you tried to call on me to tell me the truth about Kurkov, but instead I believed his lies."

"Your Grace need not apologize to me," she protested softly.

"But I do! And to this gentleman, as well. Lord Alec," Westland said, offering his hand, "I misjudged you, Knight. I have worked often enough with your brother Hawkscliffe to have known better than to doubt the blood in your veins, sir. You have saved us all from deep disgrace."

"And not just from disgrace," Parthenia added, gliding forward to press a light kiss on Alec's cheek. "Thank you, Lord Alec. And thank *you*," she reiterated, turning to Becky with a repentant smile. "We are, all of us, in your debt, my mysterious 'Abby.' But none so much as I." Becky blushed now that her ruse had been revealed, but Parthenia showed no sign of holding it against her. "Thank you for your courage in coming forward to let us know what a villain Mikhail was. Otherwise I might have truly married him." Becky returned her smile shyly as Parthenia leaned near and pressed a sisterly kiss to her cheek, but then Parthenia noticed the welt and fussed over her with abundant concern. "Oh, my dear!

What's happened to you? Well, don't worry. I'm sure it will fade before the Winner's Ball tomorrow night."

"Winner's Ball?" Becky echoed.

Parthenia nodded. "And mark my words, when you come into Society, my dear, you will have no firmer champion than me—*Lady* Draxinger," she added in a whisper by Becky's ear.

Becky's eyes widened.

Drax appeared just then, grinning, a blush in his cheeks. "There he is! Good man. I knew you'd manage to come back alive." He clapped Alec proudly on the shoulder.

"Ow, stab wound," Alec muttered, flinching.

"Blazes! Sorry, old boy. I say, is there a surgeon in the house for my good friend?"

The surgeon was by his side in an instant, but Alec brushed him off.

"In a moment, thanks. First, there's something I have to give to Becky."

A general murmur of curiosity rippled through their midst.

Everyone followed as Alec escorted her inside. He didn't mind if they watched this momentous occasion. Slowly, he took the deed to Talbot Old Hall out of the drawer, scrolled and tied with a ribbon.

"There, my darling," he said softly as he placed it in her hands. "The Hall is finally yours."

"No, Alec," she answered, lifting her teary gaze from the document. "It's *ours*."

He smiled tenderly at her.

Tears of pure love and gratitude shone in her beautiful violet eyes as she searched his face for a long moment. "Can I show it to you, Alec? The Hall, my village? Will you go there with me?"

"Of course I will," he answered as he drew her into his embrace. "I'd love to take you home."

"Our home."

"Yes," he whispered. "Forever."

She flung her arms around his neck and pulled him down to kiss her. His smiling lips touched hers. The whole room burst into applause and raucous cheers as they kissed each other joyously.

✑ EPILOGUE ✑

A fortnight after the Winner's Ball, they arrived in Buckley-on-the-Heath.

Riding in an open landau, with the convalescing Fort and Rush following in a second carriage, they all stopped in the village, where the whole populace turned out to cheer the man who was to be their new lord of the manor and had saved them from Mikhail and his Cossack horde.

Becky could barely believe how tiny her village looked to her now, after all of her adventures in the larger world, but her heart clenched with eager excitement as she introduced everyone to Alec, bursting with pride in him. Her betrothed, in turn, dazzled the simple country folk with his offhand elegance and gracious warmth, spreading his charm like an effortless mantle of sunshine. He promised to come down to the tavern soon to sample the local brew, but Becky, eager to get up to the Hall, did not wish to linger.

As they moved on, leaving the tiny village, Alec gazed warmly at her. "You didn't tell me it was so quaint. And the people are so friendly!"

She smiled, then glanced back, for their convalescing friends had fallen behind.

"Uh-oh," Becky murmured. "Trouble."

"What is it?"

"Fort and Rush have just met Sally and Daisy."

Alec followed her gaze and saw that the second carriage had halted. The two notorious rakehells were leaning over the side, captivated by a buxom redhead and an overly flirtatious blonde.

"I don't think we'll be seeing them for a while," Alec remarked.

"No."

They exchanged a look of amusement, and then drove on.

Becky sighed happily and rested her head against his shoulder, which had healed well. The poor roads gave them a bumpy ride, but she didn't mind. Her thoughts drifted back to the whirlwind of events of the past fortnight, especially to the Winner's Ball—her first real Society function. She had been so terrified leading up to it, obediently following Alec's advice to wear the rose-red gown with the low heart-shaped neckline. She thought he was merely being his usual fashionable self, but then the package had arrived, from Brighton Pavilion, no less.

As she soon discovered, he had tried to buy the original Rose of Indra from the Regent to surprise her, but his royal friend gallantly refused the money, making the jewel his wedding present to them.

It seemed His Royal Highness was smugly pleased with Alec's triumph over Kurkov, for it was not every day that a humble British subject had the chance to do a favor for the arrogant Czar.

Alec had fastened the ruby necklace around her throat, and then bent to kiss her cheek as he stood behind her at the mirror. "My love, you are magnificent."

His ardent whisper had infused her with confidence and readiness for the ball.

Her heart still fluttered when she thought of dancing with him, whirling lightly around the glossy parquet floor. They had broken the three-dance maximum most scandalously, but what else could be expected of the captain of all London rakehells and his lady? Then the Duke of Westland had called for everyone's attention, announcing his daughter's betrothal to Lord Draxinger. At last, Drax and Parthenia had found the courage to admit their love to each other. And now, Becky mused, how pleasant it was to know that Alec and she would both have friends so close, merely on the neighboring estate.

Surely, though, the highlight of the evening had been when the Knight brothers arrived in response to their youngest brother's summons for help a few days earlier. The crowd had gasped as Robert, the dark-eyed duke, burst through the tall white doors at the ball and strode in, flanked by the identical twins, Lucien and Damien. Having ridden for days from the other end of England to arrive on the scene like Alec's own personal army, they were shocked that their "baby brother" had already handled the crisis quite nicely.

When they heard how he had single-handedly thwarted half a dozen Cossacks, they marveled, and they congratulated him with pride and admiration, clapping him on the back and finally acknowledging him, it seemed, as not just the wayward charmer of the family, but their equal. Somewhat abashed, Alec swiftly put all that aside, presenting Becky to them.

The added news of their engagement left his stern elder brothers nearly agog. They gasped and stared and gawked at Becky as though she were the eighth wonder of the world.

"You mean . . . ?"

"Actual marriage, Alec? You?"

"Is this true?" Robert had finally uttered. "This is not one of your pranks?"

"Oh, it's true," he vowed with a soft smile, drawing her closer. "I love this girl, and she is to be my wife."

With exclamations of wonder and awe, they had nearly fallen over themselves in their eagerness to welcome her to the family. Each one was kinder to her than the next, treating her as though she were made of most delicate porcelain. With their solicitous care, it was easy for Becky to get over her shyness, warming up to her future brothers-in-law with ease.

"My dear, what have you done to him?" Lucien murmured by her ear.

"Never mind that," Robert interrupted. "Whatever it is—thank you."

Damien had simply given her a big, jolly hug.

As for Nelyudov, upon returning to Brighton from his unsuccessful pursuit of Lady Campion, the Russian master-spy had interviewed Alec and Becky, as well as Vlad, the captured Cossack, for his report to his superiors in St. Petersburg.

The Cossack had bargained for his life by agreeing to show them where Dmitry Maximov was buried on the moors. Nelyudov then dispatched some of his men to Talbot Old Hall for this purpose. With the Cossack to guide them to his unmarked grave, they had collected the fallen agent's remains so he could be returned to his grieving family.

This done, Nelyudov had then set out again to track down Lady Campion, but if he ever cornered her, it was hard to say who might capture whom.

Presently, the landau turned in at the Hall's dusty drive. Becky had been anxious, and half dreaded laying eyes on her home, fearful that Mikhail might have harmed it before he had left, just to spite her. Alec pointed to the demolished gatehouse, and she shook her head. But as the Hall rose over the hillcrest, she felt her heart lifting.

Her home was unharmed.

Against the azure sky, the rooftop angels, carved in oak, stood guard with swords and shields, just as they had for centuries, one posted at every corner of the house. She let out a low exhalation of relief, for the ancient, half-timbered pile looked exactly the same as she remembered it: countless sagging gables jutting this way and that, their upper stories jettied out in late medieval fashion. Ivy climbed thickly up the walls, encircling the diamond-paned windows.

And yet, somehow, everything was different. Or perhaps only she was, she thought. Perhaps because she knew that it was hers now, not her relatives' possession from which she could be evicted at anytime. But no, she amended, glancing at Alec. Not hers.

Theirs.

The place where they would raise their family. Becky prayed that Alec would like it. When she glanced at him uncertainly, his face was rapt with boyish enthusiasm as he stared at the house.

He jumped down from the carriage, took a few paces forward. "This place is *fantastic*," he exclaimed, then whirled toward her suddenly. "Is it really haunted, Becky? Honestly?"

Her smile grew. "I'm afraid so." She should have known.

"Well, come on, then!" he exclaimed. "I want to meet the ghost."

Becky laughed. He grabbed her about the waist and set her down beside him. Hand in hand, they dashed into the house, shocking Mrs. Whithorn, who had just come to answer the door. Becky could see that Alec would have no trouble at all taming that termagant with his charm, but she was in no mood to loiter with her huffing, scandalized housekeeper.

She gave Mrs. Whithorn a pointed look that said, *"One wrong word and you are fired."* No longer would she be bullied by the woman in her own home. She turned once more to Alec, taking both his hands.

"Come," she whispered.

Laughing at his enthusiasm over the many intricate

details of their house, Becky tugged him from room to room, showing him the great hall with its secret doorway, the library with its creaky, towering bookshelves, and the fine oak-paneled salon. But when Alec paused to kiss her, nudging her hungrily against the wall, she knew it was time to make a beeline for her chamber.

She trailed a finger down his chest and gave him *that* look—the one he knew so well.

"Aha," he murmured, instantly getting the message. "Yes, quite. But won't Mrs. Whithorn have a fit of apoplexy?"

"Who cares? I'm the lady of the house, and I want my man. Come."

Half stumbling, they moved up the ornately carved staircase, kissing and groping and undressing each other on the way; minutes later they fell into Becky's humble, narrow bed.

"I love you," she whispered, wrapping her arms around his neck.

"I love you, too, sugarplum."

She smiled as she pressed her lips to his in a slow, sensuous caress, and then captured his plump lower lip lightly, playfully, between her teeth. Alec gathered her closer with a soft moan; his tongue stroked hers. Becky dug her fingers hungrily into his broad shoulders.

"Sweeting?" he breathed a few moments later, brushing his warm, smooth lips against hers in a dizzying caress.

"Yes, Alec?" She thrilled to the heated intent in his hand moving slowly up her thigh beneath her skirts.

"Make love to me now. Hurry."

She smiled dreamily, reveling in his touch. "Shall I?"

"Yes."

"Very well, then. Since I'm practicing wifely obedience . . ." She lifted her already unbuttoned gown off over her head.

He let out a low, breathy *woof* of appreciation, surveying her body, and leaned back, shirtless, against the headboard. She licked her lips as she held his smoldering half smile. One hand stroking his smooth, muscled chest, she pushed the sheet away and slung her thigh across his body, sitting astride him.

He grasped her hips appreciatively and watched her every move with anticipation burning in his eyes. Becky planted her hands on his wide shoulders and leaned nearer, plying his sculpted mouth with her kisses. She cupped his face, skimming his elegant cheekbone with the pad of her thumb, and coaxed his lips wider, stroking his tongue with her own.

In many ways it was a reversal from their first night together, as if this time Alec was the virgin and Becky the tender, patient lover, easing his fears, breaking down the last of his defenses with a reassuring whisper, a velvet touch. Quiet wonder reflected in his innocent expression; his guard was down as never before, allowing her to read the open mirror of his soul in his blue, blue eyes.

Soon, with her fingers linked through his, she rode him gently.

Becky held his gaze in aching sweetness, only longing to fill the emptiness that had driven him so relentlessly for so long. *May it never return.* She would flood his heart with her love for the rest of their lives. After a time, Alec closed his eyes and rested his head back, allowing himself to simply receive. Becky gave him all she had.

"Never let me go," he said starkly, gripping her hips as the pleasure took hold of him.

"I never will," she promised, breathing hard. "I told you, Alec, whatever happens, I'll never leave you. I love you. Surrender to me, darling, and know that I am yours."

She kissed him again. He clenched her desperately, letting out an anguished groan as he thrust more deeply into her. Endless moments passed; they both were in a trance of love, moving with a slow, powerful rhythm that quickened as their fever climbed. Soon Becky's heart was racing; she could hold back no more.

She dropped her head back, climaxing with her arms wrapped tightly around his neck, her swollen breasts crushed against his sweat-dampened skin. Alec arched his neck as he came, spilling himself inside her with an anguished groan. She gasped, clutching him to her, and savoring his deep and satisfying release.

Slowly, she caught her breath. Pressing one more soft but possessive kiss to his lips, she lay down flat atop him and folded her arms across his chest.

She gazed into his hazy eyes, enjoying the glow and his sated look; for a long time, she simply stroked his golden hair in silence. He kissed her forehead after a while, and pulled her onto the side of him.

"Thank you," he murmured softly as he cuddled her close.

"For that?" she purred. "You're welcome, sir."

"I meant for loving me."

"Oh Alec, my angel man," she whispered, leaning in to kiss his cheek as he caressed her shoulder. "Loving you is the easiest thing in the world."

He met her devoted gaze with a smile like heaven and quiet joy shining in his eyes, the clear blue color of eternity.

∞ AUTHOR'S NOTE ∞

Gambling was probably *the* favorite vice of the Regency period. Stories abound of great aristocrats and lesser mortals ruining themselves left and right at the tables. In fact, one Lord Foley was bankrupted during the Regency when his grandson gambled away the family fortune!

Though the "annual Brighton whist drive" is purely my own concoction, such an event could very well have existed; whist drives are commonly held as charity fundraisers even today. Alec and the other players involved had to put up £10,000 in order to enter the whist drive. At the modern equivalent of about $500,000 U.S., such a sum would have qualified these high rollers as what Las Vegas casino men term "whales," with the lure of a jackpot valued at approximately $22 million split between the winning pair. So, as you can see, Alec did pretty well for himself.

Regarding one of the settings of this book: the Althorpe. London-lovers will probably recognize it as being modeled on the hallowed grounds of Albany. By the way, if you are skeptical about the existence of heated running water for bathing tubs in 1817, see the Regency-era print of *The warm bath* on page 123 of Steven Parissien's *Regency Style* (London: Phaidon Press, 1992). The painting shows a lady getting ready to take a bath in a luxurious built-in alcove bath with two spigots for hot and cold running water clearly visible. A great rarity and a luxury, no doubt, but a sybarite like our Lord Alec would have spared no expense on the most basic pleasures of life while he was winning and could afford them.

The Cossacks were a paramilitary, semidemocratic, strongly independent people who started out as bandits and mercenaries but evolved by the 1800s into the Czar's elite cavalry units. Since the Czars couldn't break the Cossacks, they hired them, granting them special rights and privileges not given to other groups within their domain, such as land grants and tax exemptions. In addition to terrorizing enemy armies, Cossack forces were often brought in to suppress peasant uprisings and urban disturbances.

As to Prince Kurkov's plot to overthrow Czar Alexander I, just such a conspiracy was uncovered. The grandson of Catherine the Great, Alexander started out as the golden boy of Europe and the great hope of Russia, but he was more of a thinker than a man of action, and he steadily lost credibility for his high-strung nervous nature that resulted in wavering and indecisiveness. The army grew to despise him for ignoring his seasoned military advisers; the Czar preferred to decide himself how to direct his army, resulting in many unnecessary defeats.

For all bits of Russian dialogue in this book and advice on Russian names, I am indebted to up-and-coming romance author Sylvia Day, a former Russian linguist for U.S. Army Military Intelligence (*Bad Boys Ahoy*, Kensington Brave, February 2006).

In closing, I hope readers will rejoin the Knight family for the next installment in the series, featuring Lord Jack Knight. Previous books in this series, in order, include: *The Duke, Lord of Fire, Lord of Ice, Lady of Desire,* and *Devil Takes a Bride.* More information about each story is available at my website at www.gaelenfoley.com, along with various history articles about the Regency period. I want to thank all my readers for coming along with me on this imaginative journey. I hope you've had fun! I sure have. Until next time. . . .

With fondest wishes,

Gaelen